From internationally bestselling author
Paul Cleave—a gripping new thriller about a
former private investigator's search for redemption
and a mental patient's dark obsession

PEOPLE ARE DISAPPEARING IN CHRISTCHURCH. COOPER
Riley, a psychology professor, doesn't make it to work one day.
Emma Green, one of his students, doesn't make it home. When
ex-cop Theodore Tate is released from a four-month prison stint,
he's asked by Green's father to help find Emma. After all, Tate was
in jail for nearly killing her in a DUI accident the year before, so he
owes him. Big time. What neither of them knows is that a former
mental patient is holding people prisoner as part of his growing collection of serial killer souvenirs. Now he has acquired the ultimate
collector's item—an actual killer.

Meanwhile, clues keep pulling Tate back to Grover Hills, the
mental institution that closed down three years ago. Very bad things
happened there. Those who managed to survive would prefer keeping their memories buried. Tate has no choice but to unearth Grover Hills' dark past if there is any chance of finding Emma Green
and Cooper Riley alive.

For fans of Dennis Lehane's *Shutter Island*, Thomas Harris's *Silence of the Lambs*, and Jeff Lindsay's Dexter series, *Collecting Cooper* is
another "relentlessly gripping, deliciously twisted, and shot through
with a vein of humor that's as dark as hell" (Mark Billingham) novel
by this glimmering new talent in the crime thriller genre.

ALSO BY PAUL CLEAVE

PAUL CLEAVE

COLLECTING COOPER

A THRILLER

ATRIA PAPERBACK

New York   London   Toronto   Sydney

ATRIA PAPERBACK
A Division of Simon & Schuster, Inc.
1230 Avenue of the Americas
New York, NY 10020

First Atria Paperback edition July 2011

ATRIA PAPERBACK and colophon are trademarks of Simon & Schuster, Inc.

For information about special discounts for bulk purchases,
please contact Simon & Schuster Special Sales at 1-866-506-1949
or business@simonandschuster.com.

The Simon & Schuster Speakers Bureau can bring authors to your
live event. For more information or to book an event, contact the
Simon & Schuster Speakers Bureau at 1-866-248-3049 or visit our
website at www.simonspeakers.com.

Manufactured in the United States of America

10 9 8 7 6 5 4 3 2 1

Library of Congress Cataloging-in-Publication Data

Cleave, Paul, date.
  Collecting Cooper : a thriller / Paul Cleave.—1st Atria pbk. ed.
    p. cm.
  1. Murderers—Fiction. 2. Christchurch (N.Z.)—Fiction.
3. Psychological fiction. I. Title.
  PR9639.4.C54C65 2011
  823'.92—dc22

                                              2011002934

ISBN 978-1-4391-8962-7
ISBN 978-1-4391-8964-1 (ebook)

To Paul Waterhouse and Daniel Williams—
we've been friends for over thirty years with much more to go

COLLECTING
COOPER

prologue

Emma Green hopes the old man isn't dead. It's one of those moments that come along in life where you think one thing and pray for another. The one thing dead for sure is the café. There have only been two customers over the last hour and neither ordered anything beyond a coffee, and her boss isn't the kind of guy to let anyone go home early even on a slow Monday night, and just as equally he isn't the kind of guy to be in much of a good mood because of it. The parking lot out back has her car and her boss's car and a couple of others. There's a dumpster off to the side and some milk crates stacked against it and the air smells of cabbage. There's not much in the way of lighting. But some. Enough to see the old guy slumped in the front seat with his mouth open and his eyes closed, his head angled to one side, looking exactly the same way her granddad looked a couple of years back when they had to bust down the bathroom door after he went in and didn't come out.

She walks up to the car and peers in. A string of saliva dangles from his lower lip to his chest. His hairline has receded about as far as a hairline can go before being considered bald. She recognizes him. He was in a couple of hours ago. Coffee and a scone and he sat in the corner with a newspaper trying to solve the crossword puzzle. "The devil lives here," he kept whispering over and over while he tapped his pen on the table, and she glanced over his shoulder thinking she knew the answer and saw there was only space for five letters. Christchurch has twelve. "Hades," she had told him, and he had smiled and thanked her and been pleasant enough.

She wants to tap on the window hoping he's sleeping, but if he is sleeping then she may startle and frighten him and then it's all going to be very embarrassing. But if he isn't sleeping, maybe his heart only stopped beating a few seconds ago and there's a good chance it can be kick-started. The sums don't add up, though, because he left the café over an hour ago. No reason for him to sit out here for an hour before dying, unless he was working on the crossword. Well, maybe the devil got him. She stares through the window. She reaches out to it but doesn't touch it. She should just let the next person deal with it. But if she did that the old man would still be just as dead in the morning only he'd be poorer, and his car stereo would have gone too.

If she was the one sitting freshly dead in a parked car, would she want people to keep passing her by?

She taps on the window. He doesn't move. She taps again. Nothing. Her stomach drops as she grabs the handle. The door is unlocked. She swings it open and places a few fingers on his neck, her wrist snapping the drool from his chin where it dangles over her arm like a strand of spiderweb. His skin is still warm but there's no pulse, not there, and she shifts her fingers and . . .

He gasps deeply and pulls back. "What the fuck?" he blurts, blinking heavily to clear his vision. "Hey, hey, what the hell are you doing?" he shouts.

"I . . ."

"You goddamn thief whore," he says, sounding nothing at all like her granddad—at least nothing like him before the Alzheimer's set in—and he grabs her hand and pulls her in. "You were trying to . . ."

"I thought . . ."

"Whore!" he shouts, then spits on her. She can smell old man sweat and old man food and his clothes smell of old man and his bony grip is strong. She feels sick. Her back hurts from the angle, her back has hurt pretty much from every angle since the car accident last year, and she reaches for his hand and tries to break his grip.

"You were trying to steal from me," he says.

"No, no, I work at the . . . the . . ." she says, but the words get caught up in the tears, "coffee and a . . . a scone and I, I thought you . . ." This close his breath is almost hot and humid enough to start her makeup running. She can't finish what she's trying to say.

He lets her go and slaps her across the face. Hard. Harder than she's ever been slapped by anybody in her seventeen years on this earth. Her head twists to the side and her cheek is burning. Then his hands are on her chest, at first she thinks he's trying to feel her up, but then he's shoving her and the stars come into view and swirl overhead, and her back is hitting the pavement, her hands behind her breaking the fall.

The car door slams shut. The engine starts. He winds the window down and shouts something else at her before pulling away, but she doesn't hear him over the car and over the blood rushing in her ears. He races toward the exit, hugging the wall too closely and clipping the edge of the dumpster there. It grinds a long dent into it, and she expects him to pull over and scream at her some more, but he carries on, racing out onto the street where there's the squeal of another car's breaks and somebody yells out "Asshole."

She sits on the ground crying and angry, her handbag next to her, the contents in a puddle across the tarmac. Her first thought is to go inside and tell her boss what happened, but he'd tell her it was her own fault. Another thing about her boss is that everything is always somebody else's fault, and in this case he would think she was somehow trying to blame him. She gets onto her feet and looks at her palms. The skin has torn on her right palm, the skin stretched up like a balloon. At least there's no blood.

She wipes at the tears on her face. "Asshole," she whispers. The warm wind pushes against her and tugs against the torn skin on her palms, puffing it out like small parachutes. She gets her handbag packed and then has to rummage back through it for her keys, but her keys aren't there. She crouches back down. She was holding her keys when she was walking out to the parking lot, wasn't she? She isn't sure, but she starts to turn, then spots them behind the back wheel of a dirty and beaten-up Toyota. She moves over and bends down and reaches for them. At the same time footsteps race toward her. She looks up and can see a man silhouetted against one of the lights, thank God somebody is here to help.

"Thank . . ." is all she can say, then just utter panic as he jumps on top of her.

She has no idea what's happening. She tries to fight him and he rewards her by pounding her head into the ground so hard the parking lot lights go dark. She can feel the world slipping away. She thinks she is fighting against it, but she isn't sure because it feels like she's falling into a dream. Her grandfather smiling at her, the old man in the car, dropping one of the coffees earlier in the day and getting told off from her boss, her boyfriend wanting to spend the night, then she thinks about Satan living in Christchurch, setting up residence and inflicting His friends upon the city before deciding this isn't even happening, but for all her good hopes the world drifts away.

When the world comes back, it arrives without any reference to time. It's just like last year when she had the accident. Back then she was hit by a car, but she has no memory of it. Can't remember the hour before the accident, or the day following it. This time she can remember. She's lying down on a mattress, but when she rolls to the side the mattress doesn't end. Her wrists are painfully sore and are tied behind her, and her legs are tied too, they're connected to whatever is keeping her wrists together. The headache is the worst, the pressure so strong behind her eyes that whatever is covering them is probably holding them in. She's thirsty and hungry and the air is hot and stale. It must be ninety degrees. Everything is dark. She starts to cry. This isn't a hospital. She's tied up to bake in this oven of a room.

Footsteps. A floorboard creaking. A lock disengaging and then a door opens. Somebody approaches her. She can hear breathing. She tries to talk but can't. She thinks of her parents, her friends, her boyfriend. She thinks of the old man at the café and she makes a promise to herself that if she gets out of this alive she'll never help anybody again.

"Drink."

It's a man's voice. The pressure is removed from her mouth. There has to be something she can say to get out of this. Something she can say to make him let her go.

"Please, please," she cries, "please don't hurt me. I don't want to be hurt, please, I'm begging you," she says, the tears soaking her face. She doesn't think she's ever cried so much. She knows she's never been this frightened. This man is going to do bad things to her, and she's going to have to live with what he's done to her, it will haunt her and make her insane. The person she was is about to die.

But she will get through this. She will survive. She knows that because, because . . . this was never meant to happen to her. It's not possible her life is about to end. It doesn't add up. Doesn't make sense. She cries harder.

"Please," she says.

The plastic neck of a bottle is pushed against her lips.

"It's water," he says, and he tips it up. It pours into her mouth. She hates him, but the thirst is overpowering and she accepts the drink. He pulls it away before she can swallow more than a few mouthfuls.

"There'll be more soon," he says.

"Who, who are you? What are you going to do with me?"

"No questions," he says, and the pressure is back on her mouth, some form of tape. "You're going to need to keep your strength," he tells her. "I have something very special planned for you over the following week," he tells her, "and you won't be needing these," he adds, and she feels a blade slip beneath her clothes and he starts cutting them away.

5

chapter one

The dust from the exercise yard clings to the hot air. Flies and mosquitoes are trying to use my neck as a landing strip. Giant concrete walls separate me from the sounds coming from the other side where men are ticking through life, kicking a football or playing cards or getting stomped on. Cranes and scaffolding are off to the right, workmen creating additions to a prison that can't keep up, dirt and cement dust hugging the air like an early winter's fog, so thick the details are hard to make out, could be a stampede of cows just came through, could be a stampede of prisoners are trying to escape. My clothes smell stale and feel stiff; they've been folded and jammed inside a paper bag for the last four months, but they're sure as hell more comfortable than the prison jumpsuit I worked, slept, and ate in. Sweat and confinement is still on my skin. Heat is radiating up from the blacktop pavement into my feet. When I close my hands, I can feel the metal and concrete walls that would isolate me from the world the same way an amputee can feel a phantom leg. My last four months have been all about isolation. Not just from the world, but from other prisoners too. I've spent day after day surrounded by cells full of pedophiles and other pieces of human trash that couldn't be thrown into the general population for fear of having their throats ripped open. Four months that felt like four years, but it could have been worse. I could have had my teeth smashed out and made to play fetch-the-soap every night. I was an ex-cop in a concrete-and-steel world surrounded by men who hated cops more than they hated each other. I felt nauseous being surrounded by child molesters, but it was the better alternative. Mostly they kept to themselves, spending their days fantasizing about what it was that got them arrested. Fantasizing about getting back to that life.

The prison guards watch me from the entrance. They seem worried I'm going to try and break back in. I feel like a character in a movie; that lost guy who wakes up in a different time and has to grab somebody by the shoulders to ask them for the date, including the year, only to be looked at like they're a fool. Of course I know the date. I've been waiting for this day ever since I got thrown inside. My clothes are a little bigger because I'm a little smaller. Prison nutrition is malnutrition.

The nine o'clock sun is beating down and forming a long shadow behind me. In most directions it looks like there is water resting on the surface of the ground, a thin pool shimmering in the heat. The blacktop grabs at the soles of my shoes as I walk across it. I have to hold my hand up to my face to shield my eyes. I've been out of jail for twenty-five seconds and I don't remember a day as hot as this before going in. I haven't seen much sun over the last four months and already my pale skin is starting to burn. The longer I was trapped behind those walls behind me, the further away this particular Wednesday seemed. Prison has a way of fooling with time. There are a few cars around belonging to visitors, and one has a guy leaning against it staring at me. He's wearing tan pants and there are dark rings in the armpits of his white shirt and he's lost a bit of weight since the last time I saw him, but the buzz-cut hair is still the same, and so is his expression, of which, lately, he seems to have only the one. I can smell smoke from something big burning far off in the distance. I close my eyes against the sun and let it warm my skin, and then burn, and when I open them again, Schroder is no longer leaning against the car. He's covered half the distance between us.

"Good to see you, Tate," Schroder says, and I take his hand when he reaches me. It's hot and sweaty and it's the first hand I've shaken in a long time, but I can remember how it goes. The prison food didn't rot all of my brain away. "How was it?"

"How do you think it was?" I ask, letting go.

"Yeah. Well. I guess," Schroder says, summing things up. He's just looking for words and not finding them, and Schroder won't be the last. A couple of exhausted-looking birds fly low past us, looking for somewhere cooler. "I thought you could do with a lift home."

There's a white minivan waiting near the entrance, the bottom half of it covered in dirt, the top half only marginally better. There're a couple of other guys released today sitting onboard, both have shaved heads and tattoo raindrops streaming from their eyes, they're on opposite sides of the van staring out opposite windows wanting nothing to do with each other. Another guy, a short, powerfully built man with all the fingers on his right hand missing, turning his fist into a club, is swaggering out from the prison, his arms puffed out to the side to encompass his large chest and even larger ego. He stares at me before climbing into the back of the van. I give it a week tops before they're all back in here.

Four of us are getting released today and I wasn't thrilled about the prospect of spending twenty minutes in a vehicle with any of them. I'm not exactly thrilled about spending time with Schroder either.

"I appreciate it," I tell him.

We head over to his dark gray unmarked police car that's covered in dust from the drive out here, making all the letters on the side of the tires stand out. I climb in and it's hotter inside. I play around with the air-conditioning and get some of the vents pointing in my direction. I watch Christchurch Prison get smaller in the side mirror before disappearing behind a large belt of trees. We hit the highway and turn right, toward the city. We drive past long paddocks with dry grass and barbed-wire fences. There are guys in those fields driving tractors and whipping up clouds of dirt and wiping the early-morning sweat from their faces. Away from all the construction and the air is clear.

"Any thoughts to what you're gonna do now?" Schroder asks.

"Why? You want to offer me my old job back?"

"Yeah, that'd go down well."

"Then I'll become a farmer. Looks like a pretty nice lifestyle."

"I don't know any farmers, Tate, but I'm pretty sure you'd make the worst kind."

"Yeah? What kind is that?"

He doesn't answer. He's thinking I'd make the kind of farmer who'd shoot any cattle being mean to the other cattle. I try to imagine myself driving one of those tractors seven days a week and moving cows from one field to another, but no matter how hard I try I can't get any of those images to stick. Traffic gets thicker the closer we get to town.

"Look, Tate, I've been doing some thinking, and I'm starting to see things a little different now."

"What kind of different?"

"This city. Society, I don't know. What is it you say about Christchurch?"

"It's broken," I answer, and it's true.

"Yeah. It's seems like it's been breaking down for a while. But things . . . things are, I don't know. It's like things just aren't getting better. You're out of the loop since leaving the force three years ago, but we're outnumbered. People are disappearing. Men and women leave for work or home and just never show up."

"My guess is they've had enough and are escaping," I suggest.

"It's not that."

"This is your idea of small talk?"

"You'd rather tell me about your last four months?"

We pass a field where two farmers are burning off rubbish, most of it bush that's been cut back, thick black smoke spiraling straight up into the sky where it hangs like a rain cloud without any breeze to help it on its way. The farmers are standing next to tractors, their hands on their hips as they watch, the air around them hazy with the heat. The smell comes through the air vents and Schroder shuts them down and the car gets warmer. Then we're heading past a gray brick wall about two meters high with *Christchurch* written across it, no *welcome to* in front of the name. In fact, somebody has spray-painted a line through *church* and written *help us*. Cars are speeding in each direction, everybody in a hurry to be somewhere. Schroder switches the air-conditioning back on. We reach the first big intersection since leaving jail and sit at a red light opposite a service station where a four-wheel drive has backed into one of the pumps and forced all the staff to stand around in a circle with no idea what to do next. The board out front tells me petrol has gone up by ten percent since I've been gone. I figure the temperature is up about forty percent and the crime rate up by fifty. Christchurch is all about statistics; ninety percent of them bad. One entire side of the petrol station has been covered in graffiti.

The light turns green and nobody moves for about ten seconds because the guy up front is arguing on his cell phone. I keep waiting for the car tires to melt. We both get lost in our own thoughts until Schroder breaks the silence. "Point is, Tate, this city is changing. We catch one bad guy and two more take his place. It's escalating, Tate, spiraling out of control."

"It's been spiraling for a while, Carl. Way before I ever left the force."

"Well, these days it seems worse."

"Why am I getting a bad feeling about this?" I ask.

"About what?"

"About why you came to pick me up. You want something, Carl, so just spit it out."

He drums his fingers on the steering wheel and gazes straight ahead, his eyes locked on the traffic. White light bounces off every smooth surface and it's becoming harder to see a damn thing. I'm worried by the time I make it home my eyeballs will have liquefied.

"In the backseat," he says. "There's a file you need to take a look at."

"I don't need to do anything except put on some sunglasses. Got some spares?"

"No. Just take a look."

"Whatever it is you want, Carl, it's something that I don't want."

"I want to get another killer off the streets. You're telling me you don't want that?"

"That's a shitty comment."

"See, the man I knew a year ago would have wanted that. He would have asked me how he could have helped. That man a year ago, he would have been giving me his help even if I didn't want it. You remember that, Tate? You remember that man? Or did those four months in the slammer fog up your memory?"

"I remember it perfectly. I remember you shutting me down when I knew more than you did."

"Jesus, Tate, you have a strange perception of reality. You got in the way of an investigation, you stole, you lied to me, and you were a real pain in the ass. Reality saw you kill somebody, it saw you crash your car into a teenage girl and put her in the hospital."

Last year I tracked down a serial killer, and people died in the process. Bad people. At the time I didn't know one of them was bad, and killing him was an accident. That guilt, it changed me. It got me drinking. And drinking led to the car accident which led to me getting sober again.

"You don't need to lecture me on reality," I say, thinking about my daughter, cold in the ground for three years and never coming back, then thinking about my wife in her care home, her body nothing more than a shell inside of which used to live the most perfect woman in the world.

"You're right," he says. "You're the last person who needs a lecture on reality."

"Anyway, I'm a different man now."

"Why, did you find God while you were locked away?"

"God doesn't even know that place exits," I tell him.

"Look, Tate, we're losing a battle and I need your help. That man a year ago, he didn't care about boundaries. He did what needed to be done. He didn't care about consequences. He didn't care about the law. I'm not asking any of that from you now. I'm only asking for your help. For your insight. How can a man who did all of that last year not want to offer that?"

"Because that man ended up in jail with nobody to give a damn about him," I say, the words more bitter than I intend them to be.

"No, Tate, that man ended up in jail because he got drunk and almost killed somebody with his car. Come on, all I'm asking is for you to take a look at the file. Read it over and tell me what you think. I'm not asking you to track anybody down or get your hands dirty. Truth is we're all losing perspective, we're too close—and hell, no matter what you've done or the actions you've taken, this is what you're good at. This is why you were put on this earth."

"You're stretching," I tell him. "And trying to appeal to your ego." He takes his eyes off the road for a second to flash me a smile. "But what isn't a stretch is the fact that you can do with the money."

"Money? What, the police department is going to put me back on the payroll? I seriously doubt that."

"That's not what I said. Look, there's a reward. Three months ago it was fifty thousand dollars. Now it's two hundred thousand. It goes to whoever can offer information that leads to an arrest. What else you going to do, Tate? At least take a look at the file. Give yourself a chance to—"

His cell phone rings. He doesn't finish his sentence. He reaches for it and doesn't say much, just listens, and I don't need to hear any of the conversation to know it's bad news. When I was a cop nobody ever rang to give me good news. Nobody ever rang to thank me for catching a criminal, to buy me some pizza and beer and say *good job*. Schroder slows a little as he drives, his hand tight on the wheel. He has to swerve out wide to avoid a large puddle of safety glass from a recent accident, each piece reflecting the sunlight like a diamond. I think about the money, and what I could do with it. I stare out the window and watch a pair of surveyors in yellow reflective vests measuring the street, planning on cutting it up in the near future to widen it or narrow it or just to keep the city's roadworking budget ticking over. Schroder indicates and pulls over and somebody honks at us and gives the finger. Schroder keeps talking as he does a U-turn. I think about the man I was a year ago, but I don't want to be him anymore. Schroder hangs up.

"Sorry to do this to you, Tate, but something's come up. I can't take you home. I'll drop you off in town. Is that okay?"

"Do I have a choice?"

"You got any money for a taxi?"

"What do you think?" I actually had fifty dollars stuffed into my pants pocket for this day, but between the time I took my clothes off four months ago and got them back, that fifty found a new home.

We hit the edge of town. We get caught in thick traffic where a lane has been closed down so some large trees overlapping the power lines can be trimmed back, the trucks and equipment blocking the way, but the workers are all sitting in the shade too hot to work. We reach the police station in town. He pulls in through the gates. There's a patrol car ahead of us with two cops dragging a man out from the backseat, he's screaming at them and trying to bite them and the two cops both look like they want to put him down like a rabid dog. Schroder digs into his pocket and hands me thirty dollars. "This will get you home," he says.

"I'll walk," I say, and open up the car door.

"Come on, Tate, take the money."

"Don't worry—it's not that I'm pissed at you. I've been locked up for so long I need the exercise."

"You try walking home in this heat and you're a dead man."

I don't want his help. Problem is the heat is already close to blistering the paintwork on the car. It blasts through the open door, passing over my skin and sucking away any moisture. Even my eyes feel like they're being lubricated by sand. I take the money. "I'll pay you back."

"You can pay me back by picking up the file."

"No," I say, but I can feel it back there, pulling at me, this magnet for violence whispering to me, telling me within its covers is a map which will take me back into that world. "I can't. I mean . . . I just can't."

"Come on, Tate. What the hell are you going to do? You've got a wife to take care of. A mortgage. You've had no income for four months. You're slipping behind. You need a job. You need this job. I need you to take this job. Who the hell else is going to hire you for anything? Look, Tate, you nailed a serial killer last year, but do you think anybody is going to care about that? No matter how you justify it, or weigh up the rights and wrongs of what you did, the fact is always going to be the same—you're an ex-con now. You can't escape that. Your life isn't the same life it was back then."

"Thanks for the ride, Carl. It was about halfway useful."

It isn't until I'm on the street with the gates to the police parking lot closing behind me that I look down at the file, pages of death crammed inside its covers, waiting for me, knowing all along I couldn't turn it away.

chapter two

The thumb is inside the jar, suspended in liquid murky with age. The lid is sealed tight and the jar safely cuddled by bubble wrap. The whole thing is packed inside a cardboard box the size of a football, the corners crushed in slightly, the contents surrounded by hundreds of pieces of jelly bean-shaped polystyrene packaging, each about the same size as the very thumb they're protecting. The box is in the hands of a courier driver with an untucked shirt with the bottom two buttons open. He looks impatient. He looks frustrated by the heat. His eagerness to leave is evident in the way he thrusts his electronic signature pad into Cooper's hands. The pad is the size of a paperback and Cooper awkwardly scrawls his name onto it. The driver gives him the box and tells him to have a good day, and a few seconds later he's reversing from the driveway, the wheels spinning up small pieces of tar-coated shingle from the road that plink against the undercarriage. Cooper stands there watching him, holding on to the box that feels very light. He plays his fingernail along the side of the stamps—there are a dozen of them, slapped onto the side along with a declaration form that lies. The stickers and stamps give it an exotic look, as though it has traveled from faraway places, routed through distant lands, that the contents could be anything—just not that of the severed thumb. None of the seals have been broken. If they had, it would have been the police coming to his door, not a courier driver.

He locks his front door against the heat of the morning sun. Headlining the news all week has been the heat wave. It arrived in Christchurch six days ago and set up camp. It's started a death toll that's still in the single figures but expected to hit double digits by the weekend. It's melting the tar seal in roads and burning tussock and trees and killing farm stock. Drownings and road rage are up and every day the sky somewhere in the city is clouded with smoke from a burning house or factory. He makes his way along the air-conditioned hallway to his air-conditioned study on the second floor, where diplomas line the walls, each of them perfectly level and equidistant to the next, the glass covering them clean, each of them small windows to his past achievements. He rests the package on his desk. He can only imagine what other people in his field would be saying right now.

He runs a knife blade along the tape. He'd like to know where the other thumb was posted, whether the recipient ripped into their box like a Christmas present. The cardboard edges spring upward on their folded creases. The jelly bean polystyrene whispers against his hands as he searches inside. His fingers close around the lumpy exterior of bubble wrap.

This is it.

The thumb looks fresh. The reality, however, is different. The thumb hasn't been attached to its owner for over a year. In an ideal world he'd be looking at the whole set. Thumbs and fingers all attached to the hands, but they were all separated soon after death and the thumb was all he could afford. Other parts, bigger parts, all went to higher bidders. He licks his lips, his mouth so dry he can't swallow. He drops the bubble wrap and moves to the first of his two bookcases. He sits the jar on the top shelf into the gap he made the day he won the auction. In a world of collectors, in a world of addicts, collecting the works of serial killers or saving the weapons they use, or the words they have written and the clothes they wore, or the paper their original confession was written on or the handcuffs they were arrested in is no different from collecting stamps or bobble-head action figures. Eighty percent of his own collection is made up of books. The rest is made up of a few knives, a few articles of clothing; he has some private police reports too which he shouldn't have. Until now the most unique piece he owned was a pillowcase that was used by a bellboy in an Australian hotel to cover the faces of three different women he killed. He turns the jar, studying the thumb, aware of how creepy it is, and also how creepy it is that he bought it. He won it online through a private auction, one he was invited to bid on through contacts he's nurtured through previous auctions. He's still not entirely sure why he wanted it. He didn't, not in the beginning. He saw it and thought it was crazy to own a body part, but the more he thought about it, the more he wanted it. He must have been crazy. What was he thinking? That he could put it on display and show people the next time he threw a dinner party? The shelves of his study are full of the other memorabilia he's won over the years, both from killers and victims. It is for others to debate whether the collecting of these items creates a market for death. His focus is purely educational. If he is to learn, if he is to teach others about methods and a killer's drive, then he must surround himself with these objects. It isn't a hobby, it's a job. And the thumb is more of an . . . he isn't sure. *Indulgence* is the wrong word. *Curiosity* works better. Yet it's more simple than that—it came down to him wanting it.

The arrival of the package has left him running late. His criminal psychology students will soon be staring at a whiteboard and no lecturer. The thumb has pushed him enough off schedule that he's going to have to skip breakfast and head straight into getting caught in traffic. He swallows a couple of vitamin pills and heads through to the garage and backs out the car.

The sun is climbing steadily into the sky, shortening the shadows from the trees and making the floating strands of spiderweb glint in the light. The radio is on and he's listening to a talk-back station, the current debate one that's been raging in the news lately—whether or not New Zealand should bring back the death penalty. It started as a flippant remark, the prime minister making a bad joke when asked what they were going to do to try and curb the country's growing crime rate and growing prison population, but it snowballed into other people backing the statement and asking why the government can't really consider it. After all, if death was good enough for the victims, why not give that same courtesy to their killers?

Cooper isn't sure where he stands on the issue. He isn't sure a first-world country should be practicing third-world punishments.

He puts the gear stick in park and climbs out to close the garage door because the damn automatic opener broke about two months ago and the service agent is still waiting on parts that were supposed to arrive back then. He can feel the warmth from the ground through the soles of his shoes. He breaks into a sweat a few paces from the door. The breeze is light and feels hot enough to ignite. All week people have been walking around with short sleeves and shortened nerves. He can smell marijuana from the goddamn surfer across the road who likes to spend his mornings and evenings and the hours in between using his lotto money to get as high as a kite. His shirt dampens with each stride. He's so distracted by the thumb and the heat that he suddenly realizes he's picked his briefcase back up and is carrying it with him.

"Weird," he says, and when he turns back to the car it gets even weirder. A man he's never seen before is standing next to it.

"Excuse me," the man says, and even though he's in his midthirties there's something about him that makes Cooper think of him as a kid, it could be the floppy hair hanging across his forehead, or it could be the corduroy pants twenty years out of date. "Have you got the time?"

"Sure," Cooper says, and he looks down at his watch, and when he does a sharp cramp explodes in his chest. He jerks the briefcase into his body with enough force to pop it open. The contents spill onto the driveway and a moment later he collapses next to them, every muscle and limb well beyond his control. The pain extends to his stomach and legs and groin, but mostly it's his chest that hurts. The man lowers the gun and crouches down next to him, brushing his hair out of his eyes.

"It's going to be okay," the kid says, at least that's what Cooper thinks he says, he can't really tell, because at the same time a chemical smell wafts over him and something is pushed into his face and he can't do a thing to fight it. It's at that moment the darkness rushes in and takes him from his collection.

chapter three

The sign says *Lost puppys for sail–$5 each.* It leans against the side of a brick wall held together by mortar and graffiti. The wall is two hundred meters closer to home than the police station. Leaning against that same brick wall in the shade it offers is a guy in a tattered blue shirt and tattered blue shorts and a hat made out of cardboard that came from a cereal packet. It doesn't fit quite right but he doesn't seem to mind. He hasn't shaved in a while by the look of it and hasn't eaten real food in about as long. I walk past him and he smiles and asks for loose change, only one side of his mouth moving when he talks, revealing teeth pointed and gray. All I have is the money Schroder gave me, and I give ten of it to him, hoping he'll spend it on spelling lessons rather than beer. His smile widens and clean white lines appear around the corners of his eyes between all the grime, and I figure his last four months have been worse than mine.

"That gets you two lost puppies," he says, arithmetic his strong point. "Take your pick."

I don't want a puppy, but I look anyway, turning left and right and not seeing any.

"They're lost," he reminds me, and tucks the money into his pocket.

I walk into the heart of the city, past office blocks with large glass doors and shops with large glass windows; banks and cafés scattered among them, even the occasional place of worship. Many of the buildings in the city are almost a hundred years old, some even older, the old English architecture looks fantastic when you're in the mood for it, and it's hard to be in any kind of mood other than a pissed-off one when the temperature is above a hundred. Most of the buildings are stained with exhaust fumes and soot from over the years, but the beauty of Christchurch isn't in the architecture, but in the gardens. Christchurch isn't known as the Garden City for nothing—there are trees almost on every street, the Botanical Gardens are only a few blocks away, and it breaks up the old look of the city more than the occasional modern hotel or office block being built. A couple of the shops still have Christmas decorations in the windows from a few months back, or they're getting them up earlier this year. It's creeping up to ten o'clock in the morning and the streets have never looked so empty. It's as if in the time I was away the Ebola Circus came to town, but of course it's nothing as scary as that; the heat is keeping people indoors. Those unlucky enough to be out and about are walking slowly to maintain energy, shirts and blouses damp with sweat, people carrying bottled water they've bought from the supermarket even though Christchurch has the best water in the world coming straight out of the tap. I cross the bridge going over the Avon River. The water level is lower than normal, and the trees lining the banks are drooping and look like they're trying to dive in. There are a couple of ducks hidden in the shade of some flax bushes, and another duck floating along the water on his back, his head twisted backward, dark bloated flies swarming its body. I pass a four-wheel drive double-parked at a set of lights, forcing cars to swing out into the opposite lane to get past. The vehicle is coated in dirt, and somebody has written *I wish my daughter was this dirty* across the back window with their finger. I walk to the central bus terminal and get blasted by the air-conditioning. The terminal smells of cigarette smoke and the electronic board displaying the departure times has had a brick or something equivalent thrown through it. I wait with ten other people for the next ride, a few of them helping to give a pair of lost tourists directions. For the first time in about twenty years I catch a bus in my own city. At the back of the bus a couple of school kids are rolling cigarettes and talking about how wasted they got last weekend, how wasted they're going to get this weekend, their drunken antics a badge of honor for them. They use *fuck* as a noun, a verb, an adjective, their conversation littered with the word.

The bus driver barely fits in behind the wheel and there is no obvious sign where his forearms end and his wrists start, and his head seems to come straight out of his shoulders, his neck engulfed by the fat of doughnuts past. We drive past a large group of teenagers with shaved heads all wearing black hoodies and jeans and looking like they've all just come from court and getting ready to do something that will send them back. I watch the city and see nothing dramatic has changed; a couple of new buildings and altered intersections, but for the most part it's identical to how it was before; those who don't look defeated by it are those doing the defeating. On the outset of my prison stay, four months seemed like a long time for me, and it seemed like time on the inside would come to a standstill while on the outside it would fly by. Now it looks like I haven't missed a thing.

Clouds of smoke erupt from behind the bus and add to the smog stain that's building on the back window. The bus pulls over every few minutes and the numbers on board shrink and grow. By the time we hit the suburbs there are only two other people onboard besides the driver. One of them is a nun, and the other is an Elvis impersonator decked out in full Elvis-Vegas-style sequins, and I feel like I'm in the middle of a setup to a joke. The folder Schroder gave me stays on my lap—unopened—the entire time. It has a green cover that is held closed by two rubber bands that I flick with my fingers every now and then. It takes a little under thirty minutes to reach the bus stop closest to home, and it's a five-minute walk from there that takes me eight in this heat.

Normally this time of year you can't go fifty meters without passing somebody mowing lawns or planting flowers, but the weather has pushed those activities to the end of the day when the heat has died down, so I walk the distance to my house in relative silence. Ninety-nine percent of my neighborhood is identical to how it was before. The remaining percent is made up of recently subdivided properties with brand-new homes. The sun bakes all of it, me included, and Schroder's money has almost turned to soup by the time my house comes into view.

I've never been more pleased to see it. Part of me was sure I'd never see it again, that the only way I'd be leaving prison was in a body bag after being shanked. It's a three-bedroom house with a black, concrete tile roof and gardens that are tidier than I've ever had them. My parents have been looking after the place. I find the key they hid along the side of the house for me. I head inside and it certainly feels like coming home. It's a lonely house but it's nice to be in a room that doesn't have concrete walls. The fridge is stocked with fresh food and there's a vase of flowers on the table with a *Welcome Home* card leaning against it. I call for my cat. He doesn't show up, but there's a half-empty food tray on the floor, so my parents have fed him this morning. I sit the flowers outside before my hay fever kicks in. While I was in jail my house was broken into but nothing stolen, the window they smashed has been replaced. I leave the file on the table and take a long shower, but the feeling of prison remains on my skin no matter how hard I scrub it.

When I get out I examine myself in the mirror. I haven't seen myself in four months. I've lost weight. I jump on the scale and find I'm almost ten kilograms lighter. My face is thinner, and for the first time ever my stubble is coming through gray in places, matching the gray coming through around my temples. Great—I'm on my way to looking like my father. My eyes are slightly bloodshot too. This is how I used to look last year when I was drinking.

I put on some summer clothes and feel more relaxed. I want to go and see my wife more than anything. Bridget has been in a care home for the last three years. She sits in a chair and stares out at the world and doesn't speak and hardly moves and nobody really knows for sure how much of her is still alive. There has been progress—or at least a hope of progress. The accident that nearly killed her left her with broken bones and torn flesh and in a coma for eight weeks, it punctured her left lung and shattered vertebrae and people tell me she was lucky to live. My daughter wasn't so lucky. Nobody ever tells me my daughter was unlucky enough to have died. People hardly mention her anymore.

Schroder's money will only get me about halfway there. Instead I have to wait for my parents. I don't have a car—it was damaged in the accident last year that led to my conviction. My parents wanted to pick me up today but couldn't. They visited me twice a week every week while I was locked away, but the day I'm due out they're busy, Dad with an appointment with a specialist at the hospital to fix the kind of prostate problems men get when they get to Dad's age, problems I'm hoping they'll cure with a pill by the time I get to sixty.

It's too hot to head back outside, and ironically, after four months of wanting nothing more than to come home, I'm hit with an incredible sense of boredom. I stand at the kitchen sink and stare out the window. Though tidy, the backyard looks tired, the heat having drained much of the life from every living thing planted out there. My cat, Daxter, comes in and gives me a sad look, then comes back in a minute later with a bird in his mouth. Daxter is an overweight ginger cat who, for a piece of food, will be your best friend. He puts the bird on the floor next to my feet and steps back and meows at me. I don't know whether to tell him off or cuddle him. I do the latter, then toss the bird into the garden recycling bin outside.

Like I knew I would, and like Schroder knew I would, I turn my thoughts to the folder with the green cover and rubber bands—a folder full of death. It couldn't hurt to look. Schroder's hoping there is something I can see that nobody else can. It's unlikely, but possibly I can offer a different perspective. Plus I have a mortgage to pay and nothing in the way of job prospects. I pick the file up from the dining table and carry it to the study.

chapter four

The heat is bad—not as bad as earlier this morning when Adrian set fire to his mother, but still hotter than he'd like. People complain about the heat. His mum did. She complained and screamed until the pretty-colored flames melted her tongue to the roof of her mouth and then she couldn't scream anymore. People like to walk around complaining that it's too hot and six months ago those same people walked around complaining it was too cold, and people, he knows, just can't be pleased. Adrian doesn't like the heat, but he isn't making a fuss about it. He knows you just have to be careful enough to stay in the shade and drink enough water. If you don't you can get skin cancer or your skin gets old quickly and gets blotchy and he doesn't like the idea of that. When he gets too hot he sweats, which makes his clothes stick to him and makes him itch, and he hates itching, because his are the kind of itches that he can never quite get to, they travel as he scratches at them, forcing him to chase them with chewed-up fingernails, which roughs his skin and makes him bleed.

He doesn't know how to work the radio in the car so he can't hear the temperature on the news. He wishes he could. He loves to listen to music, any kind of music as long as it's not that heavy metal stuff you rip your throat up trying to sing along to, or worse, hip-hop. For twenty years he never heard a single song, a life without music, only sad, lonely humming from some of the others he lived with. When music came back into his life, he just didn't get it. It was like all the rules had changed. Even records and cassette tapes had been replaced with songs you listened to on a computer, and he barely even knew what a computer was let alone how to use one. He listened and adapted to the new styles and now he hates to be without it. His favorite is classical. As a kid he never liked classical music. He used to have a paper route, and he'd save his money, and he was always spending it on cassette tapes. He used to collect them. He liked bands and he liked solo artists, but he didn't like women singers that much. Every week he would spend his pay on another tape, building his library of music. All those bands and artists are in the past and didn't date well, but classical music stays the same forever, and now he can't fall asleep without listening to his tape player.

The car stereo isn't the only thing not working. For air-conditioning he has to make do with having the window down. He doesn't have a driver's license and isn't sure he'd pass the test if he tried. The thought of it makes him nervous. He could have every piece of information memorized, he'd know in the little diagrams presented if the blue or red car had to give way, he'd know how much tread your tires needed, how much alcohol you could drive with in your blood, but if he sat in front of an officer who watched him trying to complete that test, it would be like a magician came along and made his answers disappear. It would be worse trying to pass the physical part, the part where he had to drive through town with somebody next to him, judging every move he made. He knows he'd only manage a few hundred meters before throwing up all over himself. No, he doesn't need a license as long as nobody ever pulls him over, and there's no reason anybody should. He's a careful driver, and the body in the trunk isn't making any noise.

He just wishes he could get the air-conditioning to work. He isn't sure whether it's his fault or the car's. The car is at least ten years old—surely not everything can be working right on it. The same goes for the radio.

There aren't many people on the streets as he drives through them. All the faces look the same. The houses seem to fall into two categories—nice ones that he'd like to live in, and bad ones he wouldn't. His last house was in that second category, but he's moved out now and living in the house where his mother, God bless her soul, raised him. It's not a nice place, but it's home, and there's a certain something to be said for that. He just doesn't know what that *something* is.

The driveway leading to that certain-something house has never been paved. It's made up from loose tooth-sized pieces of shingle that over the years have compacted into the dirt. Some of that dirt blankets the air behind the car as he drives over it, and when he comes to a stop it settles over the warm metal. He sits in the car and waits for the air to clear, humming to himself, not wanting the dust to stick to his damp body and make the itching worse. Soon the tranquillity returns. He loves it out here—the isolation, the peacefulness—out here there are no such things as home invasions and loud cars and people being rude.

The thumb he took from Cooper's house is sitting on the passenger seat in a glass jar filled with fluid that, if he holds it up to the light, is full of small gray flecks. He shakes it and the flecks float aimlessly like a snow globe but nowhere near as pretty. The thumb doesn't move much. The nail is longer than he grows his own, and he remembers hearing somewhere that people's nails still grow after they died, but he isn't sure that's true. It makes sense the nail stays the same and the fingers and toes shrink as the body dries out. Cooper would know. Cooper is a professor and a smart person, and this would be just one of a hundred things that he knows. He can't tell if Cooper cut the thumb from a man or a woman. The nail doesn't have any polish on it, but that doesn't mean anything. The cut that removed it from the hand is clean and the bone doesn't look splintered, but would be under a microscope. Something pretty sharp must have been used. He knows serial killers like to collect moments and . . . and no, not *moments*, and not *moment-o* either—he knows the word, has read it a hundred times, but for the moment it just won't come to him. Whatever it is, he knows that serial killers collect them and that it's normally a piece of jewelry or clothing they save somewhere private. It's dangerous for Cooper to have taken an entire thumb, and even more so to have put it on display. Adrian climbs out of the car and rests the jar on the roof where it forms a ring in the dust. The air is full of grasshopper sounds and birdsong. He moves to the back of the car and pops the trunk.

Cooper Riley's face is grazed from the fall he took when the Taser hit him, and he looks beaten up from banging around in the trunk of the car. His face is puffy and his wrists have swollen and turned purple from being tied behind him. Next time, Adrian thinks, he'll pad the trunk with blankets first. If nothing else, he's learning. Cooper would be proud of him.

There's a line of drool running from the corner of Cooper's lips. Tiny pieces of dirt have gotten caught in it. He brushes them away knowing Cooper would appreciate it, and wipes his hand across Cooper's shirt, hoping Cooper wouldn't mind. He knows this entire ordeal is going to be one giant learning curve, and it gets proven again when he discovers pulling a man out of a trunk is much harder than putting him in. He drags Cooper over the rim, the limp body catches in places, first his belt, then his arms, then his chin, and then there is a loud *thunk* as his head hits the bumper on the way down. Cooper lies on the ground as lifeless as he looked when he was in the car. Adrian leaves the rope around Cooper's wrists and ankles, heads inside, and returns with a red dolly that once, a lifetime ago, when he was supposed to be in his bedroom but wasn't, he saw a dead boy strapped to it. Age and use has chipped away over half of the paint, but the wheels still turn pretty good. The tires are half flat, and look even flatter once he has Cooper strapped in.

Negotiating the steps leading inside is the most awkward bit, and he manages them by turning around and dragging the dolly backward. Getting Cooper down into the basement is equally as hard, but he does the same thing, only in reverse, keeping the dolly low and carefully taking one step at a time, knowing if he lets go Cooper will crash down and break his nose and teeth. Cooper doesn't make any noise, other than his head bouncing against the frame of the dolly with every step.

The basement is segmented into two separate rooms, a dividing wall running across the middle is made of concrete block with a door near the middle acting as barrier to the second, internal room. The outer part used to be used as storage, though not these days. The inner room, the Scream Room as they used to call it, years ago contained a furnace that was stripped out and sold for scrap, not long after Adrian came to live here. He can still remember the workman coming and taking it away. He was young then, curious as to what was going to happen with the empty room. It was only a matter of days before he found out. In that room now is nothing but bolts sticking out of the walls and floor that were never important enough to spend the time or resources on removing. There's an old bed with a worn mattress and flat pillow that has absorbed thousands of tears, not all of them his own. There are extra blankets and a bucket in the corner with a lid and another bucket full of fresh water, a cup, a toothbrush and toothpaste, and a towel. He's filled a large plastic container full of water for Cooper to drink, there must be five liters in there. The door to this cell is made from iron except for a square patch of reinforced glass at head height. There is a sliding arm across the front that can't be accessed from the inside. At the bottom of the door is a panel that can be hinged open like a cat-flap so items can be passed back and forth, big enough for the bucket or for somebody very small. It opens outward and has the hinges on this side of it and the bolts are on the outside and can't be opened from within. From no point within the basement can the outside world be seen. There used to be a single lightbulb that hung down from the ceiling, but a long time ago that was removed after one of the boys pulled enough of the wire through to make a noose. His name was George, and George's tongue bloated to the same size as his mouth and his skin turned gray and George never came back. After that all the rooms in the house had the cables shortened. So now the only light comes through the open basement door, which isn't much, but enough to see by.

He wheels Cooper into the inner room and unties him, then helps him onto the mattress. The mattress is slightly damp and cool, which Adrian thinks Cooper will appreciate, especially this week with the temperature almost topping one hundred and ten every day. The bedsprings sag and it's the first time they've had weight on them in three years. He lifts Cooper's head and secures a pillow beneath it then steps out of the cell, taking the dolly and ropes with him. He locks the door behind him and leans with his forehead on the glass and watches Cooper, who, for the moment, is still. He knows when Cooper awakes he won't be happy, and Adrian is fully prepared for it.

Back outside the day has continued to grow hotter. The glass jar with the thumb has trapped some of that heat and nearly burns his fingers. He collects it, along with a few other things he's taken from Cooper's home, and heads back inside. Over the years Adrian has met other killers. He has lived with people who have killed families, people who have killed strangers, people who have killed for no real-life reason, who have taken lives because of a voice telling them to, or an instinct, or a hidden message in a newspaper from God. He's shared rooms with people who have sliced others apart, only a few without emotion, most of them dumbfounded and upset at what they did, all hoping pills and talking about feelings would cure them. There haven't been many—he's met less killers than he can count on both hands, but he believes they are the reason he now has a fascination with them. He would have been just like them if he hadn't been sent here and locked away when he was a teenager.

There was one, he remembers, that was impossible to warm to, a man who had killed his parents and brother and sister the day before he turned sixteen. Not really a man, but more of a boy, certainly a boy younger than Adrian when they met. His name was Hutchinson, and Adrian always thought it was a strange name, and he also thought that Hutch was a boy before he took the knife to his family but a man immediately after. Whenever Hutch had to spend time in the Scream Room he never complained. There were many trips down there for him, and never did he speak a word about what happened. Adrian has always wondered what it would be to be a man like that.

Hutch stayed here for a few years and then moved on and Adrian has no idea what became of the man, whether he's alive, whether he's still a killer, or whether he's in a grave mourned by no one. It was these years that shaped his obsession . . . no, his mother has told him it's wrong to be obsessed with anything . . . it was these years that shaped his *interest* in killers. Last year with the papers continually feeding him information about the Christchurch Carver and the Burial Killer, his interest in serial killers became extreme. He suspects the thing inside him creating that interest isn't normal. It made him want to move back here. It made him want to learn to drive so he could do something with that interest. He stacks Cooper's belongings on the shelves in the basement where Cooper can see them through the small window that, yesterday, Adrian cleaned especially.

"Cooper?"

Cooper does not answer. He does not move.

"Cooper?" This time a little louder. He knows you have to speak up to be heard through the door, but not much, only a little really.

Satisfied Cooper is still asleep, he tidies the basement. He doesn't need Cooper to wake into this mess and form an instant bad impression. He straightens the memorabilia on the shelves, tidies the bookcase that has dozens of autobiographies of serial killers. There is a couch down here and a scarred coffee table but not much more. Anyway, today is only day one, and as he learns he will begin to improve.

"Cooper?"

Nothing.

He heads upstairs and turns on the radio. It's small, and has a belt clip so he can hang it from his pants, and it can play tapes and even record things too. He's sure Cooper will enjoy the same kind of classical music, and he carries the radio back to the basement, but when he starts to climb down the stairs the reception fades. He plays with the dial but can't get any of the stations to work, not until he climbs back up the stairs into the corridor. He replaces the batteries, but the same thing happens and he doesn't understand why. Can the music not get past the concrete walls from the radio station? He could play a tape, but playing tapes uses up the battery faster, and he doesn't want to use it up that way. He's disappointed. Hopefully this will be the only setback.

Suspecting Cooper will be hungry as well as confused when he wakes up, Adrian, not wanting to be a rude host, heads to the kitchen where the radio works again, and he clips it onto his pants and listens to one of the modern rock bands he's come to like, and starts preparing lunch for his new housemate.

chapter five

They're calling her Melissa X. It's not a Roman numeral—she isn't the tenth Melissa in the city to have killed a cop, or the tenth Melissa to become a serial killer still on the loose, or the tenth Melissa to fill what I imagine to be boxes and boxes of evidence stored in an evidence warehouse. It's an X because it's an unknown. The media, normally quick to come up with catchy names for crimes and killers, have dubbed her The Uniform Killer. She became famous when a videotape found in the Christchurch Carver's possession—a serial killer named Joe Middleton who was caught last year—showed her stabbing a knife into the chest of a currently missing detective. The Christchurch Carver was arrested the same day I killed the serial killer I was hunting last year, a man dubbed the Burial Killer. In the month between the accident I caused, the sentencing, and then being put in jail, I saw on the news that Melissa was still on the run and was now the suspect in other homicides. She was big news back then, and I guess she's even bigger news now because the police still have no idea where she is or who she really is. Another day, another serial killer—each one trying to outdo the other. For the last few years the city was under siege by the Christchurch Carver, now it's dealing with his girlfriend.

I open the windows in the study and let the outside air force its way in; it's warm air but at least it's fresh. It's circulated slightly by an oscillating fan that I drag out of a wardrobe and plug in, thick dust blowing off the blades and clouding the air for the first ten seconds and sending me into a sixty-second sneezing fit. The contents of the folder are two inches thick and I stack them on the desk into different piles. The fan lifts the corners of the pages every twenty seconds as it passes by. There are reports, statements, copies of forensic evidence. There are photographs of bruises, cuts, blood; there's a DVD with a recording of Melissa X murdering Detective Inspector Calhoun. Four dead bodies and a lot of paperwork, and Melissa is on the loose. They have DNA and fingerprints and even footage of the woman, and with all of that she's a ghost. Her face has been plastered in the papers, headlining the news. Three episodes of *New Zealand's Most Wanted* have been dedicated to finding information about her. Even the psychics have come out of the woodwork. Nobody knows where she is, and even stranger, nobody has come forward to identify her. Family, friends, colleagues, schoolmates, doctors, teachers—if these people are in her past or present, they don't recognize her. Melissa may be her name but it also may not be. At one point during the Carver investigation she showed up at the police station to help identify a suspect—giving false information to help the Carver evade capture. She gave her name as Melissa Graves, and nobody at the time had any reason to doubt her. The name, of course, isn't real. Since then it's been narrowed down to Melissa X, and it's unlikely Melissa is her real name either.

Days after that the Carver was caught and nobody has seen Melissa since. For the first few weeks after the Carver's arrest, the consensus was Melissa X was dead, another of his victims. Then the bodies started showing up and Melissa X went from suspect to victim and back to suspect again.

Since the Carver's arrest five months ago, multiple attempts have been made to get him to offer up information on the woman, and each time he shoots them down. Melissa X is a monster with the blood of at least four people on her hands. I can't blame Schroder for wanting all the fresh perspective he can get.

The report details each of the homicides, leading with Calhoun's. All three of the other men worked in uniform—though no uniforms were found near the bodies, which were stripped down to their underwear. Two security guards and one police constable. The constable was found in a park, naked. He'd been tortured. One security guard was found in his home, the only thing reported missing was his uniform. The other guard was found on a golf course where he patrolled, his almost naked body pitching distance from the fourteenth green with the same signs of torture as the other men—a completely crushed testicle, the same injury Melissa gave the Christchurch Carver. No connection has been made between the men other than the way their throats had been opened up by a blade, and the fact they all had missing uniforms. There was nothing to link them to the Carver. There are two theories floating around as to why the uniforms were taken—either for practical use to impersonate one of these men or as a trophy. The reason for the torture is unknown—again two possibilities—one was to extract information, the other was for fun. I watch the DVD in the living room and my take on Melissa is she hurt these men for fun. Detective Inspector Calhoun is bound to a chair. The chair is in a bathroom and there is tape over his mouth. There are patches of blood on his shirt and the skin around the duct tape is dry and raw. His eyes are wide with fear and his face is soaked with sweat and he looks like he hasn't slept in a week. The footage is taken two days before the Carver was arrested.

"I don't understand what you're playing at, Joe," Melissa says. There aren't any background sounds. Her voice comes from somewhere to the side of the camera. The report says the angles in the footage and an examination of the apartment show the camera was hidden in the wardrobe pointing out. It means Melissa didn't know she was being filmed. It's possible Joe was going to try and blackmail her. The report doesn't say.

"He's my witness to what you really are." They are Joe the Carver's words, and his voice is also off to the side. The footage still only shows Calhoun, his eyes wide in panic. Every ounce of his being is seeping fear. Calhoun didn't need to be a detective to figure out what was going to happen to him. My stomach tightens and I tighten my grip on the remote control to try and stop my hands from shaking.

"Oh? And what do you have on him?" Melissa asks.

"Enough."

I wonder what "enough" means, and I'm sure I'm not the only one wondering. Calhoun's fingerprints were found on a knife used to kill a prostitute only days before his death, but the scene was staged. Calhoun was innocent.

"You're forgetting one thing, Joe."

"And what's that?"

"I don't need him."

Melissa steps into view, this tall woman brimming with sex appeal, but her eyes don't fit with the package, her body and face transmit the kind of beauty you'd expect from a woman used to showing off the latest fashions on a runway, but her eyes tell a different story, her eyes reveal somebody you'd expect to spend her nights skinning kittens. She moves gracefully toward Calhoun and the veins stand out in her neck from the effort of plunging the knife into his chest. The camera doesn't move. Joe doesn't enter the frame. I want to put the TV on mute because I don't want to hear the sounds Calhoun makes because somehow they're worse than seeing him convulse beneath her. There's a long gargling sound, like the last of the water draining from a bathtub. When it's over, Melissa tucks her hair over her right ear and looks toward the camera, but not right at it. The Carver never comes into view.

"You stupid bitch. How could you do such a thing?"

She pulls the silver duct tape away from Calhoun's mouth and blood spills out of it and down his front. "I'm surprised that you thought I wouldn't."

I'm surprised too.

She carries on. *"I told you no tricks, Joe."*

"No you didn't."

"Well you should have assumed it. I still want my money."

After that the footage gets even worse. There is a coldness with this woman that I've never seen before, a cold beauty that remains even when she withdraws the knife and drags it across the dead detective's throat. Not long after she walks away the footage ends. Melissa said no tricks, but filming her was a trick. I wonder what the money is she's talking about. According to the file the question has been posed to Joe, but he hasn't given an answer.

I switch off the TV and walk slowly down the hallway to the study with a stronger determination to help Schroder. This is why he included the DVD. The connection between Melissa and the Carver is hard to understand. She tortured him, they became lovers, and he won't give up any information on her. It doesn't make sense. If the Carver hadn't been arrested, would they have stayed together until one of them killed the other?

By the end of the first hour there aren't any spare surfaces on the desk and I've had to lock down the fan to keep it from blowing the papers away. By the end of the second hour parts of the floor are covered and some of the images are taped to a whiteboard I have in my study and the fan is back in the wardrobe. All the windows in the house are open. I can hear a stereo thumping from one of the neighboring houses and somebody singing along to it. I wanted to think in silence, but I turn my own stereo on preferring to listen to my own music rather than somebody else's. I listen to a Beatles album and think things were easier back then before figuring things are never easy. In the two hours I've created piles of chaos with no real clear insight to who this woman is.

The security guard on the golf course was the last body found, and that was three weeks ago. I wonder what Melissa wants their uniforms for. All that wondering, though, tires me out, and by the end of the third hour I start moving through the house, putting some distance between me and the collection of evidence. I pause in the kitchen and make a sandwich. I'd planned on arriving home and somehow making my way out to see my wife, but somehow three hours have gone by and I haven't even thought of her. I feel like getting a drink. Start with a beer and see what follows, but there's no alcohol in the house. I end up sitting at the dining table with my lunch and a glass of milk the same way I did when I was a kid.

There is a world waiting for me back in the study, a world that I thought I had escaped. I finish my lunch and I'm halfway down the hall back toward that world when somebody knocks on my front door. My parents said they'd call first, so it isn't them. Anyway, through the blurred glass I can see only one figure. I feel like not answering it. I just want to tell whoever is there to go away, but the knocking continues so I head toward it. I open up the door. It's my lawyer. A year ago my lawyer wanted to kill me. He tied me up and dragged me into the woods. He threw me into the dirt and made me stare down the barrel of a gun while he considered pulling the trigger. My only thought now is that he's come to finish off what he couldn't finish then.

chapter six

Cooper can taste carpet and dust and something metallic, along with something he can't place, something that makes him think of decaying coffins being opened in ancient black-and-white movies, where the inside lids have claw marks and the dead men have torn and broken fingernails. His eyes are too heavy and sore to open. The darkness is connected optically to a mind that feels raw. His head is pounding and he wonders what sort of hangover this is, and quickly decides it must be the worst kind, the kind where you wake up and wish you were dead instead of drunk. There is a ringing in his ears and his chest is burning.

The first memory to return is the heat wave. A city under siege by the sun. That could be why he started drinking. Hell, it's a good reason for anybody to start. Drink what you can then pass out someplace cool, because wherever he is at the moment, it is certainly that. He bets his wife is equally as drunk somewhere before remembering he doesn't have a wife anymore, that they separated three years ago though he can't quite remember why, not off the top of his head, and since his wife there haven't been any other women, not serious ones, and there's nobody at the moment, so probably he started drinking alone. Only he's given up drinking, or so he'd thought. In the past the drink has gotten him into trouble. He rolls onto his side, the bed squeaking and grinding beneath him, not his bed, though, because he doesn't recognize any of the sounds. Then he thinks *hospital*. He's been in an accident, that whatever has happened has nothing to do with an indulgence of too much scotch. He listens for but can't hear the chatter of patients, the scuffle of feet, the *bing bong* of the intercom shouting code blue or code red in room one-oh-something. Last time he stepped into a hospital was two years ago when his uncle was sick, his uncle being eaten alive from the inside out by cancer. He remembers another old man in the same room having to shit into a plastic container suspended beneath the seat of a chair next to the bed, the stench of it wafting through the room enough to make him leave. None of that is with him here, none of the sounds or the smells. This isn't a hospital.

He massages his closed eyes with his fingertips and winces when he finds a bump on his forehead sticking out like a golf ball. He gets his eyes open and everything is blurry and gray-looking. He blinks heavily until things start to clear a little, but it doesn't help. Wherever he is, there isn't much light. His face is grazed and stings to the touch. He remembers walking to his car after closing the garage door. He was carrying his briefcase and he can't remember why, there'd be no purpose for that, and then there was . . . was . . . what?

"Oh Jesus," he says, and he tries to stand up, but his body won't work, he manages to get up onto his elbows before collapsing back down, his arm banging off the edge of the bed, his knuckles hitting the concrete floor and scraping away the skin. He sticks them in his mouth and the blood tastes sweet. He needs to get up. Needs to get away from wherever this is. The man. The man asked him for the time and then . . . and then he lost control over his body. He lay on the ground with the sun in his eyes until the man shadowed it. He couldn't move. Couldn't even speak. There was confetti on the ground next to his face and he couldn't figure out why it was there.

The man crouched down and held a cloth over his face and there was nothing he could do to fight it. Then . . . then this.

He pushes his hands into the bed. Forces himself upward, slower this time, trying to maintain control, desperate to get onto his feet, pausing to sit on the edge of the bed while the world spins. His eyes begin to adjust. The room comes into focus, but there's not much to see. It's some kind of bomb shelter. The only light coming into the room is through a small glass window in a door. Everything is concrete and steel. With small cramps and electrical-like charges, feeling begins to arrive to the rest of his body. First pins and needles through his feet and hands, then it spreads up his limbs into his core. He stands up. There's a heavy ache behind his eyes. He's tired and scared and has no idea how long he's been unconscious.

He realizes he was shot by a Taser. That's what the confetti was. Tasers spit out twenty or thirty bits of paper with serial numbers on them every time they're fired. It identifies the user. Then he was drugged. He remembers the rag on his face, the smell, the darkness.

He supports his weight against the wall and makes his way to the door. It's a short walk. The room is twice the size of a prison cell, with a view out to what looks like another prison cell, this one not as dark, with light coming through an open door that he can just see the bottom of on an upper landing. The window in the door is clean, but has some scratches on this side of it and, if broken, wouldn't leave a hole big enough to climb through. The window fogs up from his breath, he wipes his hand over it, his thumb following some of the scratches. He doesn't want to think about the people trapped on this side of the door who made them, not yet anyway. There's a bookcase out there but he can't make out any of the titles. There's a couch with holes big enough for him to see, through which springs are sticking out. He looks back at the bookcase. He keeps staring at it, the shapes becoming clearer . . . if only there was a little more light. On the top shelf he thinks he can see the thumb he bought in the auction, and suddenly it all makes sense to him—the auction was a trap. Whoever sold him the thumb never intended to part with it—in fact, all along the seller wanted more thumbs to add to his collection. Next to the bookcase, the leather scuffed up and one of the catches twisted, is his briefcase.

The nausea hits him like a punch to the stomach. He turns around and everything is dark until he moves from the window. There's no sink or toilet, only two buckets. There's a cup for drinking and a toothbrush, which indicates the seller's intent isn't murder, at least not immediately. He picks up the empty bucket and sits on the edge of the bed and throws up into it, wiping the bottom of his shirt across his mouth when he's done. His head is pounding, and having to squint to see a goddamn thing isn't helping. He rubs his hand over his chest and finds the two small holes where he was shot by the Taser, the barbs pulled out by his attacker.

He closes his eyes and takes himself back to the moment he first saw the man, he holds on to the image, and no, he's sure it's not somebody he's ever seen before. How many other people did this man post that thumb to and then abduct? It's a hell of a signature. A hell of an MO. One he'll teach about if he ever gets out of here.

He moves around the cell, slowly exploring the walls with his hands, the back of the cell almost in complete darkness. The stench of his vomit hangs in the room with nowhere to go, making him feel sick all over again. There are bolts jutting out of the floor and the walls that he finds when he trips on one and lands against the other. Once something large used to be in this room. There are pipes leading up into the ceiling that have been capped off, and a thick piece of steel that's been bolted into the roof, probably covering a hole. If the hole is close to the size of the piece of steel, then it would be big enough to squeeze through. He steps onto the bed but can't reach it. He tips the bed up onto its side and scales it and when he's within reach he sees that the nuts on this side of the metal have been filed into a smooth surface. Even if he was strong enough to loosen them with his fingers, there's no way he can grip them. He tries digging his fingers under one of the edges of the plate but it's no use. He climbs down and resets the bed to how he found it. On another wall an iron eyelet has been welded onto another of the bolts, this one half a meter from the ceiling. There are a couple of holes in the walls that have been filled in with cement. Whatever was taken out of this room was taken for the purpose of turning this place into a cell, and that's exactly what this place is. Christ, it's like something out of a textbook. Something he would teach.

Is that the point of this? Is that why he's here?

He checks his pockets. There's a piece of tinfoil that he didn't put in there and a couple of coins which he did. He unwraps the foil. There are two painkillers. He wraps them back up. He studies the ceiling looking for signs of surveillance and sees none. He has two options: keep waiting, or start banging and yelling.

He pounds against the door. "Hey? Hey? Who's out there? Hey? Where the hell am I?"

No answer. He pushes at the glass, not expecting to see it flex, and flexing is exactly what it doesn't do, nor break, nor shatter. He bangs against it with the heel of his fist and each bang vibrates through his head, making the headache worse. He takes off his shoe and bangs with the heel of it and gets the same result. He looks out at the bookcase. The harder he stares at it the more his head hurts, and he finds peripherally he can make out some of the items, but when he looks straight on they merge with the darkness. Before disappearing, he's sure what he was looking at were weapons and ropes and pieces of clothing; things he himself has collected.

He starts banging again. He keeps his eyes closed and tries to ignore the throbbing deep in his brain. His arm is getting sore from swinging his shoe into the door. He switches from hand to hand and is getting ready to give up after five minutes of it when the light coming through the door upstairs dims, and he knows somebody is standing up there. He stops banging and his headache thanks him for it. When the man comes down, he comes down surrounded by a cold blue glow. Cooper sees him in stages, the feet are first, brown leather shoes scuffed from use. Pants frayed around the hems with a couple of coin-sized holes—not the kind of fraying with holes that are in fashion, but the kind that comes from years of wear. Then the hips, the top of the pants coming into view, a leather belt, then he sees the lantern, a battery-powered lantern for camping, not bright enough to hurt his eyes. The man carrying it is wearing a short-sleeve white shirt with a thin leather tie, and the same corduroy pants from earlier. He reaches the bottom of the stairs and turns toward him. The lantern gives his skin a pale sheen. His hair is slicked to the sides with wide comb teeth marks through it, with a clump of it falling over his forehead. He has brown, droopy eyes and chapped lips and dozens of acne scars. He reaches the cell door, the lantern to the side of a tray carrying food that Cooper can't smell.

Then the man smiles. "Welcome to my collection," he says.

chapter seven

My lawyer's name is Donovan Green. He's my height and built about the same and I met him late winter last year—the afternoon after I got drunk and ran my car into Emma Green, his daughter. I didn't know who he was when he bailed me out and offered to represent me. I took his help because there was no real alternative. Thirty minutes after meeting him his help turned out to be the kind that had him dragging me unconscious through the woods. He held a gun to my head and in the end didn't have the stomach to finish the job. He left me with the promise that if anything ever happened to his daughter he'd be back. I keep my hand on the door and my stomach sinks. If he's here to kill me, then his daughter must have died from her injuries. Which means I won't get to see my wife one last time. Which means I have to go along with whatever it is he wants to do. That's the way things work in my world. Last year I wanted him to pull the trigger. Now I don't.

"Remember me?" he asks.

He looks about as run-down and tired as he looked last time I saw him, as if the heat has gotten to him the same way it's gotten to the trees outside my house. His hair is messed up and his clothes are wrinkled and he hasn't shaved in a few days and he smells like he hasn't showered either. My mouth goes dry and I struggle to answer him. It must be obvious that I remember him. The kind of time we shared together is impossible to forget. I let my hand fall from the door and I take a step back.

"You might as well come in."

"I know what you're thinking," he says, and he sounds tired. "I remember what I promised you. But I'm not here for that. I'm here for your help."

For him to want my help it must be bad. Bad enough he'd come to the one man he hates more than any other. I move aside and he comes in. I lead him through the house. He doesn't comment on any of the furniture or décor. The stereo is on repeat, and the Beatles album has started back up. I take him outside onto the deck where the outdoor furniture has gathered some rust and a whole lot of cobwebs over the last four months. I don't offer him a drink. The sun beats down on us and I figure he won't want to stay long, and imagine he'd want to stay even less if I showed him the DVD I watched earlier. We sit on opposite sides of the table, balancing it out and giving the yard good feng shui.

"I want to hire you," he says.

He's beginning to sweat and he has to keep squinting to look at me because the sun is in his face but on my back. He's wearing a T-shirt and shorts and not a suit, so he's not here in any lawyering capacity, which means I won't have to take out a second mortgage to talk to him. He looks like he's slept in that shirt for the last few days.

"I don't need the work," I tell him.

"Yes you do."

"It's a moot point. I lost my PI license so I can't help you."

"That works out okay because I won't be paying you. You'll be doing this for free so it won't be professional. You're not going to need a license because you're going to want to do this for free anyway. You owe me."

"Thanks for sweetening the deal. You want to tell me what's bad enough for you to have come to me? You do realize I only just got out of jail today."

"I know. If that had been up to me you'd have been put away for much longer. You could have killed my daughter."

I don't answer him. I've already apologized and I could apologize a thousand more times and he wouldn't accept it. I know that because I've been in his shoes. I dragged the man who killed my daughter and hurt my wife into the woods and handed him a shovel. There was a lot he tried saying. He tried telling me how sorry he was that he'd been drinking so much, how sorry he was at all the other driving convictions in his past. He apologized for running down my wife and daughter by accident and doing nothing about it. He cried as he dug the hole, he got dirt all over his face and shirt. He was a mess. His face was covered in snot and tears and he kept blubbering that he was sorry, and in the end I didn't want to hear it. I didn't see it as an accident. I saw it as murder. A man with that many convictions behind him, that many warnings, a man like that who keeps on drinking and driving, that makes it only a matter of time before he kills. It was no different from a man firing a loaded gun into a crowd of people.

I put a bullet in his head and filled in the grave he had dug.

My lawyer knows I did it. I told him. When he pointed the gun at me wanting to do the same thing, I told him how it was going to feel.

"She's gone missing," he says. "Emma."

"What?"

"Nobody has heard from her in two days. She was at work Monday night and left to go home and never showed up."

"You've gone to the police?"

"What?" he asks, almost flinching as though my question is the most stupid one he's ever heard. "Jesus, of course we have. But the police, the police only care once somebody has been missing twenty-four hours, so they've only cared since last night, and they haven't cared much because they're not out there looking for her, and even when they do start looking there are things I know you can do that they can't."

"The police, you have to trust them. They know what they're doing."

He starts drumming his fingers across the tabletop then stops and stares at his fingernails as if disappointed by the tune they made. He looks back at me and there is genuine pain in his eyes and I know the feeling and I know I'm going to help this man.

"When girls like Emma go missing," he says, and the words are slow and considered and must hurt to say because I know where he's going with this, "there's only one way they're ever found."

I don't answer him. He looks up toward the sun and I know he's fighting back tears.

"When was the last time somebody her age went missing and there was a happy ending?" he asks.

I still don't answer him. I can't tell him the truth, and I don't want to lie to him. Girls like Emma who go missing normally show up a few days later floating naked in a river.

"I already know she's probably dead," he says, and the words come from him in small stops and starts, like he really has to force them.

He looks back at me. "Statistically, I know the deal," he adds. "My wife, she knows it too. Right now she's sedated because she's borderline hysterical. The police tell me in cases like this, they never really know whether the girl just ran away from home or got herself a new boyfriend and is holed up in a bedroom somewhere. It's bullshit. They know it's bullshit when they're spinning that possibility to me and my wife. If there's a chance she's still alive, she won't be by the time they find her, and if she was alive in the time they were looking and not finding her and I didn't do everything I could . . . then . . . I don't know. I think you know, right?" he says. "I think you can figure out how it would feel. So I'm doing everything that I can, and that means coming to you. It means you're going to do everything you can because you owe me and you owe her. Then . . . and, if she is, you know, dead, then the police will find who hurt her and then what? Send him to jail for fifteen years and parole him in ten?"

"I know it's wrong, trust me, I really do, but that's just the way it is," I say.

"I know. Jesus, don't you think I know that? But it shouldn't be that way, and it doesn't have to be. I remember what you said to me in the woods. I know you killed the man who killed your daughter. What gives you the right to have that justice and stop others from having it?"

"You don't need to remind me of my own daughter."

"Do I need to remind you that you almost took mine away?" He slowly shakes his head. "When you ran into her it changed her life. It sent her down a different path. You jumped into her timeline, and instead of her turning A," he says, tapping his right forefinger with his left to make his point, "she turned B. It brought different people into her life. Doctors and rehab, new friends. She lost three months studying and had to take private tutoring. She almost didn't graduate high school last year. She almost didn't qualify for university this year. Her circumstances changed. If you hadn't hurt her, she'd be in a different place now, with different people in her life. If one of those different people are responsible for taking her . . ."

"I get your point," I say, holding up my hand. If one of those new people in her life took her, then it's my fault. It's like he said—I sent her down path B, and path B might have had a bad man waiting in the shadows.

"Do you? Because if you did you'd be asking me how you can help. I know about you," he says. "You're about doing the right thing. Looking for Emma, that's the right thing. That's why you're going to help me."

I look at him but all I can see is his daughter, slumped against the steering wheel with blood running down the side of her face, broken glass surrounding the car, my own car a wreck with the front of it folded around a lamppost, a billboard with Jesus turning wine into bottled water staring down at me, my clothes and skin reeking of alcohol. My ears were ringing and I could taste blood and the night was so cold there was fog in the air, and God how I wish it was all just a dream. I had become the man who had run over my wife and daughter. That was the worst part. I picked up the half-empty bottle of booze from the floor of the car and tossed it into the night and I've not had a drop since. Donovan Green's eyes are pleading with me, he knows his daughter is dead and yet is still holding out hope that she isn't.

"I'll need expenses," I say, and I hate asking for them, but I don't have any money. "I don't even have a car. Or a cell phone."

"You'll get what you need."

"And I can't give you any promises."

"Yes you can. You can promise me you'll do what it takes to find the man that has her, and that when you find him . . . when you find him, you'll come to me before you go to the police. You're working for me, not them. You come to me, not to them."

I slowly nod, images of Donovan Green walking through the woods with his daughter's killer and I'm walking with him, helping him get the revenge he needs. This time I imagine he'll have the balls to go through with it. "We don't know anybody took her," I say. "Not for sure."

"Somebody has her. I know it. I just know it."

"Tell me about her," I say, and as he does I realize there was never any chance of staying away from this world.

chapter eight

Adrian sets the tray on the coffee table and moves to the door. Cooper has been watching him walk down the stairs, and he knows that what is coming is going to be difficult for Cooper to hear. He's been nervous about it all morning, and only ten minutes ago he was hunched over the bathroom sink, vomiting into it. His stomach is burning and his throat is sore and he wishes there was a way to make this easier, but there isn't. It's his job to sell himself, to get his reasons across, and if he can do that then Cooper will agree to stay. He has to. For the last ten minutes Cooper has been banging at the cell door in the same way that Adrian, as a kid, used to do, but in the later years Adrian stopped banging because nothing good ever came from it. Since planning his collection, he's known there are only two reactions available to Cooper—he would be upset and angry, or he would be desperate and begging. The banging tells Adrian what reaction he's in for.

Cooper's face is inches from the glass. Adrian steps to the side slightly to let light from the lamp get past him. Cooper doesn't look so good, but he does look calm and Adrian is pleased.

"Where am I?" Cooper asks.

"Umm . . ." he starts, and suddenly his tongue is so heavy it won't move and all the words inside his mind have been wiped away like an eraser over a blackboard, and he can't remember a single thing. He knew this was going to be an important moment. He'd even rehearsed some big words with which he could impress. He started out with *"welcome to my collection,"* which has been the plan all along, and now he's wishing he'd written things down. It's such a rudimentary mistake, he thinks, then enlarges his smile knowing that Cooper would be proud with the use of the large word, but disappointed with the mistake. "Umm . . ." he repeats, his tongue a little looser now, and the faster he tries to think the foggier his thoughts become.

"Who the hell are you?" Cooper asks.

"The . . . the first rule of a serial killer," he says, thankful for the words—God, he's so nervous he wants to be sick again—"is, is to . . . to depersonalize his victims," he says, looking down at the floor.

"Is that what I am? One of your victims?" Cooper asks.

"Huh?"

"It's why I'm in this cage, right?"

Adrian is confused. "Cage? No, this is a basement," he says, looking around. Can't Cooper see that? "You can tell because there are concrete blocks and no bars."

"It was a metaphor."

Adrian frowns. "A what?"

"Let me out."

"No."

"What do you want? Did you send me the thumb?"

"What?"

"The thumb. Are you the one who sold it to me?"

"I . . . I don't understand. What thumb? The one in the jar that you cut off one of your victims?"

"One of my victims? What the hell are you talking about?" Cooper asks.

"What are you talking about?" Adrian asks.

"Why am I here? Are you going to kill me?"

"I . . ."

"Let me out," Cooper repeats. "Whatever is going on here, this needs to stop. You have to let me go. Whatever you have planned, it can't happen. I don't know what you want. I'm not a rich person. I can't give you money. Please, please, you have to let me go."

"I . . ." he starts, then something catches in his throat and he can't continue.

"What do you intend to do with me?"

"Umm . . ."

"You said welcome to your collection. Is that what all of this is? Is that what I am? A collector's piece?" Cooper asks, his voice sounding more angry than scared.

"You're asking too many questions all at once," Adrian says, getting confused. He lifts his hands up to his face and pushes his palms against his cheeks.

"Am I a collector's item?"

"No, no, certainly not," Adrian answers, upset Cooper would think that way. "You're more than just a piece. You're . . . you're everything."

"Everything?"

"You are the collection."

"So all of this," Cooper says, and Adrian thinks he's spreading his arms but he can't know for sure because all he can see is Cooper's face, "is some kind of zoo?"

"What? No, this isn't a zoo," he says, pulling his hands from his face and pointing them toward the opposite walls. "There would be animals here if it were, like monkeys and penguins and it would smell, and zoos have cages and . . . and you still think this is a cage? This is a collection and you're the main . . . the main attraction."

"As what? A criminology professor?"

"Partly that, and partly because of the stories you can tell me. And the fact you're a serial killer makes you even more valuable."

Cooper's face pales. A frown appears, the lines deep enough to look like long scars. "What? What did you just say?"

"A storyteller. You're here to tell me stories about killers you know. I find them interesting."

"You said I was a serial killer. Explain yourself."

He never had to explain himself in the past to his cassette collection, or the collection of comics he had as a kid. This is tough work. "A serial killer is a person who . . ."

"Yes, yes, I know what a serial killer is, you twit, but I'm not a killer."

Adrian doesn't know what a twit is, but he does know he doesn't like being called one. "Don't you get it?" he asks, thrilled he knows something Cooper does not, because Cooper is one of those people who knows everything. His mother called those people *good-for-nothing know-it-alls*, but of course Cooper is good for everything. "You study killers, you know killers, and you are a killer. You are an entire collection in one piece."

Cooper takes a deep breath then slowly exhales. He closes his eyes for a few seconds and rubs the side of his head with his fingers. Adrian thinks the man is either trying to collect his thoughts or fall asleep while standing. He decides on the first of the two options because it's not late enough in the day to start sleeping. Then he decides the collecting your thoughts trick might work for him too, so he closes his eyes and takes a few deep breaths, and it helps, just a little.

"I'm not a serial killer," Cooper says.

Adrian opens his eyes back up. "Yes you are. I know you are. That's why you're here."

"No, I'm here because you abducted me, and because you're delusional."

"I am no such thing."

"What's your name?"

"What?"

"Your name. Surely you have one."

"The first rule of a . . ."

"Shut up about the damn rule," Cooper says, banging the door. "Just tell me your bloody name," he says.

"But . . ."

"Your name. Tell me your name," he shouts.

"Adrian," he answers. He didn't want to answer, he certainly had the intent to always keep his name to himself, but he hates being shouted at, always has, and his name comes out before he can stop himself.

"Does Adrian have a last name?"

"You have to stop," he says, getting mad now. "No more, no more questions." He covers his ears and shuts his eyes, but he can still hear Cooper asking him things. He takes a few steps away from the door. After a minute Cooper goes quiet and Adrian moves his hands away.

"I made you something to eat."

"I don't want anything to eat. I want you to let me out of here."

"You get used to the cell," Adrian says. He starts scratching at a sudden itch on the side of his head. "And I'm going to try and make it more comfortable for you. See all of this?" he asks, spreading his arms and encompassing the small view. "I brought these things from your house, all your serial killer memorabilia, I brought it here so you could have your own collection nearby because I know how important it is to you, just as you are important to me. It's still all yours," he says, "I don't want it, I want you to still have it. If you think about it, we're not that unalike really. You collect serial killer memorabilia, and . . ."

"And you collect serial killers. I get the point."

"I am so lucky to own you," he says, hardly hearing what Cooper said at all.

"You don't own me, you crazy son of a bitch," Cooper says, the defiance in his voice is annoying.

"Don't be mean," Adrian says, then remembers that of the two of them, it really is his job to be the calm one. After all, he has had days to think about this, and Cooper has only had a few minutes. This is going to be quite an adjustment for Cooper. He can't just expect the man to wake up and accept it. "You should eat," he says, hoping the change in topic and the food he made will hasten the bonding they have to do.

"Listen, Adrian, Adrian, I can't stay here. This isn't going to work. You're going to see that soon, and then you're going to let me go, but by then it'll be too late and the police will lock you away and . . ."

"You need to keep your strength up."

"Jesus," Cooper yells, and bangs something against the window that looks like a shoe. "Doesn't anything get through to you?"

"Stop with the questions," Adrian yells, and before he can stop himself, he kicks out at the coffee table, sending the sandwich he'd made all over the wall and floor. The lantern hits the floor, flickers for a few seconds but doesn't go out, just rolls across the ground sending shadows moving over the walls.

"Great, just great," he screams, "now look at what you've done? That's it—that's it—no more lunch for you today. Now you go hungry," he says, and he kicks at the coffee table one more time, picks up the lantern, and heads upstairs. He wanted nothing more than to make a good impression, a lasting first impression, and he's failed, all because of Cooper.

"You can't keep me here," Cooper shouts out from the basement.

Adrian stops at the door and looks back down at the cell. Cooper is staring up at him through the window. "We'll make it work," he says. "Soon we'll be friends. I forgive you for making me make a mess."

"You're delusional."

"I'm. Not. Delusional," he says, biting down on each word. Why do people always think he's crazy? He's had to deal with that his whole life and he's sick of it. He looks down at his feet, at his polished shoes. He cleaned his shoes as part of his attempt to make a good impression, and now he isn't even sure why he bothered. Did he not clean them enough? Is that the problem? The right one is scuffed up from kicking the coffee table. The fifteen dollars he paid last week for his shirt and tie from the thrift store is looking like a waste of money. He flicks the hair out of his eyes. He can feel the tears starting to come. This has gone nothing like he expected.

He slams the basement door on Cooper's shouts, angry, embarrassed, wondering if it wouldn't just be easier to set fire to his collection the same way he set fire to his mother.

He races down the hallway and up the stairs to the first landing, his hip hitting the wall and the radio bouncing off his belt onto the floor. He wouldn't really set fire to Cooper, that's just his frustration talking and trying to convince him to do something stupid. He bends down to pick up the radio and is relieved it hasn't broken. He rewinds the tape a little and can hear Cooper's voice, then rewinds it the rest of the way so he can record over it. He doesn't want to hear any of the conversation.

If he wanted to, he could give Cooper the gift he got for him to smooth things over, but he wanted that to be a surprise for tomorrow. He quietly opens one of the bedroom doors in case Cooper's gift is sleeping, and she is. There are other, perhaps more appropriate rooms for her, but he liked the idea of keeping her more comfortable, of giving her a bed. Her hands are bound to the rails of the bed in the same place he tied them two nights ago. Her skin is flushed and the skin around her lips is dry and has chipped and there's a plastic drinking straw hanging from her mouth. There's a pitcher of water on the floor next to her that he helps her drink from, but unfortunately there's no bathroom in here and he didn't want to risk untying her all the time for her to urinate, so the room smells from where she's soiled herself, and the smell reminds him of his days at school, which makes him smile, but then reminds him of the day he got beaten into a coma and the smile disappears. The girl is no more than twenty, he thinks; he isn't sure of her name and the time for asking was before he glued her lips together around the straw, but he had to do the gluing before she could say mean things to him. She looked the type that could be pretty nasty if she wanted to be. Right now she just looks unhealthy, and he doesn't think Cooper will be happy with his gift covered in sweat and urine, and he's going to have to do something about it. Probably he'll just hose her down and leave her naked. Cooper will like her that way.

chapter nine

Donovan Green leaves me the car he arrived in—a rental—and catches a taxi. The rental is a white four-door sedan about a year old. It tells me Green knew I would take on the case, that he knew I had no car, and from the moment he realized his daughter was missing he knew he would be contacting me if she didn't show up. If there had even been any doubt, he would have decided that Fate or Destiny played a part in this—his daughter going missing thirty-six hours before I'm released from jail—there has to be something in that, and thank God it wasn't the other way around, otherwise, instead of coming to me for help, he may have come to blame me for her disappearance. He's given me a thousand dollars in cash for expenses with the promise of more if I need it. The cash is to smooth any wheels that grind to a halt along the way. He's given me the gun he threatened to shoot me with last year. It brings back memories. I hide it beneath my wife's side of the mattress. He's given me a photograph of Emma when she was ten years old, taken at her birthday party. He's asked me to carry it with me until I find her. He wants that photograph burning in my pocket as a constant reminder to find Emma, as if I need reminding. I fold it into my wallet. And he's told me how he thinks Emma would react. She's a smart kid, he said, one who wanted to study psychology because she thought she was good at figuring out what people thought. He said no matter what the situation, she would adapt and she would survive it. I just kept nodding the entire time hoping he was right, but knowing there wasn't a lot a young girl like Emma could say to talk her way out of the situation some sick bastard has put her in.

He's also given me a photograph of Emma taken a month ago. She's an attractive girl. Last time I saw her she was lying in a hospital bed with tubes coming out of her body. She was awake and didn't know who I was. I didn't go into the room, just stood outside it arguing with her father, telling him I was sorry. Her black hair is hanging to her shoulders, framing a face with an easygoing smile, the kind you love to see on any attractive girl, but the kind you don't see on many of them. There's no doubt that smile could break some hearts. Her eyes are squinting a little on account of the sun, the background a park or a backyard somewhere.

My parents arrive only moments after my lawyer leaves. I hear them pull up and go back outside and meet them. They climb out of the car and Mum runs over and hugs me and Dad, who has never hugged a man in his life, shakes my hand and I invite them inside and we sit down drinking cold drinks while we catch up on all the same things we caught up on when they visited me twice a week in jail. Dad is in his midseventies, his hair white but full, no signs of it receding out of existence, a fact he's proud of. He has a beard with no mustache, which is a real shame. He is relieved when I tell him I no longer need to borrow a car. Mum is in her early seventies and knows she may not be around in twenty years, and is making up for that by getting in as many words as she can before passing away. She has thick glasses that hang around her neck, a holdover from her years working as a librarian in town, and dark blond hair that's been coming out of a bottle for the last twenty years. She offers to stay longer so she can help me around the house but I turn her down. My parents are lovely people, but spending the last four months without them calling me every day or popping in all the time certainly gave jail an upside. There aren't any uncomfortable silences because my mum doesn't give them time to develop. Mostly she updates us on what other family members are doing. I don't have any brothers or sisters, but I wish I did because it'd spread Mum's attention toward me a little thinner. I hear about my cousins, uncles, and aunts; new jobs; new additions to the family; who's sick. I almost need to take notes just so I can keep up.

It's nice seeing them, but it's also nice seeing them leave. When they're gone I drive to a nearby mall. I was once told that Christchurch has more mall space per capita than anywhere else in the Southern Hemisphere. The rental is quiet and easy to speed in by accident. The air-conditioning works a treat and the seats are comfortable enough to fall asleep in. There's a huge bouncy castle set up in the parking lot, with dozens of laughing children jumping in or around it, a couple of clowns making balloon animals, and a few barbecues endlessly cooking hot dogs that nobody seems to be eating, all of it covered by large sun sails set up to make shade. Parents are standing around and chatting while keeping an eye on their kids, the occasional *calm down, Billy* or a *don't sit on her, Judy* coming from them.

I find a parking space and head inside and spend two minutes looking at cell phones before deciding on a cheap model, figuring any extra features won't do me any good with the luck I have when it comes to keeping a cell phone in one piece. The guy behind the counter has earrings in each ear and a small one in his left nostril and to be honest I just don't get the point. He tries to sell me an expensive plan to make the phone cheaper and I have to turn him down four times before he lets it go. He puts in a new SIM card and lets me know my phone will take about an hour to connect to the network. I use some of the cash Donovan Green gave me. Somehow I manage to leave my wallet on the counter, and don't realize it until the guy who sold me the phone catches up with me in the parking lot and hands it over in what looks like a reverse mugging. I try to offer him some money as a reward, and he waves it away and tells me that's not why he returned it, that doing the right thing is about doing the right thing, not about getting something out of it.

From the mall I hit a thin flow of traffic, which gets even thinner the closer I get to the care home. The driveway leading up to it has been paved since the last time I was here. The trees on each side of it are drooping in the heat. The building is gray brick and about forty years old and doesn't have the kind of appeal to make you think you could live here. The grounds are scenic, there are five hectares of them, beautiful enough to be on postcards. I step through the doors into an air-conditioned foyer and nothing in here has changed and I figure nothing ever will, including the nurses. Nurse Hamilton greets me with a small hug and tells me it's good to see me and I think she means it. She's been looking after my wife for three years, and before my jail sentence I would try to come out here every day. I've seen Nurse Hamilton hundreds of times and there's nothing I know about her other than the fact that she's a woman and a nurse and never wears any perfume and is at that timeless age where you can't tell whether somebody is fifty or sixty or seventy. She follows me to Bridget's room and updates me—but there isn't much to update. Bridget has gotten four months older and nothing else. She's sitting in a chair looking out over the grounds where a gardener without a shirt is riding a lawn mower, cutting stripes into the lawn. She has a slight tan, so before the heat wave struck somebody was wheeling her outside to sit in the sun for small periods at a time. I hold Bridget's hand and it's as warm as it was the last time I held it, and I spend an hour with her. In the room are photos of our daughter.

"I've missed you," I tell her, and I hope that she's missed me when the reality is she doesn't even know I've been gone and doesn't even know I'm here now. My wife is a sponge that absorbs the words but can't do anything with them. "And I'm sorry," I add.

I check the cell phone on the way back into town and it's connected to the network. I punch in Schroder's number and the line is clear.

"What can you tell me about Emma Green?" I ask.

"The girl from the accident? Why would you ask that, Tate?"

"You didn't tell me she's missing."

62

"It's not my case, and as it stands we don't know that she's missing."

"Yeah you do. She's been gone almost two days and that makes her missing, only you're hoping she's taken off somewhere with a boyfriend, right?"

"Like I said, Tate, it's not my case. Why are you asking about her?"

"Her father came to see me."

"Oh, Jesus, don't tell me he tried to hire you to find her."

"No."

"No he didn't try and you offered? Or no he didn't hire you and you're doing this for free? Which is it?"

"A bit of both."

"Jesus, Tate, you're not even a licensed investigator anymore."

"Like I said, he didn't hire me. I'm not doing this in a professional capacity."

"You can't do this in any capacity."

"That didn't stop you from asking for my help this morning."

"That's different."

"Yeah? You really think so?" I ask.

"Look, Tate, we're looking into her disappearance. We really are. We've got people at her work right now taking a look around. Nobody thinks she's run away. We're sure something bad happened to her. Nobody knows a damn thing. She just vanished. But people go missing every day in this city. We've got boxes and boxes of files of people we just can't find, but we're looking, we truly are."

"And no leads?"

"If we had leads then her father wouldn't have contacted you so fast."

"So what do you think? You think she's dead?"

"I hope not."

"That's not much of an answer, Carl."

"Let it go, Tate."

"I can't."

"Why? Because you hurt her last year? You've paid your debt, Tate, you don't owe her or her dad anything."

"Is that really what you think?"

"It's really what I think," he says.

"I don't believe you. You'd be doing the same thing if you were in my shoes."

"Look, Tate, I get why you're feeling this way, I do, I really do, but it's a bad idea."

"It can't hurt if I at least try."

"Come on, how can you say that?"

"It'll be different this time."

"Yeah? How's that? You're going to find the guy and let him live?"

"That was an accident," I say. He's referring to the Burial Killer I caught last year. There was a fight in the cemetery where I caught him. He was digging up coffins, pulling out the occupants and replacing them with his victims. The original occupants he was dumping into the small lake nearby. During the fight we both ended up in an empty grave and the knife we were fighting with ended up inside of him. If you wanted to put a label on it, you could say it was a *deliberate accident*. "Come on, you know I'm going to do this anyway. Give me a copy of the file. Think of it this way—the more I know to begin with, the less people I'm going to upset along the way. That has to be good for everybody, right, including you."

"Goddamn it, Tate," he says. "You have some strange logic in your world."

"But it works."

"Look, I gotta go," he says.

"The file?"

"I'll think about it," he says, and breaks the connection.

The first person I want to talk to is Emma Green's boyfriend. They weren't living together, not yet, but according to her dad it was only a matter of time. Donovan Green isn't a fan of the boyfriend, but only in the same way I wasn't going to be a fan of my daughter's first boyfriend when she was old enough to start dating. The boyfriend's name is Rodney and he's the same age as Emma and still lives with his parents. Donovan Green gave me the boy's address, and I drive to his house and he's home because he's taken today off because of Emma's disappearance. The house is a single-story A-frame from the seventies, the roof steep enough to slide down and break the sound barrier along the way before breaking your neck. The front yard is brown grass with lots of bare patches and a large pine tree in the middle of it all, big roots breaking out of the ground and sucking the moisture from all the nearby plants. The bell on the front door rings loudly and there are some shuffling sounds on the other side of the wooden door before a woman with almost white hair swings it open. She's wearing a pair of shorts and a cream blouse and looks about as tired as the big pine tree out front. She adjusts her glasses and smiles at me and I tell her hello, and when she answers it's obvious the woman is deaf, and I'm sure we're not far away from a time where *deaf* will be considered an insult, and we start going with *hearing impaired*. She says hello and talks exactly the way people talk when they don't know how they sound. I speak slowly and ask to speak to Rodney and she holds her finger up and taps her watch, telling me she'll either be one minute or one hour and then disappears. Rodney comes to the door thirty seconds later. He's a skinny kid with beer-colored eyes and black hair and his cheeks are flushed from the heat. He's wearing jeans and his T-shirt is salmon pink and he looks well fed and tidy and not on drugs or wearing any dark eyeliner, and therefore I have no reason to immediately hate him. Except for the T-shirt, which hurts my eyes.

"I'm Rodney," he says. "You're here about Emma?"

"That's right."

"What are you? A reporter? I'm sick of reporters. I swear to God if you're a reporter I'm going to kick your ass."

I suddenly like him even more. "Her dad hired me. I'm a private investigator."

"He hired you to talk to me? Why? He thinks I had something to do with her going missing?" he asks, his voice starting to raise. His right hand grips the door frame as if he has to stop himself from lunging at me.

"So you're confident that's what she is? Missing? That she hasn't gone away for a few days?"

"Emma's not like that. I recognize you, you know," he says, "but I can't tell where from."

"I have one of those faces," I answer. "And her dad doesn't think you've done anything to hurt her. I'm here to help, to try and get her back."

He relaxes his grip on the doorframe. "Is she dead?" he asks, and his question is so genuine that it really seems he has no idea one way or the other, but I've been fooled by grieving boyfriends before.

"Can I come in?"

"You didn't answer the question."

"I don't know."

"But you think so."

"I hope not," I say, giving Schroder's answer from before.

"What's your name?" he asks.

"Theo."

"Theodore Tate?"

"Yeah," I say, and for a second I look down.

"The man who . . ."

"That's why I'm here," I say. "It's why her dad came to me. He knows I'm going to do what it takes to find her. That gives you two options. You can stand there and be pissed at me like you deserve to be before closing the door, or you can answer my questions and help me find Emma before it's too late. What's it going to be?"

He leads me inside to a living room that nobody could come to an agreement on how to decorate. I sit down in a chair that tries to swallow me. Rodney's mother carries out a tray with a teapot on it and three cups. She sits on the couch next to Rodney and pours me a cup, then points to the milk. I can't stand tea and nod at the milk figuring it will help dilute the problem. There's a light on the wall above the door that I figure must flash when somebody rings the doorbell. The mother signs something to Rodney, and he signs something back, and I feel like an outsider.

"Mum recognizes you too," he says.

He doesn't say it in an accusing tone and his mother doesn't sign it in any aggressive way. I don't apologize because it's not why I'm here. His mum nods, not hearing us but knowing what's being said. I look at her. "I'm here to find her," I say, and she nods and smiles.

I turn back to Rodney. "How long have you been dating Emma?"

"About four months."

"How'd you meet?"

"School. I've known her for years. She was off from school last year for some time because of—well, you know why, and when she came back we just kind of started talking. I was in an accident when I was a kid and Mum got pretty hurt and Dad didn't make it, and we spoke about her accident and my accident and we found out how we were both going to university this year, and then we found out we were both taking psychology. We're in the same psych class. It's weird. I mean, I've always seen her around at school, just never, you know, just never thought she was my type."

"Your type?"

"Yeah. Any girl who talks to me is my type, which pretty much narrowed it down to Emma and nobody else in the world."

"You share many classes with her now?"

"Just psychology."

"Anybody at university giving her a hard time? Anybody creeping her out?"

"Not that she mentioned, and I think she would have. We haven't been there long yet—I mean, this is only our second week of the term. Plus a bunch of classes have been canceled because some of the students have been passing out from the heat."

"You sure nobody was making her uncomfortable?" I ask.

"Pretty sure."

"Did you see her on the day she disappeared?"

He shakes his head. His mother has made him a cup of tea and placed it on the coffee table ahead of him and he stares at it untouched, as if he's too scared to drink in case Emma's fortune is at the bottom and the news is bad. "Sunday night I went around to her flat and we hung out for a few hours."

"Hung out?"

"Yeah," he says, and he finally picks up the cup of tea. He holds it in front of his mouth but still doesn't drink from it, but it shields his lips so his mum can't see what he's saying. "Hung out," he says. "In her bedroom." He takes a sip and puts the cup down. His mum looks over at me, smiles, and rolls her eyes. I smile back. "I got home about eleven," he says, "then went to class the following morning only to find class was canceled because of the heat. We swapped a few texts during the day and she had to go to work, then that was it. We weren't planning on meeting up Monday night at all. Yesterday she wasn't answering my calls so I spoke to her flatmate who thought Emma was with me. Her boss was calling, looking for her too. I knew it was weird and I was worried, but not worried enough to call the police because bad things like that only happen to other people, right?"

"If only that were true," I say.

"Yeah, but I didn't know that then. So I called her parents. Then they rang everybody they knew and then the police and the police don't even think anything bad has happened."

I don't tell him that's not the case.

"Was she enjoying her job?" I ask.

"Who enjoys their job?"

"What about any old boyfriends?"

"I'm her first boyfriend," he says.

I take a sip of the tea trying to be polite. It tastes exactly how I knew it would. The mother smiles at me and nobody says or signs anything for about ten seconds and in that time I try to get a read on Rodney, knowing full well my reads in the past have been way off the mark. Could this kid have killed Emma and dumped her somewhere?

"She could still be okay, right?" he asks. "I mean, if something bad happened and somebody hurt her, she could still be okay. She could still be alive."

"Absolutely," I say, unable to tell him what both Schroder and I suspect—that Emma Green is dead somewhere, and the devastation Rodney is already feeling is only going to get worse.

chapter ten

The cell has been plunged into complete darkness. The shoe in his hand has gotten warm from the last few minutes of continuous banging against the door. Adrian isn't coming back. Yelling at the man was a mistake, he knew it when it was happening but he couldn't stop himself, it was a rush of blood to the head, some animal instinct that told him to lash out and ignore the voice inside telling him to shut up, stay calm, and be smart. Or maybe that voice couldn't be heard over the still pounding headache. If he wants any chance of getting out of here alive, he has to keep his emotion in check. He has to listen to that voice.

In the dark, the cell feels colder, and his breathing is louder, ragged breaths that make his head spin. He leans against the door and slips his shoe back on before following the wall back to the bed, the concrete feeling damp, his feet dragging over the floor. He sits down and waits for his eyes to adjust, but they don't. The only light coming downstairs is what sneaks through the edges of the door upstairs, and it doesn't sneak far, enough to see part of the top step but nothing more. The bed squeaks and he puts the pillow between his back and the wall and leans against it, hooks his legs up in front of him, and rests with his wrists hanging over his knees and thinks about Adrian.

Come on, every time somebody gets murdered in this city you create a profile of the killer and compare it to the newspapers once he's caught. It's like a game, and Christchurch has given you plenty of practice. This is the same—if you want to get out of here you have to start by building up a profile.

He has to play the game.

Over the years, his profiles have helped identify a suspect, have narrowed down the kind of person doing the killing. In this case it's to identify what the suspect wants, how to make him think he's going to get it, and how to escape this bloody cell. If he had his notepad here, he'd write *Completely loony* at the top of the page and draw a ring around it so many times the pen would chew through the pages. In fact, thinking about it, Adrian is so completely loony that if he had his notepad, Cooper would also write and underline the words *Mental Patient / ex mental patient?*

Mental issues aren't such a bad thing. In fact, given the choice, he'd rather be captive to somebody like Adrian over a cold-blooded, calculated killer. Being deranged makes Adrian unpredictable and dangerous, but there's a flip side to that, it gives Cooper more room to try and play him, to gain his trust and talk his way out of this cell. If it were simply a case of being smarter than Adrian, then he'd already have gotten out of here. That means he has to rely on luck too, and unfortunately Cooper's never really been one for having much luck. Today is a perfect example of that. He's dealt with some seriously deranged people over the years, and no matter how smart they are or he is, you have to take common sense out of the equation and replace it with luck, and without that, he's going to die down here—or worse, he'll manage to live down here for twenty years. He imagines Adrian being excited about bringing food and water down every day, then imagines Adrian becoming tired of that, of bringing down supplies less and less because the novelty of having a *serial killer* has worn off. Well, the novelty of starving to death will sure as hell wear off fast. The stomach pains, the dehydration—there's no point in thinking about it.

Instead he focuses on Adrian—that's what is going to get him out of here—which leads him in a circle, because immediately he imagines Adrian going out one day and getting arrested for something, or being hit by a truck, or having a heart attack or getting shot shopping for milk, then nobody ever knowing where Cooper is, starving down here in the cold and dark and suffocating in his own stench. Kidnapping cases normally have a twenty-four-hour window in which to solve the crime—after that you're looking for a corpse. He doesn't know if it's the same for him.

"Jesus," he whispers. "A collection," he says, "I'm part of a goddamn collection."

If he did have his notepad, he'd tear it up right now. Everything he's read, everything he's learned and taught over the years, it all turns into a blur, the texts and references hit by a tornado in his brain, scattering all the relevant data too fast to hang on to, and even if he could hang on to it, he doubts there'd be anything there to help. He stands and moves over to the door. He lifts his fists back and is ready to start banging on the door, punching at it, wanting to vent the frustration, but somehow, somehow, he keeps it in check. He thinks he can smell the sandwich in the next room, but he knows it's unlikely. He picked the worst day to skip breakfast. Even if the food wasn't all over the floor, even if he could reach it, he isn't that sure he would touch it. He figures he can go twenty-four hours without food. People do that all the time. People in other countries last days without anything. Homeless people seem to make do.

His stomach starts to rumble. He has to get a grip on his surroundings and, more important, get a grip on the man who has him locked down here. In the basement. Of a house. As an exhibit. In wonderland.

Questions start coming out of the tornado. He begins plucking them out of the air. Is Adrian the only person who will see this collection? Or is he more a zookeeper, and others will come to look?

Are the police looking for him, does anybody know yet he's missing? Who is Adrian, what has he done in the past, have others died in this room? What of those others, did they admit to being serial killers in the hope of gaining Adrian's trust, or deny it?

He can feel the onset of panic. He pushes at the door and the walls and kicks at the cinder blocks but it's all pointless. He takes one of the coins out of his pocket and drags it back and forth against the mortar between two of the cinder blocks and can feel a sprinkle of cement come away, blunting the edge of the coin. He figures if he had a thousand dollars in change he could cut his way through if he stuck at it for about two years.

He hangs his head against the window and asks himself the big question—what should he do next? The way he sees it, he has two options. He can play the professor and try to puncture Adrian's version of reality, or he can go along with it. He can't imagine Adrian taking too kindly to his attempts at proving him wrong. Best option is to play along to gain his trust. Tell this loony what he wants to hear. Go down that path for a bit, test it out, see how it feels.

If he were a betting man, he'd give himself three-to-one odds of getting out of here. Adrian's IQ is half of his own. Cooper knows what he's talking about and Adrian doesn't. He has to gain Adrian's trust. Compliment him. Take baby steps. Use his name as often as he can and try to form a connection. Tell him stories about how good it feels to kill. Become friends. Then start asking for privileges. Start small, like asking for certain food. A change of clothes. Build up the requests until he can convince Adrian to let him outside to see the sun.

Can he do all of that within twenty-four hours? He doesn't think so. Maybe forty-eight.

He lays on the bed and waits for his headache to pass and for Adrian to come back. The only thing he can do now is be patient. Baby steps. He'll try to take them as quickly as possible. And now that he has a plan, he already feels calmer. He's no longer feeling like his odds of getting out of here are three-to-one, more like two-to-one. Good odds. A betting man's odds.

chapter eleven

If the reaction at the boyfriend's house could be considered cool once they realized who I was, then at the café I'm in need of a winter jacket and scarf despite the summer heat. I knew it was only a matter of time. People know Emma's missing and they know the police are looking into it, and they don't want to talk to a man who put the missing girl into hospital last year. At least at the boyfriend's house things thawed out. After only a couple of words to the café owner, the only thing thawing out are half a dozen chicken breasts in the kitchen. The café is a small mom-and-pop affair with swirling patterns of broken glass in flower-petal shapes glued to the oak veneer walls, serving up croissants and sandwiches with meat and egg and salads in them, chicken or mince pies, rich-looking palm-sized cakes and custard treats that all look pretty damn good after four months in the slammer. The coffee looks good too, but I get the feeling if I ordered a cup I'd have to sink some antibiotics to the bottom to balance out whatever the barista would add with his back turned. The café is located in Merivale, a block away from the Main North Road—one of the central roads heading out of the city. Merivale is one of those suburbs that defines its own housing market, where you pay far more for far less, where if you don't own a four-wheel drive and expensive clothes the neighbors would ask you to leave. Everybody has the collars on their shirts and jackets turned up, many of them walking around as though they were living in a country club. There's a parking lot behind the café and no sign of Emma's car. I walked around it when I arrived, passing a *Help Wanted* sign in the window that I hope isn't advertising the spot Emma isn't filling. Not even two days missing and the world is moving on.

The café owner's name is Zane Reeves. He has a toupee that at the most cost what he'd make off about eight cups of coffee, and he's one of those guys who always has to lean against something when he talks, propping himself up against the counter and putting his fist on his hip, his stomach extending out. He smiles for the first five seconds until I introduce myself and he realizes I'm not there to buy something. The café smells of warm food and coffee and is full of people hovering a year or two either side of twenty, all of them drinking hot coffee from small cups on an incredibly hot day, the café full with the low murmur of conversation and some kind of classical music folk guitar blend being pumped through the speakers that is already making me drowsy. Reeves's smile turns into a grimace and he takes me through a door into the kitchen to talk.

"I've already spoken to the cops," he says.

"Then it will still be fresh in your memory."

"Speak to them. If they want you to know then they can share."

"Did she mention any weird customers? Anybody watching her, or giving her weird vibes?"

"We all want Emma back, and mate, you have a bad track record when it comes to people you get involved with. Emma is better off without you trying to help."

"That's not what her father thinks."

"People make bad decisions when they're grieving."

"Grieving? Why, you think she's dead?"

"Don't you? Mate, last thing I want is anything to have happened to her, she's a great kid, a good worker, but I watch the news as much as anybody. I'm not an idiot."

"That why you already have a new help wanted sign in the window?"

"Fuck you, man," he says, pointing a finger at me. "I have a business to run. I can't just keep her position open. See those people out there? They don't care who serves them as long as they get served. It sucks, but that's the way it is. There's nothing here for you, mate. You've already hurt her, and I'm not going to help you hurt her family."

"Where does she park normally? Out back?"

"We all park out there."

"Security cameras?"

"Does this look like a bank to you? Now get the hell out of here."

I try to make eye contact with the other staff, hoping one of them will want to talk to me, but they all look away. I head again into the parking lot. There's some crime scene tape that's been left behind from the search earlier, it's fluttering in the breeze and caught up against the side of the dumpster. Nobody is around, and no cars are parked there. It's a likely site for Emma's abduction, at night it would be fairly dark, nobody around, lots of shadows. Emma could have walked to her car and been attacked, her abductor throwing her into the trunk of her own car then speeding away. I walk over to the dumpster and open it up, knowing the police have already searched the area, but I suddenly have a bad feeling Emma Green is inside that dumpster. She isn't. There are bags of trash and nothing else. The front corner of the dumpster has been edged with red paint from a car. Somebody hit it on their way out.

I get down on my hands and knees, looking for anything that may be out of place, or something dropped in the struggle. All I can see are patches of oil and weeds poking through the cracked pavement, a few old oil stains, and some old pieces of dog crap. The sun is beating down on my back. My back aches a little as I stand back up. If there was anything here, the police have found it already.

I head back to my car thinking I'm in the wrong line of work.

There isn't much I can do until I get the police file, other than talk to more of Emma's friends, most of whom I figure won't want to talk to me. Donovan Green may have picked the last person on earth that may be of any use. Like Zane Reeves said, a grieving man makes bad decisions.

The day is moving on and has cooled off a couple of degrees. I still need to talk to the flatmate but that will have to wait until tonight. I head back home, picking up some Chinese takeaway on the way. It's around six o'clock by the time Schroder shows up. I've been on the case six hours and Emma Green is either six hours deader or six hours closer to becoming it. My dining table is covered in empty plastic tubs and smells of good food.

"This is a bad idea," Schroder says, holding up the Emma Green file. "Got any beer?"

"That a joke?"

"It's been a long day. You ever seen a body so badly burned it had to be peeled off the floor?" As soon as he's asked it, he remembers that I have. We both have. And on more than one occasion.

"Wanna talk about it?"

"No."

"You looked over the file?" I ask, nodding toward it.

"Yes," he says, "but it's not my case," he says. "My case is figuring out who started today's fire. You looked over the file I gave you?"

"I've been busy. Is there anything you can tell me that isn't in here?"

"Sure there is, but you're not listening. I keep telling you to let it go, even more so since it's personal. Come on, Tate, you know if it becomes personal it becomes messy."

"Thanks for the advice."

"So, look, I know I asked this morning, but what was it like? Prison?"

"You know when you go on holiday and you're never sure what the hotel is going to be like, or the restaurants and clubs, or the beach, and it's always a little different from what you're expecting? Well, prison isn't like that. Prison is exactly how you think it's going to be."

"Sorry," he says, but it isn't his fault and not a very useful apology. He slaps the file down on the kitchen table but keeps his hand on it. "You owe me," he says. "When this is done, I want your help on the file I gave you this morning. You get this out of your system, and then you give me one hundred percent on helping me figure out who this Melissa woman is. Deal?"

"That depends on whether you're going to hold out on me, or give me the information I need along the way," I say. "You came to me for a reason, Carl, you came to me because you're going to want me to do things that you can't do."

"That's not it."

"Bullshit. You're one of the good guys, Carl, and that restricts you. I don't know how you justified it to yourself, but when you gave me that file this morning that wasn't just you asking for my insight, that was you asking me to get my hands dirty."

"You're reading too much into it," he says.

"And you're doing the same thing now."

He picks the file back up. "You want me to walk out of here to prove how wrong you are?"

"I just don't want you complaining when I've crossed a line you knew all along I was going to cross." I reach out for the file. "We're on the same side here, Carl. Let me find this girl and then I promise I'll help you find Melissa."

He takes his hand off the file. "I don't feel good about any of this," he says.

"This isn't about feeling good," I tell him. "It's about getting Emma back. Her dad thinks she can talk her way out of anything. Seems to think she knows how people work, and if anybody could survive, it would be her."

"Any father would be saying the same thing."

I nod. It's true. "She is a psychology student," I point out.

"Yeah, for barely two weeks. I doubt she's learned enough to talk some lunatic who wants to probably rape and kill her into letting her go."

I keep nodding. That's also true.

"Just remember, Tate, when you find something, you come to me with it, okay? You're helping me out now, not Donovan Green. You come to me first. You clear everything with me."

"Of course," I tell him.

He doesn't believe me, but he doesn't say anything. He stands up and I follow him to the front door.

"Look, Tate, there's some info in there that's new. There was a search this afternoon in the parking lot behind Emma's café."

"I know. I was there earlier."

"Yeah, well, I really hope her father is right about her being able to handle herself, because right now it isn't looking good."

"Was it ever?"

"Good luck, Tate," he says. "And this time do me a favor."

"Yeah? What's that?"

"Try not to kill anybody."

chapter twelve

Adrian found happiness hard to find when he was a kid. He found it with his music and his comics, and he also had a collection of toy cars that he loved more than anything. They were all small-scale metal cars with moving parts, and each time he got one he'd dream that when he was older he'd be able to afford the real thing. No matter what happened to him at school, those cars would be waiting for him at home, so would his tapes and comics, and nobody could ever take that away from him. He would space his cars along a shelf he had in his bedroom, he would measure them so they were the same distance apart, and every week he would dust them. His music collection he would line up by color, so the spines of the tapes merged into each other. His comics he would never bend the covers, never. That made him happy.

The other thing that made him happy was Katie. When he was thirteen years old he fell in love with the new girl in school with the green eyes and long red hair tied into a ponytail and frazzled on the ends. She was a little taller than him and a little heavier, but not by much, and it would have taken a day to count the freckles on her cheeks and each one of those freckles he wanted to collect. Her family had moved up from Dunedin, a city down south that made Christchurch look large. When he first saw her his stomach felt tight and his chest warm and his mouth went dry. She had a nervous smile that he took with him wherever he went and he dreamed of holding her hand and walking her home. She was put into his class and sat on the opposite side of the room, but forward a little from him, where he could steal glances at her all day long. He didn't know what he'd do if she ever looked back and caught him, but she never looked back. As it was with every new student who came to the school, there was one of two ways things would go—the other kids would be interested and befriend them, or they would tease them. In Katie's case, they teased her. Occasionally, on lunch and recess breaks, they would push her and try to make her cry, and sometimes she did.

Adrian loved the idea of standing up for her as much as he loved her, but he was a coward and he knew it. The girls were stronger than him. The boys could crush him. One of the horrors of school was public speaking. He hated giving speeches. He had to stand up in front of the class in his secondhand uniform, the shorts too baggy on him, his arms and legs stick thin, and no matter how many times he rehearsed he could never remember the words. No matter how much water he drank his mouth would always be dry. Every time he could hear the others sniggering, could feel his face turn red, and every time all he wanted to do was run from the classroom and just keep running. A few months into the new school year and the sun was lower as the mornings grew cooler and the leaves from the ground were being trudged into the classroom. They were giving speeches on people who inspired them. He had chosen Neil Armstrong because, since the age of ten, Adrian wanted nothing more than to be able to run as far away as the moon. Truthfully, and he didn't mention this in his speech, he fantasized about captaining his own starship and exploring the galaxy. He wanted to be the first man to step foot on Mars. He gave his speech talking about the Gemini and Apollo missions and about Armstrong's test pilot days, and he stuttered through much of it, the nerves getting the better of him to the point where his hands were shaking so hard he dropped his cue cards, getting them out of order, which was a problem because he hadn't numbered them, so in his speech Neil Armstrong grew up and flew to the moon before joining NASA. At the end nobody clapped and the teacher, Mrs. Byron, with her horn-rimmed glasses that magnified her eyes to twice their size, told him to take his seat, before telling Katie it was her turn to go next.

The girl Adrian loved stood up in front of the class and spoke about Beethoven. Adrian didn't know much about Beethoven except that Beethoven had cut his ear off, though Katie didn't mention it in her speech and he wasn't sure why, but she did say the composer had gone deaf, and cutting your ear off would certainly make that happen. Halfway through the speech some of the kids started laughing. Mrs. Byron told them off. Mrs. Byron was the kind of teacher who was always telling people off, the kind of woman who looked like she may have been born at the age of forty. Katie slowed down and carried on, then the laughing began again, and then she started to cry. She ran out of the room. Adrian wanted to go after her. He thought it would be an amazing gesture and she would have to love him back. The coward living inside of him wouldn't let him. He hated that coward. He wanted to kill it, but didn't have the courage. Not then—but he decided in that moment he would at least try to fake it.

When lunch came he went up to the boy who had started the laughing.

"I want you to leave Katie alone," Adrian said.

"You what? Fuck you, you're kidding, right?"

"I mean it."

The boy, his name was Redmond but everybody called him Red, was holding a rugby ball that he was about to start throwing with his friends. Redmond was one of those fat kids with fat cheeks who later on in life would call himself big-boned. "You mean it?" Red said, then pushed a fat finger into Adrian's chest. "Little Aids," he said, because that's what they called Adrian, "doesn't want us teasing his girlfriend."

"She's not my girlfriend."

Red pushed him again, only this time one of Red's friends had knelt down behind Adrian, so when he moved backward he tipped over, the ground knocking most of the fight out of him, the rest being knocked out a moment later when Red jumped on top of him, punching him hard twice in the stomach, and then rubbing his face in the dirt. There was nobody to help him. Other students started to come over to watch. Including Katie. A couple of the bigger girls brought her over. Adrian looked up at her. He tried to smile at her but couldn't. He was in too much pain, and he was using all of his effort just to keep his bowels in check.

"He's not your friend is he?" asked one of the girls, a big girl, one of those rapidly growing girls with big jaws and mean eyes and curly hair. It was common at school that if you grew faster than the majority you became a real bastard.

Katie didn't say anything.

"Because if he's your boyfriend, then you're about to be on the ground next to him," the girl added. "That's your future." They were deep words for a thirteen-year-old girl.

Everybody fell quiet as Katie thought about her future. "He's . . . he's not my boyfriend," Katie said.

"Then who is he?"

"I don't know. Just some . . . some loser in my class," Katie said— there were tears in her eyes but they didn't fall.

"A what?" the girl asked.

"A loser. A loser," Katie said.

Adrian can still remember it, word for word. He doesn't have problems with those memories, only with the ones he's developed over the following years. That day he fell out of love as easily as he fell into it, or at least that's what he thought at the time. His life at school got worse. The girls began to tease him as much as the boys. Katie became popular. To her credit she never teased him directly. Sometimes he'd come home with a bloody nose and grazed elbows and knees and his mother would call the school and complain, and the following day the bullying would be worse. Bullying was like that, the more you complained the bigger the problem became, the teachers never able to do anything about it. His classmates took any chance he had of becoming a confident student and squashed it. It was months after Katie called him a loser that he learned the only way to find happiness was to take it from somebody else.

He also knew how.

In the morning, while his mother was making him breakfast, he would go into the bathroom and urinate into a plastic bottle that would hold half a liter. He would screw the top on really tight. The bottle would be warm when he put it in his school bag but cold by the time he got to school. He would take one of his many moments of isolation between the taunts and the beatings, and he would go into the locker rooms and unscrew the plastic bottle and pour the contents into the bags of anybody who hurt him. There was a time, about a week into it, that he had to pour it over his own bag so the others wouldn't think it was him, but he diluted it with so much water that it wasn't really that bad and he took the things out of his bag he didn't want damaged. If he couldn't pour it into their bags, he'd pour it into their desks, over their uniforms while they were in gym class when he could manage it. He lasted a full month before he lost the courage to continue regularly. By then there were too many people watching out for the *Urinator* as he was called, with a promise from the principal that the Urinator would be expelled. It didn't matter, because by then school was nearly over for the Christmas holidays. He carried on when they went back seven weeks later, not as often, only once or twice a term. He never soaked Katie's bag, but he soaked some of the other girls' bags. The occasions lessened. Once a month became once every three months. Then only a couple of times a year.

It all ended three years later when he was sixteen. He doesn't know the boy's name who walked in on him during the act, he was pouring his urine through the grill holes of another boy's locker, a boy who had walked past him the day before in the corridor and slapped him in the face for no reason. In that moment of being caught his future flashed ahead of him, it would start with his mother finding out, he would be expelled, he would carry the Urinator name with him wherever he went. He was old enough to know his astronaut fantasy wasn't going to pan out, young enough to have no idea what he wanted to do in life, and old enough to know that whatever dreams he would have were now over. The boy stared at Adrian, said nothing, and then walked away.

The rest of that afternoon was the worst. He couldn't concentrate in any of the classes. He thought the teachers were giving him a funny look. He kept waiting for somebody to bring a message for the teacher, asking for Adrian to be sent to the principal's office. The school bell rang and it was time to go and still nothing. When he got home, every time the phone rang he knew it was going to be the school talking to his mother, that expulsion was next, but the call didn't come.

If the first day was bad, the second was by far much worse. He didn't eat breakfast that morning. He felt sick all day. On recess breaks and during lunch he would sit in the bathroom with his stomach holding what felt like a bucket of water.

It was the third day the boy came for him. He didn't come alone. They took him at the end of the school day and dragged him into a park. Together they held Adrian down and tied him up. They didn't kick or punch him, not in the beginning, and when he was securely bound they stood around him in a circle and they all pissed on him, eight of them in total. It splashed over his skin and ran down his body. It pooled beneath his back and buttocks and soaked into his clothes. They strapped a stick in his mouth so he couldn't form a seal with his lips. They aimed for his face, it streamed into his eyes and burned them, it rained onto his tongue and felt like acid at the back of his throat. He gagged and coughed and spluttered and it stuck in his throat and he felt like he was drowning. It felt like it lasted forever. When they were done they laughed at him and one of the boys kicked him in the head. The kicking caught on the same way fads tend to sometimes, because then another boy did it, and another. Soon they were all kicking him, and when he finally blacked out, their laughter followed him into the darkness. He dreamed of Katie. He dreamed of better times.

When he came to, the ropes were gone. He couldn't stand. The world was off balance. A passerby found him. An ambulance was called. He was in hospital for six weeks. His brain had swelled and holes had to be drilled into his skull to relieve the pressure. He was put into an induced coma for two weeks. Six of his ribs had been broken. So had his right arm. When he came out of it, he didn't name the boys who had done it to him. He told the police he couldn't remember who they were. Only he could remember.

His balance came back after a month. It took him a couple of days to start walking straight. Things he'd learned at school no longer made sense. The simplest things were no longer that simple. He didn't like listening to his music anymore. He hated it. The comics didn't make him laugh anymore, and he hated the stories because they were about people who had unique abilities he could never have. Instead he started to make his own comics. He wasn't a good artist, but he was good enough, and he'd draw those kids who had hurt him, and he'd draw himself standing over those boys, and he'd draw different types of weapons and different ways to use them. Sometimes, when he wasn't drawing, he'd sit in his room snapping the doors and wheels off his model cars. He heard his mother telling his aunty that he had changed, that something inside his head had been broken. He didn't know what. His mother knew, and she'd explain it to him, but it just didn't make sense. He was the same person, he felt the same—and yet he knew he had changed. Sometimes he'd forget things. Things before the beating were locked inside his memory for good, but some new things struggled to stick. He was always losing things, he couldn't remember people's names. But he didn't forget the names of each of the boys who had done this to him. The police were still asking questions, only not as many now. They had moved on to other things. People forgot about what happened to Adrian.

He got his strength back. His balance came back. His mind started to heal. He would never be a hundred percent, but at least he could remember new things if he tried hard enough. However he saw things differently now. The kicks to his head, the swelling to his brain, it changed his perspective on life.

School was over for him. Even if he could have gone back, he wouldn't have wanted to. What was he going to do, study to become an astronaut? The worst part was he couldn't pour urine into the lockers of the boys who hurt him.

The best thing was it gave him more time to think about what he was going to do to them. Ever since then, he's struggled to make friends. Now it's looking like it might be the same with Cooper. Before the beating he wasn't popular, but there were a couple of equally unpopular kids who would at least speak to him on occasion. If his mother were here, then at least there'd be somebody to comfort him, to calm him, to care that he's upset. At least that's the fantasy. His mother would do no such thing. She used to, a long time ago, until he started waiting outside his school and following those kids home who had hurt him. That's when things got bad. It wasn't long after this that his first mother sent him out here to the Grove and stopped being his mother.

It's not fair, but things never are. Collecting Cooper is supposed to be the most exciting thing he has ever done, and these thoughts, along with Cooper's actions, are bringing him down. There has to be a way to make Cooper like him. Cooper likes other people, which means it's possible. He should go downstairs and ask Cooper who else has ever shown him such a respect as to want to own him for a collection! Who else thinks so much of Cooper's work? Nobody!

He tries to tell himself Cooper just needs time to adjust, and remembers what it was like for himself when he was first brought out here, what it was like being in a foreign world, only for him it was worse, for him he was locked out here with dozens of other patients, some of them crazy, some of them mean, some of them crazy-mean, all of them set free three years ago when Grover Hills was shut down. He reminds himself he knew Cooper's anger was always going to be a possibility.

Tomorrow his gift will go a long way to fixing any problems between them. For now, he should rest for the remainder of the day, and then sleep on it. Like his mother—not his real mother who abandoned him, but his second mother who looked after him and the others who were different—used to say, *"A problem with rest becomes a solution most best."* He's not so sure if his mother was right on that one.

He paces his bedroom, counting the footsteps, finding comfort in the familiar. He used to pace this room a lot as he grew from teenager to man. Sometimes he'd have the room to himself, other times he'd have to share it and there would be less room for his footsteps. The higher the number, the calmer he becomes. He prefers even numbers over the odd, and makes sure he always finishes his steps on a multiple of ten, having to either shorten or lengthen his stride to make it happen. He pushes everything from his mind until he reaches a thousand. A thousand is a good number, twice as good as five hundred, half as good as two thousand. A good, solid number, a multiple of ten and also a hundred, which itself is a multiple of ten. He sits down. He thinks about second impressions. He thinks about what he can do to make Cooper happy, and decides that giving the serial killer some books to read might help. It's a great idea.

As quickly as the excitement comes, it disappears, replaced by a feeling of utter uselessness, a feeling he has been intimate with his entire adult life. Giving Cooper reading material is an idea to be proud of, but what he isn't proud of is the fact it took so long for the idea to come. He should have known all along a man like Cooper needs to keep his mind active, stimulated, otherwise he'll become stagnant. Collector's items aren't meant to be boring.

"Cooper will be so happy," he says, knowing once he shares the idea the two of them will start to bond. For the last three years he's been collecting books about serial killers. He loves reading them. They fascinate him. He picks up a handful of books from his bedroom and carries them to the basement. Cooper watches him coming down the stairs, his face in the small window, motionless. He looks gray, hollow, like a ghost who's moved on to somewhere else.

"I brought you something to read," Adrian says, holding up the books.

"Thank you. I appreciate that," Cooper says and Adrian is pleased at his politeness. "Are you going to leave the lamp for me?"

"It's the only one I have," Adrian says, "and I'll need it for when it gets dark."

"Then how am I going to read?"

Adrian straightens up the coffee table and sits the books on them, embarrassed because he doesn't have an answer. Parts of the sandwich have stuck to the surfaces it hit, and the bread has gone hard. He'll clean it up tomorrow.

"Are you mad at me?" Adrian asks, not looking up. "Don't you feel special?"

"I feel trapped," Cooper answers. "You seem like an intelligent guy, you must be to have accomplished all this by yourself. You must have plenty of friends you can talk to, why do you need to keep me here?"

"I don't have any friends," Adrian answers, fiddling with the books so all the spines are perfectly aligned. "I used to, but they all left."

"Come now, that can't be true," Cooper says. "A guy like you, you must have lots of friends."

"Are you mocking me?" he asks, looking up.

"I don't mock."

"You should feel special," Adrian says. "I mean, you're one of most special people in this city at the moment. You're a serial killer, and if that isn't special, I don't know what is."

"Why do you think I'm a serial killer? What have I done to make you think that?"

"For one, you have a thumb in a jar. Serial killers collect things like that from their victims."

Cooper smiles. "You think I cut the thumb off somebody I killed?"

Adrian likes seeing the smile, and he smiles too. "Didn't you?"

Cooper nods, the smile still there. "Okay," he says. "No more lies. You got me. Of course I cut it off one of my victims."

"Why did you ask me before if I had sold it to you?"

"I'm not sure. I woke up feeling groggy and confused. Did you shoot me with a Taser?"

"Yes."

"And then held something over my face. What was that?"

Adrian doesn't know. It's stuff he picked up last week when he got the Taser. He shrugs. "Something that makes people sleep," he says. "Who did you cut the thumb off?"

"A man I killed."

"You kill men? I thought you only killed women."

"Sometimes both," Cooper says.

"Why did you kill him?"

"Because I wanted to. How did you figure out I was a serial killer, Adrian? Lay it out for me. The police don't know I'm one, so you must be smarter than the police."

Adrian smiles. It's been a long time since he's had any emotional warmth well up inside of him, and it feels great. This is exactly why he wanted to have Cooper so badly. They will become best friends. Cooper can tell him how it feels to be a serial killer, and Cooper can tell him about all the other killers he's known. He's glad he re-wound the tape earlier and is recording over their previous conversation. He hopes it comes through clearly—he has his shirt hanging over the radio so Cooper can't see it.

"I started watching you because I remembered you were writing a book," he says. "You used to come out here years ago and ask us questions, but you never had any questions for me."

"Here? Where is here? One of the abandoned institutions?"

"Grover Hills," Adrian says, "and it's not abandoned because we're here. And it's not an institution, it's a home. You were writing a book about us, and I've looked for it but haven't found a copy anywhere."

"It's not finished," Cooper says.

"I'd like to read it."

"Sure, I'd like that too. I'm interested in what you have to say on it. How can I give you a copy, Adrian? It's on my computer. We could go to my house and I could show it to you."

"Maybe," Adrian says, knowing Cooper is trying to trick him, "but not today. You never had any questions for me. Do you remember me at all?"

"No, I'm sorry."

"You only spoke to killers, that's why," Adrian says. "They were my friends."

"And now they've all gone," Cooper says.

"Yes, but I'm back, and since I can't have them, I can have you because you knew them all, you can tell me their stories, and you're a killer just like them."

"People go missing every day, but not like this," Cooper says, looking around the cell. "What you've done here is nothing short of . . . brilliant."

"Oh," he says, and then it sinks in. "Oh! That's great," he says, and he can feel himself blushing.

"You know, Adrian, you seem like a pretty cool guy. I just wish you'd talked to me first before bringing me here. I'm sure we could have figured things out a little better. A little more . . . smoothly."

Adrian wants to believe him, but doesn't think he can. Not yet. "Can I ask you some questions?" he asks.

"Sure, sure you can, Adrian. Ask anything you like, and I'd be grateful if I could ask you some as well. Is that okay? I'm really interested in what you have to say."

"Really?"

"Of course."

Adrian isn't sure. Nobody has ever been interested before in what he has to say. Serial killers are clever people, they're . . . what's the word? *Man-ip-you-la-tive.* They're certainly that, and suddenly he isn't so sure Cooper really does think he's a cool guy. He has to be careful.

"What made you interested in serial killers? What made you want to become one?" he asks, and he sits down on the couch in the lamplight and waits for Cooper to tell him.

chapter thirteen

Emma Green's flat is exactly what you'd expect from any flat rented by university students: run-down with long lawns and windows covered in films of dirt and a recycling bin overflowing with empty beer cans and wine bottles standing sentry by the front door. It's one of those student neighborhoods where alcohol consumption equates to social standing, where the more you drink the cooler you become and the better friends you get. Donovan Green has smoothed the way for me to talk to Emma's flatmate, which I do, along with her boyfriend and a couple of the boyfriend's friends who are hanging out in the living room drinking instead of studying as they hope for the best and fear the worst for Emma. The furniture is all the kind of stuff you see dumped on the roadside with signs attached saying *Free*. I stay standing. The flat smells of cigarette smoke. The boys are stacking their freshly empty beer bottles on a coffee table in a formation like a house of cards. The flatmate is a pretty girl with bouncy blond hair styled from some latest sitcom. She keeps picking at her cuticles, snapping away splinters of skin from the sides of her nails and dropping them onto the threadbare carpet.

She wipes at her eyes as we talk, there are mascara stains beneath them, what my wife would have called *panda eyes*, which she'd get sometimes if we fought, which, thankfully, wasn't often. She tells me a similar thing that Emma's father told me, that Emma's a smart girl and can talk her way out of anything.

"She even talked her way out of a speeding ticket a week ago," she says. "She told the officer she was in a rush to get to the hospital because her mum was undergoing cancer treatment."

"I hadn't heard."

She shakes her head. "That's the thing. Her mother hasn't got cancer. Emma has this idea that everybody knows somebody with cancer, or who has died from it, and you can use that to talk your way out of anything because people are sympathetic and they can relate. She's been reading about psychology for the last year even though she only started studying it a few weeks ago. She has this way of seeing how people tick, you know?"

I talk to everybody and don't get any more information than I already had. The boys are more interested in shooting each other on the big-screen TV, their thumbs flying over game controllers and their eyes locked on the action. The volume is turned down so at least we can talk. Two mornings ago Emma Green woke up and went to class. She finished studying and had lunch with two of her friends. She went to work, pulling a four-hour part-time shift at the café. Then somebody abducted her.

The file Schroder gave me has information that Donovan Green didn't have. The police searched the parking lot behind the café and found a makeup compact and a small patch of fresh blood with skin and hair stuck in it. The flatmate identified the compact as belonging to Emma. The hair matched the color of Emma's hair, and the blood matched Emma's blood type. DNA testing takes weeks, but it's a safe bet it'll be a match. It all adds up to a struggle. Emma dropped her bag and the compact rolled out. Her head banged into the ground or somebody banged it into the ground for her.

Paint scrapings were taken from the side of the dumpster I looked at, which had been driven into. They were red and Emma's car was yellow. If somebody was speeding away from the scene with Emma in the trunk of their car, why come back for her car later on? No, most likely whoever hit the dumpster had nothing to do with Emma's disappearance. Could have happened yesterday, could have happened three days ago. It's not useful. Sales receipts are being run from the café, a list of people there on the day is slowly being built, but the problem is most people spending five or ten bucks on coffee and a muffin don't use credit cards. If the suspect did take Emma's car, how did he get there? Bus? A taxi? Does he live close enough to have walked?

There have been no unusual visitors to the flat, no maintenance men or gardeners or a creepy landlord, no strange phone calls, nobody hanging around outside. The flatmate lets me look through Emma's room about twelve hours after the police already have, and everything is out of place from this morning's search and anything they found relevant taken away. I spend an hour at the flat with my questions and leave feeling more frustrated than when I arrived.

I get home just before nine o'clock. It's been a long day, and one that started with me waking up in jail. There are kids out in the street racing on skateboards, some throwing a football, others playing a game of tag. The sun is moments away from sliding off the edge of the horizon, but at the moment it's reflecting brightly off the windows, a blistering orange ball of fire trying to melt the glass. It's the first time in four months I've seen the sun sink from view, and the sight has never looked so fantastic. For four months day and night were brought in with the flick of a switch. It's hard to imagine that tomorrow I'll be waking up in my own bed. Hard to imagine Emma Green can see the sunset. It's the perfect evening for a beer but I've made a promise never to touch another beer again.

I stay outside until the sun is completely gone and I can no longer hear the kids in the street. The temperature drops down to a more livable seventy degrees. I watch the late-night news and there's no mention of Emma Green, no mention of Melissa, but the news is no different from the news I was watching before being shut away for four months—bad people doing bad things to good people all across the city, across the country, all across the world. The news becomes blurry as my eyelids become heavier. There's a brief mention of the fire Schroder attended today. The victim peeled from the floor was a nurse by the name of Pamela Deans. It shows a picture of Pamela in a nurse's uniform. It makes me think about Melissa for a moment, but all her victims have been men and the fire doesn't fit. The picture has to be at least a few years old and in it she looks around fifty, hair streaked black and gray pulled tightly in a bun, perhaps her downcast smile is a result of her extra chin weighing down on her lips.

I make some coffee and go back through the file Schroder gave me. I call Schroder for an update but his phone goes through to voice mail. I leave a message. Some of the facts in Emma's folder are things I learned about her last year when I ran into her life. Her birthday was the day after I ran into her with my car. She'll be eighteen this year and has an older brother, Jason, living in Australia. She has blond hair and hazel eyes and a look that would have men watching her anywhere she went. It could be that look that got her abducted.

My cell phone rings and I'm hoping it's Schroder, but it's Donovan Green. He's wanting an update. I tell him I've spoken to the boyfriend and her boss and her flatmate and I'm going to speak to some of her classmates in the morning. I tell him there will be many who won't want to speak to me, and he tells me to remind them why I'm there—to help find Emma. He reminds me in an almost pleading way why he's come to me. I don't tell him about the blood and hair. I hang up and a minute later Schroder calls.

"We're working on something," he says. "We got a report of a car speeding away from the café just after Emma finished work. Another driver had to slam on his brakes to avoid a collision."

"He get a plate?"

"He got the first two letters. Said if he'd gotten the rest, he'd have reported the guy for reckless driving yesterday. He said he forgot about it, then Emma's case made the news tonight, and he thought it might be relevant. He said it was a red four-door sedan, maybe five years old. Couldn't pin him down on any other details. You saw the dumpster?"

"Yeah. Red paint. But if he sped away from the scene, where's Emma's car?"

"That's the key question. You take another look at the Melissa file?"

"Not yet. I'm going to talk to some of Emma's classmates," I tell him.

"Yeah, I figured you would. You still think you can do a better job."

"It's not that . . ."

"I know, I know," he says. "I didn't mean it like that. Hell, maybe you can do a better job. There could be something to what you said earlier."

"Yeah?"

"Yeah. Or I'm just frustrated and tired, that's all. The fact is you do have a good insight and one that can save lives," he says before hanging up, and I hope he's right, I hope that we can balance the scales of this city a little by finding Emma Green alive.

chapter fourteen

Cooper has to be careful with Adrian's questions: *What made you interested in serial killers? What made you want to become one?* His instinct is to say he isn't a serial killer, but instead he has to play the game. He didn't set the rules, but he can follow them. Already he has made wrong assumptions. He thought Adrian had been the one to sell him the thumb, but that's clearly not the case. The thumb is a coincidence in a day full of random shit. The basement is getting cooler. It's too dark to see if there's damp or mold, but he can sense it there, growing in and around the concrete blocks, leeching the warmth from his body. He'd rather freeze to death than wrap the sheet laying on top of the mattress around himself. He takes a deep breath and plunges into the delusion, answering the question with one of his own. "Do you know how many women I've killed?"

Adrian, smiling now because he is being drawn into the conversation, smiling because he's getting everything he wants, raises up two fingers, and then says "Two," confirming it. "Plus the man who owns the thumb. That's three in total that I know of. Are there more?"

Be careful. And be believable. Just what is a good number to start with?

Christ, it's like bidding in one of the auctions. Ten is way too many, but he likes the idea of going higher than three because it will give Adrian the feeling of being drawn into a secret. He settles on five.

"Six," he says, changing his mind at the last moment. "Four women and two men," he says.

Just hope he doesn't ask you to name them.

Making up the names won't be the problem, no, the problem will be remembering them. He struggles enough as it is to remember somebody's name when he's introduced to them. What he'll do is go with some of his students. Surely Adrian wouldn't recognize the names. He pushes forward, hoping to get past that. "I enjoyed the women," he says, "but the men were necessities."

"Why?"

"One of them was a boyfriend of one of the women who was in the way," Cooper says, then pauses. It sounds unbelievable to himself and surely to Adrian too, and he waits to be called a liar, and when it doesn't happen, he carries on. "And the other one owed me money."

"And the thumb belongs to one of them?"

"Yes. The one who owed me money," he answers, wishing he'd gone with four people. Or just the two Adrian said in the beginning. Wait—three—because of the thumb in the jar. This is going to be harder than he thought. He can feel those two-to-one odds tugging in the wrong direction.

"What did you use to cut off the thumb?" Adrian asks, stepping closer to the window. "Who was he? Why did he owe you money?"

Shit. Cooper can see this quickly getting away from him. "He was a friend of mine," he says, "and I lent him some money a few years ago, but then he refused to pay it back," he says, and he has lent money to friends before and every one of them has always paid him back and there was no need to remove any thumbs. "So I strangled him, and I used a knife to cut off his thumb, and I buried his body."

"Where did you bury him?"

"In the woods."

"What woods?"

"It doesn't matter," Cooper says, slumping his shoulders. "What matters is it's over now," he says, and he looks away, but not away too far because he needs Adrian to see just how sad he's pretending to look.

Adrian takes another step forward. "What's over?"

"The killing." He rests his forehead against the window. "The very thing you like about me is the very thing I won't be able to do anymore." *Unless you let me out,* Cooper thinks but doesn't say. It's too soon. Baby steps. Anything more than that and he'll blow it.

"I have thought about that."

"You have?" he asks, looking up, genuinely curious.

"Yes. And I have something that can help."

"What?"

"It's a surprise. I'll tell you tomorrow."

Baby steps. He's clenching his fists but Adrian can't see him. He can only imagine what it's like to strangle somebody, his imaginary friend didn't struggle, but when he gets out of here he'd like to find out how it feels with Adrian.

"Okay, Adrian. Thank you," he says, and it's a struggle not asking what the surprise is. "You know, I always knew the killing was going to come to an end."

"I guess," Adrian says, scratching at a red blemish on the side of his face. "But it doesn't have to."

"How's that? You're not going to start bringing me people to kill, there isn't much . . ."

He trails off when he sees Adrian smile. Oh, Jesus, that's his plan! He's sure of it. The surprise Adrian has for him is going to be somebody for him to kill. His stomach tightens at the thought.

"Just wait until tomorrow," Adrian says, almost confirming it. "You didn't answer—why did you become a serial killer?"

Is the person he's supposed to kill already here? A man or a woman? Somebody he knows?

"Cooper?"

Wait, this can be a good thing. It can be somebody who can help. They can help each other.

"Hey, Cooper?"

"Huh?" He looks at Adrian. Adrian is looking concerned.

"Are you okay?"

"Sure I am."

"Why did you become a serial killer?"

"What?"

"Are you listening to me?"

"What? Yes, yes, of course. It's just that, well, it's a hard question to answer," Cooper says, trying to focus, trying to recall what he's learned and taught all these years. "It just kind of happened. The first one was almost accidental. I was breaking into somebody's house," he says. "I was looking for money and this woman just, you know, kind of just came home at the wrong time." It's a standard answer. Every day somewhere in the world somebody comes home to find a stranger in their house and gets killed for it. A burglar goes in to steal money and is presented with a career changing opportunity, it happens all the time, burglars upgrading from thief to rapist to killer.

"That's how it can often start," Adrian says, nodding. "It's in the books."

"One thing just led to another."

Adrian stops scratching at the blotch on his face to study his fingers. "Did you rape her?"

"Like I said, one thing just led to another."

"Did you kill animals when you were a kid?" Adrian asks, returning to his scratching.

"Did you?"

"Umm . . ."

"Remember the deal, Adrian? I was going to answer your questions but only if you answer mine."

"I remember."

"Was it a cat or a dog?" Cooper asks.

"How did you know?"

"But it's never gone beyond that, has it? You've never killed a person?"

"No, never," Adrian says, looking down, and Cooper can tell he's lying. Adrian is a killer. The odds at getting out of here slip a little more. Hopefully the other people Adrian has killed haven't been people he collected in this room.

"Tell me about it," Cooper says.

"It was a long time ago," Adrian says. "At school, I used to get bullied."

"So did I," Cooper says, though that isn't true. He never got bullied and he wasn't a bully. He was more of a ghost—people didn't really see him.

"It was all the time. I didn't get beaten up every day, but I got teased every day, and punched or pushed at least every week. I hated school."

"It can be tough," Cooper says, "but you survived it."

"One day these kids beat me up really bad. I had to go to hospital. I was in there a while. They kicked me heaps and put me into a coma. The coma didn't hurt, but the rest of it did."

"That sounds awful," Cooper says, wishing the kids had finished the job.

"It *was* awful. I wanted to get revenge on them but they were all bigger than me and there wasn't anything I could do. I wanted to kill them. I would follow them home, but, but . . . like I said, they were all bigger than me."

"So you started killing animals?"

"Pets. I started killing their pets. There were eight boys that beat me and they all had pets. Cats or dogs. At night I'd sneak out of my house and hang outside their homes. It took only a few days to learn what kind of pets they had. I didn't think they'd all have them, but they did." Adrian moves back to the coffee table. He begins to straighten up the books again. "Eight cats and two dogs because some of them had more than one pet. I started with the cats because they were easier to get to. I took a packet of cat food and when I caught one I held it down and wrapped it in a blanket so I wouldn't have to see it, then I'd just jump on it. They would move around like a thousand volts was being pumped into them, and then they'd stop moving. When I unwrapped it the cat would always feel floppy and warm, like it was fast asleep. I'd leave the animal on their front lawn. Because I wasn't going to school anymore, I could hang out near their house most of the day. I'd watch where they buried the pet, then that night I'd go back to visit the grave."

Cooper says nothing. He can feel his mouth hanging open. The room still smells of vomit, and he is sure he's going to be sick again. He takes a deep breath and thinks about what he's just listened to. "You went back to the houses to gloat?" he asks, knowing it's extremely common for serial killers to visit graves of their victims. The original theory had killers doing this out of guilt or remorse, but they learned serial killers were doing it to relive the excitement, to gloat. But not when the victims were animals.

"No. Not go gloat," Adrian says.

"You felt bad?"

"No."

Cooper doesn't understand. It's always one of those two reasons. "Then what?"

"I used to dig them up."

"What?"

"It wouldn't take long because the earth was always loose. I'd dig them up and hang them outside the front door. The people stepping out in the morning would always scream, and I'd be standing a few doors down to watch. There was a lot of waiting involved, but the payoff . . . the payoff was always worth it. I loved seeing their faces. I wanted to kill every pet those kids had. I got caught jumping on the fifth cat. The police came and then everybody thought it would be best if I got sent away, not just for their safety but for mine. So I got sent here, to the Grove."

"The Grove?"

"It's what we called it."

It's unlike anything Cooper has ever heard or read about, and it's one of those rare moments in his life where Cooper just doesn't know what to say next. He gets the idea there may be many of these moments over the next day. Adrian's behavior back then is certainly outside the scope of the textbooks.

Even under the circumstances, part of him is thinking there has to be a paper in this. Maybe even a book. He just has to get out of here.

"Can I ask you something else, Adrian?"

"It's my turn to ask you questions," Adrian answers. "How do you feel when you kill somebody?"

Like you don't already know.

He can tell Adrian that he feels nothing, no ecstasy or remorse, but he takes the other path instead. "I like to hear them beg for their lives. Is that why I'm here?" he asks. "Because you want to be like me?"

"You wouldn't want to be like me," Adrian says. "I'm too average for anybody to want to be like me."

Adrian is right. Being like him is the last thing Cooper wants. "I doubt you're average, Adrian. None of this seems average."

Adrian doesn't answer. Just shrugs the way an average man would when he can't make a decision.

"What do you do for a living? Do you have a job?" he asks, wishing he could take notes.

"You think you already know, don't you," Adrian says, and he shuffles the books around so they're no longer straight. "You've already built up a profile of me."

It's true, and part of the profile Cooper has come up with has Adrian sorting out colored buttons from other colored buttons, or sweeping floors, or he receives disability benefits. Does he drive? Yes, because he brought Cooper here. Does he have friends? No. Does he live here alone? Yes.

"No, I haven't built up any profile," Cooper answers. "Only thing I've been thinking about is how my friends and family are going to miss me. My mother relies on me, Adrian, to look after her."

"You hate your mother."

"Why would you say that?"

"Because all serial killers hate their mothers."

True. Most serial killers do hate their mothers. Cooper loves his. "You're right, Adrian, I hate my mother," he says, the words sitting uncomfortably. He can't stomach the idea of her finding out he's missing. "But she still relies on me, and I'm worried about what she'll do if I'm not there to help her. I'm scared of her."

"It's all going to be okay. I promise."

"And the police? They're going to be looking for me. Have you thought about that?"

Adrian smiles, and Cooper can tell that he has. "I've taken care of that. For you. You don't want them finding out you're a serial killer, I mean, you don't want them knowing, right?"

"How have you taken care of it?"

"I'm tired," Adrian says. "I'm not used to staying up late. We can talk again tomorrow if you like. I know I want to. I hope you want to too."

"Of course I do, buddy," he says, and Adrian winces and Cooper knows he's pushed too far.

"I'm not your buddy," Adrian says. "You're trying to trick me."

Shit. Now what? Own up? Or jump further in? "It's true," he says. "I don't know what it is, but there's already a connection between us. Come on, Adrian, you must feel it too, right?"

"You think I'm a fool," Adrian answers, and with that, he turns away and runs up the stairs, leaving Cooper alone in the dark, angry and disappointed with himself.

chapter fifteen

It's my first day waking up as a free man. I put my phone on charge and refuel on a bowl of cereal before heading out into the heat to find Emma Green alive and well. That's the goal. That's the frame of mind I'm going to keep. Yesterday was hot and today is even hotter. There are no clouds in the sky and if there were they'd probably catch fire. Mother Nature is holding her breath because there isn't the slightest hint of any breeze. Smoke hangs to the south over the Port Hills, blazing scrub fires turning the sky out there gray. Last night I left the rental in the driveway and I suffer for that now, the steering wheel hot to touch and my sunglasses, which I left on the dashboard, burn the bridge of my nose. I leave the doors open and let things cool before hitting the road. It's nearly ten o'clock and the traffic is much thinner than it would have been an hour ago. Everybody looks tired. Everybody looks like they want to take the day off from whatever it is they're doing and spend it inside sleeping. It's no different when I reach Canterbury University. The parking lot is a quarter full and the silver birches lining it are less tree than they are kindling. The people climbing out of their cars are all in a daze.

Canterbury University is a mismatch of old and modern buildings—many how you'd imagine a Soviet university to look at the peak of the cold war, the rest how you'd imagine a university to look if it were built on the moon. There are older, Gothic-style buildings of the same era as Jack the Ripper, gray stone covered in soot and bird shit and dirt picked up and dumped on them from the nor'west winds. Mixed among them are modern buildings with big steel beams and long glass frontages covered in fingerprints and streaks from whoever cleaned them last. None of the buildings have much in the way of curves, any extra shape outside of a square being a cost the university wasn't prepared to spend. Most of the students are in T-shirts and shorts, but there are still those in black trench coats from thrift shops with black or white shirts and black jeans, badges on their jackets, both men and women with eyeliner, defying the hot weather to show off their angst. At least half of the students are walking along with their faces down, their eyes locked on their cell phones as their thumbs dance across the keys sending out texts, just the occasional glance upward so as not to walk into a wall or another cell phone user. Even more of them have white wires leading from their ears to a pocket somewhere. I ask for directions and to these people it's like helping the elderly.

I reach the lecture hall where Emma Green's next class is. Outside is a sculpture painted bright colors and made from wooden beams that looks more like bad carpentry than good art. I'm not sure what it's meant to represent, or whether Superman just came along and meshed together all the bus stop benches he could find. There's a group of students hanging about outside in the shade, sitting on the lawn. They tell me their lecturer hasn't shown up yet. I ask them about Emma and most of them remember seeing her in the class but never really knew her. Some have been questioned by the police, and those who did know a little something about Emma are eager to go over what they told them. I spend a productive hour waiting with them; their psychology professor never shows up. It turns out their professor also teaches criminology but only to students who have taken psychology for three years. The fact it's a psychology class means everybody offers an insight into Emma's disappearance, some of them likely hoping an accurate assessment of the situation will get them an A. I figure that's the norm. I figure about two weeks into studying psychology you start self-diagnosing yourself, and then everybody else. As helpful as they all are, I'm saddened by them too, there's an excited atmosphere surrounding them, brought on by the knowledge that one of their own is about to hit the headlines in the worst way possible, and some relief too that it isn't any of them.

"This lecturer that didn't show up today," I say, speaking to a girl with a dozen earrings in her left ear and hair not much longer than her nails. She's wearing a skin-tight T-shirt with the words *Underage Sperm Bank* across it. "I'd like to talk to him as well. What's his name?"

"He's actually a professor," she says, "and he doesn't really like it if you make that mistake," she says, summing him up in one sentence. "You got a cigarette I can have?"

"I don't smoke. The professor's name?" I ask because she appears to have forgotten I asked.

"Oh yeah, Cooper Riley," she answers, "but I can't tell you where you can find him. This is the second day he hasn't shown up. It's like, totally random, you know? Looking at him you'd kind of think he had never been late for anything in his life. Maybe the heat got him."

"Maybe," I answer, thinking about the timeline, about Emma being missing for two and a half days and Cooper Riley not showing up for two. Riley wasn't mentioned in the file—no reason he would have been questioned because it was only yesterday Emma was officially considered missing. I get directions to the faculty lounge and thank the students for their time. I phone Schroder on the way.

"The name Cooper Riley mean anything to you?" I ask.

"Nothing. I don't even know who he is."

"He was one of Emma's professors."

"Come on, Tate, I've told you already, it's not my case."

"And he didn't show up for work yesterday or today."

"Shit. So now you're jumping to conclusions, right?"

"I think he knows something."

"Tate, he may be sick, or was called away because somebody else is sick."

"Either way I still want to talk to him."

"Doesn't matter what you want. We'll be the ones to talk to him."

"Damn it, Carl, I'm coming to you with this, just like you asked, remember? I'm not holding back. Don't cut me out of the loop."

"I'll call you back," he says and hangs up.

The psychology department has its own faculty lounge. In fact the psychology department is actually one of the largest departments in the entire university, and I think that sums up Christchurch pretty well. All the corridors are like hospital wings, linoleum floors and pastel colors. I learn the same thing from another professor that I did from the students—that Cooper Riley hasn't shown up for work in two days. I ask if I can see Riley's office and the woman I'm talking to tells me I'd have to ask Cooper.

"How can I get hold of him?"

"You could ring him, I suppose," she says, "or you could try. His phone has been switched off."

She gives me his cell phone number and landline and I try calling the cell on the way back to my car and get a message saying the phone is off or out of range. The landline goes through to an answering machine and a promise of a returned call.

I give Schroder another call but his line is busy. I borrow a phonebook and match up the home number I was given with Riley's name to get his address, wondering, wondering, was Cooper Riley the last person to see Emma Green alive?

chapter sixteen

It's a brand-new day. His second mother used to tell him anything can happen on a brand new day, that a fresh start each morning gave you a chance to redeem yourself for the things that angered you the day before. That never helped much when he was locked in the Scream Room and didn't have the chance to prove himself, but it certainly helps now.

He's noticed Cooper using his name as often as he can. Part of him likes it, he likes the connection forming between them and hearing his name makes him genuinely hope that connection is real. His mother hardly ever used his name, only when he was in trouble, the kind of trouble that got him locked downstairs.

Ultimately he isn't sure whether Cooper is trying to bond with him or fool him. Reading about all this kind of stuff, he learned if you're ever attacked by a serial killer, you should use their name as much as you can if you know it. That's why Cooper is using it. He doesn't know this for sure—and he doesn't like the confusion that comes with not knowing. It actually makes him angry. He tries to think of an adage his mother would use, but can only come up with "*A frown is a foe that certainly must go.*" Cooper is hoping to humanize himself so Adrian won't hurt him—but of course there is no chance of that. He hasn't gone to all this effort to hurt the one thing he cherishes the most.

Today he will give Cooper his gift, and from there any bonding between them will be genuine. The gift will reset the mistakes from yesterday. The gift is his redemption. He learned years ago that you can feel better giving rather than receiving. It will be like that today. He is sure of it. He also learned years ago he felt good taking things. Like the lives of those cats.

The sun is pouring through the eastern windows as it makes its way around to the north. He fell asleep last night after listening to his conversation with Cooper, and then listening to classical music. The radio is still on, and the news is on, the announcer is talking about the temperature. People have been dying in the heat and Adrian doesn't fully understand why. People should just stay inside if they're getting too hot, or drink more water. He turns the radio off and a few minutes later he sits outside and drinks an orange juice. He likes the heat. He's spent too many days locked in cold rooms to want to hang out in the shade. The trees forming a barrier between him and the neighboring paddock and the road are absolutely still, no breeze or birds to create any movement. There's a forest about a kilometer away covering a shallow hill, the trees in there thick and old, the branches gnarled and twisted. The air is sticky. A persistent fly keeps landing on him and he keeps swatting it away until it falls into his orange juice. He starts to wonder what will happen if Cooper doesn't like his gift, and that makes him sad. "*Depression is a sad man's joy,*" his mother used to say. This is one she said to him many times, but he never really understood. He picks the fly out with his finger, studies it for a few seconds, then gently sits it on the porch. Its wings are stuck together. He moves it into the shade so it won't burn.

He walks inside where the temperature drops a little. There are flies on the walls and ceiling and he's never known how they do that without falling off. There isn't much in the way of furniture to land on. He rinses his glass in the kitchen and makes his way upstairs to the bedroom next to his own. The girl is awake. He enters the room and holds up the pitcher of water and helps her tilt her head forward and she sucks it in greedily through the straw. He gives her ten seconds and then pulls it away. She makes sounds inside her mouth; he thinks she's trying to form some words but he has no idea what and doesn't want to know. He holds the water back up and she takes another drink then slumps her head down. Her arms and legs are flushed the most, her face and stomach a close second, and he doesn't know how attracted to her Cooper needs to be to do what it is he does best. He could try to put some makeup on her once he's cleaned her up, but he doesn't know how. It can't be difficult.

When he goes down to the basement Cooper is standing at the cell door, looking out the small window as Adrian walks down the steps. The sun is still low outside, coming in through the windows and hitting the basement door, and for the next hour or so, as long as that door's open, it's almost as good as it used to be when this place had electricity.

"Good morning, Adrian," Cooper says. "Did you have a good sleep?"

"Not really," Adrian says, suspicious at how friendly Cooper sounds. Suspicious . . . and happy.

"That's a real shame. So what are we going to do today?"

"Today you get your surprise. In fact I have two of them. One will have to wait until tonight. It's a nighttime kind of surprise."

"And the other one?"

"You haven't made the news yet," Adrian says. "When the police go looking for you, they're going to find out you've done bad things."

"True," Cooper says. "That's good thinking, Adrian. Excellent thinking. And we need to do something about that, because they'll come looking for me and eventually they'll come here."

Adrian frowns. "Why would they come here?"

"Because they're the police. They'll look for me. They'll figure out who took me, and they'll figure out where you have me."

"No they won't," Adrian says, and he's confident of that. "And that's one of the surprises. See, I don't want them to figure out you're a serial killer because then they'll look even harder for you. That's why I'm going to burn it down."

"Burn *what* down?"

"With your house gone the police won't be able to learn as much about you."

"Wait, wait, hang on a second, Adrian," Cooper says, putting his hand on the glass. "Listen to me. There's no need to do that. I've been careful. There's nothing there for them to find."

"But it's for the best! You don't need it anymore, and it's safer this way. I'm doing this for you! It's about being careful," he says. "I'll be back in an hour or two and I'll bring you some lunch," he adds, and he makes his way back upstairs, shaking his head as Cooper continues to call to him, thinking, *who knew being a collector was so much work?*

chapter seventeen

Cooper Riley lives in Northwood, one of the newer subdivisions in the north of Christchurch that came into existence around the same time the twentieth century ended. Out here half a million dollars can buy you a badly built house that looks nice, but is nowhere as strong as a home built across town fifty years ago where land and life is cheaper. People come to Northwood for the safety of a community that isn't addicted to drugs or murder, but like all things, the violence is already catching up. Today it doesn't matter where you live in Christchurch, everywhere is being blasted by the heat wave equally. Paint has peeled from letterboxes and iron fences, and the only grass that hasn't been burned off is in thick shade. All of the houses have manicured gardens, and there aren't any weeds in sight. Each house falls in line with a similar design. It's the kind of community where everybody's uniqueness conforms with the collective agreement. If somebody built a front fence or painted their house something that wasn't a shade of fawn, they'd be lynched. There are garage-sized sculptures every few blocks that are supposed to look like pergolas but instead look like incomplete garages. Cooper lives on Winsington Drive, surrounded by other pretentious-sounding street names that could have come out of some 1940s golf clothing catalog, *the Winsington Jacket is a collaboration of style and elegance, a must for when one is taking lunch on the 19th hole.* Cooper's street is part of a subdivision less than five years old, the tar seal road has bubbled from the heat and there are potholes where it's melted and stuck to the tread of passing cars. I drive slowly because it's impossible to know what direction other drivers are wanting to take because the residents of Northwood are allergic to indicating.

The price tags increase as the houses get bigger, two-story places with columns leading up from the front door to the top floor, columns that in another time and country would have been made from marble. Here, however, ninety percent of the homes are made from plaster that's been slapped over polystyrene sheets, a great idea until some kid punches a hole in a wall with his soccer ball and then the moisture is sucked into the wooden framework of the house where the rot spreads. It's an expensive problem and a common one across the country. People here are paying for the area and for the look and for the illusion of quality. There's a big jet boat parked up on a trailer out on the street next to Cooper's house, taking up most of the lane. It looks expensive, and I guess the nice house wasn't enough by itself for the owner to prove to the neighbors he has wealth. I get past it and there are two cars on the other side and they certainly don't look like they belong to a detective. The smaller car parked out front is yellow and looks out of place in this neighborhood because it's not European. If it were here for more than twenty-four hours it would get picked up by the sanitation department. The second car, the BMW, is in the driveway. I pull in ahead of the cheaper car. I've seen it before. Emma Green's file is next to me on the passenger seat. I open it and there's a photo of her car with her standing next to it, taken about four months ago. I look at the registration plate in the file and then the one in real life and they're identical. Since Tuesday night there has been a report out to look for that car, but the problem is there are more cars than cops in this city, and the report to look for it doesn't mean anything unless it enters the orbit of a patrol car. This is the car the insurance company gave her after I ruined her other one. In the photo she has a big grin on her face. In the photo she thinks the worst is behind her. She has no idea she's about slap-bang between two tragedies, one that almost took her life and one that may have. I close the file and step into the sun, her smile staying with me and pushing me forward, making me desperate to find the man who took that smile from her.

I walk carefully up to the house, the lenses in my sunglasses ready to drip from the frames. Schroder must have made a call by now and somebody will be on their way to talk to Cooper Riley. That means soon a police car is going to arrive and a detective along with it. But something here isn't right. The front door to the house is ajar. The keys are hanging from the lock. The driver's door to the BMW is closed, but hasn't latched. The interior light isn't going so either the bulb has blown or it's switched off or the door has been open all night and the battery has died. The BMW is dark blue and about ten years old and can't have been the car that hit the dumpster behind the café.

I take a deep breath and pop the trunk and breath out slowly when I see Emma Green isn't in there. If she ever was folded up into it at any point there's no sign. If Cooper did take her he could have wrapped her in something. When I walk around the car there's something plastic on the ground sticking out from beside the tire. I bend down. It's a camera. There's a crack running across the back of the display screen and the lid to the battery compartment has busted off. I open up the small compartment covering the memory card and pop it out. I sit the camera back on the ground and look under the car. There're a couple of papers, a teaching schedule, a sandwich wrapped in clear wrap, and an apple that's wrinkled and soft. Wedged beneath the edge of the tire are some tiny pieces of paper, disk-shaped with a serial number across them. There are others further beneath the car, and when I stand back up I can see some against the edge of the lawn. They are from a Taser gun. I slip the memory card into my pocket and walk around to the trunk and take out the tire iron.

I don't knock on the door. Instead I take the keys and pocket them before swinging the door all the way open with my foot. The stench of petrol wafts out. My eyes water as I move forward. There are two empty petrol cans just inside the doorway. I wipe at my eyes while holding my breath. The tiled foyer floor is wet and slippery. To the left are a set of open French doors leading through to a carpeted living room with large dark patches where petrol has been splashed around. Ahead are more French doors, another living room, a dining room, and a kitchen. To the right a staircase twists up to the second-floor landing, a ninety-degree bend halfway up, all of it edged with iron wrought bars connected by a white wooden handrail.

I step back outside. I suck in a breath of clean air. Somebody was shot by a Taser, and somebody is about to set fire to the house. All that petrol—it's going to burn quick, and it's going to happen any second now. If Emma Green is inside she's going to burn quick along with it.

I have no choice. I head back in. I take the stairs, moving quickly past prints and photographs, my feet squelching into the carpet as petrol comes up out of it. If I'm quick I can get in and out of here before this place goes up in flames, or maybe I can stop it from happening. I check the rooms upstairs. A study to the far left, a guest bedroom, two bathrooms, and two more bedrooms. My chest is sore from breathing hard, my legs are aching, the lack of exercise over the months clearly evident. The fumes are much thicker up here. It doesn't add up—torching your own house doesn't seem the way a criminology and psychiatry professor would deal with hiding a body. A guy like Cooper wouldn't have brought a victim here, then become desperate enough to burn down his own house to hide the evidence. He also wouldn't be foolish enough to leave her car parked outside. Cooper Riley is quickly sliding down the scale from suspect to victim. Something bad has happened to him, or about to if this place burns, and I'm thinking it's the same bad thing that might happen to Emma Green.

I get through all the rooms. No blood. No Emma Green. No

Cooper Riley. No sign of any struggle except for the broken camera outside and signs somebody used a Taser. Every second I expect to hear the rush of flames erupting from below. I head back toward the stairs. Maybe I'll have more luck on the ground floor.

From downstairs a toilet flushes and the urgency is replaced with caution. I reach the staircase, my grip still tight on the tire iron, looking down into the foyer, when a man I don't recognize steps into the hall. He has a box of matches in his hand and one of them is already lit. He drops it into the petrol on his way out the door without even seeing me, picking up the empty containers on the way. Before I can move or even yell out, there's a *whoomp* as fire erupts over the tiles, through the French doors and onto the carpet and up the curtains. The arsonist disappears behind a haze of heat and smoke. The flames reach the staircase where it forks, heading along the ground floor and at the same time climbing the steps toward me, the flames blue at the bottom, yellow at the tips, the heart of it dark orange, the furniture in the foyer and living room already burning, the air blanketed with smoke and toxic fumes, all of it taking only seconds.

There is no path to the front door. The entire foyer is engulfed in fire. I take a few more steps down toward it. Somehow I have to get through those flames and find Emma Green.

Only I can't. Those flames are suicide. There is no path through them. The only direction is up.

Smoke rolls like water beneath the ceiling. Petrol splashes from the carpet onto my legs. I start coughing as raw dark air is pulled into my lungs. I run the length of the upstairs hallway to the bedroom at the end where there isn't any petrol on the floor. I slam the door closed hoping it will form a barrier to give me more time. The flames downstairs sound like a freight train. I can feel the floor heating up but I'm not sure if it's real or just my imagination. I try the windows. They open but not far enough to climb through. Emma Green's car is doing a U-turn. Badly. It bounces up over the opposite curb and hits a letterbox then shudders as it stalls. It stays that way for a few seconds before lurching forward again, the engine hiccupping, the letterbox crushed flat beneath the front wheels. The skeleton of the house groans as it weakens, the ground floor readying to have the top floor fold into it. The polystyrene walls are melting as the timber framing crackles and burns. It's only a matter of seconds until the bedroom is the next victim in the inferno.

I use the tire iron on the window, smashing it, taking out some of my frustration on the glass, angry that on the ground floor Emma may be burning to death. The quicker I get outside, the sooner I can make my way back in downstairs and look for her. Most of the shards of glass rain down outside, but some are pulled back in as the tire iron hooks toward me. A couple of pieces slide into my hand and cut deep. I drop the iron and drag the mattress from the bed and twist it out over the windowsill, shark tooth-shaped fragments of glass biting at it, making it difficult. I get it far enough to let it fall and allow gravity to take over. It disappears through the smoke and I can barely see the shape of it hitting the ground. Landing on the mattress is such a cartoonish thing to attempt, but it's all I have. The window in the bedroom below shatters and flames erupt outside and heat rushes over my face. I will have to pass through the flames, no choice there. People are appearing on the other side of the road. They're standing there staring at me with no idea what to do, some of them with their hands over their mouths, others pointing at me, some making calls on their cell phones, others pointing their phones at me and taking pictures or shooting film, some of them probably even annoyed I'm devaluing the neighborhood by being burned alive. None of them come any closer or offer any encouraging words of survival. I drape a blanket over the edge of the window to cover the remaining glass. The bedroom door is on fire. Smoke is being sucked in under it and toward the broken window. I wrap another blanket over my body, covering as much of myself as I can, holding it over my face by putting it between my teeth. I lower myself outside as far as I can to lessen the impact. The flames hit my feet. I let go, pushing back slightly, unable to see the mattress but remembering where it landed. I watch the house race past me. I pull the blanket down further to cover my face as I pass through the flames. I tuck my knees up slightly and I hit the mattress with my feet and butt at the same time; something in my left knee popping. I roll onto my back and away from the fire, leaving the blanket behind. The cuffs of my pants are smoldering. I slap at the flames with my hands and kill them, having to stretch forward because of my already swelling knee. I crawl further from the house, and at the same time two men appear. They grab me under the arms and drag me away, asking if there is anybody else inside.

I look at the house. Fire is coming through all the windows, it's overlapping every surface. I tell them I don't know, but I think there might be—I think Cooper Riley might be somewhere among those flames, Emma Green too, but I can't send these men in there.

"Let me go," I tell them, and try to shrug them off.

"You can't go back in there, buddy," one of them tells me.

"I have to. There's a girl in there."

"Not anymore there ain't," the other one says, "at least not one that's alive."

"Let me go," I say again, but they don't let me go, instead they drag me further from the fire and I let them do the dragging because they're right, I keep protesting but even if they let me go I don't know if I would try to go back in there, not now. If Emma Green is in there then it's already too late for her. Nobody can go in there and come back alive.

We watch as the house loses the battle, as clouds of smoke flood the air and extend out to the car and gardens and the heat pushes us back.

chapter eighteen

Adrian drives two blocks. He parks the car and locks the door and slowly works his way back to the fire. People have their eyes glued to the spectacle. A growing crowd has formed, and in that crowd he will not stand out. He should have kept driving, but there is something about the fire that called to him and made him return. When he was a kid, before he became the Urinator, he used to love lighting fires. Nothing big. Just small, contained fires, normally in rubbish bins on the side of the road, sometimes he'd drop a match into piled-up cardboard or newspapers waiting to be picked up for recycling. Less than ten fires in total, the addiction broken for him when one of the neighbors told his mother he'd seen him trying to set fire to a letterbox. Since the beating there have only been two fires. One yesterday with his mother and one today. Both big-scale fires impossible to drive away from without watching the show. Watching his mother burn was far better than trying to set fire to a wooden letterbox, and watching Cooper's house burn is even better again. Giant orange and yellow flames climbing over the houses, smoke billowing high into the air, the raw power of a contained inferno. It's a beautiful thing.

The group watching numbers almost twenty. He doesn't know where they've come from. Most of them are women, some surely stay-at-home mothers. There aren't any kids, which is great, because he doesn't like kids. Most of the people seem to be at least forty and he thinks that's because young people can't afford to live in this neighborhood. He wouldn't have thought any of them would want to stand in the sun and feel even hotter as the air around them heated from the flames. There are cars parked up and down the street with more arriving. There's a jet boat next to Cooper's house with the paint blistering along the side of it, the wheels of the trailer it's in are completely flat. There aren't any police cars or fire engines, but he can hear sirens in the distance. He enters the crowd but doesn't ask anybody what's happening. On the front lawn of Cooper's house are three men and one mattress and a blanket. The mattress wasn't there earlier, and looks like it's been thrown from the upstairs bedroom. One of the men is being helped by the other two. He's limping. His clothes are scorched and there is blood on his hands. Was that man inside the house? And who is he? A neighbor? A cop?

Yes. A cop. That feels right. But why was he there? Looking for Cooper because he's missing? Or looking for Cooper because he's killed six people? And he recognizes him too, he knows him, knows him, but can't place him.

The first fire engine arrives. It's bright red with lots of chrome, and big men wearing smoke-stained yellow uniforms jump out of it, moving quickly despite their size, hooking up large hoses and getting into place, they're in time to fight the fire but nothing can be saved. The house collapses in on itself in a crash of violent sound that hurts his ears, sending a shower of sparks into the garden where dry bushes and plants start to smolder. Cooper's car is also on fire. Another fire engine arrives. More yellow uniforms. Then come the patrol cars, two of them at first, and he can hear the siren of a third a few blocks away. The crowd grows bigger. Has to be at least forty people now. More firemen start piling into the street. Police officers start trying unsuccessfully to push back the spectators. The fire is getting louder. The flames larger and more beautiful. Adrian is caught between staring at them and the man. His mind is ticking over, trying to remember.

The fire hoses grow fat and tight, the pressure moves them across the ground where the folds snap into straight lines. Water arcs from nozzles into the fiery pit that was once a house, the firemen bracing themselves against the pressure. People are yelling at each other over the noise. There are more sirens of approaching vehicles. The crowd has reached fifty, their voices growing louder to be heard over the noise. Adrian is constantly pushed back as newcomers nudge forward for a better view. If he fell he would be trampled to death. It isn't fair—it's his fire and everybody else is getting a better view. He moves further down the street where he can get a better line of sight even if everything looks smaller, and even back here he can still feel the heat from it on his face. More and more he focuses on the man. The two men who helped him away from the flames have gone. The man is leaning against a car having an argument with somebody. It's Detective Inspector Schroder. Adrian has seen him on the news. He's on there a lot. In fact he thinks that's where he knows the other man from. As far as he knows, Schroder has never killed anybody. Schroder would never be worthy of collection.

The crowd ebbs and flows as people come and go. Adrian walks back to the car. There is a moment where he's scared the car will have disappeared, and another moment when climbing into it he suddenly realizes it might be a trap and police are watching, but it comes to nothing and he pulls away.

Adrian watches the news, but not obsessively, and only if it involves serial killers, which isn't often, and he hasn't seen it since leaving the halfway house he's been forced to live in over the last three years since the institution closed. He thinks about the man on the front lawn as he drives, then has to pull over. He finds it hard sometimes to focus on two things at the same time, especially if one of them is driving. So he sits with his face in his hands and closes his eyes and thinks about the serial killers this city has had, he pictures them from the news and it only takes a few moments to put a name to the face he just saw. Theodore Tate. He remembers now. Theodore Tate used to be a cop and became a private investigator, and last year he was in the news because he caught and killed a serial killer. Adrian found the whole case fascinating. He remembers wishing he could figure out who the killer was before the police did, just so he could meet the guy.

Does that mean Theodore Tate has also figured out Cooper Riley is a serial killer? With his face still buried in his hands, Adrian decides that it does. Theodore Tate is hunting Cooper Riley. He doesn't know how Tate figured it out, all he knows is that it's what Tate does.

Not only is he trying to ruin Cooper Riley's life, but Theodore Tate is going to try and take away Adrian's collection. That's not fair. When he pulls his hands away his eyes are assaulted by the sun and he has to close them again, opening them for a second at a time until he can bear the light. He drives to a service station. He fills up the two plastic containers that an hour ago were full of petrol but are now empty. He fills up the car too.

He pays with cash. He asks the woman behind the counter if he can borrow a phone book and she says yes, which immediately makes him like her. Women normally do their best never to speak to him. He borrows a pen to write down Tate's address. He spends five minutes with his map sprawled across the passenger seat trying to figure out the best way to Tate's house, not recognizing any of the streets because he doesn't know the area. He draws a line with his finger, humming as he decides on the best way to go.

chapter nineteen

In total, five fire engines, four patrol cars, and one ambulance show up. Only three of the fire engines are used, the other two park at the back, the excess firemen standing around watching the blaze, one of them talking to a young blond woman in the crowd and making her laugh. I sit in the back of the ambulance with my view of the burning house obstructed, but there are still some pretty clear views of lots and lots of smoke. We're parked far enough away to no longer feel the heat, but close enough so we still have to talk loudly to be heard over the crackling wood. I've drunk about a liter of water since being dragged away from the flames, my lungs are sore, I'm no longer coughing but my hands are shaking. I could have gotten back in there. I know I could have. Wouldn't have mattered if only one leg was going to support me, I could have made it back in there and found Emma and made it back out. Instead I let those two men drag me away and I could have done more.

I try to focus on the positive. The positive in this case is that I didn't see Emma, so that means she may not have been in there. The positive is that I'm still alive.

It only takes one paramedic to look me over, and the second one stands outside with everybody else. My knee has swelled up to twice its size from the impact of my fall and has almost no movement. The paramedic is a guy in his midthirties and is completely bald, his scalp glistening with so much sunblock you can see the ambulance walls reflected in it. He gives me anti-inflammatories and painkillers and the pain disappears somewhat but the tightness remains. He jabs my hand with a needle and injects some local anesthetic and digs out a few pieces of glass before cleaning the wound.

"You're going to need stitches," he says.

"Can't you do it?"

He shakes his head. "You're gonna have to come to the hospital for it."

Now I shake my head. "I don't have time. Can't you just patch it up?"

"You cops are all the same," he says, and he secures some gauze and padding around my hand, followed by some bandaging and tape. "It's still going to need stitches, and unless you want more damage, you should get it done today."

"I'll try my best."

"Good. And as long as you're trying things, try to keep it dry," he tells me, "and try not to use it."

"Not even for swimming?"

"Is that a joke?" he asks.

"It was supposed to be," I say, but with the fire still burning, no joke is going to come out sounding funny.

"You won't be laughing if it gets infected," he says, "especially if we have to cut off your hand."

"Is that a joke?"

"No."

"I'll keep it clean and dry, I promise."

My feet are slightly burned and he smears ointment on them and covers them with gauze and a lighter layer of bandaging than on my hand. Schroder waits outside while I'm being looked at, the argument we were having until the ambulance arrived put on hold. My hands have some blisters on them from patting down the flames on the bottom of my pants. It'll only take a couple of days for everything to heal except for the cut in my palm, which is going to take at least a week if I get around to having it stitched. When I'm all patched up they help me out of the ambulance and I lean against it, taking all the weight off my bad leg. I grab my shoes from the ambulance floor. The leather has charred and the tips of the laces and the soles have melted. They're a tight fit with the new bandaging.

Schroder comes in and puts his hand on my shoulder. "I'm sorry," he says, "and, if it helps, we don't know she was in there."

"I could have saved her," I tell him.

"And on that note," he says, pulling his hand away, "now I have to lay down the law. You fucked up, Tate," Schroder says. "It was only a matter of time before somebody tried to set you on fire."

"People are always warming up to me," I say.

"Jesus, Tate, this could have been much, much worse."

"Well, I'm grateful for your concern."

"Don't be. I mean people could have gotten hurt here, Tate. People could have gone rushing in to save you when you weren't supposed to be there in the first place."

"I've told you why I went in. You got a picture of Riley yet?" He holds one up and it matches up with the Cooper I saw in a couple of the shots inside, Cooper with friends, with family, Cooper on holiday, Cooper not being burned alive or attacked in his driveway. This one looks like it could be an ID photo from the university. Cooper has a short gray beard, he's bald on top with hair running around the sides.

I shake my head. "That's not the guy I saw. This guy was younger by ten or fifteen years."

"Then who?"

"Like I said earlier, I didn't get a good look at him, only from above, but it certainly wasn't that guy," I say, nodding toward the photograph.

"Okay. Work with a sketch artist. See if you can put something together."

"I'll do my best," I tell him. I look toward the smoldering remains of the house. "Even if Emma isn't in there, I think you're going to be scraping your second dead body out of a fire in two days."

"Yeah, that's what I'm thinking too."

"He live alone?"

"Yeah. He divorced three years ago. No current partner, according to anyone we've questioned."

"You think they're related?" I ask. "Two fires in two days."

"Could be. Both were obviously arson," he says, "though it's anybody's guess what the connection between Pamela Deans and Cooper Riley could be."

"She was a nurse, right?"

"Goddamn it, Tate, isn't there an off switch in there somewhere?" he asks, tapping me on the forehead. "Let it go. I know I said earlier I was happy to let you look for Emma Green, but this has advanced beyond that now. You see that, right? You see how you can fuck things up for us by getting in the way?"

"I'll back off," I say, not really sure if I mean it.

"Sound like you mean it," he says.

"I mean it," I say, still unsure.

"No you don't."

I shrug. "I'm sorry," I say, but I'm not sorry, and I don't know what else to add.

"No you're not. You've been out of jail for twenty-four hours and you're running around like a damn cowboy. I should have known it'd be this way. If you had just used that goddamn phone of yours to call me the moment you saw Emma Green's car, things would be different. You'd have seen the arsonist come out. You could have followed him. We'd have somebody in custody, Tate, if only you had waited."

"Come on, Carl, I had no choice but to go in once I smelled that petrol. I knew from the moment I stepped inside that place might burn down around me, but I couldn't take the chance Emma was alive in there getting ready to be cooked. How'd it have looked if I just waited out here while she died? You'd have done the same damn thing, so stop acting so pissed at me."

He looks mad, and then he sighs and slowly shakes his head. "Okay, Tate, point taken," he says. "Are you sure you didn't recognize the arsonist? I wouldn't put it past you to recognize him and not tell me because you wanted to find him yourself."

"Screw you, Carl."

"Hey, I'm just putting it out there," he says, holding his hands up. "And don't pretend to take offense. It's exactly the kind of stupid thing you'd do."

"Not this time."

"You sure on that?"

"Positive."

We both look toward the fire. The car has been put out, and the house is now just a smoldering wreck. "If we're lucky," Schroder says, "one of those Taser ID disks survived the flames."

We both look at the driveway and at the car, it doesn't look like we're going to be lucky.

"It's not the car that sped out from behind the café," Schroder says.

"I know. You got any leads on that at all?"

"Not yet. The café doesn't have any surveillance, and the owner says it's pretty much a cash business. We're still waiting on testing to see if the paint can be matched to any specific car, but that'll take a few more days."

"Emma doesn't have a few more days. Nor does Cooper," I say. "If he wasn't in there," I say, staring at the house, "then he's been taken somewhere. Why Taser him if you're planning on killing him right away?"

"Maybe it was the only weapon somebody had."

"Then he'd have Tasered him and stabbed him and left him in the hallway. I don't think he's in there. No reason to drag him that far into the house if you're planning on killing him."

"There's always a reason," Schroder says.

It's a good point; however, I'm thinking Cooper isn't in there. I'm hoping that means Emma isn't in there either.

"Okay, Tate. Look, go home. I'll send somebody around in half an hour to draw up a description. We'll get it into the papers. Maybe somebody will recognize him. Get some rest and take care of that leg of yours."

I take that leg of mine along with the rest of me back toward my car. It isn't parked far enough away from the house to not be affected by the heat, and the paint on the hood and passenger side has bubbled. I have to walk swinging my leg out to the side because I can't bend it. I get the door open and am easing myself inside when a guy steps out of the crowd and comes toward me.

"Hey bro, you were lucky to get out," he says. He has long blond hair twisted into dreadlocks that are a meter long and smell like wet dog. He's wearing army green cargo pants and a T-shirt that says *You're not in Guatemala anymore Dr. Huxtable*. His face is deeply tanned and his lips chapped by the sun; he has one hand stuffed into the pocket of his pants and an unlit cigarette in the other. "You're a cop, right?"

"You see who lit the fire?" I ask, standing back up, my knee complaining. Along with the smell of his dreadlocks is the smell of weed. His eyes are bloodshot.

"Nah, sorry bro. Is the professor okay?"

"You're one of his students?" I ask.

"Nah, man, one of his neighbors."

"You think something happened to him?" I ask.

He shrugs. "I think so. First I gotta tell you, man, you can't arrest me. I got no weed on me."

"Oh man," I say.

"Deal?"

"Sure. I promise I won't arrest you."

"I saw something yesterday morning. I was sitting outside, you know, just sitting, right, relaxing with a smoke, you know what I mean? And I saw this dude approach that professor dude and the professor dude fell down or something so the other dude helped him and I thought I was hallucinating or something. You know, from the smoke."

"Which house is yours?"

"That one, bro," he says, pointing to the one opposite Cooper's place. It's a single-story home, tightly packed into a compact lot like all the others on this street, painted the same kind of color, the only real difference between his and the neighbors being that it hasn't seen a lawn mower since winter.

"Why didn't you call the police?"

"Because I was . . . you know, wasn't real sure what I'd seen and you'd have just ended up arresting me. I kind of forgot about it all until his house like, totally caught on fire, right, oh man that's a hell of a sight, a real sight. Anyway I thought I should tell you."

I have the urge to see if the bandaging on my hand will pad my knuckles like a boxing glove. "You should have reported it yesterday!"

"I didn't want to get in trouble. I had to, you know, man, finish what I had. Jesus, I'm hungry," he adds.

"Shit."

"Geez, dude, Gandhi yourself down a notch," he says, holding up his hands. "You think Professor Mono's going to be okay?"

"What?"

"You think he's going to be okay?"

"What did you call him?"

"Professor Riley."

"No. You called him something different."

"Oh, yeah," he says, and he starts to grin. "Don't tell him, but some of us in the neighborhood like to call him Professor Mono, you know, on account of his accident."

"What accident?"

He starts to laugh. "Oh man, I shouldn't laugh, but it's the one he had . . . let me think, must have been three or four years ago. Yeah, four years I think, nah, maybe it was three. I've been here five. Like it here too, man. Guess how I bought the place? Go on, guess."

"What accident are you talking about?"

"I won lotto, bro. How sweet is that?"

Now I feel like kicking him too. "The accident?" I say, reminding him.

"Oh, yeah. Well, I don't really know how it happened, but I have a friend, right, and his girlfriend's a nurse at the hospital, right, and she told him that she recognized Cooper because she used to be one of his students way back whenever," he says, "and . . . and where was I? Oh, yeah, anyway the professor rushed himself in there after he got one of his nuts ripped off."

"What?"

"Yeah, she said it was crushed like a grape. They had to remove it."

"He was attacked?"

"He said he got it caught in a door, but how the hell does a man get his nuts caught in a door?" He spreads his legs and pushes his waist forward and tries to twist his body. "You'd have to, you know, have one leg out like this," he says, "and maybe if the door slammed and you were . . ."

"This nurse, how can I get hold of her?"

"Oh man, that's a bummer."

"What?"

"You can't, ay. She was stealing medical supplies and prescription drugs and sold them to a patient who ended up dying. She got caught and she killed herself because she didn't want to go to jail. It was really sad, bro, real sad. She had a real great rack," he says, holding his hands up to his chest and looking sad.

"So which was it—when he had the accident? Three years ago, or four?"

"What's it matter?"

It matters because Schroder said Cooper got divorced three years ago and there could be a connection. "See that guy over there?" I say, and point toward Schroder.

"Another cop?"

"Go and tell him the same thing you just told me. It's useful."

"Okay, man. Sure," he says, then walks in the opposite direction, heading away from Schroder.

I'm able to bend my leg enough to get behind the steering wheel. Thankfully I'm driving an automatic. I pull away from the curb, smoke still drifting up from the house into the sky. I think about the nurse stealing pills and getting caught and taking her own life and wonder if any of what I was just told is true. My leg is throbbing but it's too early to pop any more of the painkillers the paramedic gave me. Last year my addiction was booze; I haven't been out of jail long enough to start a new one. Traffic is thick in and around the blocks surrounding the fire, and there are plenty of parked cars, but once I get through it all it's a pretty easy drive. I drive past a service station and the attendant out front is up on a ladder changing the prices on the sign, putting petrol up another five cents a liter. I call Schroder on the cell phone.

"You checked Riley for any criminal record, right?"

"Right."

"You check if he reported any crimes?"

"What?"

"Was he the victim of a crime?"

"What kind of crime?"

"Look it up. If there's a record of it you'll have all the details. If not, call me back and I'll tell you. And one other thing. Riley's house was doused in a lot of petrol. Maybe you should check some service stations. Maybe one of the attendants helped somebody fill up a few containers of fuel."

It's way too early for rush-hour traffic, and most of what's on the roads are parents picking up their kids from school. There are groups of kids cycling with their bags slung over their backs, their shirts untucked, yelling and swearing and laughing at each other. Others are walking on the pavement, their feet scuffing the ground, they're lighting up cigarettes and practicing what passes for being cool these days. I get home and park up the driveway and support my weight on my good leg and am halfway to the front door when I see Daxter. He's lying by the doorstep.

"Hey, Dax," I say, and Daxter doesn't respond. "Dax?"

He doesn't move, and the closer I get to him the more my heart starts to sink, and the slower I walk.

"You okay, Big Fella?" I ask, knowing that he isn't.

Daxter is laying on his side stretched out in a position that he never adopts. It's a struggle to crouch down next to him but I manage it, sliding my unbending leg out to the side. I put my hand on Daxter and he's not as warm as he should be. I shake him a little and there's nothing. His head lolls around. I hold his face and turn it toward me and his eyes are half closed and there is blood down the side of his face. I pick him up and he's heavier than normal and he sags, gravity pulling every limb straight down, some of his ribs have broken and changed the shape of his body. I lean against the side of my house and I cradle Daxter against my chest and I start stroking him, rubbing him beneath his chin and scratching the top of his head. Tears well up in my eyes and I can't contain them. It takes a minute or so to realize my lap is wet, and when I lift Daxter up urine and water is leaking out of him. I hug him against my chest and push my face against him, fully aware I'm cuddling a dead cat and I must look insane doing it, but unable to do anything different. We bought Daxter for Emily five years ago, and he was more her kitten than mine or Bridget's. After Emily died Daxter was never the same. He would always sleep in her room and only ventured to the rest of the house when he was hungry or desperately in need of attention. Daxter is with my daughter now, and I truly am alone.

I carry him through the house to the backyard. I change into some fresh pants and throw the urine-soaked ones into the trash since they're burned anyway. I find the shovel in the garage. I struggle to dig a hole, and it hurts, but I need to feel the pain, it should never be easy burying something you love. It's the first grave I've dug in over a year, and it's certainly by far the smallest. I pick a spot against the back fence opposite the deck, beneath a small tree whose roots aren't big enough to interfere with the digging. The ground gets harder the deeper I go. The dirt piles up on the lawn, it gets darker the deeper I go. When the hole is deep enough I head inside and find a shirt I'll never wear again. I wrap Daxter inside it, careful to make him look like he's still sleeping, careful to lay him on his side with his back curved slightly and his front paws up over his face covering his eyes the way he used to do it. I scrunch up a handful of shirt so I can lift him, and again he feels heavier than he ought to. I lower him into the ground and I can't contain the tears anymore. I shovel the dirt back into the grave. I pat it down and I sit on the deck and I figure if Daxter could choose a place to be buried, this would be it.

I stare at the grave and my emotions take hold. The tears come quicker. Daxter has been family from the day we got him, and now he's another family member I've lost.

chapter twenty

Adrian is exhausted. Stopping at Theodore Tate's house added over an hour to his journey. The house was in the base of a cul-de-sac, with the back fence looking out over a different street. He was able to see through a gap into the backyard. He watched Tate break ground with a shovel, but didn't hang around after that. He was pushing his luck as it was. He had parked down a side street a few blocks away, where he seriously doubted Tate would be driving, and had killed time walking up and down the street trying as hard as he could not to be noticed while he waited. He figured everybody was too busy being hot to pay him any attention. They were certainly too busy to pay him any attention when he convinced the cat to come to him. Adrian was good with cats. He always has been. He thought cats and dogs would have a sense about what he was capable of doing to them, but they didn't seem to. It was weird. He didn't know for sure the cat belonged to Tate. It was laying in Tate's yard, but cats tended to get around. He took the gamble, and it's obvious from Tate's reaction that the gamble paid off.

He's returning home much later in the day than he wanted. Cooper will be angry at having been kept waiting so long, but Adrian knows the present will make up for that. The sun is peaking in the sky and there is dust in the air and a hot wind is steadily picking up speed from the northwest. In warm winds like that he finds his itches become worse. He pours a glass of water and sets about making some sandwiches. The house doesn't have any power, and the best he can do to keep the slices of sandwich meat fresh is to store them in a cooler. As long as he replaces the meat every couple of days it doesn't go off too much. He'll try to remember to pick some up later on today on the drive back to Tate's house.

The more he thinks about Tate, the more he starts to think about what he would be like if added to the collection. Both cop and killer. It's certainly worth considering.

The girl in the bedroom wakes up when he opens the door. The look of fear that was in her eyes for the first two days is no longer there, instead there is seething hatred. He imagines part of her wishes he had killed her already, but of course he's not going to kill her. He moves his gaze from her eyes to the curves of her body, and sometimes he wants to touch those curves, to feel them beneath his fingertips, and sometimes, and thank God his mother never found out, he'd lay awake at night and imagine what kind of curves Katie, the girl from school, would have. She actually reminds him of Katie, similar hair, similar eyes, and he wonders if she remembers him from months ago when he first approached her. He's aware he smells of petrol, but she smells far worse. He was stupid, he realizes, to have stood among that crowd of people smelling the way he did, stupid for that and lucky nobody noticed.

"I have these for you to wear," he says, and he rests the clothes on the end of the bed. Her own clothes weren't appropriate for what he wanted, so he had cut them from her and discarded them in the bin. "I'm going to clean you down a little," he says, and rests a wet towel over her leg.

She flinches but doesn't answer him because she can't, just the same murmurs that can't take shape around the straw to become words.

"Do you remember me?" he asks.

She shakes her head. The hate has gone from her eyes and now it's back to fear.

"I tried talking to you," he says. "It was the last Monday night before Christmas. You were working. I told you that you looked like a girl I used to know. It was hard for me to talk to you," he says, "hard for me to talk to anybody. It went against all of my instincts, but I found the courage to come up to you and you rejected me. You shouldn't have done that," he says. "You shouldn't have been mean to me."

All the hardness falls from her eyes and she starts to cry.

"It's going to be okay," he says, "but don't try anything, he adds, holding up a knife. "You've been here for nearly three days and you don't have the strength to fight me. Trust me, I've been in your situation," he says, which isn't exactly true but close enough. He leans over and cuts through the rope. She doesn't move. She's lost weight since being here and doesn't look good. Her face is more . . . hollow, he would say, for lack of a better word. And pale too, white and damp with sweat.

"I'm not going to hurt you, I promise," he says, and it's true. He isn't going to hurt her. But she shouldn't have made him feel bad. "You can't go around being mean to people," he tells her, wiping the towel over her, her skin wet and breaking out in goose bumps. "You made me feel bad about myself."

She tries to slap him and he pulls back, she mostly misses but one of her nails stings his face. He grabs her by her ankles and drags her off the bed. She flails at him with her arms but can't reach. She hits the floor, her head bangs heavily against it and her eyes roll upward. She goes limp.

He is disappointed in her. He drags her away from her own mess, leaving a greasy trail. He picks her up and carries her into the bathroom and rests her in the bath and rinses her down then dries her. When he undressed her a couple of days ago it was new to him. He'd never undressed a woman before and it felt kind of, well, kind of nice. Kind of like how he always imagined it would be with Katie. When all this is over, he might look for more women to undress. Of course, dressing her is much harder. He can't use a knife for that. He struggles with her, rolling her over the floor while tugging on her clothes, thinking this is pointless since Cooper will strip her down anyway, but doing it because stripping her down will be important to Cooper. It will be part of the ritual. As much as he enjoys the idea of undressing future women, he certainly doesn't want to go through this process again. The dress is a little big for her, which makes it somewhat easier. His face is sore, and when he reaches up his finger comes away with a spot of blood from where she scratched him. He looks at the scratch in the mirror, then wipes away the blood. It's not very long, only a few centimeters, but now that he knows it's there it hurts.

"You hurt me," he says, but she doesn't respond. He's tempted to try and remove the glue from her lips. He could wipe nail polish remover across them, but he'll wait because Cooper will like her more this way. Her chest raises and falls steadily, a soft, raspy wheeze comes from her throat, the sound identical to the one the old fridge at the halfway house used to make.

He lifts her up and carries her to the basement door. She is much lighter than Cooper and he thinks even lighter than when he first brought her here so he doesn't need the dolly. He knocks first on the basement door before opening it, thinking Cooper would like that more than just barging in. It's a small simple sign of respect, one that was never afforded to him whenever the Twins locked him down here. The Twins were a pair of orderlies who used to work here, and for fun they would lock patients down here and make them hurt. The sun has moved to other parts of the house and not much light is getting downstairs, so he hooks the lamp under his fingers before heading down.

"She's for you," he says. He lays her on the floor, careful to keep her limbs from tangling beneath her, before turning on the lamp. Cooper is standing at the cell door looking at him, an expression on his face that Adrian has seen on other people before this, notably his own mother when he started soaking her in petrol yesterday morning.

"What . . ." Cooper says, but doesn't finish.

Adrian hopes Cooper isn't turned off by the dress. He'd have liked to have put her in something sexier, but all he had was a dress he took from his mother's house. He took other things too that morning. Food, mostly. And money. "I found her in town," he says. "Isn't she perfect?"

Cooper's face is pressed up against the glass. "Jesus, Adrian, Jesus, this is insane. Totally insane."

"I found her on Monday night," he says. "Isn't she perfect?"

"I . . ." Cooper says, then nothing else.

"You're lost for words," Adrian says. "I know what that's like. See, I told you I can take care of you. I took care of your house. I burned it down."

"Oh Jesus, my house," Cooper says. "And this girl. Adrian, Adrian . . ."

"I wanted to do something nice for you," he says. "And I know you like women and I thought you'd like this woman and I used my own initiative. I want to help you, Cooper. I like helping my friends," he adds, hoping Cooper believes he has other friends.

Cooper says nothing. Adrian finds the silence unsettling. He's spent many days and nights down here in silence, and back then he got used to it. Now it hurts. "You said the very thing I liked about you the most is the one thing you can't do locked up down here. But you were wrong, Cooper. See? I can bring them to you. As many as you need," he says, hoping Cooper won't want many, hoping that if Cooper does, taking girls like this one will only get easier.

"I . . . I don't know what to say," Cooper says. "Is she mine?"

"Yes."

"Okay, okay. Good, that's good," Cooper says. "So . . . so I can do with her anything I want?"

"Of course," Adrian says, smiling. He's happy Cooper is getting the point. "Are you going to have sex with her?"

"Is that what I did with the others?"

"I think so."

"Then yes, of course, I'd love to have sex with her. It's just that, well . . . ah, it doesn't matter."

Adrian is confused. "What doesn't matter?"

Cooper sighs. "I'm going to have to say no, Adrian. You're going to have to take her back, or kill her yourself. I'm sorry."

"Why?" he asks, his voice gaining in pitch.

"No reason. But I appreciate the gesture, I really do. If only . . . ah, nothing."

"If only what? Please, just tell me," he asks, desperate to know.

"This is stupid," Cooper says. "It's just that if I'm going to have sex with her, I can't do it in front of anybody. I can't have an audience. I'm going to need privacy."

"Privacy?"

"See, I told you it was stupid, and now you probably hate me and think I'm being ungrateful and a bad friend." Cooper turns away.

Adrian steps up to the door. "I don't hate you," he says, desperate for Cooper to believe him. I think I understand," he says. "You don't think you can . . ." he searches for the right word, and settles on *perform*. "You don't think you can perform if I'm watching."

"Exactly."

"So if I don't watch, you can sex her?"

"And kill her, if that's what you want, Adrian."

"Is it what you want?"

"Of course."

"Then it's what I want too," Adrian says, smiling.

"There's one more thing."

"What?"

"Ah, now I feel really silly, and you're going to say no."

"Go ahead and ask," Adrian says. His eyes are wide open and unblinking as he stares at Cooper, hanging on his every word. This is why he wanted Cooper here. For the stories. For the excitement. For his collection.

"I was thinking it would be cool if I had sex with her, and you were to help me kill her when I was done."

"You want me to kill her?"

"Just help me. You've never killed before, right?"

"Right," he says, but that's not true.

"So, I'm thinking that as a favor to you for bringing her to me, and to make sure you'll bring me more, I'd like you to join in. Just on the killing, though, not the other stuff."

"I don't know."

"I really want to kill her, Adrian, I really do. I have a strong need growing inside of me. Also . . . there's one more thing. I'm going to need a knife."

"A knife?"

"Exactly! I appreciate it, Adrian, I really do," Cooper says, and he claps his hands together and starts rubbing them. "See, sex isn't the same unless you can do some cutting along the way. It doesn't have to be a big knife, but it needs to be sharp. I'll wait here while you get it."

"I don't know . . ."

"Trust me, Adrian, it's going to be fantastic. And she'll be the first of many. How long until she wakes up? What did you to do her?"

"I knocked her out," he says. "I don't know when she'll wake up. Are you really going to kill her?"

"Of course."

"How do I know you're not just saying that so you can try to escape?"

"Where would I go? You've burned down my house. This is all I have now, I've accepted that, and I'm not going to sit in my cell brooding for the rest of my life. I'm going to make the best of it."

Adrian realizes he's made another mistake. Even if he believes Cooper, there's no way of getting the woman into that cell without being vulnerable to attack. Why didn't he think this through better? He's learning, that's why, and things will only be better next time. One of two things will happen—Cooper will hurt her, and then they can become best friends. Or Cooper will try to hurt him. There has to be another way. Has to be. His mother would know what to do. He's starting to think he killed her too soon. He can hear her voice. "A blessing is only half a miracle." He doesn't need a miracle here, he only needs to be smart.

"I need to think about it," Adrian says, "and then I'll decide," he adds, and then it comes to him. There is another way. It's perfect too. Cooper will get his gift and then Adrian will know if what Cooper is saying is for real or just another lie.

"I'll be back in half an hour," he says. He leaves the lamp on the coffee table, makes his way upstairs and closes the door behind him.

chapter twenty-one

The sun seems to get a degree hotter for every degree it moves further to the west. The shadow from the fence grows slimmer. The sun comes around the tree and Daxter's grave is flooded with sun and the bandages on my feet and hand are stained with dirt. I feel angry and frustrated that I couldn't have done anything more for him. I feel stupid for feeling so sad for Daxter while Donovan Green and his wife are going through much worse with their daughter. I stare at the grave thinking a lot of things, many of them stupid, many of them morbid, none of them motivational. My knee has swelled more since the digging. The paramedic would be upset with me if he were here.

I finally push myself away from the table and go back inside. I pop a couple of anti-inflammatories and a few more painkillers and I go hunting for some bandaging in the bathroom. I call Schroder and he doesn't answer. A minute later Donovan Green calls me and I don't answer. It's the circle of life. What am I going to tell him? That I might have just seen his daughter burn to death? That when I went inside I took the stairs before searching the ground floor, that there was no reason to that decision, that next time I might have taken the ground floor first, that his daughter might have burned in there because of a fifty-fifty chance that I got wrong?

I hobble outside to the car. I'm able to keep my left leg straight while using my right to switch between the accelerator and brake. My face is feeling a little sunburned from yesterday and when I scratch at an itch on my nose it feels like I'm clawing my nail an inch deep. Traffic is blocked near town where an RV has turned the wrong way into a one-way street. It hasn't hit anything, but none of the drivers coming toward it felt like pulling out of the way to give it room to turn back around, and there's a chorus of swearing and advice being thrown from dozens of directions as more traffic backs up. I switch on the radio and there're a couple of DJs talking about the death penalty. They talk about Emma Green and how her disappearance is proof that New Zealand needs to bring back capital punishment. They're saying what the rest of are thinking—that whoever took Emma has hurt other girls in the past, and harder sentences would save future victims. It's all commonsense stuff. Kill the really bad people and they can't hurt good people, and who could argue with that? Only really bad people. The DJs are saying they should start with the Christchurch Carver. They're coming up with ways in which they would execute him, starting out with the clichés like hanging or lethal injection before delving, or devolving, into more imaginative ways that make me seriously wonder about the two men giving the commentary. Then they throw open the lines to the public, to Steve from Sumner who thinks they should start setting these guys on fire, to James from Redwood who thinks we should go old school and stone these bastards in front of rugby-sized crowds in rugby-sized stadiums, then to Brock from Shirley who says nothing beats a good, slow cutting in half right down the middle where they dangle the guy upside down to keep the blood in his brain so he doesn't pass out as fast. I turn off the radio and pray to God I never piss off Steve, James, or Brock.

Once I get past the blocked RV, traffic thins out. I miss two more calls from Donovan Green. I pull into the university parking lot and stop in a handicapped spot. There's a student sitting in a shopping cart with another student pushing him along a sidewalk, both of them laughing.

I limp to the psychology department wishing I had crutches. I struggle with the stairs, leaning on the handrail along the way. A couple of people pass me and stare at me while pretending not to stare at me, I can see part of them wants to offer to help, but the bigger part doesn't want to suggest that I need the help. It's like opening a door for a person in a wheelchair and not knowing whether they're going to say *thank you* or *fuck off.* I reach the second floor where all the offices are lined up. There's a montage of photographs on the wall of faculty members, the kind of thing you'd see where dead people were being remembered, small hand-sized portrait shots forming a grid. I search through them for the man who lit the fire and decide it could have been about half of them. Cooper Riley is among them, his hair not so gray and more of it in the photo. I head down the corridor. Everything up here looks old enough to predate the very subject of psychology. All the office doors are blue and they're all labeled by name and Cooper's office is no different in that aspect, but very different in the fact there is crime scene tape crisscrossed over the door. There's a large poster pinned to the wall between two of the offices labeled *Personality Study* with flow diagrams and long complicated words that give me a headache. Nobody is around. I try the door. It's locked. I take out the keys I found in the front door to Cooper's house. One of them fits. I pull down the tape and toss it onto the floor. The blame will go to the students.

The air in the office is thick and stale. The desk is pine and there are dents and scratches covering the surface, and nothing on top of it shares any of the same angles. The desk drawers are open and the filing cabinet is open and the computer is running and there's fingerprint powder on plenty of flat surfaces. The police came here looking for any clue as to what happened to Cooper Riley. I can imagine Cooper being the kind of guy to keep everything in straight lines and if he were to come into his office right now he'd be pretty upset. My cell phone rings and it's Schroder.

"Where are you?" he asks. "The sketch artist just showed up at your place."

"Shit. I completely forgot. Tell him I'm on my way."

"Listen, there's no record of Cooper Riley reporting any crime," he says. "Why did you want to know?"

"So you're on the case now?"

"Two fires in two days. It could be connected, so yeah, I'm on the case. The fire department will know for sure hopefully later on today."

I tell him about what the neighbor said.

"And you think our Melissa X did that to him?"

"I think so."

"Why wouldn't Riley report that?"

"That's the question. Why wouldn't a victim report being a victim?"

"Happens every day, Tate," he says. "You know that. Only about one in seven rapes are reported. Could easily be the same psychology behind that as what happened to Riley, assuming what the neighbor said is true," he says.

"Can you access his medical records?"

"I'll try to get a warrant."

"How'd the search of Riley's office go?"

"It hasn't turned up anything. We're hoping forensics will find something at the house or Cooper's car once we can go through the ruins, but it's not looking hopeful."

"I'm thinking of taking a run out to his office," I say, leaning against the edge of the desk. "See if I can spot something you missed."

"Are you trying to offend me?" he asks.

"No. It's like you say, I have an eye for this kind of thing. So, are you cool with that?"

"That depends, Tate. Are you already there?"

"What if I was?"

"Then you'd be entering a crime scene, which can go a long way to damaging whatever case we're building up here."

"Technically it's not a crime scene," I tell him. "Come on, Carl, what can it hurt if I take a look around?"

"I'll meet you there in twenty minutes," he says. "Last thing I want is you messing things up."

He hangs up. I start flicking through the files on Cooper's desk the same way somebody else would have earlier today. They've gone through all the student and staff files because so far that's the only link between Cooper Riley and Emma Green. Maybe an ex-psychiatry student who was pissed off about a failing grade wanted to get even. Maybe he blamed Emma Green somehow too.

I check the filing cabinet and the files have been jammed in one direction and obviously thumbed through, they cover this year's students and last year's students but don't go back any further. I think about Melissa and whether she's the reason Cooper Riley has become Professor Mono to his neighbors. If she was, she could have been a student here. He had to interact with her somehow.

I step out into the corridor and move down to the next office. A plaque on the door says it belongs to Professor Collins. The door is slightly ajar and I knock on it and open it the rest of the way. A man sitting behind a desk looks up at me. He has wiry gray hair and eyes that are too big for his face and his ears stick out almost ninety degrees. The office has the same layout and same view as Cooper's, only nowhere near as messy.

"Can I help you?" he asks.

"Professor Collins?"

"Just like the door says," he says, smiling and leaning back in his chair. "You're not a student," he says, "so you're either a reporter or a cop. I'm going to go with cop. Am I right? You're here to ask questions about Cooper Riley? I've heard his house burned down this afternoon, and you guys were searching his office an hour ago."

"Well done, sir," I say, stepping inside.

"Please, take a seat," he says, and I sit opposite him, stretching my leg out in front of me. "So, any word on Cooper?"

"None yet. How long have you worked here?"

"Going on fifteen years," he says.

"You know Cooper well?"

"What do you think happened to him? Do you think he's going to be okay?"

"We're looking into it," I tell him. "Please, anything you can tell me might help."

"Sure, I knew him well. We have offices next to each other. We've both been working here the same amount of time. We both went to each other's wedding and sometimes we'll still have dinner together."

"How long has he been divorced?" I ask, aware these are things that Schroder already knows.

"Hmm, let me think. Three years ago, give or take. His wife moved on, you know. Met somebody else. I heard they met online. Happens all the time these days. It's an interesting psychological phenomena, really, how people form online relationships to find a connection in the offline world. I'm actually thinking of writing a paper on it."

"She still around?"

He shakes his head. "Australia, last time I heard, but Cooper never talks about her. Just one day she was in his life, the next day she wasn't. It's a shame. They're both good people, but it didn't work. It happens that way sometimes," he says, but he doesn't follow it up by saying he's thinking of writing a paper on it. "Cooper took it pretty hard."

"Can you tell me when he had his accident?"

He looks confused. "Accident? What, a car accident?"

"Not quite."

"Then what kind of quite?"

"Can you recall a time when he was off work, maybe for a month or so? Quite suddenly? Would have been around three years ago, around the time of his divorce."

His eyes flick to the left as he tries to recall, then slowly he shakes his head and his mouth turns into an upside-down smile. "Not that I can remember."

"He wasn't sick all of a sudden and couldn't show up?"

"I'm sure he was. It happens to us all at some point. Life does get in the way of work, detective. Why, does his being sick in the past relate to his disappearance now?"

"I'm not sure," I tell him.

"Try the administration office," he tells me. "They'll have all those kind of records there."

I follow Collins's directions to a building more modern than the rest, large tinted glass frontages overlooking a concrete fountain that's currently home and toilet to a dozen pigeons. There's a foyer that is like a doctor's waiting room, with students sitting in chairs reading textbooks or magazines while waiting to talk to somebody. The woman behind the desk is in her late forties and has hair pulled tightly back into a bun and glasses that hang around her neck on a thin chain. Her perfume is sharp and I can feel the hint of a hay fever attack lurking. She's wearing a blouse that has cat fur caught around the buttons.

"How can I help you?" she asks, smiling up at me.

"You know we searched Cooper Riley's office earlier?" I ask, hoping she's going to make the same mistake Professor Collins made, and she does.

"Yes, of course. Everybody knows."

"There's something else you may be able to help us with," I tell her. "There was a time when Riley took a month or more off work. Possibly around three years ago. Can you look that up for me?"

She doesn't answer me. Instead she puts on her glasses and adjusts the distance between the lenses and her eyes as she looks at a computer monitor, then her fingers fly across the keyboard.

"It'll take a minute," she says, and about ten seconds later she finds it. "Here we go. You're right," she says. "Almost three years ago. April through to May. Five weeks in total."

"I need to get a look at names and faces of his students from that year."

"Why?"

"Please, it's important. We're trying to save Cooper's life," I tell her.

"Is it true his house was burned down?"

"It's true."

"There are hundreds of students from three years ago," she tells me.

I need to check them all for the arsonist, but that can wait till Schroder gets here. "Just the female ones."

"I guess I can print them out," she says. "It'll take an hour, unless you can narrow down who you're after."

"What about students who dropped out during the year? Around the same time Professor Riley was off work?"

"Why? You think that means something?"

"Please," I tell her, "we need to hurry."

"Hmm . . . let me see," she says. She taps at the keyboard again. "Four female students dropped out during that time."

"Any of them named Melissa?"

"Melissa? No, none of them."

"Can I see their photographs?"

She twists the computer monitor toward me and I have to lean over the desk to get a better view, entering her perfume zone in the process. She cycles through the photos. She gets to the third one when I stop her for a better look. The eyes look familiar.

"I remember this girl," the receptionist says.

"You do?"

"Not so much her, but her parents. They came in here looking for information."

"What kind of information?"

"Anything that would help them track her down. She went missing. Oh no," she says, making the connection. "You think the same thing that happened to Emma Green happened to her?" she asks, tapping the monitor.

I don't think so. I think these two girls ended up with very different fates. I think the girl on the screen might be the woman who attacked the Christchurch Carver and killed Detective Calhoun. This could be the woman that put Professor Riley in hospital three years ago. Her image has been in the papers and all over the news, an image taken from the video I watched yesterday, but that image isn't the same as the one I'm looking at now. Similar, but not the same, different haircut, different color hair, a little less weight around the face—but it's the eyes. Those eyes are the same, I'm sure of it.

Cooper Riley would have known it too. He would have seen the news and he would have known who she really was, and he never came forward to the police.

Why would that be? Is he still afraid of her?

Or is there something he's hiding?

chapter twenty-two

Cooper's head is much better today, but it's still throbbing a little and he's tempted to take the pills he found in his pocket yesterday. The wound on his chest is starting to itch and when he touches it with his fingers they come away damp with blood and something else too, something that's not quite yellow. If he doesn't eat something soon he thinks he's going to go crazy.

He recognizes the girl. Shoulder-length red hair that is knotted and frayed. Her skin is pale and flushed. She can't be any more than twenty. A student? Perhaps a former one. Even one from this year—there are always so many. Or it could be somebody from the supermarket, a checkout teller, some girl he's made idle chitchat with while his groceries were scanned before he swiped his credit card. Maybe a hairdresser from the mall, a Jehovah's Witness who banged on his door one morning, a receptionist at his doctor's office. He's seen her around but can't place where. She's in a dress that's too big for her and covered in flowers that, under the lamplight, all look pale blue. It's something his mother would wear in the summer.

Jesus, his mother . . . she'll be a mess. His mother will be eighty years old in July, and already the family is planning a huge party for her. His sister is going to fly back from the UK—and he suspects she might be flying back now because of what's happened, assuming people even know he's disappeared, which they must do if it's true what Adrian said about burning down his house. He hopes his mother is holding up okay. She's a strong woman. Has been ever since his dad walked out on them when Cooper was twelve years old. He hasn't seen him since. Has no idea whether the man is even alive and doesn't care. But his mother . . . he owes her everything. With a weaker mother, his life would have taken a different path. When he was fourteen years old, he stole a car. He and his friend got drunk, and they crashed it. Neither of them were hurt, but his mother came and picked him up from the police station and didn't say a word on the way home, didn't say a word until the following morning when she made him breakfast.

He had apologized, and she had told him she wasn't the one he should be apologizing to, that he should be apologizing to his future self, that it was his future self he was damaging. He didn't care. Back then he didn't care about much except that his dad had left, and how good beer tasted when he snuck out at night to meet his buddy. She made him write himself a letter for the future, in which he told himself how sorry and how stupid he was. She made him write down how much he had hurt his mother. He did that too. Then she went into her room and cried. When she came back out she sat down with him and ate breakfast and told him she felt sorry for the man she was going to give that letter to in ten years' time. She never gave him that letter. Instead things changed. Every day she would tell him whether his future self would be happy or disappointed with his actions. He started to care about that future self. He didn't want to grow up to be like his dad. He started to study harder. His grades were good.

When he was twenty years old, he had an affair with the next-door neighbor. She was fifteen years older than him. He thought he loved her. One day her husband came home with a shotgun and put a hole in her before putting one in himself. Nobody saw it coming. Cooper was never sure whether the husband knew his wife had been cheating, and he suspected that if he had known and who with, there would have been a shotgun shell reserved for him too. The husband was the cliché, the quiet man who didn't speak much to people, and Cooper couldn't figure out how he hadn't seen it coming. It fascinated him. People were different, they ticked differently, and he wanted to understand them. He felt the loss of losing his lover, but he felt no guilt, and that interested him too.

Right now, he needs to understand Adrian and, if he can get this woman to wake up, get her to understand what's going on.

"Hey," he says, loud enough to be heard but not loud enough to be heard by her. He bangs against the door and gets the same result. Adrian said he'd be half an hour. The clock is ticking. He'll aim for twenty minutes to be on the safe side. Cooper bangs against the window. He needs the girl to wake up, and to wake up now.

And she does.

Slowly.

Her eyes stay closed and her hands creep up to her face and start probing. She looks like she's coming out of a very deep sleep, probably a nightmare. Her skin is red and patchy and her face is flushed, except for the dark gray smudges beneath her eyes. Her hands explore the straw sticking out from her mouth. She pulls on it gently but it doesn't budge. For the first time he realizes her lips are glued shut. He calls to her again but she doesn't respond. In fact she looks like she's passed back out. Her fingers have stopped moving and her hands have collapsed onto the floor. It takes what feels like an hour but is only two minutes before there's any further movement. She rubs at her eyes slowly and then they open. He can see her looking around but she can't focus on anything. He taps on the glass and she looks in his direction but doesn't register his presence.

He has eighteen minutes left.

"Miss, hey, miss, wake up, wake up. Please, you have to wake up."

He watches her jaw move as she tries to speak. Then he sees it all coming back to her, her memories flooding with emotions. Her face tightens and her eyes grow wider and her hands probe faster at her face, especially at her lips, and she starts to cry. She sits up and looks around the room before holding the edges of the dress up to stare at it for a few seconds. Finally she locks her gaze on him. Her jaw moves again and he thinks she's trying to scream. She turns away from him and her head pauses in the direction of the bookcase, the lamp casting her shadow over the books and trophies, and he's sure if she could another scream would be coming.

"It's okay, it's okay," he says, holding up his hands even though she can't see them. "You're going to be okay. I'm going to help you."

She puts her palms on the ground and pushes herself further away from him. Looking through the cell window, and with her lips glued shut, it's like watching a show on mute.

"Please, please, I'm not here to hurt you," he says. "I'm a friend. I'm in the same situation as you."

Sixteen minutes. Maybe more.

She gets to her knees. Both of them are scuffed and become even more scuffed as she tries to get to her feet. She loses balance and falls forward and he can hear something in her wrist crack. He winces at the sound. She starts to cry again. Another minute is lost. "Please, can you open the door?" he asks. "Is there a latch there? Or a lock?"

She doesn't look at him. She cradles her arm and curls up into a fetal position. She's wasting time and he can feel himself becoming increasingly frustrated. Even angry. He wants to get out of the cell and shake her. She's going to blow their chance and she's going to die and he's going to die and if she just focused, if she could just get hold of herself . . . Christ, if only he could slap her!

"We're going to die down here if you don't start helping me," he says, only she isn't listening. Out of a desperate need to do something, out of instinct, he turns and looks around his cell for something to help, but of course there's nothing, only a ratty old mattress and a spring bed and a bucket a quarter full of his own piss and vomit that smells worse today than yesterday. He looks back at the window. She hasn't moved.

Stay calm. Baby steps.

He takes a deep breath. "My name is Cooper," he says, clenching his fists down low where she can't see them. He tries to smile at her but ends up grimacing. He has to return to the basics, he has to return to psychology 101. "I bet your family is worried about you," he says. "My family is worried about me. Help me help you see them again. Can you open the door? Please, please, take a look at the door."

She looks up at him. She seems to figure out if she's a prisoner here and he's a prisoner here then they're on the same side. She tightens her jaw and her eyes clear and for the first time since waking up she seems fully aware of herself.

Twelve minutes left.

"We need to be quick," he says, "before the man who took us comes back. You have to help me, then I can help you. I promise we're going to get out of here," he says. She looks around the room, and it seems to Cooper that she's seeing it for the first time. She turns in a circle and stops when she's looking directly at him.

"The door," he says. "Can you unlock it?"

She nods, but doesn't move.

"We have to hurry," he says, "and we have to stay quiet."

She takes a step toward him, and then another, and finally she's directly on the other side of the glass. He keeps waiting for her to back away and curl into a ball again but she doesn't. She looks through the window at him and tries to see beyond, and he steps aside slightly so she can get a better look, only the lamplight doesn't hit much of it. Up close, her face is sunken in and she looks tired and underfed and there are small blisters growing around the edges of her mouth. At least he thinks they're blisters.

"I can find something to remove the glue," he says, keeping his voice low and calm, no traces of panic, no hint that he desperately wants her to hurry the fuck up. "It won't be hard, I promise."

She nods again, and then she looks down at the door. She continues to cradle her injured wrist under her opposite armpit as she works at something with her free hand. There is squeaking as metal is hinged up and down, a dead bolt he assumes. It's tight, and she has to work it a few times and then *bang* as it slides open and hits into place. The door opens a crack. He puts his hand on it and pushes, thinking this is too easy, then thinking it ought to be easy when the person holding you captive has the mind of a child.

Ten minutes left.

The door swings open. He steps into the basement. The air is just as cool on this side of the door. She flinches when he wraps his arms around her and holds her tight. "Thank God," he whispers, and he has the urge to sob into the side of her neck. He pulls back. "I'm not going to hurt you," he says, holding her shoulders, but she doesn't seem to believe him.

"We need to find something to use as a weapon," he says, and he moves over to the bookcase. He couldn't get a good look from his cell window, but there is plenty of history on these shelves, including a couple of knives that have come from his house. He picks up the largest one, it's a dull blade that forty years ago belonged to a man who stabbed his parents, a dull blade that he bought in an auction for just under two hundred dollars. Right now the blade feels priceless. It makes him feel as powerful as the previous owner must have felt. His briefcase is on the floor. He kneels down and pops the catch that does work and opens the lid. Everything inside is messed around. He rakes his fingers through the contents.

The camera is missing.

If it fell out when the briefcase got damaged, if Adrian doesn't have it . . .

This changes everything.

He closes up the case. He picks up the lamp and heads to the steps. Even though he was banging on the door a few minutes ago, he's desperate to stay as quiet as he can now. In a world well away from this, his house has turned to ash, his life ruined, but nothing could be worse than being stuck down here forever. The basement door will probably be locked, but compared to the cell, even the basement feels like freedom. If it's locked he'll just wait on this side of the door until Adrian comes back. He can't see things playing out any other way than him being forced to kill his captor. He has to. If he doesn't, he risks too much. He'll kill Adrian and the police will give him a hard time. The one thing he knows for sure is how eager the police are to get a conviction, no matter what the circumstances are. He's seen it before. He's seen them lock away men they've known are innocent, and there have been proven instances where they've planted evidence to get a conviction.

He's going to kill Adrian and save this woman's life and end up going to jail.

He comes to a stop halfway up the staircase.

The police are going to be a problem.

The missing camera an even bigger problem.

He carries on up the stairs. He crouches down and puts his head against the door but can't hear anything beyond. There are so many possibilities waiting out there.

The girl is two steps behind him. She looks unsure of what's about to happen.

Ultimately it's the missing camera that makes his mind up for him. If it'd been in his briefcase, then things could have turned out differently. It's a shame, because he truly was grateful for the girl's help.

He still has eight minutes left. That's plenty of time.

"There's something I should tell you before I open this door," he says, "because so far I haven't been completely honest with you."

chapter twenty-three

I stand outside Cooper's office, reading through Melissa's file while waiting for Schroder. Only it isn't Melissa X anymore. It's Natalie Flowers. She was nineteen years old when she became a student at Canterbury University. She was studying here for two years before wanting to get a degree in psychology. She took it for three years before taking criminal psychology, where she entered Cooper Riley's class. One and a half months after joining his class, she dropped out. At the same time Cooper Riley took five weeks off work. I do the arithmetic. Melissa X in the video I saw would have been around twenty-six years old. She looked a little older, but maybe she has an old soul.

I get tired of waiting in the hall, and my leg is hurting from all the walking, and in the end I decide there's no harm in waiting in Cooper's office. I sit down behind the desk. I go through the basics, opening the drawers, going through anything I can find. I keep looking outside, I have a perfect view of the path that leads to the psychology department. I'll have time to get out when Schroder shows up. I move the mouse and the computer monitor becomes active. There's a desktop showing an island surrounded by clear water Cooper might have dreamed of visiting. I navigate my way through the files, finding nothing of interest. There isn't anything personal on it, only work related. I glance over a few of the topics that Cooper is teaching and it's very dark stuff, the kind of stuff that gives good people bad dreams and bad people good dreams. I look for any mention of Natalie Flowers and there's none.

I look at the photograph of Natalie taken on the day she enrolled here, I try to imagine what kind of thoughts she had back then, I wonder if she knew the person she would become, or if the Natalie back then was a completely different person. I imagine her sitting in front of the camera just as Emma Green would years later, each of them with smiles on their faces, a click of the shutter, a flash going off, a *say cheese* and then a *next please* as the photographer ushered them through, their image stored onto a . . .

Memory card!

Jesus, I'd completely forgotten!

I reach into my pocket, and there it is, the card I took from the camera in Cooper's driveway. I slot it into the computer and it grumbles for a few seconds trying to read it. If we're lucky, he has a photo of the man who took him. Or there'll be a location, or at least something we can use to track him down. A new icon appears and I click on it to open the files, and it goes about the process slowly. I click on the first one and it takes about ten seconds to open, the computer drawing the image from the top, the rest of it coming into view an inch at a time. The second image opens much quicker as the computer gets into the swing of things. There are just the two images, and I flick back and forth between them until the door opens and Schroder steps inside.

"Jesus, Tate, how the hell did you get in here?"

"Emma Green," I say, pushing my chair back from the computer. Despite the heat of the office, my skin has gone clammy and my spine feels chilled. "Jesus, Carl," I say, my mouth dry. "I think Emma Green is still alive."

"Look, Tate, you can't . . ."

"For once, Carl, just shut up," I say, and he does. "Take a look," I say, and I nod toward the computer. He comes around the desk and I watch him as he looks at the photographs, the only sound in the office is the computer fan whirring and the occasional click of a mouse button. There is laughter and yelling from outside, students at work. Schroder's sleeves are rolled up and he's leaning forward with his hands on the desk and I can see goose bumps littering his forearms. He's slowly shaking his head and I'm slowly doing the same thing. I stand up and Schroder takes the chair. I move to the window and stare out at the students in the sun below, all of them hovering a year or two either side of twenty years old with so much to learn, but there are things in the real world I pray they never have to see. The saying goes that a picture tells a thousand words. Looking at them, it couldn't be more true. What they don't tell us is an ending.

"We need to search the office again," I say, still looking out the window. There's a couple of students beneath a tree making out in the shade for everybody to see. They notice others are watching and start to get into it more, putting on a show. I want to throw a bucket of cold water over them.

"We've already searched it," Schroder says.

"Yeah, but you were looking to see what happened to Cooper. You were looking at him as a victim."

"And not a suspect," he says. "Where the hell did you get these?" he asks.

"They were on a memory card. I found it at Cooper's house."

"Jesus Christ, Tate. You didn't think of mentioning this earlier?"

"Actually, Carl, no, I didn't. I forgot I had the damn thing," I say, snapping. "Why the hell do you always have to assume the worst?"

He doesn't answer.

"I'm sorry," I tell him, and then I tell him how I found the card. "And if I hadn't been there on time, it would have gotten destroyed like everything else and you wouldn't have those," I say, nodding toward the computer where there are images of Emma Green lying on a floor with her hands tied behind her. In one photo she's wearing the clothes she went missing in, in the next she isn't wearing anything. She has duct tape over her eyes and none over her mouth. "You wouldn't even know there was a connection."

"We don't know that she's still alive," he says.

"And we have no reason to suspect otherwise. What if Cooper was interrupted? What if he was planning on going back?"

"Back? You don't think these were taken at his house?"

I shake my head. "I doubt it. She's not gagged. These were taken where nobody could hear her scream."

"We'll know soon enough if there were any bodies in the fire."

"Listen, Carl, there's another connection too."

"With who?" he asks. I hand him over the file. "Natalie Flowers," he says, looking at the picture. "Who is she, another of Riley's students?"

"She was."

"Was? What happened, she go missing too?"

"In a sense."

"You want to be more specific?"

"Take a closer look at the photo."

He does, but he still doesn't get it. "What am I looking at here? You think Riley took her too?"

"I think so. Only things didn't go the way they did with Emma Green. You don't recognize her?"

"Should I?"

"Yes."

"Well, stop playing around," he says, "and just tell me what you want to tell me."

So I tell him. What color had managed to return since first seeing the photographs of Emma drains out of his face. He takes a closer look at the picture and slowly starts nodding. I explain about the Professor Mono comment, about Riley being off work three years ago on sick leave the same time his wife left him, the same time Natalie Flowers went missing. I explain the chain of events that have led me to handing over the file.

"Jesus," he says, and for the moment it's all he can say. "You think Melissa X is involved in this somehow? You think she is the one who took Cooper?"

"I don't think so. None of her victims were shot by a Taser, and she wasn't the one who burned down his house."

Schroder snaps on a pair of latex gloves. He opens up the drawers. He starts going through them. Then he starts pulling them all the way out and sitting them on top of the desk. He checks behind them and under them for anything taped out of sight. People always think they're being clever when they hide things in those sorts of places, under drawers, under the carpet, behind books or above a suspended ceiling or in the tank above the toilet. They're all places the police wouldn't have checked because earlier Cooper Riley was only a man who had gone missing. He wasn't a man who knew Melissa X, and he wasn't a man who had tied Emma Green up and photographed her.

"So what about the car?" he asks. "The paint on the dumpster. The witness said it pulled out around into the street in a hurry, and the timeline proves he saw it just after Emma finished work."

"I don't know," I say.

"Maybe it's unrelated," he says.

"Yeah, it's possible, but like you say, it's around the same time."

I get up on the desk keeping the weight on my right leg. I push up at the ceiling tile.

"What the hell, Tate? Leave that to me," Schroder says.

I reach into the ceiling cavity and pray I'm not about to be bitten by a rat. I search with my fingers but don't find a thing. My knee jars a little as Schroder helps me down. He continues to check beneath the drawers. I twist the filing cabinet away from the wall. There's a USB flash drive taped to the back of it. I thought Cooper would be different because I thought he'd have an insight into where he shouldn't hide things, but he either thought he'd never be the victim of an office search, or he thought his hiding place was suitably sufficient. I hold it up and Schroder stops searching. I hand it over to him and we stand adjacent to each other staring at it. It's as if whatever bad news is stored on there can be averted if we don't open it, and we know it's bad news—we've both been doing this for long enough to have a sense of what we're about to see. The horror isn't in seeing the images, the horror is in the quantity. How many others has Cooper killed?

Schroder plugs the flash drive into the computer and we go through the same process as I went through with the camera card. The first image loads up and he clicks the arrow to move to the second and then the third. There are thirty pictures in total. All of the same girl, which is an awful thing to be thankful for, but we are. Scared and clothed in the beginning, naked and dead in the end. The photos are a progression of the last week of her life according to the time stamps on the files. She's laying on the same floor as Emma Green. The photos are in a sequence, and looking through them is like reading a story. The sequence shows the girl become paler as the days pass, she loses weight, blisters and a rash appear on her face, mean-looking welts appear on her skin. Seven days of hell. Seven days of knowing you were going to die but praying for the best. There is duct tape over her eyes in all of them except the last. Cooper liked the idea of not being seen but being able to converse. I bet the bastard loved hearing them cry or beg for their lives.

"She's alive," I tell him.

"What?" he asks, lost in his own thoughts.

"I said she's alive. Emma Green. If he was going to do to her what he did to this girl then . . ."

"Jane Tyrone," he says.

"What?"

"That's who this girl is," he says, tapping the monitor. "She went missing nearly five months ago. "She was a bank teller at that same bank that got held up just before Christmas. A woman was shot and killed."

"You thought she was involved with the robbery?"

He shakes his head. "No. She went missing three months before the robbery. Her car was found abandoned in a parking building in town with her keys in the trunk along with traces of blood. Whatever happened to her, it started there." He turns toward the window and looks at the same view I was staring at earlier. "He kept her for a week," he says. "A whole week she was begging for us to find her and we never did."

"Emma Green is begging for the same thing," I tell him. "Come on, Carl, she has to still be alive. We've got two photos of her from his camera. He hadn't copied them to the flash drive yet. He wasn't done with her."

"And Melissa X?"

"I'm thinking three years ago she was Riley's first, but something went wrong and she ended up attacking him. He kept quiet, because what was he going to say, that a woman he was trying to rape and kill assaulted him?"

"You think this is what got her started?"

"I don't know," I say. "She could have gotten a taste for doing bad things and just kept on doing them, and I think there aren't any pictures of her because she was the first and it was an impulsive act. After her Cooper was too afraid to try again. Could be it took him three years to get up the nerve."

"So what in the hell happened to him? Who abducted Cooper and burned down his house?"

"Maybe it's somebody Cooper has hurt in the past. One more thing that doesn't make sense is why wait a day between kidnapping Cooper and burning down his house? And why use Emma Green's car?"

"You don't think Cooper torched his own place to try and hide evidence, faked his own abduction, then ran?"

"No reason to," I say. "Nobody was on to him. Only reason he became a suspect was because he didn't show up for work. And why torch his house and leave these," I say, nodding toward the photographs, "in his office?"

"They weren't exactly on display."

"Still, he wouldn't try cleaning up one scene by torching it without getting rid of the USB key from another."

"He would if he killed the girl at his house," he suggests.

"He wouldn't have left his camera in the driveway, and we have a witness who saw him taken. And those were definitely ID tags from a Taser I was looking at."

"Okay, so what about Donovan Green? He could have done it."

"Possible," I answer, "but why come to me about it?"

"Because he wanted an alibi. He wanted to make out he had no idea what happened to his daughter. You think he's the kind of guy who could do it?"

"I don't know," I say, thinking back to last year when he wanted to kill me. Absolutely Donovan could have done it. But Donovan Green was waiting for me to give him a name. It's possible, I guess, that he had that name first, that he killed Cooper Riley, panicked, and then came to me to start building a story to make him look innocent. I think about the look on his face, the grim determination to get his hands on the person who hurt Emma. No, he didn't know who took his daughter. I'm sure of it. "Donovan Green wouldn't kill the only person who knew where she was."

"Maybe he's torturing it out of him."

"Wasn't him who lit the fire."

"He could have hired somebody."

"Then why drive around in Emma's car?"

He doesn't have an answer.

"You looked into a connection with the fires?" I ask.

"There could be a link there between Cooper Riley and Pamela Deans, but it's a very tentative one if it is."

"Want to share?"

"Look, Tate, I have to call this in. You should go. If you're here when the other detectives arrive, you'll get me fired."

"You'll call me later today?"

He nods. "I'll keep you in the loop and update you later. Tate, you've done a good job with this Melissa X thing," he says. "If what you've learned leads to an arrest, don't worry—you're still looking at the reward money."

I look down at the photographs. "I'm not doing this for the money," I tell him.

"I know. But you need it."

I head back into the hall and close the door behind me. I think of the girls wandering these halls and how close any one of them came to being Cooper's next victim.

Donovan Green calls again before I reach the parking lot. It's no longer blue skies in every direction. There are white fluffy clouds to the north and it's completely overcast out to the east, the cloud cover over the ocean stretching the length of the horizon. The temperature must have dropped a few points too. I answer the phone and give Green an update. I don't tell him about the photographs of his daughter tied up and naked. I don't share with him my theory that she may still be alive. Last thing I want to do is feed him false hope only to have to confront him with the worst news of his life a day later. I tell him that I have made some progress, that I have some leads, and am hoping for some more news soon.

I head for home. Peak-time traffic makes it a long trip. I make some strong coffee once I walk through the door and fire up the computer. I go online. Rain starts to splash on the windows, just a couple of drops every few seconds. I get up and close them, the breeze coming through is warm and feels charged. The trees outside the study window are being thrown about by the wind. The pre-autumn leaves that have already fallen are scuttling across the lawn. There is no more blue sky, no more white clouds, just darkness in every direction. I step out into the rain as it starts to come down heavy, and I'm not the only one. Neighbors are standing in the street with their faces turned up to the sky, their arms stretched wide and smiles on their faces. For days on end this city has felt like it was going to burn, and for the moment everything is okay. Children are laughing. People are dancing in circles. It's absolute pure happiness, and it's infectious. I start laughing too. I let it soak my clothes, my first touch of rain in four months, and like the sunset last night, I've never seen rain looking so good. When the lightning comes, I head back inside, then thunder rolls over the city, loud enough to rattle the pictures on the wall. The house lights up like a camera flash as more lightning splits the evening apart. I dry off and put fresh bandages on my feet and hand, then I sit in front of the computer.

I look up articles about Natalie Flowers. She was reported missing almost three years ago, but the police didn't look into it. According to the articles, Natalie cleaned out her bank accounts and packed up all her clothes and moved out of her apartment, telling her flatmate she had somewhere else to be. There were no suspicious circumstances. Her parents reported her missing, they pleaded in the media for their daughter to come home.

Eight years before that Melissa Flowers, Natalie's sister, was raped and killed by a police officer. Melissa Flowers was thirteen years old, an unlucky number for some, especially unlucky for her. I can still remember the case. It wasn't an officer I knew, but I knew all about him after the fact. There was no investigation because he confessed to the crime within an hour of doing it, confessed with a note and by putting a bullet in his head, his body found next to the young naked girl. The note had an apology, it told what he did but didn't say why. It stunned the whole country. I think whatever happened that night with Cooper Riley, Natalie Flowers died and Melissa X was created. She walked away from her old life and started a new one. Either something inside of her snapped, or something inside of her lit up with the excitement of what she had done and needed more. Three years later she would murder Detective Calhoun while the Christchurch Carver filmed her, and she would go on to kill others. Maybe when Cooper attacked Natalie, whatever had started to break when her sister had been killed finally snapped. She was no longer Natalie. She became Melissa, and Melissa wanted revenge for what that officer had done. Is there a connection to the men Natalie has killed, other than the uniforms? Did these men remind her of the man who murdered her sister?

I read the rest of the articles on them both and there are no answers. So I start to look for the connection between Cooper Riley and Nurse Deans, and before I can find anything there's a knock at the door. It's the sketch artist. We sit at the kitchen table, and he goes to work and I keep thinking about Cooper Riley and Pamela Deans, I keep trying to figure out a way they can connect, and keep coming up with nothing.

chapter twenty-four

Cooper Riley hasn't killed six people like he told Adrian, but six sounded much better than the truth—which was one, but this isn't about the truth, this is about escaping from a man who's purely delusional. Technically, having killed only one person doesn't make him a serial killer even though he has a second one all tied up waiting for him, so in that sense he wasn't lying when he first told Adrian he wasn't a serial killer. He guesses that now he is, because now he's up to two.

He really did want to help the girl who saved him, but the missing camera may be in the hands of the police, they may have seen photos of him with Emma Green, they may have searched his office and found pictures of him with Jane Tyrone. He needs to find that out before going to the police, and if he walked out of here with the girl, what could he say to her to keep her quiet until he knew for sure the police didn't know he was a killer? The moment they escaped she would be calling for help. It was unfortunate, but he couldn't take her with him. It was too risky.

The blade is deep inside the girl's stomach. Her eyes are wide and he can see all sorts of thoughts running behind them, the foremost one her regret at unbolting the door. She's no longer struggling. Blood rolls along the edges of the blade and warms his hand, and in the thrust he gave the knife to enter her he has managed to cut himself, his hand jarring forward and dragging the web of this thumb along the sharp edge. He lets go and repositions his grip on the handle. It's getting slippery.

Seven minutes left.

He presses his body weight against her, holding her against the wall. There are tears in her eyes and her face is red. She is losing a battle she no longer even has the strength to fight. With his free hand he pinches shut her nose, and at the same time crumples the end of the straw into his palm. Her eyes grow wider, her face redder, veins stand out in her neck and her forehead. Her eyeballs, he really believes, are in jeopardy of popping right on out. It's something he'd be curious to see happen, but at the same time he thinks it would gross him out. Something inside her nose clicks loudly. Then her mouth opens, the lips tearing, glued skin hanging from them like tiny leaves, the straw dangling from her bottom lip like a cigarette as blood splatters across her chin. She inhales loudly but her lungs don't even fill before he twists the knife, any air sucked in immediately rushing out.

He doesn't want this to take much longer, and it doesn't. Her eyes are asking the question she cannot.

"Because it's who I am," he tells her, then, when that isn't enough, he carries on. He feels as though he needs to. "I'm sorry," he adds, and he thinks he means it.

Her eyes roll up and then she sinks to the floor. This is different from the other girl who died. This way is more enjoyable, and it's the way he always wanted to do it. There is nothing sexual here, and he misses that, but that hasn't made the experience any less rewarding. The last girl died while he was gone. She just gave up. He can't help but wish he knew what his peers would say, not only other killers, but those who study them too. What would they say about a man whose need is so strong he kills the very woman who set him free and could possibly help? That makes him a step above any other killer. It makes him brilliant. If he could tell them, he'd say it wasn't just a need, it was also about semantics. He couldn't take her with him. He has to kill Adrian. Camera aside, his personal life has to stay personal—any talk of him being a serial killer could end up having the police dig deeper than need be, and then it's all over for him, then he may as well have stayed down here because at least it would have been safer than real jail.

He looks down at the woman. There are tattoos on the insides of her arms and needle marks on the insides of her elbows. There's something about her that makes him think she's a prostitute, that her body has been polluted with the needs and anger of hundreds of men. Her blood has flecked onto his face. He wipes at it with the back of his arm. His shirt is covered in dark red patches. Annoyed, he plucks the wet material away from his body, and when he lets it go it clings back to his stomach. The blood is already cooling down. He looks at the cut on his hand. Jesus, all that blood mixing with his wound—fuck, he's going to need to take a shower. The way things are going, he's going to get out of here, get his life back, only to find out he's just become HIV positive or has hepatitis, or maybe he's struck the jackpot and has AIDS.

He makes his way to the top of the stairs. He puts the webbing between his thumb and finger into his mouth and pinches down softly with his teeth, tasting the blood. He sucks it into his mouth then spits it onto the floor. He holds his ear against the door. He can make out classical music. There is some natural light showing around the edges of the door but not much. He puts his hand on the handle. It's unlocked. He has four minutes left. Maybe longer. He slowly opens the door and the music gets louder.

The corridor looks the same as the last time he was here three years ago, back when he had ideas of writing a book that people were going to care about. Movement. Out from the shadow of one of the other doors. He knows what's about to happen, just as he knows he has been played, that he has been fooled by a man who is nothing but a fool, and before he can move the pain hits him, a blinding pain that makes his entire body shut down and he drops like a rock, his mind trying to move his arms and legs but all the wiring in between has been switched off. He watches Adrian come over and can do nothing as he crouches down and holds the rag over his face. The sweet chemical smell, the taste, and then there is nothing.

chapter twenty-five

Friday morning and the rain is still hanging about. There's some fresh bacon and eggs in the fridge, courtesy of my mother, I manage to burn the bacon but not the eggs. I'm feeling tired, last night after the sketch artist left I spent three hours online looking into the pasts of Pamela Deans and Cooper Riley and eventually finding a connection thin enough to tear, a connection involving an abandoned mental institution. I turn my cell phone on and check my messages. There are three, two from Donovan Green, and one from Schroder. Schroder tells me there were no bodies found in the fire and that the fire department is of the belief both fires were set in the same manner. Schroder goes on to say he has been unable to get a warrant for Cooper Riley's medical records from three years ago on account of medical records being one of the hardest things to be given.

From the clouds outside you'd never know we'd just come through a heat wave. Rain is pouring from the gutters of my house into the garden, and the roads are overflowing, water rushing toward drains mostly blocked with leaves. I want to start my day by driving out to see my wife, I want to hold her hand and escape the world for an hour, but it's not going to happen and, strangely, I'm okay with it. I don't feel guilty at not seeing my wife, but I feel guilty at not feeling bad about it.

I switch on the TV and eat my breakfast in the living room, watching the morning news. Emma Green's disappearance has finally become newsworthy. The story about her lasts ten minutes, and then it mentions Jane Tyrone, the girl on the memory card who disappeared five months ago, around the same time the Christchurch Carver was being arrested. I looked her up online last night and read the articles about her when she disappeared. She made the news for two weeks and hasn't been mentioned since until now.

The description I gave the sketch artist is shown. The problem is it's very generic, not all of the details have come from me, but from other witnesses; the dope smoker and a woman at a nearby service station where Adrian filled up two cans of petrol. The shading and the frown of the arsonist makes him look like a killer, but the killer looks like my next-door neighbor and everybody else's next-door neighbor. After they show the sketch, they show some footage from the service station of a man stepping out of Emma Green's car and paying for petrol. The problem with service station footage is that it's the same quality of film used to shoot Bigfoot, but what it does do is give a more accurate description of height and weight of the man who took Cooper Riley.

I clean up the dishes and come back into the living room. The news has ended, replaced by a breakfast show. A woman in her forties is dressed like a woman in her twenties, she's sitting on a bright red couch all relaxed with her arm propped up along the top of it, and sitting opposite her on another bright red couch is a man in a pin-striped suit with slicked-back hair and teeth so white there must be some supernatural element involved. The man's name is Jonas Jones, and I used to run into him a lot when I was on the force. He's a *psychic* who tries to scavenge information from the police department so he can make what he likes to call his *in-tune psychic readings*. You know there's something wrong with the country when somebody green-lights the kind of show tailor-made for Jonas Jones—this one a reality TV show where psychics, including Jones, solve crimes. Not once have any of their *insights* led to an arrest. They like to hold clothing or keys or puppies that belonged to the victims, they like to sit in a dim room with a few candles, they close their eyes and tilt their heads slightly and crease their brows as they connect to a different plane of consciousness before spewing forth their predictions, putting on a show, never giving a damn about who they are hurting, each of them about as psychic as a brick. Jonas Jones has earned a pretty good living from this sham. He wrote a book, then another, and somehow people keep buying them, not caring that he's exploiting real victims and their real pain, capitalizing on those who have died at the hands of somebody else. The author bio overlooks the fact that ten years ago Jonas Jones was a used-car dealer who filed for bankruptcy after two sexual harassment lawsuits were filed against him.

I turn up the volume.

". . . police can only do so much, which is why there's always going to be a need for people with skills such as myself," he says.

"I have to say, I love the show, it always gives me goose bumps seeing you work," she says, "and I especially love your new book," she adds, leaning forward before sweeping her hair back and giving him the look a hungry man would give a pizza.

"Thank you, Laura, that's always nice to hear," he says, his teeth flashing at her. "It's available now and if you buy it today through my website you'll receive a ten percent discount, or twenty percent if you buy two. It does, as you well know, Laura, make a wonderful gift."

"It certainly does, Jonas. I know if I had a man in my life I'd certainly be buying one for him," she says, and it doesn't take a psychic to see she's interested in him. "It appeals to everybody." I roll my eyes and can't decide between reaching for the remote or a vomit bag, and during my indecision she throws another line at Jonas and it's an interesting one. "Now, you were telling me before the show you know something about Emma Green, the young Christchurch girl that's gone missing."

"Yes, yes, a very sad case I'm afraid."

Well that's the only thing he's ever gotten right.

"Christchurch is becoming renown for that kind of thing," she tells him. "In fact, the police now refer to the city as 'Crime' church."

"*As well they should,*" he says, and that's the second thing he's gotten right. He's on a roll. That means I should hear him out.

"*What can you tell us about Emma going missing?*"

An image of Emma Green comes up on a big screen in the background. She's smiling. There are extra arms and shoulders to the sides, friends or family cropped out of the picture. The photo looks recent. There's some generic greenery behind her, a tree or some shrubs.

"*Not missing,*" he says, "*she was abducted.*"

"*And you think she's still alive?*"

Jonas looks glum at the same time still managing to show his teeth. It's a look he must have practiced in the mirror, back when he was selling used cars and telling his customers there was nothing he could do about the faulty water pump on the car they just bought. Copies of his book are standing on a small coffee table between him and his host, a bunch of flowers behind them, everything arranged just so.

"*Unfortunately no,*" he says, playing the percentages. That's what psychics do. They read the situation and go with the statistics. A young girl goes missing in Christchurch, then the statistics say she's been abducted. They say she's dead. And assholes like Jonas Jones come along and use that to promote their new book. The plane of consciousness he's on with these in-tune readings of his has his bank balance on it too. I turn off the TV before he can say another word.

I sit back down in front of the computer and go through the same information I found last night. Pamela Deans was fifty-eight years old, and for the last three years worked at the Christchurch Public Hospital. Before that, she spent twenty-five years working at Grover Hills, a mental institution built outside of Christchurch during the First World War. Joshua Grover was a businessman who made most of his money importing mining equipment into the country back when people were flocking to the south island searching for gold. Grover had three sons, the oldest was nineteen years old when he killed another schoolboy. The problem was Grover's son had the mental capacity of a five-year-old. Back then there was no room for sympathy in the justice system, and Grover fought hard to keep his son alive but failed, and for the first time since making his money Grover found there were some things that couldn't be bought. What he could do was make a difference. Within months of his son being hanged, he petitioned for and finally won the right to build a mental institution where people like his son could be contained. He was granted the right, as long as the institution was well outside the city limits where the mentally ill could be swept under the carpet. Over the years it became one of a handful of institutions, all of them flourishing until, over the last few years, one by one they were shut down, the costs too high and the funds to run them put to use elsewhere by the city council, money spent on trees, on roads and recycling, money being spent trying to solve the teenage drinking epidemic rather than being spent on keeping the mentally dangerous at bay. Patients were kicked to the curb and told to fend for themselves, many with nowhere to go, all of them with instructions that no matter what, they must keep taking their medications. They spilled back into society, those who went on to kill would wind up in jail, but of course it was always too late, the damage was done.

For a quarter of a century Pamela Deans worked with these people, and then three years ago Grover Hills closed its doors and hung up a *Closed for Business* sign.

For nearly thirty years Cooper Riley has studied serial killers and murderers. Along with psychology, he has taught about them at Canterbury University for fifteen years. Some of the cases he speaks about happened here in Christchurch. He studied people who were mad, and Pamela Deans looked after people who were mad.

The connection this morning is just as thin as last night—but it's all there is.

I ring Emma Green's boyfriend, tell him that I don't have any news yet about Emma, and then ask him if he knows anything about Grover Hills.

"Like what?"

"Have you heard of it?"

"Yeah, it closed down a few years ago, right?"

"Right. Has Professor Riley ever mentioned it?"

"Not really. I think it's something he covers in later years if you start moving from psychology to criminology."

"Do you know if any classes in the past took any field trips? Anything like that?"

"I doubt it," he says, and I doubt it too. Nobody would take a class field trip to a mental institution. "He's missing, right? Professor Riley? Somebody took him and burned down his house."

"Yes."

"It's connected to Emma?"

"Yes."

"Did he kill her?"

I think of the photographs, Emma Green naked and bound in a chair but still very much alive. "You sure he never mentioned Grover Hills?"

"It's only my first year with him, and we're only two weeks into it, and we're only doing psychology one-oh-one, not criminology. You should ask one of the other lecturers, or a past student, or you should get hold of his book."

"His book?"

"Yeah. There's a rumor Professor Riley was writing a book about killers in Christchurch. You know, the crazy ones, sociopaths and multiple killers. He's an expert in that kind of stuff. If it's true, he'd be writing about people who might have ended up in Grover Hills."

"Where can I get a copy?"

"You mean if there really is one? See, that's part of the story. He never got it published. It was kind of a joke for some of the students. Professor Riley acts like he knows everything there is to know, but he couldn't get a publisher to sign him up. We figured that meant he didn't know enough."

"Do you know anybody who's ever seen it?"

"No. But I don't even know if he really wrote one. Could just be one of those urban legend type deals. But if he did write one it must be on his computer or something, right?"

"Right," I say, thinking about the lump of plastic his home computer has become.

After I hang up I call Schroder. He lets it ring half a dozen times before picking up.

"Look, Tate, I'm glad you called," he says. "I've been thinking hard about this, and the way things are running now, it's best you leave things to me. I know it's about finding Emma Green, but it's also about getting a conviction. Having you running around, that puts any conviction at risk."

"I thought you were going to keep me in the loop."

"It's beyond that, Tate."

"And Natalie Flowers? Have you spoken to her parents?"

He sighs, and I think he's about to hang up, but instead he carries on. "We've spoken to her mother. The father died a month after Natalie went missing. The mother says it was from a broken heart. She said that if nothing bad had happened to Natalie, then she would have gone to her father's funeral, but she never did. You remember the Melissa Flowers case?"

"Pretty much."

"Yeah. That took a toll on that family, and when Natalie went missing, well, you can figure out the rest. We showed her the images we had of Melissa X. She says it looks like her daughter, but it's not her. She saw the photos in the papers last year and thought the same thing. I think she can't get her head around the possibility of what her daughter was capable of, that's why she can only see a stranger in those pictures. Look, Tate, if we do it your way then maybe we get the guy and we find Cooper and they take a walk because their defense attorney points out how a convicted felon was contaminating the crime scenes. We do it that way then I lose my job too and then I'm no good to anybody else that goes missing."

"The connection between . . ."

"Jesus, Tate, let it go."

"I'm trying to help you here."

"No you're not. You're trying to help yourself. You feel responsible for Emma Green, but you're not."

"I . . ."

"I'm hanging up now, Tate. It's for your own good."

I start pacing the study, loosening up my knee. It's still swollen but not as tight as yesterday. The rain has eased off and the gutters on the roads are no longer overflowing. There are patches of blue sky far in the distance. I understand what Schroder is saying, but it's hard to give a damn when I'm trying to save Emma Green's life. I'm talking short term and he's talking long term. I'm talking about saving one girl and he's talking about saving future girls.

There has to be a copy of Cooper Riley's book somewhere. If he was working on it at home, then any trace of it there would be destroyed, but Riley seems the kind of man who would keep it backed up. Maybe it's hidden on a flash drive somewhere taped to the back of a filing cabinet. Or, more likely, it'll be on his office computer.

I step outside and there's a warm wind flicking rain water from the trees into my face. By the time I get to the university all the dark clouds have disappeared, the sky out to the east is gray but in the west it's all blue, the sun beating down on half the city. There are more cars in the parking lot since yesterday and more people around. Everybody seems more awake than the last few days. Though that might change, because the morning is getting muggier by the minute. In my lifetime I can remember Christchurch going above one hundred degrees less than a dozen times. It'll hit ninety degrees ten times in a good summer, perhaps once in a bad one. Last week it kept closing in on one hundred and ten, and I get the feeling today isn't going to be any different.

I park in the shade of a silver birch and leave my windows open a crack so the pressure inside from the heat doesn't punch a hole in the roof. There's a patrol car parked outside the psychology building. I walk past a set of double doors with a sign out front saying *Psychology Loading Bay*. Maybe they load crazy people into the lecture halls for the students to practice on. I make my way upstairs and keep walking past Cooper's office, nodding toward the two constables stationed outside. When I'm out of the hallway, I call Donovan Green. I can hear pigeons up on the roof through the air vents, they're loud enough that I have to jam my finger into my other ear.

"I heard about the photographs," he says. "But the police won't show me."

"It's for the best."

"You were the one to find them?"

"Yes."

"And yet you didn't call."

"I'm calling now."

"We had a deal, remember? You were meant to report to me first, not the police."

"That just puts Emma in greater danger."

"At least she's alive. I told you she was a survivor."

"I think Cooper Riley being abducted may have saved her life," I tell him, "but we just don't know."

I walk up and down the corridors of the psychology department until I find the server room. Inside I can see lots of computers all hard-wired together. I can hear the fans going and the air-conditioning unit inside keeping the room cool. There's a guy inside so pale-looking he can't know there's a heat wave outside because he hasn't stepped into the sun since turning thirteen. He's about twenty now, with messy hair and long sideburns and I watch him and try to figure out how much money we're going to need. I figure I'm going to need more than I have on me.

"So now where do we look?" Green asks.

"I have a lead, but I need some cash."

"How much?"

"Five grand. Hopefully less."

"What for?"

"I'll explain when you get here," I say, and I tell him where I am and hang up and wait.

chapter twenty-six

Adrian is settling into the routine. For the three years he's been gone from the Grove he's missed the place, which, honestly, he doesn't understand because for the twenty years he was here he hated every minute of it. When he was forced to leave, as they were all forced to, groups were put into halfway houses, where they would be integrated into the community, some successfully, some not so, others killing themselves, others dying homeless in the streets. They were given bank accounts and sickness benefits, almost two hundred dollars a week going to them from a government that didn't care where they ended up. Adrian had never had nightmares until he began living in the halfway house, a run-down wooden version of his real home run by a man who called himself the Preacher. The house was less than a quarter of the size of Grover Hills, with only one kitchen and two bathrooms they all had to share, his bedroom shared with a man the same age as him but in a wheelchair, wheeled in from another institution that closed down around the same time. In all that time the man never spoke a word to him, and for a long time Adrian resented him for that, but that resentment faded once he learned the man's silence was brought about by the fact he'd had his tongue bitten out. Adrian was unclear whether the man had bitten his own tongue out or if it had been done for him, and either possibility made his muscles contract around the back of his neck and his stomach sag. The most noise that man ever made was about five months ago when he choked on a chicken bone and died, the color drained from his face leaving dark bags under his eyes. The halfway house always stunk of food and the carpets were damp and his shared bedroom was smaller than his room here. The windowsills in the bathrooms were full of rot and the ceilings in them sagged and if you put your face against the wall it would be sliced up by flakes of dried paint. He hated it there. His mother never came to visit, even though she promised she would.

Adrian's real mother never visited him at all since he left home twenty-three years ago, not since the incident with the cats. He has two mothers, the one who abandoned him when he was sixteen, and the one who abandoned him three years ago when his home was closed down. Both were hard women. Both left him to fend for himself. Both he holds in contempt, as well as loving them fully. His original mother died eight years ago. Nobody told him it had happened, and he only found out when he was released. He has no idea if she died being the same person he remembered her being when he was a kid. He doesn't even know how real his memories are, whether they're true accounts of their relationship or whether they faded and twisted over time. He knows he was sad when he found out about her. He had it all planned—a trip back home, a knock on the door, his mother would hug him and everything would be okay. Only back home wasn't home anymore, it still felt that way until he knocked on the door and a stranger answered. The stranger was a man in his fifties, he had bought the house years earlier and knew nothing about Adrian or his mother, but the neighbors next door were still the same. So it was from next door that he got the news his mother had died, and he broke down and sobbed, the old lady there doing her best to comfort him. His mother had died of a brain embolism. He doesn't know what that is, what causes them, but was told an embolism is basically a ticking time bomb inside your head that can go off at any time. His mother's had gone off while she was standing in line at a supermarket. The checkout aisle was the last thing she ever saw. One second she was alive and the next second she wasn't.

He went to the cemetery to see her. It took him over an hour to walk there from town. A priest, Father Julian, helped him find her grave and had stood with him, answering Adrian's questions about God, promising him if he had any more he was free to return at any time. Adrian didn't have much of an opinion about God. The Preacher—the man who ran the halfway house—tried to convince Adrian that God was somebody worth having on your side, but Adrian already knew God wasn't on his side, otherwise he'd never have been put into that coma all those years before. Adrian returned to the grave a few months ago only to learn that God wasn't on Father Julian's side either, because, for all his worshipping and loyalty, Father Julian had been murdered. Adrian has never fully understood what irony is, but he thinks that may have been it. A new priest had taken his place, much in the same way a new mother had taken his original mother's place.

His second mother's name was Pamela and he met her the first day he came here to live. He doesn't know when she became more a mother figure to him than his nurse, and he guesses, just as he thinks Cooper would guess, that it happened because he was still very young. She insisted he call her Nurse Deans, and never Pamela, and the couple of times he accidentally called her *mum* he was locked downstairs in the basement, each time for one full day and night. She was never cruel to him over the years, just strict, and the times she had to hit him, or as they both grew older have one of the orderlies hit or restrain him, he knew were for his own good. He didn't like it, but the abuse was the only way to fix whatever was wrong with him and make him a better person, and they sure spent a lot of time trying to make him better. She never saw him as a son and he never forgave her for not visiting him in the halfway house. After all their years together she made it seem as though she had never cared.

He hated the halfway house and three years . . . three years were just too many. He wanted to come back here. The problem was he couldn't. He would go to the hospital and wait for Pamela Deans, he would hide in the parking building across the road, other times shadowed by a tree in the park opposite, and he would watch her, always wanting to approach but always too nervous to do so.

Then one day everything changed.

Adrian learned how to drive.

He was petrified the first time he got behind the wheel of a car, but soon that grew into mere nervousness, which itself became excitement. His teacher, Ritchie, was not an experienced driver himself, but he certainly knew more than Adrian. Ritchie was older than him by twenty years and lived out at the Grove for five of them before it was shut down. There was a lot Ritchie had done that Adrian never would—he'd been married, he had children, he'd had the same job for over fifteen years teaching people how to play the guitar. He tried teaching Adrian too, but the guitar had five strings too many for him to figure it out. But he had taught him to drive. In the end it was one of the most fun things he had ever done. They laughed a lot as he learned, and there were a few shrubs and letterboxes that became victims, but at no other time has he ever felt so much at peace as he did with his best friend talking him through braking and steering, teaching him the art of changing gears, an art that needed to be so precise in the beginning because any mistake would stall the car. He even learned how to pour in petrol and fill the tires with air.

Learning to drive brought about his freedom. With freedom he could do whatever he wanted, go wherever he chose. It opened up an entire new world of possibilities. It gave him access to Grover Hills, to the people who hurt him, it gave him access to a new life, and what he wanted the most from his new life was to be just like his old life—minus the Twins.

So that was the plan. He would live at the Grove again, and Nurse Deans would look after him. He just had to make sure the Twins weren't going to be there to hurt him.

A few years before the Grove shut down, the Twins had left. It was pretty easy to find out where they lived. It was a beautiful moment showing up at their house last week, and it was the first time he ever killed anybody. Boy, he was nervous. So nervous that he almost dropped the hammer. He got through it. He clubbed them both to death, and then he took their car. They weren't ever going to need it again.

He wanted to live here, he wanted Grover Hills to be the way it used to be now that the Twins were dead, and he wanted Nurse Deans to live here with him.

Only she didn't want to.

He moved what he owned out here but quickly became lonely. His best friend had met a woman and their friendship had taken a back-seat to the new relationship. Adrian was jealous of them and happy for them at the same time, but not happy enough to ask them to join him out here. He wishes things had gone differently. Being back here he can clearly remember the good times, and there were many. He remembers some of the killers that came to stay, young men and women who weren't fully aware of what they had done, or so they pretended, but sometimes at night they would tell him in detail and their stories would take on a life, he could see the details through their eyes, both sickening and exciting him. Some were so vivid he could almost lay claim to the memories and call them his own.

After hearing them, he would go back to his room and work on his comics. He was getting better at them. No matter what the story was he had heard, he would draw that scenario. He would put himself into the killer's shoes, he would imagine he was the one swinging the ax or holding the knife, and the victims he drew were always the eight boys who had hurt him all those years ago. As he drew them, he could feel himself killing them, and it was magnificent.

But then the orderlies and nurses started to find his comic collection. Each time they would destroy it and he would be sent into the Scream Room. He wouldn't be allowed pencils or paper anymore, but there was always a way to get some, and he'd start over again with the new stories until he lost those too.

When he left the Grove and went to the halfway house, the people who inspired him were no longer with him. It affected his work. He found he couldn't get the shapes right, or the shading, and the details in the faces disappeared. The characters just didn't want to be there. After six months of trying, he gave up. The memories had faded, just as the people who told them have faded from his life.

He has his books, but books aren't the same. Those people who came and went over the years, he would tell them his story too, and those people are what made the Grove a home. You can't tell your story to a book.

He remembers everything about Cooper Riley from when Cooper used to come out here with his questions. Part of him felt jealous in the beginning, because Cooper was stealing the stories that were meant for him, but of course that was stupid, and he came to realize that in the end. Cooper would come out here once a week over the final year the Grove remained open, and he would interview a handful of patients, all of them committed for taking lives. Adrian found the process fascinating, and he couldn't wait to read the book when it came out, and he hoped it would have pictures too. When the Grove shut down, Adrian looked for but was never able to find a copy. Nobody at the book stores had ever heard of it. That meant Cooper wasn't done writing it.

Last week he looked Cooper Riley up. He was a professor at the University of Canterbury who taught psychology to some students and criminology to others. Adrian began to follow him. He began to think—if he couldn't be friends anymore with the men who had told him those stories, men who had moved on, he could have the man who had recorded them, the man who was the keeper of those stories as well as a storyteller.

Only Cooper was so much more.

Because a few nights ago he learned Cooper was part of the story. Following him, Adrian watched as Cooper hurt the woman behind the café. Cooper dropped her into the trunk of his car and drove away.

Adrian followed.

When it was all over, Adrian drove back to the parking lot. He wanted the woman's car. He didn't know why, but he wanted to own it. He wanted to collect it. Even more, he wanted to collect Cooper. He had been using a car that belonged to one of the Twins. He left it several blocks away and walked back to the café. He was lucky—the keys to the woman's car were laying on the ground. What started as an idea was now a must have. He would bring Cooper back to Grover Hills. He would store him in the Scream Room, and over time Cooper would grow to trust him, to befriend him, and tell him story after story.

He knew keeping Cooper would be a lot of work. He had his savings, and he was still receiving a sickness benefit. The government was giving him money and he didn't have to work for it, all he had to do was tell the doctor he had to go and visit every six months that he was taking his pills even if he wasn't. He knew once in the Scream Room the professor would get bored, and the way to combat that was to bring home a victim. So from the café he had driven his new car into town and parked near the corner where the woman had rejected him months earlier, back when Christmas lights had decorated the city. It had been the week before Christmas and he had known for months what he wanted, and what he wanted to do was spend some money and be with the woman from the street corner who reminded him of the girl who changed his life. He had seen her many times over the previous year, each time she looked more like Katie than the last, until finally he was convinced that it was her. He should have known it wasn't—after all, Katie would have been his age, and this girl on the corner was no more than twenty. The memory of it still makes him feel bad, almost embarrassed to tell the truth. He had approached her and asked how much it cost to be with her, and she had given him a varying range of prices for things he didn't understand.

They had walked to an alley less than twenty seconds away. She had looked him over and then asked for the money first and he had paid it. Then she had undone the front of his pants. He had never been with a woman before and didn't know what to do, but she seemed to know plenty.

"Don't be shy," she had said, but he was shy and his heart had been banging like a drum, so nervous he was that by the time he felt sick it was too late to warn her, his mouth had opened and a stream of vomit hit her in the middle of the chest.

"Ah, shit, you goddamn freak," she screamed, jumping away from him.

"I'm sorry, Katie."

She looked up from where she was wiping the vomit off with her hand and flicking it into the ground. "What did you just say?"

"I said I'm sorry."

"You called me Katie."

"I didn't mean to."

"How much money do you have on you?"

"None."

She stepped forward and poked him in the chest. He was afraid of her. "How much?"

"I . . . I don't know," he said. He had already given her sixty dollars. He pulled out his wallet and she snatched it from him. She took out all the cash that was in it and threw the wallet back.

"This is to cover the dry cleaning," she said, "and don't let me ever see you again."

But he had seen her again, sometimes a few nights in a row, but he had never approached her.

Not until this week. She didn't recognize him. She seemed *softer* for lack of a better word, and he suspected she was high. Plus he had a car—and last time he didn't. She climbed into the car willingly and he Tasered her when they drove into an alley half a block away. He probably could have just held the rag over her face, but this way there was no struggle. It was the same Taser he would use on Cooper and she collapsed into the same kind of heap, only she was supported by the passenger seat.

The Taser came from the Twins, and so did the extra cartridges, a dozen of them in total, meaning he can shoot twelve people, or less people more than once. He also found the chemical they used to use on him sometimes. They would soak it into a rag and hold it over his face and he'd fall asleep. He would have collected the Twins and listened to their stories if he hadn't hated them so much. He considered putting the woman in one of the padded rooms and decided to rope her to one of the beds instead. The bedrooms got more air and he figured were more comfortable. He used rope and glue and she stayed asleep the entire time.

After that he went back out. Driving was amazing. Having a car was changing his life. He drove to the hospital. He waited outside. He followed his second mother home. He needed her help to look after all the people he was collecting. She called him a freak just like the street girl had, only this time she didn't have any orderlies to back her up. He lashed out at her. She told him she would call the police and he would go to jail and that jail was far worse than anything she had ever done to him. So he lashed out again and, when he was finished with the lashing, he tied her to the bed, went out, and bought a container of petrol.

He slept in her house most of the night on the couch, waking up at five o'clock in the morning to load his car with all the food he could find. He took some of her dresses for the girls he would bring home for Cooper, said goodbye to his mother, and set her on fire.

It meant he was going to have to do everything by himself. He could handle that. After all, the last three years in the halfway house proved he was capable, and look at what he's learned in that time—he's learned how to drive, how to cook, how to clean up after himself, how to go into town and buy groceries and clothes. He's been back at the Grove for a week now, and each morning he has sat on the wooden deck out front in the sun, sometimes for only a few minutes, other times for the entire day. This morning was a little different because of the rain, but it's cleared up now pretty good. He drinks his orange juice and he thinks about Cooper and how, last night, the two men bonded over the killing of the woman. Violence is . . . is sit-u-ation-al, that's what all the books say. That's what makes criminals model prisoners in jail—there are no women to rape and murder in there. He knew when the situation changed, so would Cooper's attitude. He's read that somewhere.

Adrian also feels betrayed. He knew the woman would let Cooper out of his cell, and what Cooper did next was going to impact their relationship. If he tried to escape, it meant he didn't really like Adrian at all, and that everything he had said was a lie. The killing brought them closer, but the betrayal has driven them apart. He guesses that means he's exactly where he was in the beginning.

He finishes breakfast but doesn't go downstairs. He cleaned up the mess last night. He wrapped the body in an old blanket and took her around the back to bury her with the others. He doesn't want to face Cooper right now. He's still too annoyed at him. And anyway, he's got other plans for this morning—he has some digging to do, and maybe some collecting too.

chapter twenty-seven

Donovan Green doesn't look like he's had any sleep since the last time I saw him. He hasn't changed either. His hair is a mess and his eyes are red and keep flicking left and right as if he's being followed. He looks like he's just walked out of a bar where he's been holed up for the last twelve hours drinking hard.

"Here's the money," he says, handing me an envelope. When it comes to finding your daughter, there's no limit to what you'll spend. "What's the lead?"

"Cooper Riley wrote a book," I tell him. "It may have something in it we can use."

"It's five thousand dollars for a book?"

"It is for this one. I'll call you later on today."

He seems about to argue the point, that he wants to hang around and watch me work, but in the end he just nods slowly. He's a broken man holding out the kind of hope that may kill him if things don't work out the way he needs them to.

"The sketch in the news," I say, "you recognize him?"

"Looks like the prime minister."

"You know if the police have shown it to Emma's flatmates and friends?"

"One of them thought it was their cousin Larry. I told you she was still alive, and the photos prove it," he says. "I know you think things might have changed since they were taken, but they haven't. She's alive and I can feel it," he says, and I really hope that he can. "She's strong," he tells me. "You know that for a fact. She survived what you did to her, and she'll survive what's being done to her now. She can talk her way out of anything."

I hope she can. I hope she has the ability to talk.

"My wife, Hillary," he says, "she was always the strong one. Last year, when you hurt Emma, my wife was a rock. I was the one falling apart. This time, Jesus, she's a mess. All she does is sit in Emma's old room holding on to some of the clothes Emma left behind when she moved out. Hillary is the strongest woman I know, but this . . . if we don't get Emma back alive," he says, "she's . . . she's . . . I don't know. I just don't know," he says, shaking his head. "Just . . . just find her, okay? Find her alive. Please, I'm begging you, find my daughter alive."

I want to tell him that's exactly what I'm going to do. I want to tell him he can tell his wife everything is going to be okay, because by the end of the day, tomorrow at the latest, they'll have their daughter back. I can see in his tired face and tired features that he wants me to tell him this, that hearing it would make him feel a whole lot better.

And I almost tell him.

I nod, and he takes meaning in that nod because he nods back, turns around, and I watch him walk away, maybe he's going to head back home, maybe to the hospital, maybe to go and see Jonas Jones Psychic or a priest because he's desperate to try anything.

I head back into the corridor. The idea of money isn't as powerful as money itself, which is why I hold up two thousand dollars in the window of the door to the computer server room and knock on it. I could try holding up fifty dollars and hope for the same result, but the risk of having him call the police fades more with every hundred I hold up. The door is locked and the guy comes over and stares at the money then at me and then back at the money.

Keeping his eyes on the money, he asks "What do you want?"

"To ask you some questions," I answer. "About Cooper Riley."

"You a reporter?"

"Come on, this is cash I've got here, not a check that's going to bounce."

"What are you then?"

"I'm somebody trying to find Cooper Riley and you're somebody who looks like they could do with some cash."

"How much is that?"

"Two thousand," I say, beginning to grow impatient. "It'll only take two minutes. You ever earned a thousand dollars a minute before?"

He unlocks the door. The room is the coldest room I've been in since getting out of jail. There are fans blowing and an air-conditioning unit running hard with small ribbons taped to it fluttering in the breeze. There are LED lights coming from every surface and lots of light radiating into the room from a dozen switched-on computer monitors and overhead fluorescent lights that I can hear humming. Throw in the sound of a hundred ticking hard drives and we're listening to an IT symphony. The door swings closed behind me. He can't take his eyes off the cash.

"Okay, so what's the deal?" he asks. Then he adds, "You shouldn't be in here," almost as though he's reading off a cue card.

"I need some information."

"I'm not at liberty to . . . to . . . this is two thousand?"

"That's right. And I'm not after anything illegal," I say, which is a complete lie. "Listen, all I need you to do is access any files belonging to Cooper Riley."

"I thought you only wanted me to answer some questions."

"It's a little more complicated than that," I tell him.

"Police have already had me access them."

"Then this shouldn't be too hard for you."

"I . . . I don't know."

"I'm looking for something in particular. I need to know if he's backed something up. You take a look, and you get this," I say, waving the cash.

"Just for looking?"

"Just for looking."

"Okay. Okay, that doesn't seem too illegal," he says, justifying it to himself and holding out his hand. I give him the cash.

He walks over to one of the terminals. It only takes him thirty seconds to punch up the information he needs, having accessed it yesterday. A list of files and folders comes up.

"He was writing a book," I tell him.

"What kind of book?"

"About criminals."

"Hang on," he says, and starts scrolling through the files. "Yeah, there's a word processing document here that looks pretty big that the cops took a copy of yesterday. Let me check," he says, and double clicks on the icon. Page one of a manuscript appears. "This looks like it could be it," he says, and when he turns back around I'm holding out another thousand dollars in my bandaged hand.

"I need it printed," I say.

"I don't know . . ."

"Nobody will ever know."

"If it comes back I did this . . ."

"It won't. Trust me. There's no way I'll get caught with it, and it's not like Cooper Riley is going to be in any position to complain about his book being printed—even if he ever does find out, and since the police have a copy anyway, it's only a matter of time before it becomes public. I just need a head start on it."

"I don't . . ." he says, but keeps looking at the money.

"Just print it out and I'm gone."

"And nobody ever has to know?"

"Not from me."

He turns back to the computer. He reaches into his pocket and grabs a flash drive and slots it into a USB port. "Printing will leave a record," he says, "plus it'll take too long. It's about three hundred pages. It'd take close to fifteen minutes."

He copies the file, which takes about two seconds and hands me the flash drive. I'm halfway out the door when I turn back toward him. "One more thing," I ask. "Can you tell me when he last accessed the file?"

"I can only tell you when he last backed up this particular one. He may have been working on it at home, or have a different version saved somewhere. But this one was last saved three years ago."

Three years ago. The same time Natalie went missing. The same time Cooper got divorced.

The dashboard of the rental tells me it's almost eleven o'clock and one hundred and six degrees. Traffic starts to back up from the north where there's another house fire. Hardly anybody is walking the streets. A few stray dogs are sniffing the gutters for food, the gutters having dried out now and full of fresh litter. I get past the fire only to get boxed in by traffic a few intersections later where two taxis have collided, the drivers both unhurt but yelling at each other in different foreign languages neither of them can understand. It takes ten minutes to get past them, glass pooled out over the road like diamonds.

When I get home I leave the front door open and crack open the windows in the study and try to get some airflow going. I get the fan up and running and plug the flash drive into my computer. It takes a few minutes for my computer to boot up, it takes longer than last time and will take longer next time, the eighteen-month-old components inside making it an antique. I sit in front of it and massage my knee, which is feeling better and bending more than it did this morning. Three hundred pages is a lot to read through, but I'm only going to be scanning it for a connection between Pamela Deans and Cooper Riley and Grover Hills. I set it printing and pick up the first few pages as they come out. Before the pages have even cooled off I can see the connection. It's in the introduction Cooper Riley has written. Riley was visiting Grover Hills. He was interviewing some of the criminals out there for his work. Nurse

Deans was helping him. He was building up a study and writing this book and I imagine at some point was going to approach some publishers, or maybe he did and was rejected. He was heading out there on a weekly basis, Nurse Deans the liaison between him and the patients. More warm pages are ejected from the printer. I pick them up. It looks like Riley interviewed at least a dozen or so patients. A couple of things come to mind. First off, how far down the path was Cooper Riley toward abducting Natalie Flowers, killing Jane Tyrone, and abducting Emma Green when he conducted these interviews? Second, was the thought of torturing and killing a young woman something he never thought he'd do back then, or something he was dying to do? Impossible to know whether these interviews brought his desire forward or repressed it.

Almost a hundred pages are finished printing. I tap them against the desk to level them then carry them out to the living room. The house is stuffy at this end and the smell of toner has followed me down the hall, making the house feel even stuffier. I open the French doors to head out to the deck.

I drop the pages. Daxter is hanging from the gutter, his eyes half open, and while yesterday he looked like he was sleeping, today he looks exactly the way dead cats look when a noose has been fashioned from a piece of wire and hooked up to the roof.

chapter twenty-eight

The payoff is in the expression. It's been more than twenty years since he last saw that look. It brings a flood of memories that makes his insides warm and gives him a sense of longing for those days. There will be more cats, he tells himself, because there are more people who have hurt him. Through the gap in the fence he watches Tate drop the pages. They hit the deck and slide apart like a deck of cards, the top few peeling away and drifting onto the brown lawn. Tate reaches up to the cat and Adrian doesn't stay to see what happens next, instead he runs down the street to where his car is parked, mission almost accomplished, drives to the end of the street, turns left, then turns left again and comes up the parallel street into the cul-de-sac and stops outside Tate's house.

The front door to the house is open, which makes this easier. He was going to knock on the door and shoot Tate when he answered it, which is always risky, but now he steps inside. He can't hear anything except a mechanical sound being repeated over and over from the first room on the left, a *whirr-clunk, whirr-clunk*. He takes the Taser out of his pocket. His hands are sweating and he almost loses his grip on the handle. He keeps it pointed ahead of him, but close to his body where he can protect it. The rag is in his back pocket, along with the small plastic bottle of the fluid that makes people sleep.

Ideally he'd like to shoot Tate in the back. The whole thing would go that much easier, but it's not necessary. Either way, once Tate is down and unconscious, Adrian can back the car into the driveway and pick him up. He's not the best at reversing a car but he's done it enough times that he's confident he can do it again. He'll park next to Tate's car because the driveway is wide enough. Then he'll pop the trunk and load Tate in and drive back to the Grove. He'll put him in one of the rooms with the padded walls. Not as comfortable as a bed, but much safer when dealing with somebody like Tate.

Theodore Tate—both killer and hunter of killers—the perfect collector's piece. He will have stories too—good ones.

The room making the sound is a study. There are pages coming out of a printer, being ejected through a slot like an envelope being mailed. The pages fall into a tray. There's a bunch of them already, and there are lots of other papers and photographs scattered across the floor and desk. He takes hold of the next page rolling out of the printer. He scans it then picks up other pages from the tray and scans those too.

Oh my God, is this the book Cooper was working on? He recognizes some of the names. It is! It really is! He can't believe it, and he's so excited that his hands start shaking even more. More pages come out of the printer. He snatches them up. How did Tate get hold of a copy? And why? He glances around the room as if the answer is going to be there for him, but it isn't, but what is here are lots of other papers and photographs to do with another case, one that he's been reading about lately. Tate is not only looking for Cooper, but also for the woman who's been killing men in uniform.

He can't believe his luck in coming here.

He doesn't think the smile will leave his face for hours!

He steps into the hallway. He can hear Tate talking to somebody and his heart slams harder in his chest and his smile disappears. There are two people here! He steps back into the study and scoops up the manuscript and all the papers scattered around the room, and the papers he jams into an empty file. He doesn't get them all and he can't wait for the rest to come out of the printer. Cooper will love getting his hands on this Melissa X information. What a way to make him happy! He feels like he's raiding a treasure chest. He feels like, at any second, Tate and his friend are going to burst into the study and capture him. It makes him both excited and anxious.

He gets back outside and runs down to the car. His racing heart slows down, but he's still dripping with sweat. He starts the car and is about to pull away when he realizes that Tate may not have had somebody with him, but may have been on the phone. He feels stupid. He bets that's what it was, that Tate was calling somebody. Probably the police. He still has time to go back inside and try to collect him.

Only he's too nervous, way too nervous now, and he's ridden his luck for the morning, getting in and out of the house without being seen, getting all that information, and digging up the cat. He can come back any time. He can come back tonight, or tomorrow, or next week. So he puts the car into gear and drives out of the street. His nerves turn to excitement. In fact he's so excited on the way home he pulls over for five minutes to look through the book. Seeing the names of people he used to know, it's like pulling the scab off an old memory, a happy scab because the memories make him smile. He drives to a convenience store and buys a newspaper, and when he finally gets home he bursts through the front door and puts Cooper's book on the floor by the basement door, then heads straight down into the basement.

chapter twenty-nine

"I have something for you," Adrian says.

Cooper is standing on the opposite side of the door. He's been asleep for a long time—two shots from the Taser within two days has made him tired. It's been a long morning in the dark, followed by a long night in the dark. This basement is like a black hole when it comes to time. The basement also doesn't vent any smells that well. The stench of vomit and urine is really getting to him, and he had to take a shit when he woke up a few minutes ago, which is making the air feel thick. Plus his hand is sore. There's a neat slice through the webbing of his thumb that looks like it would peel apart with just a little help. He's got nothing to wrap it in. Best thing he can do to avoid an infection is hope for the best.

"I have something for you too," Cooper says. "An apology. I know you thought last night that I was trying to escape, and I'm sorry if that's what you thought, but I wasn't, I really wasn't. I was coming upstairs to find you."

"Really?"

"Of course," he says, but he can tell that Adrian is feeling unsure. "I wouldn't lie to you, Adrian. After all, you're all I have."

"You're all I have too," Adrian says. "And that's why I got you something. Two things, actually."

"More women for me to kill?" he asks, hoping that it is. Next time he won't mess it up. It was his stupid ego that got in the way last time. He should have let the girl live. At least until he'd dealt with Adrian. In lieu of an answer, Adrian holds up both hands. In one he's holding a newspaper, in the other he's holding a file. If this is what he brought for him, Cooper feels disappointed. The sun is coming through the basement door and the paper is easy to read. He can see a sketch on the front page of somebody who looks like one of his old teachers from school, Mr. Maynard, who used to smoke his pipe in the classroom back when things like that were considered normal. Adrian puts the file down on the coffee table, then wraps the first page of the newspaper behind the last, then folds it back in half.

"Stand back," Adrian says.

"Why?"

"I want to slide this through the door."

"Okay."

He stands back. There's the snap of a bolt being undone, not as loud as the one last night that opened the door. It takes all of his willpower not to run forward and try to reach out and grab Adrian's arm, but he doesn't, he keeps his ground. Even if he was quick enough to grab Adrian, what then? Start gnawing at the man's fingers until he reaches up and unbolts the door?

Actually, yeah, it's a pretty good idea, but it's already too late. The flap is opened a fraction and the newspaper slid through, and then the bolt is slid into place and Adrian is back at the window. Cooper walks forward and picks up the paper.

"What's in the file?" he asks, looking out at it.

"We can talk about that in a moment," Adrian says. "The police are looking for you," he says. "Have you really killed six people?"

"Where's my camera?"

"What camera?"

"There was a camera in my briefcase. It's gone now."

"Oh, I burned it," Adrian says. "In the fire. I didn't want the police to find it."

"Are you sure it was destroyed?"

"I poured petrol on it. Take a look," he says, and he starts to scratch at his neck and Cooper wants to believe him but isn't sure. "It's in the paper. There's a photo of the fire."

Cooper unfolds the newspaper, careful not to open the wound on his hand with a paper cut. It's too dark to see anything. Adrian figures it out and steps aside so the light coming from upstairs enters the cell. There is a photo of his house, only it isn't his house anymore, it's a fireball with his address.

"Oh Jesus," he says, and he feels nauseous. He loved his house. Loved it. "My house. You completely destroyed it."

"I know, isn't it great? It's stopped the police from finding anything to suggest you're a serial killer. I thought that today you could tell me about some of the people who used to stay here," he says.

"My house," he says. "You fucking burned down my house!" He looks up at Adrian, and Adrian is looking confused. When he gets out of here he's going to burn this place down too and Adrian can watch it happen from the comfort of this fucking cell.

He tightens his grip and the cut by his thumb squeezes out some spots of blood. At least the camera was destroyed. It must have been. He can clearly see his car. It's where he dropped his briefcase, so even if Adrian is lying about burning it, it must have been destroyed anyway.

Must have been.

Or maybe not.

"I did it for you," Adrian says, his voice quieter now. "To help you."

Cooper lowers the newspaper. He folds it in half and tosses it onto the bed. *Baby steps. You're dealing with a moron, remember?*

A moron who is in control of his future.

"That's right," he says, "you did it for me. I did love that house,"

202

he says, and thank God for insurance. "But you're right, it's for the best and I'm thankful you're looking out for me."

"This is your home now," Adrian says, "and that house was an anchor to your old life. Also, I have your book."

"What?"

"It looks good," Adrian says.

"Of course it's good," Cooper says. "How did you get it? You printed off a copy from my house?"

"No. I took it from somebody."

"What? How? From who?"

"From Theodore Tate. He's trying to find you."

"I know that name," he says, and a moment later he knows from where. Theodore Tate has made the papers a few times over the last few years. It used to be with different cases, he would be part of a team looking for some guy who had killed a prostitute or held up a service station with a shotgun, and then he made the news when he lost his daughter in an accident. The man who killed her went missing, the theory being he skipped the country rather than face jail. Then Tate made the papers again last year when he tracked down and killed a serial killer.

"He's a cop," Adrian says. "Anyway, he won't find anything be- cause there's nothing to find."

"Why did he have the manuscript?" Cooper asks, and then an even more important question comes to him. "How did you get it from him?"

"I don't know why he had it," Adrian answers, "but I got it from his house."

"You killed him?"

"I'm not a killer, remember? I left him exactly how I found him."

"Why were you at his house?"

"I don't want to talk about it," Adrian says.

"Something led you there. He's involved somehow, tell me how?"

"I don't know how he's involved," Adrian says.

"Then why go to his house?"

"For this," Adrian says, and holds up the file.

"What's in it?"

"It's a case that Tate is working on."

"What case?"

"The Melissa X case."

Cooper feels a chill run the length of his spine right into his groin, where it settles. He cups his remaining testicle lightly.

"Tate is working on that?" Cooper asks.

"It looked that way," Adrian says.

"Can I see it?"

"It's why I got it. If you're nice to me, I'll let you read it later on today."

"Okay, Adrian, sure. No problem. Just remember, you have to be careful, Adrian. What if he had caught you? Then what would have happened to me?"

"I don't know," Adrian answers, "I didn't think about it. I wouldn't have told the police about you, I promise. They wouldn't have come and taken you away."

"I would have starved to death out here," he says, and he thinks of Emma Green, locked up in a cell at another abandoned mental institution. He left her some water but no food. How much water did he leave her? Two bottles, he thinks. Maybe two liters in total. More than enough for one day. He was going to return the following night. Only it hasn't been one day. It's been three and a half. If she's spaced it out, she'll be okay. If she drank it all on Monday night after he left her, she'll be dead by now. When he gets out of here Emma Green isn't going to be much fun to be around.

"How long were you here, Adrian?" Cooper asks.

"Nineteen years, eight months, and four days," Adrian says proudly. "I counted."

"You counted?"

"Sometimes there wasn't much more to do."

"And why were you here?"

"Because my mother, my real mother, she was forced to bring me here."

"Your real mother?" Cooper repeats. Insanity aside, he's in-

trigued again. If the camera hasn't been found and his life is waiting for him once he escapes, there'll be a book in this, one that the
publishers have to accept this time.

He puts the webbing of his thumb into his mouth and lightly
sucks on it, tasting it and feeling a tiny twinge of pain that actually
feels pretty good.

"I have two mothers. My real one, and the one I had here."

"Your mother here—she was one of the nurses?"

"Nurse Deans," Adrian says. "I saw you speaking to her sometimes."

He used to drive all the way out here, and for the privilege of talking to some of the patients he had to slip Nurse Deans two hundred
dollars a week in the beginning, and when he was really getting
into it, he had to start slipping her two-fifty. She let him use an
empty office to talk to whoever he wanted, as long as there was an
orderly in the room, and as long as he didn't tell anybody about the
money. He was writing about killers. Writing about people who'd
had nervous breakdowns or spent their time eating flies wouldn't
make good reading.

But Adrian will make for great reading. Especially with all that's
going on. Cooper will kill the bastard when he escapes from here,
stage the scene any way he wants, he'll come out of it a hero and
there's no way the publishers will shoot him down again.

"So why was your real mother forced to bring you here? Because
of the cats?"

"Yes," Adrian says. "Because of the cats."

"I really was coming upstairs to find you last night," Cooper says.

"I believe you. Kind of. Would you like some time to read the
paper?"

He turns back toward it. It's on the bed but he can't make out
any of the text. "Just a couple of minutes."

"Then we can talk about my friends," Adrian says, "and you can
tell me stories about other killers you met. We can compare them
against your own stories of killing once I've read your book."

"You really love the stories, right?"

"I do," Adrian says.

"Okay, Adrian. Give me some time to read the paper and get my thoughts together."

"That would be great."

"But it has to be like before, quid pro quo."

"I . . . I don't understand French," Adrian says.

"It's Latin."

"Isn't that the same thing?" Adrian says.

How the hell can a guy like Adrian still be holding him captive? It's like being beaten by a six-year-old at chess. "Also, I'm hungry. I need some food."

"Okay."

"And you need to empty out the bucket. It stinks in here."

"Later," Adrian says, "I promise."

"Then let me read the paper and we'll talk soon. Come back with some sandwiches. And leave the upstairs door open so I can see."

Adrian rushes upstairs, leaving Cooper to read the paper in peace.

chapter thirty

Yesterday there was the need to cuddle Daxter's corpse, as if I could still offer him some compassion, as if holding him against my chest was going to let him know he was loved. Today I can barely look at him.

I raise my fists and turn quickly, suddenly sure the person who did this is behind me, but there's only the door I stepped through and the living room. I feel violated. I feel like I need to take a shower, burn down my own house, even hose down my dead cat. Something dark and very creepy has just touched my life. There are footprints all around the grave in the loose dirt that I don't want to disturb. Did the person who did this kill Daxter too? Of course he did. He wasn't accidently run over. He was killed just to be dug up, just to be part of a message. I have no idea what that message is. Stop looking for Cooper Riley? Stop looking for Emma Green? Stop looking for Natalie Flowers? Or is this a message from the past, perhaps somebody I arrested years ago?

There's another possibility that makes more sense. I call Schroder. "Somebody killed my cat," I tell him, and I realize I'm almost crushing my phone. What I'd love to do right now is crush the person who killed Daxter.

"You told me yesterday."

"What I mean is somebody murdered him," I say, and then I tell him about Daxter hanging from the roof.

"Jesus," he says. "You think it's a message of some kind?"

"I'm thinking it might be somebody from Grover Hills."

He says nothing. I can almost hear him thinking things over. Can almost hear the bones creaking in his hand as he tightens it on the cell phone. He breathes heavily a few times. Then, "How do you know about that?"

"Google."

"That the only way?"

"No, Carl, I spent my childhood there growing up."

"Well it'd certainly explain a lot if you had."

"Listen, Carl, it's possible one of the patients who got turned loose three years ago has an obsession with Cooper Riley and Pamela Deans, and now with me."

"Because of your cat."

"Yes. Because of my cat. Sane people don't pull that shit," I say. "Sane people don't go digging up your fucking dead pets!"

"Calm down, Tate."

"I am calm," I say, pacing the yard faster now. "I want you to send a patrol car and some forensics," I say. "Get some officers to canvas the neighborhood. Somebody must have seen something. And there has to be a load of trace evidence here, there are footprints around the grave for a start."

"Anybody could have done it, Tate. It doesn't take a crazy person. It just takes somebody you pissed off in an incredible way."

"No, I really think it does take a crazy person, Carl. If it only took somebody who was pissed off at me then you'd be number one on my list of suspects."

"I hear you," he says, "but it's just as likely it's an ex-con with a grudge." It's true. I've arrested a lot of people over the years. Schroder presses on. "I know you're thinking it's a hell of a coincidence," he says, "but if it was going to happen it wasn't going to be done while you were in jail—no point in that."

"So why not do it before then?"

"I don't know. Maybe they were in jail too."

"Have you showed the sketch to any of the ex-staff from Grover Hills? Maybe somebody there will recognize him."

"It's getting done, Tate. I'll send out some people to take a look around your house and pick up your cat."

He hangs up. I grab the papers and head inside. There are smooth rectangles of dirt leading from the front door to my study, dirt that's fallen from the tread of somebody's shoes. I drop the papers and duck into the bedroom and pull out Donovan Green's gun from beneath the mattress. I carry it into the study. The computer is still running. There's nobody standing in the room. Most of the manuscript is missing, only the last dozen or so pages are left in the printer. All of the files Schroder gave me on Melissa X are gone. Daxter was either a distraction or a message—either way, somebody doesn't want me finding out what happened to Cooper Riley.

chapter thirty-one

Damage control.

The newspaper article is bad, but it could be worse. There could have been a big headline, nice dark letters saying *Serial Killer's House Is Burned Down.* Ten years ago there were rules, ten years ago if it wasn't fact, the papers would be reluctant to print it. Things have changed since then. Most of the media is online, news channels are on twenty-four hours a day, the business is more cutthroat than ever, and the journalists don't have time for fact-checking anymore. News isn't about letting the people know what's happening, it's about shaping agendas and making money, and money is more important than what's right or wrong. Rumors are now fact. A guy selling hotdogs outside the police department is now a confirmed inside source. The boundaries of ethics moved, then moved some more, then were eroded away. So if there had been any suspicion at all that Cooper was a killer, it would have made it into print.

The article is about his disappearance. Cooper Riley, fifty-two years old, professor at Canterbury University, abducted from his own house, his car left in the driveway, no indication as to where he's been taken, his house razed the following day. There's a photo of the fire and there's a photo of Cooper standing in front of a class of students pointing up to a screen. The photo was taken years ago, it was a publicity shot that was bundled into a magazine to promote the university. His hair was a little thicker around the sides back then, a little blacker and there was still some on top too. He wasn't going through the stress of a divorce. Five years on this side of the photo and he's ten kilograms heavier and locked in a goddamn basement.

How much do the police know?

If they suspected more, somebody would have leaked it to the press. And nothing could have survived that fire. The photo is taken from the street, he can see his car engulfed by the flames, even half of the front yard is burning. The camera only needed to be anywhere on the property and it would have melted, the memory card useless. So he's sitting good on that level. Both victims were in the trunk of his car at one point, and each time he had them on a tarpaulin. He knows there was no trace evidence in his car, but even if there was, the fire took care of it.

His house.

He loved his house.

He loved his collection.

Jesus—if he ever gets out of here, there's no way he's going to collect anything ever again. It would give him something in common with Adrian, and he's sick at the thought that even breathing is something they have in common—though soon he'll make sure that's no longer the case.

He sits on the edge of the bed and rests the newspaper on his lap. He runs his fingers over the photograph of his house, an ink stain growing thicker on the pads of his fingertips. He thinks about the first girl he killed. It was last year. He starts rubbing the newspaper a little harder. Her name was Jane Tyrone and she was twenty-four years old, almost half his age, and at the time he thought nothing in the world felt better than a twenty-four-year-old. Five months later he would learn he was wrong—nothing felt better than a seventeen-year-old.

Of course it didn't start with her. It started three years ago with another student. Natalie Flowers. That was her name back then. He doesn't like to think about her much, and Adrian having a file on her is bringing back a whole lot of bad memories. He wonders if her real name is mentioned at all in that, and doubts it. The police don't know. If they did, they'd have let the media know. He'd love to take a look at it. In fact he needs to—there could be something in there that relates to him.

Natalie Flowers.

She came into his life and brought along a change in him that he allowed to happen. His marriage was falling apart. Had been for some time, but he'd been too obsessed with his job and with his book to notice. Then his wife walked out. She told him she was leaving. He begged her to stay. She was seeing somebody else, she told him. No, he didn't know the man she was seeing, and no, she wasn't going to tell Cooper his name, only that she loved her new man and she was happy with her new man and that Cooper now owed her half of the house and half of everything he had ever owned. He bought a bottle of whiskey the same day and drank half of it, and then started on her half too. He drank it at his office after work. He didn't want to go home. Didn't want to face the empty house. He just wanted to drink, surrounded by his files and his work, his classes over for the day, the students gone home.

He's always thought about how his life would be these days if his next decision had been different. He was drunk enough to think that driving was a good idea. That's what the booze did to you—you can make a thousand right decisions when you're sober, and when you're sober you know you would never drink and drive, but the booze changes things. It gets into your blood and tells you everything is going to turn out okay. So he made it out to the parking lot. There were only six cars in it, one of them his, spaces for a few hundred more. The night was cold, the ground covered in leaves, daylight savings was over and it was dark even though it was only seven-thirty, each day darker than the last now until the downslope to spring.

His keys were on the ground before he even realized what had happened. His hand was still by his car door, going through the motions of trying to unlock it. It was a few seconds before he realized what was happening, then a few seconds more to crouch down and pick them up. He should have called a taxi. Should have done more to stop his wife from leaving. Should have realized what was going on. Jesus, he felt so stupid, being cheated on like that and never knowing.

The girl had appeared from nowhere. Sometimes in his nightmares, he imagines her clawing her way out from Hell only meters away from him, or floating just above the ground with her feet never touching it, this beautiful demon who would change his life.

"Are you okay, Professor?" she asked, and no, he wasn't okay, his wife was a cheating whore and was going to take half of his life, and where the hell did the years go, his twenties and thirties drifting by like they were nothing, the years steamrolling on, he would be fifty the following year and he hated that, really fucking hated that.

"I'm fine," he said.

"Are you sure?"

"Positive," he answered, dropping his keys again.

"I'm one of your students," she said, and God, she was beautiful.

"Well, thanks for your time," he said, unsure exactly what he meant by that. He got his door unlocked.

"Listen," she said, "can I give you a lift home?"

"I'm not sure," he said, but the truth was he was sure. He'd love to be taken back to her house. They could have a few drinks and . . . and shit, that's not what she meant. She meant she would give him a lift to his house. "I really need my car, I have something early in the morning I have to deal with," he said. "I'll be fine."

"It's no problem," she said. "We'll take your car and you can pay for my taxi to get back."

And so the scene was set and on the car ride there he spoke little, thinking about his wife, about his job, about men taking what it was they wanted, and honesty being the best policy, he wanted this girl, wanted her more than anything, wanted her to make him feel young again.

"Want to come inside for a drink?" he asked, when she had pulled his car into his garage.

"I should be getting back."

"Just the one," he said. "I promise not to keep you. I'm a criminology professor," he said, "and I can tell you it's a crime to let a man about to turn fifty drink alone."

And so she had said yes, and three years later he isn't sure why she did, or how exactly things led to him making a pass at her. Her rejection had hurt, in fact it had hurt so much he wanted her to hurt too. That's how it started, the need to make her feel bad, to make his wife suffer, only this girl wasn't his wife, just a stand-in for her. The textbooks would say all that added up was a *trigger*. He knew it at the time. It started with a ride home and led to him dragging her into his bedroom and tearing off her clothes, forcing himself on her, his hand tight on her face the entire time, covering her eyes so she couldn't see him, and when it was done he lay there panting with her body pinned beneath him and the realization of what he had done came flooding through.

"I'm so sorry," he said, rolling off her. His head was buzzing from the alcohol and he felt sick.

She said nothing. She stared at the ceiling and, God, she could go a long time without blinking. Tears had formed a small stream down the side of her face.

"I . . . I don't know what happened," he said. "Please, please, I'm . . . I'm sorry."

He touched her shoulder. She didn't flinch away. She didn't move.

"Are you . . . are you okay?"

She wouldn't answer. Wouldn't look at him. Wouldn't move.

He started to panic. She would tell the police what had happened. He would lose his job. He would go to jail. Nobody would publish his book then. He sure as hell wouldn't win his wife back. And when he came out, what would he do? Nobody would ever respect him. Nobody would hire him. His future self would be lost.

The easiest solution was to kill her. Could he cross that line?

He had already crossed one, he could cross another. He thought about bundling her up in the car and dumping her somewhere. That part he could do. The strangling or stabbing part, no, that part he couldn't do.

"I have money," he said to her and it wasn't true. He owned the house with his wife and the mortgage was small, but now that she was gone he was going to have to buy her out for her half. When she wouldn't move, he sat up on the edge of the bed and pulled his pants back on. "It's yours. All of it," he said, and he meant it. He would sell the house and if there was anything left he would give it to her. His chest felt heavy and his breathing was forced, and he bent over and vomited on the floor. Immediately he felt better. Even the buzzing died down by half.

"I'll drive you home," he said, wiping his mouth on the bottom of his shirt, but of course he was in no condition to drive. "Let me help you with your clothes," he said, and he helped her and she did none of the work, just kept laying there, letting him move her, and the clothes didn't fit that well because they were torn and damaged. "Tomorrow we can go to the bank," he said. "How much? Oh, God, please, just tell me how much you want?"

She stayed unresponsive and he needed another drink, a drink would help him think, so he went back out to the living room, passing clumps of her hair in the hallway, strands that had been pulled out when he fought her into the bedroom. He leaned against the dining table and knocked back a shot of whiskey, then slowly sipped at another. His hands were shaking and there were spots of blood on his palms. The shot glass kept clicking against his teeth.

To this day he still doesn't know what she used to hit him. One moment he was leaning, the next the living room floor was rushing up to reach him. His face slapped into it, and when he came to he was tied up. He was spread-eagled, his legs tied to couch legs. His arms were over his head, tied to the TV cabinet. Something was in his mouth. His vision was foggy.

"You want to know how that felt?" she asked. "You want to know what I just went through?"

Her questions were calm. None of the words were stressed. It was like she was asking him if she could get him a drink.

He couldn't answer. She lifted a pair of pliers in her hand. They were his pliers. She must have taken them from the garage, and he's never seen them since. She didn't say anything. She put the pliers onto his testicle and squeezed. She didn't even hesitate. He heard something pop. Felt every nerve in his body catch fire. He screamed into the rag until he passed out, and when he came to he was alone, untied and bleeding on his carpet. He made his way to the hospital. He kept waiting for the police to arrive, but they never came.

A month passed. The student was reported missing. Nobody knew where she was. He knew he was the reason she had vanished. He thought she had killed herself somewhere. Part of him felt guilty, part of him felt relief, and the part of him that had lost his testicle was angry he hadn't been given the chance to kill her himself. That first year he thought about her every waking moment. Then he started to think of her less. Two years after the attack and he still hated her, but the anger had dulled, he didn't think about her constantly. Three years after the attack she was hardly in his thoughts anymore, and then she showed up in the papers last year. Her name was Melissa. She was on the front page, and he was sure it was her. There were differences, of course there were, a person can change a lot physically in three years if they want to, but it was her, and she was doing bad things. He couldn't understand the psychology. There must have been more to it than his attack on her. He wanted to know. He needed to understand. He wanted to kill her. What she was doing to other people, that was his fault. He knew that. He had made her into a monster. He wanted to feel bad about it too, but he didn't.

It had all been an accident. It was his wife's fault. If she hadn't cheated on him, none of it would have happened.

He wanted to track the girl down but there was no way to do it. He wasn't an investigator. Seeing her in the papers brought the anger back. He became obsessed again. He hadn't had a drink in three years, but this made him return to it. He wanted revenge.

He wanted that night with her back so he could do it differently. It would start the same but end with his hands around her throat.

He couldn't take that night back. He would sit in his living room staring at the wall while the bottle of whiskey disappeared in front of him. He would dream about what he would do to her if he found her. He would go to work the following day disguising his hangover, and nobody ever knew what was really going on inside his head.

Then he met Jane Tyrone.

She reminded him in some ways of Natalie Flowers. Same hair, young and pretty, same smile. She worked at his bank. He had gone in to deposit a check. She gave him a big smile that was part of service. He wanted the service to include seeing her naked. He wanted it enough that he followed her after work into a parking building in town. It was an impulsive thing to do, but also very simple. Just a matter of timing, really, as long as nobody else was around, and there wasn't. He walked up to her while she was unlocking her car. He smiled at her and she smiled back and she didn't recognize him. Then he reached behind her and banged her head down into the roof, once, twice, and a third time for luck. She was out cold. He put her into the trunk of her car and left her there for fifteen minutes until he returned with his own. He had to park a few spaces down, and he killed five minutes reading the newspaper until again there was nobody around, and then he made the switch.

He kept her alive for a week. That hadn't been the plan. There had been no plan, really. He had woken up that morning with no intent of harming anybody, and had ended it at the institution with her locked in a padded cell. He thought he would use her and dispose of her the way he should have disposed of that bitch three years earlier.

Things had changed. He found he began to like her, and part of him, there's no kidding himself here, part of him wanted to be liked by her too. Sometimes, within the moments after using her, he would tell her he was sorry, and tell her everything was going to be okay. In the beginning he thought he meant it. In the end he knew he didn't.

217

He kept her alive, he used her over and over, and each time he found himself not caring as much about her as the time before. He wasn't sure how long he wanted to keep her, but after seven days she just went and died on him. It was okay, because after seven days there was nothing left to be attracted to, nothing he hadn't done a dozen times to her already that he felt the urge to do again. It had been time to move on anyway. For both of them. It was bound to happen. People drift apart.

It's common knowledge that killers like to keep souvenirs, and it was no different for him. He had a digital camera in his briefcase. He used it every day with her. He took one photo, then another, and it turned out he enjoyed taking photos. It's a good thing too, because he liked to spend time looking at those pictures. It was a week's worth of fun compressed onto a microchip smaller than a fingernail. The irony is he actually thought of bringing her to Grover Hills. He needed an abandoned building, and this one suited his needs perfectly. However there were two others that were the same, two other mental institutions he used to visit to talk to the patients to write his book, both closed down within months of this one. In the end he settled on one of the locations to take the girls, a place called Sunnyview Shelter.

If he gets out of here alive, how much of his life can he return to? The camera has been destroyed, but what of the photographs on the flash drive behind his filing cabinet? There was another one too, hidden in his office at home, surely as melted and ruined as everything else in his house. He knew it was a bad idea hiding them at work, but he needed to be able to look at them any time he pleased.

The day he took Emma Green had been a lousy one. There had been another article in the previous Saturday's paper about Melissa X, or rather, Natalie Flowers. It was a feature piece that covered three pages and had pictures of her taken from a video recording the police had. The entire weekend he read that article over and over, each time a little more fueled by alcohol. Monday he went to work. The hangover was a bitch and a struggle to hide at work, but thankfully some of his classes were canceled because of the heat wave. There was a girl in his class who reminded him a little of Natalie. She worked at a café he went to sometimes. He went there to see her and nothing more, just to take a look at her and fantasize what it would be like to hurt her, and then that old man assaulted her in the parking lot. He first went toward her to help her, he's sure of that, because he was never going to harm another of his students because then the police might have questions for him. So he went to her aid and changed his mind. Just like that. His thought process went from helping her to hurting her in under a second and it was a mistake. He knew it then but couldn't help himself.

He was going to keep her for seven days like Jane Tyrone. He liked the symmetry. Other's would call that a signature. Taking the pictures was stupid. He knew it was stupid but took them anyway. It went against everything he had learned. There were rules you had to follow if you didn't want to get caught. He had broken them. Killers always ended up becoming smug enough and arrogant enough to think they won't get caught and they take bigger risks, and he knew, he absolutely knew that he was better than that. Better than all those smug bastards. It's unlikely the police have found the photos. They would have no reason to even look. At this point he's a victim, nothing more. Emma Green being a student of his doesn't look good for him, but at least the bank teller was a random stranger.

His fingertips are completely black with ink as he continues to stroke the newspaper. He turns it over and looks at the second page. A picture of Nurse Pamela Deans stares out at him from a black-and-white square about the size of his palm. There was no warmth to her, and every time he spoke to her he was sure it took all her energy to remain cordial. However she was extremely useful in his studies and exceptionally efficient. He always imagined her living alone in a house full of straight edges and starched bedsheets, perhaps a few cats, a small TV and a radio tuned only to classical music. Now she is dead, burned in the same way his house was burned.

Burned, no doubt, by Adrian.

This is bad. Really bad. If the police make the connection between the two fires, is it possible they'll connect everything to Grover Hills? Yesterday he'd have loved it if the police showed up to rescue him. But if they come today they'll find the girl who helped him, and who he killed in return for that help.

Again, that was stupid. For a man who knows a lot about killers, for a man who knows what their common mistakes are, why can he not stop himself before acting?

There is still blood on him. His clothes are stained, and there's a murder weapon with his prints on the other side of the door. He begins pacing the cell. The police will make the connection. At some point somebody will drive out here to take a look around. They're going to find the dead woman and there are going to be some tough questions. He has to get out of here. He has to kill Adrian. He has to make it look like Adrian killed the dead woman. He needs to destroy his clothes. If he escapes he can change and he can set the stage any way he wants to. As long as the camera or the photographs in his office haven't been found, there's no reason for the police to suspect him of anything.

He turns the newspaper over and goes to the front page where he saw the sketch earlier when Adrian was holding it. Up close it looks like his brother-in-law, except it's supposed to be Adrian, only it doesn't look much like Adrian.

Jesus.

He has to escape.

He has to convince Adrian to let him out of here.

It's time to try a different tactic.

chapter thirty-two

The study is tidier than I last left it. All the files have been swept up and taken. I move into the hallway and look outside the front door. No sign of anybody. Back in the study it's only a matter of time before what pages are left in the printer start curling in the heat. The flash drive is still hanging out of the front of the computer. I snatch it out and stuff it into my pocket. I go through the house room by room before heading outside and going around the property. I do a full sweep of the section then head back inside.

I'm still thinking it could have been somebody from Grover Hills who killed Daxter, but now that the Melissa X file has gone, I'm also thinking that it could have been Melissa. I'm not sure which one of those two possibilities scares me the most. What I am sure about is that I'm the world's biggest idiot for leaving the front door open, but front doors are open all across the city, people desperate for the breeze. I lock the front door now. I plug the flash drive into the computer and print out the rest of the document.

I give Schroder a call and update him.

"Jesus, Tate, how can you have been so careless? That file is confidential! Did they take the DVD too?"

"No, the DVD is still here," I tell him, and it is—it's still in the player.

"Well, at least that's something. If that footage was ever made public . . . God, what a nightmare that would be. Still, it's bad enough you lost the file."

"You should never have given it to me."

"Ah, I see, so it's my fault then."

"I didn't mean it like that," I tell him.

"Yes you did," he says, and he's right.

"I need another copy of the file."

"I'll think about it," he says. "So now what, now you're thinking maybe Natalie Flowers is the one who broke in and stole it and killed your cat?"

"The thought had crossed my mind."

"Listen, there's been an update. We've found the car that hit the dumpster behind the café."

"When?"

"A few hours ago."

"And you're only letting me know now?"

"I'm sorry, boss, you're right—you should have been the first person I told. Jesus, Tate."

"Okay, point taken," I say.

"Yeah, I'm sure you'll remember it. Anyway, we sent out the details to all the panel beaters in the city yesterday. We figured it was a long shot. I mean, it's not like somebody is going to abduct a girl and have his car looked at two days later, but we did it because it's procedure, and because it might not have come from the car that took Emma. One of them called us this morning saying he had a match to the color, and metal transfer from what could have been the dumpster, and the damage matched the height of the paint on the dumpster. So we checked it out, and sure enough, it was our car."

"And?"

222

"And a couple of detectives go around and speak to the owner. He's seventy-six-year-old Arnold Sweetman and they can tell right off the bat that he's got nothing to do with Emma's disappearance. He goes into the café at least once a week. He says he was sitting in his car getting ready to leave when a girl tried to steal his wallet. They show him a picture of Emma Green, and he tells them that's the girl."

"What?"

"That's what he said. He said he was sitting there when she opened up the door, leaned in, and tried to take his wallet from his pocket."

"Are you serious?"

"I know. It doesn't make sense. So the detectives take him down to the station and keep on questioning him. His answer doesn't change. He really thinks Emma Green was trying to mug him. So we check the side of his car for prints, and sure enough, we find a couple on the handle that belong to her."

"There must have been a reason she was opening it," I say. "I mean, she just isn't going to walk up to a car with somebody sitting in it, open the door, and try to mug them, especially right behind her work where people could recognize her."

"There is a reason," Schroder says. "After an hour, Sweetman asks for a lawyer, so the detectives have to leave him alone. His lawyer shows up, and when they go into the interview room Sweetman has fallen asleep, only he looks like he could be dead. So the lawyer puts his hand on Sweetman's shoulder and slowly tries to shake him awake, and when he comes to he starts screaming at his lawyer accusing him of trying to molest him. It only lasts five seconds, but it's possible the same thing happened the other night. The café owner remembers Sweetman being in there, and remembers him leaving at least an hour before Emma left. He probably went and sat in his car and fell asleep, and Emma came along and saw him and was concerned. She probably opened the door and he reacted the same way he did with his lawyer."

"And then Sweetman sped away," I say, finishing the story, "and

Emma was either abducted from the parking lot, or somewhere between there and her home by Cooper Riley."

"That's how it's looking. But none of it gets us any closer to finding where she is now," he says, and hangs up.

I'm thirty pages into Cooper's manuscript when a patrol car and a station wagon pull up outside. I return the gun to its hiding place beneath the mattress. Three men come to the door and none of them is Schroder. Two of them are officers and the other the crime scene technician. I lead them through to Daxter. One of the officers looks away and the other one groans. The crime scene technician stares at my cat as though he were a puzzle. The wire that was around his neck is still there. It's an unwound coat hanger. One end is wrapped around Dax's neck, the other hooked over the edge of the gutter on the roof. I show them the grave.

"Jesus, this is sick," one of the officers remarks.

I agree with him. The two officers take a customary look around the backyard. I tell them about the break-in. They keep glancing at each other as if confirming a suspicion they had about me earlier, or out of an attraction for each other. One of them heads out to the street while the other goes through the house for a few minutes before joining him in canvassing the neighborhood, leaving me with the forensics guy. His name is Brody and I've worked with him before but he seems to have wiped any memory of that from his system. His forearms are red from the sun and his nose is peeling and he has a palm-sized bald spot that's burning and he keeps sniffing, maybe an allergy to the cat. He goes about ignoring me, spending some time inside then coming back out, taking plaster casts of the footprints before dusting the shovel for prints.

"There's a couple of sets on here," he says, "we'll need to compare them against yours."

"Probably against my parents too," I say. "They've been looking after the garden for me."

"Well, there's a few sets there, hopefully we can find a match. See there?" he says, pointing to the base of the fence. "That's dirt transfer. Your cat killer left that way, and I'd guess he arrived that way too. I'd say he watched you burying the cat and drove around the block to your front door. There's plenty of shoe prints too, which we'll try to match up, but there'll be a thousand identical shoes. There's enough wear and tear in them that if you bring me something I can match it."

"What else?"

"We've got prints inside. We got them over the computer desk. They might all end up being yours, but we'll run them. We might get lucky. Between the study and the shovel, we might get a hit if this guy has a record."

"Nothing," one of the officers says, coming back through the house. "We've gone right up and down the street—nobody saw anything."

"Yeah, that sounds about right," I say. Other than the stoned guy who lived opposite Cooper Riley, the last time somebody in this country actually admitted witnessing a crime was around 1950.

"We'll run the prints and get the cat autopsied. You should fill the hole back in and stay awake tonight in case he comes back," Brody says.

They pack everything up. Daxter is slipped into a dark black bag made from thick plastic. I follow them out to the street.

"I want him back when you're done," I say, nodding toward the bag.

"I'll make sure of it," Brody says.

I make sure the doors are locked. I retrieve the gun. My knee is getting sore again. I refill the grave. I get a strong sense of déjà vu. I hold out hope the fingerprints will get a match. If it is somebody from Grover Hills they might have been sentenced there after committing a crime. We could have a name within an hour. We could have Emma Green by the end of the day. Or they might match Melissa's fingerprints, which are on record from surfaces she touched when she murdered Detective Calhoun. If they do belong to her, how did she know I was working on the case? Only Schroder knew. No, it can't have been her.

I sit in the shade and read another chunk of Cooper's manuscript. I've read similar things before, written by profilers from the UK or the US, and I imagine this is what Cooper was attempting to do. Cooper's one reads like a textbook. There is no flair, no emotion in those words, not like other books I've read where the author is genuinely disgusted and upset about the cases they're writing about, the kind of author who you think was crying into his keyboard as he detailed each victim he had to look at. Some of the names in here I remember from when I was on the force, there's even one that I arrested, a man by the name of Jesse Cartman who raped and killed and digested parts of his sister—and not in that order. Cooper attempts to explain the criminal mind. He tries to get inside their heads. It works when police profilers do it, because they're dealing with people who for the most part are sane. Many of the people locked away at Grover Hills and the other institutions Cooper visited were purely delusional, which skews all of Cooper's data. He's not studying a criminal mind, he's studying one where two and two equal nineteen. He struggles to draw connections from one patient to the next. Some have bad backgrounds, some come from good homes, some are making stuff up. He will make one point and then a chapter later he will contradict it. This could explain why the book is still in manuscript form and not for sale in bookshops. Or he stopped trying. The version I got from the university hadn't been touched in three years. Did Cooper give up writing after he was attacked?

I jot down every name I come across, thinking of each as a potential suspect. I list them by the institution they were kept in, focusing mainly on Grover Hills. In the end I have a list of forty-one names. It's possible one of these people abducted Cooper Riley and killed Pamela Deans, and it's equally as possible none of them did. It's possible the two things are unrelated, it's possible they're related but by different means.

Forty-one names. I start with the Internet, using an online newspaper site and running their names through the search engine. I rule out six of them due to suicides. Another six are currently in jail for crimes ranging from breaking-and-entering to rape, one for repeated defecation in the middle of a shopping mall, another for killing his mother. There is little information on the others, and none on the rest. Jesse Cartman, the man who ate part of his sister twelve years ago, was released along with all the others, having served the term equivalent to what he would have done if he had gone to jail, and on the days he remembers to take his medication he works as a caretaker at the Botanical Gardens.

Other than Pamela Deans, Cooper doesn't mention any of the other staff, and I can't find any other nurses or doctors or orderlies mentioned online. Getting hold of any medical records is going to be impossible. Schroder would have shown the sketch to some of the doctors and nurses who used to work at Grover Hills. Maybe he already has a name.

Grover Hills.

It's at the center of all of this and I don't even know what it looks like.

Is it possible that's where Cooper is now? It's an abandoned building that would make an excellent place to hide out.

Is it possible an ex-patient has returned to it, thinking of Grover Hills as home?

I load up the city map on the computer and write down directions to the abandoned mental institution, grab my gun, and jump into the car.

chapter thirty-three

"They're going to come here," Cooper says.

"What? Who are you talking about?"

"The police. They're going to come here. You need to let me out. We need to go into hiding," Cooper says.

"We already are in hiding," Adrian answers, disappointed at Cooper. He doesn't want to play more of these games. Why can't Cooper just like him? It would all go so much easier if he would. To be honest, he's beginning to find it frustrating. So far he's had a pretty good day—he dug up Theodore Tate's cat and bought Cooper a newspaper and had a good breakfast and soon he's going to sit down outside in the shade and start reading Cooper's book. Why does Cooper have to ruin it with more lies?

Cooper holds the newspaper up. Watching his face on the other side of the small glass panel is like watching a small TV set. Actually, it's more like watching the news where it's one bad story after another.

"The police won't come here," Adrian says. "They have no reason to."

"They have every reason to," Cooper says, waving the newspaper back and forth. "You've given them every reason."

"You're lying."

"No, Adrian, goddamn it, I am not lying. I can't afford to be caught here covered in blood, and nor can you."

"But . . ."

"Listen to me. The paper," he says, waving it again. "You're on the front page."

Adrian shakes his head. No, if he were on the front page he would have seen himself.

"Take a look," he says, and holds the paper over the glass.

Adrian takes a look. The sketch he saw earlier stares back at him, but it doesn't look like him, not really. Well, maybe a little.

"That's not all," Cooper says, pulling it away.

"It's okay, nobody is going to . . ."

"Shut the hell up," Cooper says, and he bangs the door with his palm and Adrian jumps. He goes quiet, unsure what to do. "You need to listen," Cooper says, carrying on. "We don't have much time."

"I . . ."

Cooper bangs the door again. "I demand you listen to what I say."

Adrian is scared now. He used to get spoken to like this all the time and he doesn't like it now any more than back then, but he does as he's told.

"It's simple if you think about it. Just follow the dots," Cooper says.

"What dots?" Adrian answers, confused as well as scared.

"The dots you've made."

"I don't make dots," he says, shaking his head.

"You abducted me. You burned down my house. Somebody saw you, and somebody from Grover Hills will recognize you. And you burned down Nurse Deans's house."

"How do you know about that?"

"It's on page bloody two!" Cooper says, turning the newspaper and pushing it against the glass again. "And let me guess, you burned down her house the same way you burned down mine."

"It worked so well the first time," Adrian says, talking at the newspaper now, "so yeah, but I burned them down in a different order and . . ."

"And the police have made the connection," Cooper says, pulling the paper away and folding it up.

"I don't see how."

"They will have," Cooper says. "You killed Nurse Deans, didn't you?"

"She called me a freak," he says, clenching his fists, and damn it, he didn't want to confess that to Cooper, not yet.

"Is there anything else you've done?"

"No," he says, thinking about Theodore Tate. He killed Tate's cat, and tonight he was going to go back to the house and knock on the door and shoot Tate with the Taser. He's starting to think Tate will be an easier item to maintain.

"The police probably already know who you are," Cooper says.

"No, no, they can't."

"They're going to send somebody out here to look around."

"Why?"

"Because it's routine. Because they know I've been abducted by an ex-patient and they know that same ex-patient has to have taken me somewhere and they know this place is as good as any."

"It doesn't make sense. How will they know I'm an ex-patient?"

"You took my book off Theodore Tate. The police know about it. They'll connect the dots."

"Oh," Adrian says, understanding what the dots are now. "Is that really what will happen?"

"They're on their way, Adrian. They may only be five minutes away. Or five hours. But they'll be here. Today. Trust me. And if you don't trust me all you have to do is wait around and see for yourself. Then they'll take away your collection."

"I don't want them to do that," Adrian answers.

"And they'll put us both in jail."

"I'd rather kill you than lose you."

Cooper goes quiet for a few seconds. "Let's make sure it doesn't come to that. First thing we need to do is figure out where we can go."

"Go?"

"We can't stay here, Adrian."

"But this is my home."

"Not anymore."

He's confused. "But . . ."

"Listen, Adrian, if we stay here we're both going to jail. We only need to find somewhere else for a few days. The police will come here and they'll find nothing, and then they'll move on and have no reason to come back. We can give it two days, three at the most, then come back here. It can still be your home."

He thinks he understands, and he's certainly keen to make Cooper think he understands everything. He's completely divided. Part of him believes Cooper is right and the police may well be on their way, and just as equally he thinks Cooper may be trying to deceive him. It's a huge risk. His instinct is to hide and see if the police come, but if they do they'll take Cooper away and he meant what he said earlier, he'd rather kill Cooper than lose him.

"Where will we go?" he asks.

"I know a place," Cooper says. "A couple of them actually. Eastlake Home and . . ."

"Sunnyview Shelter," Adrian finishes. "That's where you took Emma Green."

"How . . ."

"I'm not as stupid as you think," Adrian says, enjoying this feeling of . . . of what? He doesn't know the name for it because he's never felt it before. A word like super, but longer. And with a t in it somewhere.

"You were there? Is that how you knew about me?"

"It doesn't matter," Adrian answers, not wanting to tell Cooper how he had been following him for days before collecting him. "If I agree to take you there, how do I know you won't try to escape?"

"You can do what you want to me," Cooper says. "You can tie me up if you must, but please, Adrian, we must leave now. I cannot afford to be caught here."

"Because you killed that girl."

"Yes."

"For two days," Adrian says.

"Two days."

"And then we come back."

"And then we come back," Cooper says.

"I'll pack up some stuff and hide everything away," Adrian says. "Nobody will ever know we were here."

chapter thirty-four

Grover Hills is a twenty-minute drive out of the city to the west, taking me well past the airport and the prison and beyond, into the Canterbury Plains, made up of farms with barbed-wire or electric fences keeping livestock and wheat at bay. It gets even hotter out there the further I get from the city, the extra kilometers west bringing me closer to the sun.

I take a turn off the highway and begin following a series of neglected roads. The institution is hard to find because once you start heading down these roads there aren't as many street signs as in the city. Either the council didn't care about this part of the world or the locals took them down in the hope strangers would get lost out here long enough to enter the gene pool. Roads go from tarmac to stone and back to tarmac, changing from intersection to intersection where you have to slow down every few minutes to give way to a farmer moving sheep or cows from one paddock to another, the farmer high up on his tractor, sheep dogs barking and running around with their tongues hanging out, desperate for water and attention. A few days ago, coming back from the prison, we passed these kinds of sights, and the appeal at becoming a farmer and working the land hasn't grown in that time.

I get lost and pull off the side of the road into short grass with deep tire ruts from tractor tires, the car bumping up and down. I keep the windows rolled up and the air-conditioning cranked up on maximum. I study the map for five minutes. Map reading has never been my strong suit. I trace over the lines with my finger wishing my wife was here because she'd ask one of the farmers for directions. Whenever we went anywhere new, I'd drive and she'd read the map and Emily would sleep in the backseat and it was a dynamic we were all happy with. I take an educated guess at where I might be on the map but am probably better off just flipping a coin. I carry on driving. It takes me another fifteen minutes driving over unpaved roads to find the place. I figure if you weren't crazy when the courts or doctors committed you to Grover Hills, you certainly would be after the drive.

The start of the driveway has a couple of big oak trees acting as sentries, then dozens of silver birches lining the way, their branches thin and twisted and silent in the still air. I park out front and step out and dirt and dust settles behind me and covers the car. It follows me as I walk up to the building. Grover Hills is run-down and nature is trying to reclaim it. Most of the grounds are knee deep in wilted grass and overgrown shrubs that look like giant weeds. The building started out white last century and may have been painted once or twice since then, but certainly not since the moon landing. It's a giant building that wouldn't look out of place on a plantation, lots of clapboard and small windows and plenty of rooms. Some of the boards are twisting and others are rotting but all in all the building looks to be in pretty good condition. Abandoned, no doubt about it, but certainly habitable. One whole side of the building is covered in ivy, streamers of it climbing up the walls and entwined in the clay roof tiles. The amazing thing is that nothing has been vandalized. People in this country have a habit of finding places no matter how hidden in the middle of nowhere they are. They find them and smash the windows and knock holes in walls and spray paint giant penises all over them.

The rental car is the only thing out here making a sound. No breeze, no birds, just the car engine pinging as it cools down. It's eerie. It's like I've gone way off the map and into a different world, crossing over some *Star Trek* alternate reality barrier along the way. In prison there was always sound. The humming of the fluorescent lights. A toilet somewhere being flushed. Snoring, coughing, yelling, laughing, footsteps and fighting, air-conditioning. It became white noise, one sound canceling out another. But out here there's nothing. I take a few steps forward, expecting my feet to make no sound, but they do, they pad against the ground and make exactly the amount of sound I'd expect them to make anywhere else, and the magical spell of being transported to another land is broken.

I start by walking the perimeter, the gun firmly in my hand. Out front the ground is mostly stone and dusty dirt and some areas of sand; nothing but weeds poking through it every few meters or so, there's a path that's broken up by nature and time, triangle corners of cement broken and pushing upward like merging tectonic plates. There is absolutely nothing to suggest it rained last night. Off the path and I start treading carefully, not wanting to step into a rabbit hole and disappear or break my ankle. The grass gets thicker and scratches my legs. I do a circuit of the house. Behind it there's even more vegetation than out front. There's plenty of mold all over the walls. The dirt is softer. I make it back around to the front without seeing anything of interest. No people, no cars, no graves, just two lines of compacted stones and dirt in the driveway where cars have come and gone, no way of knowing when the last one was here. There's a block of trees about a hundred meters away that is the start of a series of woods.

I keep the gun pointed down as I walk. Grover Hills feels empty. I have the feeling you get when you knock on somebody's door and you know nobody is going to answer. But I still keep the gun out. The front entrance is a pair of wide double doors. I step up onto the wooden porch and try them. The left one swings open noisily, the hinges like that of an opening coffin that's been unearthed. The sun is so high that the angle stops it from gaining entry through the doors because of the veranda. It's dark inside. Not nighttime dark, but the kind of dark you'd get stepping into a boarded-up church. The air inside is dry and a little cooler the further inside I go, but not much. It doesn't feel like anybody is here, but the building doesn't quite feel abandoned either. It feels like some*thing*, not some*body*, is here.

It doesn't look like the kind of building you'd expect an institution to be. It doesn't have long white corridors with doors locking them off every fifteen meters. Instead it looks like a giant farmhouse, lots of wood everywhere, a very New Zealand version of what we must have thought mental institutions looked like back then. The windows have wire grills over them. There are lots of rooms, and I can see that each one of them has a lock on it. There's a staircase leading up to a second floor. I haven't had much luck with staircases lately so I start with the ground floor. I follow the path of the hallway, opening doors and looking into bedrooms on my way to a large communal area where maybe there was a TV set and a Ping-Pong table. There are still couches here, all of them in poor condition, some of them facing the windows overlooking the fields. There's a door that leads to the kitchen. There is no sign of life, but there is the feeling of being watched. It's creepy. I can't shake the feeling that all the dark thoughts from the patients who were locked up out here have formed some malevolent entity that's haunting the soul of this building, and if that entity came forth my gun would do me no good. In the kitchen there's a large fridge that looks a hundred years old. I open it up and it's empty except for layers of mold and no light comes on. I flick one of the kitchen light switches and nothing happens. No power. There's a long stainless-steel bench with two sinks in it, there are clearings in the dust, circles and lines where objects have been placed and then moved very recently.

I open the rest of the cupboards and drawers and find them empty except for a dead mouse. I head back to the staircase. It's not soaking in petrol so I take it. On the top floor I find pretty much the same as the ground floor, same layout, same kind of communal area, but no kitchen. There are lots of spiderwebs caught in every available corner and nobody tied up anywhere. Mouse shit against the edges of the walls. Sunlight angles through the windows and lights up the dust raised by my footsteps. Most of the rooms still have some furniture left in them, single beds with old foam mattresses, some chests of drawers scarred by scratches and stains. The bathrooms are full of hard enamel edges with external pipes lining the walls. One of the bedrooms is cleaner than the others, no dust on the drawers. Walking around the place it's impossible to sense anything good ever happened here. Impossible to know how much help those who needed it really got once they came here.

The bedrooms on the north side of the building are hot, enough sun coming through the narrow windows to heat every room, but on the south side the rooms are cold even though it's heading up to one hundred and ten degrees outside. There are other rooms, two of them with doors that have latches on the outside of them. I open them up, the walls and ceiling and floor inside are padded.

I head downstairs. I take the hallway in the opposite direction from before. More bedrooms. More bathrooms. I open up a door that leads into a basement. The stairs are poorly lit, and I reach out and swipe at the light switch on the side of the brick wall more out of habit than hope, and nothing happens. The stairs seem to lead down into a pit, the only light to hit them coming from behind me, my body casting a shadow. I start down them, expecting my feet to disappear in darkness, but instead my eyes slowly adjust to the gloom.

I follow the stairs to the concrete floor. There's another room ahead of me, this one sealed off by an iron door. A cell of some kind. The door has a small window and I look through it but can't see much beyond. I tap my knuckle against the door and it echoes through the room. There's a latch on this side of it that is unlocked. I swing open the door where there is even less light. There's a dark shape against the wall that turns out to be a bed, and there's a bad smell in here, maybe stale body fluids. I step away from the door to let more light into the room. The bed has an old mattress and a pillow that looks like it could contain about a thousand different kinds of germs. There's nothing else in there. I step back into the main room. There's an empty bookcase on this side of the cell, an old couch, an old coffee table. I try to imagine people being brought down here, locked in this room and kept in the darkness. Did these rooms predate the padded rooms upstairs? Or was this basement used for the worst of the patients? And why the couch, did people sit down here and relax while others were locked up? How long were people kept down here, and how many people knew about it? Is this standard practice? I can't imagine that it is. A room like this may have been necessary. Jesse Cartman, the man who bit off pieces of his sister's flesh, probably spent time down here. It may have been the only way to keep the others safe. As bad as this cell is, if the padded rooms upstairs were full, then there wasn't anywhere else for those people in those moments. Only if that were the case, why not pad this cell too?

The person who killed Pamela Deans—how much time did he spend down here?

More than ever I feel like somebody is watching me.

On the way back up the stairs I notice the dark stains. They look like oil stains, dark patches on the stairs. I reach down and push my finger against it, whatever the stain is it's dry, but my fingertip comes away with a red powdery film across it. Could be blood. Could be tomato juice. There's lots of it.

I head outside and am thankful for the heat of the sun. I lean back against the car and stare at the building. No sign of Cooper. No sign of Emma Green. No sign of whoever killed my cat. Just furniture and benches with spaces in the dust and what could be blood on the basement steps, which could be a day old or five years old.

I pass Schroder on the way back into town while still on one of the narrow nowhere streets. He's parked on the side of the road with another detective, they're standing outside with a map sprawled out over the hood, two patrol cars behind him. That means he's going to Grover Hills with the idea he's going to find Cooper Riley. He looks up as I drive toward him. He sees it's me and shakes his head slowly. I give him a small salute. He rolls his eyes and grins for about two seconds before the frown slips back into place. He looks down at the map and I drive past, ribbons of dirt coming off the tires and flooding the air, a wall of it between him and my rearview mirror as I find my way back to the highway.

I drive back past the same paddocks. The same guys in the same tractors are plowing the same fields and moving the same bunches of animals back and forth. I pass the prison and don't feel any sense of longing. There's a dead cow just off the side of the road covered in flies about a hundred meters past the big *Christchurch* sign. I drive down Memorial Avenue where the houses are big and cold-looking and the trees out front are even bigger, this part of town screaming family money, women weighed down with jewelry sitting on front porches ordering the gardeners about. Traffic is thick and the air-conditioning in the rental keeps me sane. When I get into town I find a parking space opposite the museum where approximately forty Asian tourists are standing next to a bus taking photographs of each other, all smiles and waves, unaware the police might end up going through their photos later in the week to figure out what happened to one of the group who went missing. I load up the parking meter and three bucks gets me an hour's worth of parking, putting the council's greed on a par with that of the criminals. I walk the thirty meters to the entrance of the Botanical Gardens, the front of it lined with a green iron-bar fence bolted into rock and mortar and streaked in bird shit. I buy a newspaper on the way, tear off the front page, and toss the rest in a recycling bin.

The Gardens is the one place in the city you can guarantee the plants are getting watered as it's a pretty big drawing card for the tourists. The gardens cover thirty hectares of land, the Avon River winding through it like a fat black snake. Say what you will about Christchurch, but this is easily one of the most beautiful places in the country. Every direction is blanketed in color with flowers in full bloom, some pathways lined with tulips, others with evergreen bushes, trees and flowers and shrubs and ducks all living in peace, nature getting along.

There are plenty of people enjoying the day, most of them sitting in the shade. There are couples lying in the grass, men lying on their backs in the soft lawn, straddled by women, lots of bumping and grinding going on beneath the flowing skirts. Kids in kayaks are paddling up the Avon, splashing water at their friends and having a good time. I make my way to the small tourist center. A severely overweight woman behind the counter who isn't aware that wearing a tight tank-top is a crime against humanity tells me where I can find Jesse Cartman. I follow her instructions to a giant glass house in the middle of the gardens, home to about two thousand ferns with an offshoot room that houses dozens of cacti. The air surrounding the ferns is thick and warm and moist and a few breaths inside make me sleepy. There's a concrete rectangular walkway within the enclosure surrounding the plants, with a second level of the same thing above.

Jesse towers over me by about twenty centimeters but looks thin enough to slip under a door. He looks the same in some ways since I last saw him, but vitally different in many others. When he was seventeen he was diagnosed with depression, at nineteen he was diagnosed as a paranoid schizophrenic, at twenty his parents made an urgent call to the police for help. We got to the family house to find his father pinning Jesse against the floor, and his mother cradling his dead sister. He's thirty-five now, and in the years between he's been medicated and something must have worked, because now he's clean-shaven with his hair neatly combed and, as far as I'm aware, hasn't tried to eat anybody since his release. His clothes are tidy with his sleeves rolled up revealing darkly tanned forearms. He turns off the hose and turns toward me when he senses somebody staring.

"I know you from somewhere," he says, "you're either a doctor or a cop."

"I'm not a doctor," I tell him.

"You were there when I was arrested," he says, and I'm impressed with his memory. "Officer somebody, right?" he says, smiling, and for a creepy moment I think he's about to offer his hand, the same hand that dug into his sister to pull out the soft meat. He doesn't.

"It's detective now," I tell him, figuring if I'm going to lie, I may as well give myself a promotion at the same time. "How you doing, Jesse?" I ask.

240

"Good. Things are good now," he says, and they seem to be. The darkness that was in his eyes when we arrested him is gone, replaced by a light that the magic pills are giving him. "You know, the meds keep me in shape. Problem is the better they make me feel, the worse I feel about what I did to my sister, and that makes me want to stop taking them."

Before I can say anything, he holds up his hand, full of calluses with dirt packed into the wrinkles in his palms. "Don't worry, I know how that sounds, and I owe it to her to keep taking them. I owe it to my whole family to feel bad about what I done. Back then things were so different. There were so many voices and I could never sleep because they always kept me awake, so many I could never focus on them. Now the only voice I hear is my own. So why are you here? My therapist ask you to check up on me? I only missed the appointment because it was my sister's birthday and I had to, you know, spend the day out at her grave."

"I'm here to talk to you about Grover Hills."

"Why?" he asks, for the first time sounding defensive.

"You recognize this guy?" I ask, holding up the sketch from the newspaper.

He nods. "That's my dad," he says. "He died a few years ago. Why do you have his picture?"

"It's not your dad," I tell him. "It's a sketch of a man I'm looking for."

"No, it's definitely my dad. I recognize him."

I fold the sketch back into my pocket. "Jesse, I want you to tell me what happened at Grover Hills."

"I was sick when I was sent there. The doctors made me better."

"What about the basement?"

He turns the hose back on and starts watering some of the plants. Water splashes off the ferns back toward him. It soaks into the plants and the soil and a string of water runs back down from the tip of the hose onto his hand and down his arm. Cartman tries whistling but he can't do it, can only blow air hard through pursed lips. I fold the newspaper page into my pocket, then I pick up a section of the hose and bend it in half to kill the flow. He turns toward me and looks defeated, his eyes cast downward.

"The basement, Jesse."

"What . . . what basement?" he asks. "I don't remember the basement."

"It had a cell in it."

"I don't want to talk about it," he says, refusing to look up.

"Is that where you got locked away when you couldn't be controlled?"

"That's . . . that's not what the basement was for."

"What then?"

"I don't want to talk about it."

"You remember talking to Cooper Riley?"

He nods. "He wanted me to tell him about my sister and why I hurt her. He wanted to know what it was like for me growing up. He had lots of questions about my parents, the kind of questions that told me he thought part of my problem was them. I didn't like him much."

"You ever tell him about the basement?"

"Of course not. Nobody was allowed to mention it. Nobody would have believed me anyway, and if I had told him I would have been sent down there."

I keep pressing him. "What went on in that room? You were forced to sleep in there, right?"

"Sometimes, but only a couple of times for me." He wipes at some tears hanging on the edges of his eyes then sniffs loudly.

"Were you beaten down there?"

"In a sense."

"What else happened?"

"What do you think?" he asks. "Some of us deserved it, I guess, for what we did. What happened down there, they were the kind of things we'd done to other people."

"Please, Jesse, it's important you tell me everything."

"I've been reading the news and I know what you want. You're looking for Cooper Riley and he never knew anything about the

Scream Room," he says, "and . . ." He stops talking, realizing what he's said. "Shit," he says. "Please, please don't tell anybody I told you."

"The Scream Room?"

"I have to get back to work," he says.

"Jesse, this is important. If you've been reading the newspapers, then you'll know I'm looking for a missing girl."

"I know," he says. "That's what we called it. That room. We called it the Scream Room."

"You were sent down there and tortured?"

"Sometimes we were sent down there just as punishment. The room was to keep us in line. But other times the Twins would take us down there."

"The Twins?"

"They were a pair of orderlies. They were identical in the way they liked to make people hurt," he says. "A place like that, there were lots of people, you know? And the room wasn't always a Scream Room, it's like you said, it was used mostly to control people. The Twins used to charge people. They'd find relatives of those the patients had hurt and they'd offer them the chance for revenge. They'd make money on our pain. Other times they'd just take us down there for . . . for what I think passed as fun. At least for them."

"How often did this happen?" I ask.

"You don't believe me."

"I didn't say that."

"You don't need to. I can see it in you."

He's right. I don't believe him—but I do think he believes himself. Going out and finding family members and charging them for the thrill of revenge just doesn't work in any kind of reality. Too many people would have to be pretty bloody fantastic at keeping such a big secret. None of this is getting me closer to finding Emma Green.

"Convince me," I tell him. "How often did this happen?"

He shrugs. "All the time. People were always dying down there. A patient would be taken down there for an hour and come out dead on a stretcher."

"And nobody knew?"

"Of course people knew, but nobody cared. It's not hard to believe," he says, but he's wrong—it is hard to believe. "If it was your sister I'd killed and you had the chance to make me hurt for a hundred bucks or whatever it is they charged, wouldn't you jump at it?"

I don't know. It would depend on whether the person had faked their illness to get away with murder, or if they really were sick. That's how I look at it now. Under the circumstances, who knows? Others would call the police or the health-care system. A story like that couldn't get shut down no matter how hard everybody worked to contain it. It would spill out into the media, and a story like this would have been pure gold. It would have made all the papers across the country and been picked up internationally. It would have been big headlines.

"Define all the time," I tell him.

He shrugs again and water drips off the hose. "Every few months or so."

I do the math. Every few months. Six people a year. Ten years would be sixty people. No way sixty people are going to pay their money and head downstairs and beat the hell out of somebody with a baseball bat or hammer. I don't see it.

What I can believe is it happening once or twice. There could be some truth in what he's saying. If it did, it must have felt good for the person getting revenge. I wonder how good it felt when their hour was up. How many went home and threw up, how many wanted to come back for more. "And you told nobody."

"Who'd believe me? Even you don't."

"I've seen the room," I tell him, but it's still not enough. I believe people suffered down there with the bed and dirty blanket and dirty pillow, but not for money, and not by family members out looking for revenge.

"Yeah, well, I didn't tell anybody. None of us did. Rumors don't amount to much when they're being told by crazy people, and half the people who came out of that place are dead now and the other half still fucking crazy. After that first guy got killed down there, the

Twins would start taking others down there. Sometimes we'd be beaten. Sometimes just humiliated. And made to scream. And our screams couldn't be heard."

"What about . . ."

"I don't want to talk about it anymore."

"Jesse . . ."

"I mean it," he says, looking right at me and holding up his hand, and his eyes flare with the darkness I saw in them years ago. "I hate that I remember it all. You want me to stop taking the drugs so I can forget?"

"Okay, Jesse," I say, still holding the hose. "No more questions about the room."

"I want you to leave now."

"I have to find Emma Green."

"She was pretty," he says. "She reminded me of . . ." he trails off and looks down at the puddle forming around his feet.

"Of your sister?"

"I said I want you to leave," he says quickly.

"You ever see Pamela Deans once you were released?"

"Never."

"What happened to you? Where'd you go?"

He drops the hose. "What do you want from me?"

"Your help," I say. "If Emma reminds you of your sister, then you owe it to her to help her. This is your chance at some redemption, Jesse. Don't let it pass you by."

He looks up at the ceiling and keeps his gaze up there as he comes to a decision. When he looks back at me, his face is tight with anger. "A bunch of us were sent to a halfway house," he says. "I was allowed to move out about six months ago. I have my own place now and I always show up to work and I never miss my doctor's appointments and always take my meds. I'm fine now. I'm no longer a danger to society," he says, and he says it as though he's rehearsed the lines over and over, as if he were forced to memorize them on the day Grover Hills was shut down and he was sent forth into the world to fend for himself.

"The guy from the picture, it also looks like another guy who might have been there too."

"Where? The halfway house?"

"Both. The Grove," he says, "that's what we called it. He was there and at the halfway house. I really can't remember his name."

"Did he have a habit of killing and digging up pets?"

He pulls back a little in disgust. "What? No, no, not that I know of. Jesus, that's wrong," he says, and I picture the day we found him after he'd had his hands deep inside his sister. I wonder what would have gotten the same *wrong* reaction from the predrug Jesse Cartman.

"The Twins have names?"

He bends down and picks the hose back up. "Just the Twins. Twin One and Twin Two."

"Where is this halfway house?" I ask him.

"Town. Worcester Street," he says, and gives me the address.

I thank him for his time, not real sure how I feel about Jesse Cartman. Back when I first saw what he had done, all I wanted to do was put a bullet between his eyes. Now he's a different person. It's as though the man who killed his sister has disappeared, and this new version of him has to live with that guilt. For the first time it really sinks in that he was a victim back then too, a victim of a sickness he couldn't control, a victim who slipped through the cracks along with others who, with the right medication in the first place, never needed to have hurt anybody.

If he were a criminal, he'd have been locked away. He'd have been released from jail within the last couple of years, and he'd have come out a far more violent man. At least this way there's a chance he can function in society.

"I truly am better now," he says, as if reading my thoughts.

"I truly hope you are," I tell him, aware the only thing stopping him from trying to eat somebody else are a few small pills that he pops every morning along with his cornflakes when he wakes up to carry on with his normal life.

chapter thirty-five

The walls are blurry and sway a little when Cooper starts coming around. There's a metallic taste in his mouth and he probes it with his finger. He's bitten down on the side of his tongue, the flesh torn and swollen.

There is no light coming into the room. He can tell by feel that he's in a padded cell. He's either in Sunnyview or Eastlake. Most likely it's Sunnyview. Adrian must have followed him out here the other night since he knows about Emma Green, and he certainly would want to hide somewhere he was somewhat familiar with. Cooper doesn't remember any of the trip here. In the end he had to accept Adrian was going to shoot him with the Taser, but it was the only way if he wanted to change location. The police are probably already at Grover Hills and he couldn't afford to be found there covered in a dead girl's blood. They'd arrest Adrian and he'd tell them everything he knew about Cooper, including what he knew about Emma Green, which was turning out to be quite a lot. Adrian would have led the police straight here. The police would be saving Cooper only to crucify him.

He's done with the baby steps. Now he has to go full throttle. It's a three-part plan. Escape. Kill Adrian. And make up a story to put him in the clear. It's all going to work out. In fact, there's no reason he can't come out of all this looking like a hero and write his book. And, if he can get hold of the file Adrian was holding up earlier, he might be able to track down Natalie Flowers.

God, that would make all of this worth it.

Unless the cops have found the photographs.

That's what he needs to determine once he gets out of here. He'll have to return to his office and see if the pictures are still there. If they are then the three-part plan will work out. If they're gone, then the three-part plan has to change. Escape. Kill Adrian. And get the hell out of New Zealand. He doesn't know exactly how somebody goes about doing something like that, but if people dumber than him can flee the country, then there shouldn't be any reason he can't too.

He walks the room. It's completely padded. Not just the walls, but the floor too. He jumps up but can't reach the ceiling. It might be padded too. There might also be a light up there. He walks a grid formation and finds nothing else in the room with him. One of these walls has a door in it, and he finds the join in the padded wall and can pull it back barely enough to reveal the door frame. Light comes in around it. He tugs at the wall hoping to tear it away, but it's no use. He finds a mail-sized slot in the door at head height. He can't open it from this side. It's hot in here and stuffy. There will be no power to the building, and even if there was there'd be no air-conditioning in this room. These were never designed to be comfortable—only designed to stop the crazy from banging themselves into oblivion.

The room is slightly bigger than the last cell he was in, cleaner, and much hotter. He'll have to speak to Adrian, see what he can do about the heat. And he's got no bucket to piss into this time and no water to drink.

When he brought the girls here he only spent time with them at night and the only heat in the room was coming from the flashlights he brought. He made Emma Green drink a bottle of water before leaving her, but that was . . . what? He's lost track of time.

Three days? Four? And he left two more bottles with her. He kept her tied up, but the bottles were open and she could roll onto her side and sip them. He was going to bring her more when he returned, along with some food. He needed her to stay healthy long enough to enjoy her. The first night he was happy with keeping her tied while he cut away her clothes and took photos. The duct tape over her eyes kept her from seeing him. He liked exercising control. The following night he was going to do more. A lot more. But the duct tape would remain over the eyes. He didn't want her seeing him. Didn't like the disgust that would have been in her eyes.

He puts his hands against the wall. The texture is canvas, the padding beneath it thick, made up from cushions of foam. Emma Green could be in the room next to him. He tries tugging again at the material, but it's secured too tight and all he does is hurt the tips of his fingers. He begins to pace, then gives up when he starts sweating. He tries banging on the walls but can't make much of a sound. All he can do is wait. He sits in the corner and doesn't have to wait long before the slide opens. The light coming through almost blinds him and he has to look away, but then it disappears when Adrian looks through the slot.

"How are you feeling?" Adrian asks.

"It's hot in here, Adrian. Really hot."

"I know. I'm sorry. But like you said, it's only temporary. Only . . . I kind of like it here. I didn't, at first, but it's . . . growing on me."

"I'd like it too if it wasn't so hot," Cooper says.

"Sorry about that."

"Where are we? Is this Sunnyview?"

"Something like that."

"Are we at Eastlake?"

"No," Adrian answers, shaking his head.

"So it's Sunnyview then."

"Maybe," Adrian repeats.

"Okay, Adrian, why don't you let me out? I need to be in a room that's cooler. It's hot in here."

"There's nowhere else for you," Adrian says.

"Well, then how about leaving that slot open. And I'm going to need water. Plenty of it."

"I can do that, I guess. Also, umm, I wanted to, you know, to thank you for telling me the police would find us. That was really nice of you and, and . . . and what I want to know is, is it true what they say about serial killers wanting to kill their mothers?"

Like you killed Pamela Deans? Is it possible after all his years in Grover Hills Adrian formed a connection that made him look at Nurse Deans as a mother figure? It takes him only a second to decide that yes, it's entirely possible.

"In most cases," he answers. "Why?"

"If you kill your mother will that make you a serial killer?" Adrian asks.

"You think you're a serial killer?"

"No," Adrian says, looking away. "I'm just, you know, curious."

"I don't know," Cooper says. "It depends on whether you kill other people too."

"What about your mother?" Adrian asks.

"What?"

"I've read heaps and heaps of books and they all say that serial killers grow up hating their mothers. They say that the one person a serial killer wants to kill more than anybody is their abusive mother, and instead they kill other women as surr . . . surr-goats," Adrian says.

"Surrogates."

"Sir-gates. Is that why you killed all those other people?"

The answer is no. And there aren't *all those other people.* There are only two. "My mother is a good person," Cooper says, and it's true. He loves his mother. Right now she'll be sitting in her living room, photos of Cooper and his sister staring down from the walls. His sister probably in the middle of some long-haul flight back to New Zealand to be with their mum. Friends and other family members trying to keep her comforted, a damp handkerchief in her lap, an absolute blank stare on her face, hoping her son is alive but believing otherwise. When people go missing in this country they don't show back up. At least not alive.

250

"Your mother made you who you are," Adrian says. "She's the reason you became a killer."

"That's not true."

"But the books say . . ."

"The books aren't always accurate, Adrian. They're a generalization."

"A what?"

"It means the books say what works for most people, but not for all. There are always going to be exceptions."

"The books didn't say anything about exceptions."

"But there are. You didn't become fascinated with killers because of your mother, right?"

"That was different. That didn't happen to you, which means you must hate your mother."

"I don't hate her. I love her."

"Do you think she's collectable?"

For a split second the words don't make sense, at least he doesn't think they do, but he knows, he knows what Adrian means. "What?"

"If you really love her, then bringing her here is the best thing I can do for you. If you hate her and want her dead, then bringing her here is also a good thing for you."

"Don't bring her here," he says, his words low.

"What?"

"I said don't bring her here," he repeats, louder this time.

"But she'll be perfect for the collection!" Adrian says, sounding out of breath. "Both serial killer and the woman who made him that way."

"She didn't make me this way."

"We can talk about it when I come back with her."

"Wait, wait," Cooper says, moving toward the slot, but Adrian closes it and he returns to the darkness. "Wait!" he shouts, but it's no use. He bangs on the padded door and can't make much of a sound. "Adrian! Adrian!"

But Adrian is already gone.

chapter thirty-six

I take a time-out to have a slice of life moment. I've hardly eaten all day and my body is starting to crash. I hit a drive-through and pick up a hamburger and fries and some kind of Coke substitute that consists of syrup and about four carbonated bubbles. It tastes exactly how I remember it tasting, which is a real shame. I stay in my car, parked under the shade of some large elm trees as burger juice runs down my fingers onto my wrist. There are kids playing cricket, which means that school is over for the day, which means it's much later than I thought it was. I think about my daughter as I eat my burger. I think about her friends from school and wonder how many of them still remember her. Then I think about the blood on the steps leading down to the basement at Grover Hills and how, at the moment, the place is most likely now a crime scene. The ice in the Coke melts and makes the drink a little more bearable. I think about Jesse Cartman and the Scream Room. If there were any truth to what Cartman said and the room was still active and I was still a cop with my daughter in the ground, would I blow the whistle on that room and all the bad things that happened there? I finish off the hamburger.

I'd want revenge the same way many others would, but seeing Jesse Cartman, seeing he was never really responsible for his past, does that change things? I don't know. I think it should. I like to think it would have changed things enough for me not to have lost my mind, pay off a couple of orderlies, and go into a basement with a baseball bat looking for revenge.

I bundle up the mess and drop it into a trash bin.

If what Jesse Cartman said is true, then the Twins did this city a service by taking care of some of the trash—the trash being those who faked their illness. But they did the city a disservice by beating on those who were ill, hurting those who couldn't defend themselves. There's no excuse for that. After I find Emma Green, I'm going to find those twins.

It's less than a ten-minute drive to the halfway house. The friendly construction of old places being knocked down and replaced by the new in this part of town hasn't reached this block of homes, tall miserable-looking state homes with unkempt yards and junked-out cars parked up on front lawns, warped clapboards and twisted fences and dog shit every few feet. The halfway house is a two-story place that hasn't been quite as neglected as the neighboring properties, the difference being only one third of the fence is missing compared to the others, which are shooting around half. I park opposite it, thankful there's still five hours of sunlight left; this is one neighborhood I wouldn't want to be caught in after dark. The house is painted a poor choice of green, the roof a poor choice of red, the front door a poor choice of black. The whole thing would look good in orange; nice large engulfing orange flames. I separate the remaining cash Donovan Green gave me into two one-thousand-dollar piles and fold them into separate pockets. I cross the road and knock on the front door and hope I haven't just contracted syphilis.

A guy in his midsixties opens it. He's wearing a white buttoned-up short-sleeve shirt with a black tie and pants and a fedora. He looks like he's about to head to the track in 1960. There are cigarette burns all up the insides of his arms that look as old as his outfit. His blue eyes burn out from his deeply tanned face and I realize forty years ago this guy would have done well with the ladies. "You lost, son?" he asks, his voice is low and gravely.

"No. I'm . . ."

"You the police?"

"Yes."

"Somebody done something?"

"Yes."

"What exactly?"

"I need to talk to somebody in charge."

"I'm in charge."

"Are you really?"

"We're all in charge, son. We all have to be in charge of our own lives to take responsibility for ourselves."

"That's admirable. Is somebody else here responsible for everybody else besides themselves?"

He starts picking at one of the burns on his arms, but it's an old burn and he can't lift any of the scar tissue. No way of telling whether he gave them to himself or had a helping hand. My cell phone starts ringing and I reach into my pocket to mute it.

"The Preacher," he says.

"The Preacher?"

"That's not his real name, son, it's just what we call him."

"Yeah? Or is that what he calls himself?"

"Both," he says, smiling. "But I don't know what started first. I think he's just always been the Preacher."

"Can I talk to him?"

"Wait here."

I stand on the doorstep with the sun beating down on me. I can hear sirens in the distance as an ambulance speeds by a block away, maybe it's come to the neighborhood to hand out plague vaccinations like an ice-cream truck selling ice cream. Every few seconds a thick drop of sweat tickles my body as it rolls from my armpit. Even in the heat a couple of guys walking their dog out on the street are wearing big black leather jackets with gang patches on the back. The dog is solidly built with short black hair and doesn't have a tail.

Not only does it look like it could rip my throat out, it gives me a look like it really wants to. Long strips of saliva are dangling from its mouth and it starts to growl. The only thing holding it back is a thick leash and a dog collar with small metal spikes decorating it.

"What fuck you staring at, muvafucker?" one of them asks, glancing over at me and slowing down.

I turn back to the door, hoping it will be enough for them, but it's not. I hear the dog growling from a few meters behind me. They've come to the fence line. I take a quick glance back. Both men look like they weigh at least a hundred kilograms each, fat and muscle compacted beneath tattoo-covered skin. I imagine they do okay with the ladies too—but not where the ladies have any say in the matter. I knock on the door again.

"Hey, hey, fuck-knuckle," one of them shouts.

It's one of those common situations that people get caught up in all the time in this city on their way to becoming a statistic. Just random shit like this, and it pisses me off, and I feel like taking the gun out of my pocket and giving Christchurch some spring-cleaning.

"Hey, muvafucker, you got a problem with us?" the other one asks.

"You fucking deaf?" the first one says.

I check the door. It's unlocked, so I step into the halfway house and close the door behind me. A glass bottle smashes against the porch and the two men keep yelling at me, but after a few seconds their yells turn to laughter, then the laughter fades as they carry on their way.

The hallway smells of body odor and cigarette smoke so strong that the actual house needs to take a shower. It branches off to a couple of bedrooms to the left and right, the doors to all of them closed so there isn't much light hitting the hallway. There's a staircase heading up to the right, and ahead is a large, open-plan kitchen. There aren't any paintings on the walls, no pictures anywhere, no plants. I head into the kitchen. The guy with the cigarette burns up his arms is talking to a guy in a pair of flared trousers with holes in the knees, and a buttoned-up black shirt with a large, pointed collar. It must be button-shirt day at the house. He looks like he picked one favorite item of clothing from each decade and chose today to test the ensemble. They both look over at me.

"You're the Preacher?" I ask.

"You're the cop?" he asks back.

"Detective Inspector," I say.

"Got a badge?"

"It's in the car."

"That why you didn't flash it to the guys with the dog?"

"I could have flashed a sword and they wouldn't have cared. I'm here to talk about one of the men who stays here."

The Preacher is in his fifties, perhaps almost as much as sixty. He has a boxer's nose and cauliflower ears and a blink rate that's thirty percent as often as anybody I've ever met, which is a little unnerving—it's like talking to somebody who's trying to hypnotize you. He has dark hair and a lot of it, not just on his head, but thick curly hair up his arms and sticking out from the gaps between his shirt buttons. He nods toward cigarette burn guy who then wanders off, leaving us alone in the kitchen. All of the utensils are mismatched, probably from city-mission donations over the years. The only matching things in the room are a pair of holes in one of the walls, perhaps created by somebody's head. Otherwise nothing has a twin—different types of mugs, no matching chairs, different light fittings, random drawer handles.

"We make do with what we have," he says, watching me look around, his blink rate still slow. "We get very little government support, and we rely on the kindness of others, and like you know, there ain't much kindness left to go around in this world. I'm the Preacher," he says, holding out his hand.

I take it, expecting it to be strong, and it is. I keep an eye on the hair on his wrist in case it's after more real estate.

"Coffee?"

"No, thank you."

"Not a bad decision," he says. "It's bad for you, and I'm addicted to it, but many addictions are bad for you, wouldn't you say?"

"I'm looking for somebody."

"Everybody is looking for somebody, and I can tell you where to find him."

"Where?"

"In here," he says, tapping his chest, "and in the Bible."

"I . . ."

"Just kidding," he says, and laughs softly. "I mean I'm not kidding about everybody needing to find Jesus, I'm just kidding about putting you through the pitch. I try to get all of the men staying here to find God."

"How's that working out for you?"

"Life is supposed to be full of challenges," he says, "and this is no different. Do you mind?" he asks, pulling out a packet of cigarettes.

I do mind, but I shake my head. "Go for it."

"These damn addictions," he says. "Thankfully they're the only two."

"You don't count God as an addiction?"

He smiles around the cigarette as he lights it up, draws in a lungful of smoke, then exhales.

"That's good," he says. "I must remember that." He holds the cigarette out in front of him and stares at it lovingly. "Life is full of temptations," he says. "It's one of God's ironies. The things that tempt us the most are what are the most bad for us. Except for religion."

"I need your help," I say. I show him the sketch. "You recognize this man?"

He doesn't take much of a look and shakes his head.

"You sure? I heard from a reliable source this guy lived here. Take a longer look."

He takes a longer look. "Yeah, maybe. Wasn't he in *Lord of the Rings*? I think he was a hobbit."

I put the sketch into my pocket. I may as well screw it up and toss it out.

"I need to speak to anybody who came here from Grover Hills."

"Why? Somebody does something crazy and you want to blame a mentally ill person?"

"Something like that. Somebody set fire to one of the nurses who worked there."

He takes a long draw on his cigarette, sucking constantly until his lungs can't take any more air. "I heard about it on the news. You think that person had to be a patient?" he says, holding in the smoke.

"There are other things too."

"Like what?"

"I'm not at liberty to say."

"You're not at liberty to say. Well, I'm not at liberty to say anything either. The people here, they look up to me, I have their trust. I'm not at liberty to break that."

I pull a thousand dollars out of my pocket. "How liberal are you about receiving donations?" I ask. "This is your chance for some good karma. You just said there isn't enough kindness in this world. We have to start somewhere, and this is it. You're kind to me with some information, and I'm kind to you. This," I say, shaking the cash, "can buy food, cigarettes, some new pots and pans."

He stares at the money the same way he did at the cigarette, like it's another addiction but one he never gets to taste, then he looks around the room as if somebody is watching. There isn't. He steps forward to take the money but I pull it away. "Names."

"I can't remember them all. There were six or seven of them."

"Were?"

"They've all moved on."

"Where'd they go?"

"This isn't the kind of place where people stay in touch," he says. "Most of the people here are straight out of prison. They get jobs flipping burgers and scraping dead animals off the street barely making minimum wage. People don't want to make friends here."

"Any of the Grover Hills patients stand out?"

"Nobody stands out here." He reaches back out for the cash. I keep hold of it.

"That's not exactly worth a thousand dollars," I tell him. "Give me something else."

"I guess there's one guy you could talk to," he says. "One of the patients. He seemed to get on well enough with most of them."

"What? He's here?"

"Yeah. He's here."

"Thought you said they'd all moved on."

He shrugs. "I just remembered," he says, and money does help people remember. "His name's Ritchie Munroe."

"He here right now?"

He reaches out for the cash. I hand it over. I figure if I really wanted to I could take it back off him in about five seconds. He takes another draw on his cigarette. "Upstairs. Last door on the right."

I head into the hallway and take the stairs. They groan with every footstep and the handrail is worn and wobbly. The windows upstairs lining the hallway are streaked with a thicker layer of dirt than their counterparts downstairs. The view outside isn't pretty, rusting roofs of neighboring houses, gutters chock full of leaves and sludge, backyards with burned lawns and car parts scattered in the sun. I knock on the end doorway and a guy calls out for me to wait a moment before opening it half a minute later. Ritchie Munroe has a nose that's too big for him and a mouth that's too small, it's like somebody gave him the wrong-sized parts in the baby factory. His eyes look too small for the sockets, as if a tap to the head would spin them around like dollar signs in a slot machine. His hair has been dyed black, and he hasn't done a great job because there's dye on his forehead too. He must be in his midfifties, maybe even sixty. He could be the man in the sketch but he could just as easily not be. He's wearing only underwear and a T-shirt and the front of his underwear is bulging out. Behind him is a small TV set playing a porn movie with the sound turned down. The hot air rushing past him from the room seems happy to escape.

"Who are you?" he asks, and he sounds nervous.

"Detective Inspector Schroder," I say, figuring Carl won't mind. Well, more figuring he'll never know. "I need to ask you some questions about Grover Hills."

He shakes his head. "I've never heard of it," he says, and he tries to close the door.

I put my hand on it. "That's funny, considering you spent some time there. You mind turning that off?" I ask, nodding toward the TV.

"Why? It embarrassing you?"

"Guess that means you don't want to put any pants on either."

"Just ask your questions and leave," he says. "Please."

"Preacher says you were friends with a bunch of Grover Hills patients."

"Preacher tell you that?"

"He did."

"You have to pay him?"

I smile. "I did."

"You hold back anything for me?" he asks, not sounding so nervous now.

I show him the remaining cash.

"What do you want to know?"

"Somebody set fire to Nurse Deans."

He pulls back a little as his face tightens, but then it loosens off again as he comes to terms with the news. "Can't say I'm sorry to hear that."

"Any idea who would do a thing like that?"

"None."

"Heard of Emma Green?"

"Nope."

"Cooper Riley?"

"Nope."

"Not even from the news?"

"Why would I watch the news?"

"Who else wouldn't be upset at hearing Nurse Deans was dead?"

He shrugs. "Everybody who ever stayed at the Grove. Nobody really liked anybody out there. Mental institutions are like that."

"And what about you?"

"I'm easy to like."

"I meant did you want to kill her?"

"I'm a lover not a fighter," he says.

"You an arsonist?"

"What?"

"Where were you yesterday?"

"Why?"

"Just answer the question."

"Here. With Melina. All day."

"Melina?"

"Yeah. She's my girl."

"She here?"

"Where else would she be?"

"Can I talk to her?"

"She doesn't like strangers."

I wave the cash in front of his face and remind him why he's talking to me. He sees it and figures talking to strangers isn't such a bad thing. "Make it quick," he says.

He swings the door the rest of the way open. The light coming into the hallway through the upstairs windows makes no effort to enter his room, it's as though the spoiled air and smell of sex is scaring it away. Melina is lying in bed facing the TV set. The curtains are closed so most of the light coming into the room is from the TV. Ritchie takes a few steps backward and his movement creates a draft, which ripens the stench. I almost gag.

"Melina?" I say, stepping toward her, but then I don't say anything else.

"Ask her your questions," Ritchie says.

I turn back toward him. "She your alibi?"

"Why you asking me?" he asks. "She's the one telling you we were here."

I look back down at Melina, but Melina is still looking at the TV, completely ignoring me as she stares at it with glazed-over eyes made from plastic. Her entire body is made from rubber and plastic and must weigh around fifty or sixty kilograms. As far as companion dolls go, she certainly looks like a high-end model. I bet that makes her high maintenance.

"See?" Ritchie says.

"What?"

"See, I told you I was here all day yesterday," he says, looking at me. He looks down at Melina. "I know," he says. "I'm sorry, but it isn't my fault. He just showed up. He has money."

He turns back toward me. "I told you she doesn't like strangers. You've got what you came for and, like the lady said, it's time you leave." He looks back down at her. "I know, honey, I know."

He leads me to the door and I'm happy to be led. "Sorry about that," he says, in a conspiratorial whisper.

"It's hard to find the perfect woman," I say. "You know, with a thousand bucks you could buy her a few nice dresses."

"I guess I could."

"But there are a few things you need to tell me."

"Like what?"

"Tell me about the Scream Room."

"Who told you about that?"

"Another patient. You ever have to spend time down there?"

"What, me? No, never. But I never . . . never, you know, hurt anybody. That room was for the bad people and I'm not a bad people. Money?"

"Not yet. What about the Twins?"

He looks down. "Why do you have to talk about them," he whispers. "I'm a better person now. I don't want nothing to do with them." He sniffs loudly and starts to cry.

"I'm sorry, I really am," I say, and it's true. "Listen, are any of your friends from Grover Hills in the habit of killing cats and digging them back up?"

"I have to go," he says, and starts to close the door. "You can keep the money."

I push my hand against it. "Ritchie . . ."

"But Melina . . ."

"Melina can wait. Give me a name, Ritchie."

"I can't. He's my friend. My best friend."

"Who?"

"Nobody."

"He killed my cat," I say. "And he killed Nurse Deans."

"She was a hard woman," he says.

"What's his name?"

"I can't," he says.

I hold the money back up. "You can spend this on Melina," I say. "You going to choose friendship over love? Is that it? You're going to choose to protect a killer instead of buying your girl something she deserves?"

He looks down and starts opening and closing his lips like a goldfish, no sound coming out.

"Ritchie . . ."

"His name is Adrian Loaner, but he doesn't live here anymore. He used to, but then I taught him to drive and he left. He was young when he went to the Grove, real young, and he was there for twenty years maybe."

"When did he leave here?"

"A week ago. That's all I know," he says, and when he looks back up there are tears running down his face.

"You've done the right thing," I tell him.

"Melina . . . she isn't, she isn't . . . you know . . . and I know she isn't, but . . . but it's better than being alone."

"It's hard being alone," I say.

"I'm sorry about your cat," he says.

"So am I."

"Please, please don't kill him."

I show him the sketch from the newspaper. "Is this Adrian?"

He looks at it, then tilts his head to change the angle first one way, then the other. "Kind of," he says. "I mean, maybe."

"Which bedroom was his?"

"Right opposite," he says, pointing across the hall. "But it's empty. He's my best friend but I don't know where he's gone."

I hand over the cash and enter the bedroom across the hall. The curtains are open and the sun falls across floorboards thick with dust. There's a bed with the sheets and blankets and pillow missing. The bedroom drawers are all open and each of them empty. There isn't anything laying around the room light enough to be lifted in one hand. Adrian Loaner isn't coming back. I do a customary check, looking under the bed, I search for loose floorboards, I check underneath and behind the drawers but nothing has been left behind.

Adrian moved out a week ago and started a new life out at Grover Hills. Only something spooked him into leaving today.

I head back into the hall. I can hear Ritchie talking to his girlfriend but the conversation is muffled. When I get downstairs the Preacher is waiting for me by the door.

"One more thing," he says. There's a fresh cigarette in his hand and also beer. "How was prison, Detective?" he asks, and the smile he gives me has no warmth.

Back at the car, all four tires have been slashed. I call the rental agency and keep my hand on my gun as I wait for a tow truck to arrive.

chapter thirty-seven

Adrian stalls the car twice as he backs down the driveway from their new, temporary home. He's excited with the new accommodations and frustrated that he had to leave the Grove, making him happy one moment and sad the next, and that makes driving a whole lot harder to focus on. At least the day is starting to cool down somewhat, and he's finding he's having more energy because of it. His head snaps forward the third time he stalls the car so he comes to a stop, gets out, and leans against it for a minute while rubbing his neck. He needs to concentrate.

He drives into the city, the traffic around him thick with people coming home from work. He doesn't like driving at this time and tries to avoid it, but sometimes he can't. People drive differently at this time of the day. They're more aggressive. They honk their horns more and the cars are closer together, the front of them almost touching the back of the car in front. He hates it. Sometimes he's thankful he's not part of the crowd. Families and funerals, taxes and TV shows, planning holidays and painting houses—the thought of that scares him.

He has the phone book in the front seat, the phone book he took from the halfway house, it's covered in pen marks and the covers are torn and the Preacher would be disappointed in him for taking it. He hated living there. If it wasn't for Ritchie he'd have tried to move out three years ago, though he doesn't know where he would have gone without the ability to drive. The problem with Ritchie was once he met Melina, he started to change. He wasn't the same guy that taught him how to drive. He didn't have much time for Adrian anymore. It's sad, because if Ritchie were here then all of this would be going easier. It would also be a lot more fun.

He looks up Cooper's mother in the phone book. He doesn't have any intention of adding her to his collection, and he isn't sure why he lied to Cooper about it. More so Cooper wouldn't be able to predict what he would do next. Adding the mother would be another mouth to feed, another unhappy person to have around, just more negativity, and like his mother used to say, *"A sad man is a bad man,"* and that would go the same for a woman too, he guesses. The idea of collecting the mum certainly does excite him, though, there is no denying that, but the reality is just too complicated. Still, he wants to see her house, just to satisfy his curiosity. He looked her address up before, only he forgot to write it down. He knows the direction, and he rechecks the address against the map and confirms he's going the right way.

When he drives past her house he slows enough to look at the cars parked outside. He doesn't think any of them belong to the police because they're too nice. Most likely she has friends over to comfort her because she can't find Cooper. In the future those cars won't be there.

Now his stomach is rumbling. He hasn't eaten since breakfast. He hates missing meals. He could drive back out to the new home and fix something to eat, but he doesn't know where things are in the kitchen or how to use them and he needs time if he's going to do that.

He pulls away from the curb. He'll go to a drive-through and get some fast food. He's never used a drive-through before and the

266

thought makes him anxious, but then again, a few years ago he'd never used an ATM card and now he knows how. Experiences like this are good for him. They are character building. He can pull over somewhere and eat the food while it's still warm. Then he'll drive out to the Grove and watch to see if any police come looking around.

It will feel nice watching the Grove.

In a way it will be like being back home but not really being there.

chapter thirty-eight

It takes an hour for the tow truck to arrive. It's a nervous wait in case the guys with the dog come back, forcing me to shoot them and their dog and then spending twenty years in jail before getting back onto the case. It's also a frustrating hour because I want to push forward. The tow-truck driver arrives and steps out of the truck and walks around the rental. He has his arms out of his overalls so the top half of his outfit is hanging down past his legs. His white T-shirt is drenched with sweat and has become see-through. His hands are stained with oil and grease.

"You must have really pissed somebody off," he says, looking down at the wheels.

"Sometimes I'm misunderstood," I tell him.

He connects a hook and chain under the car then stands next to the back of the truck as he holds a button, a pulley winding the car forward and up onto the deck. He makes sure it's secure and we climb up into the cab. The cab is full of so many hamburger wrappers that my cholesterol level spikes when I inhale. We make the kind of small talk that small talk was invented for—the weather, traffic, sports news. He drives me to the tire shop the rental agency told me to take the car to. The people there have been advised about the problem but tell me it's going to take another hour before they even take a look at it because they're busy. I sit on a bench outside in the fading heat, spending five minutes staring at a tree, five at the side of the wall, bunches of other five-minute intervals staring at whatever else is around. The air smells of rubber. I call Donovan Green and update him on the case. I tell him I have a few names that I'm following up tonight and that he should keep his cell phone nearby in case I need more money. He tells me money isn't an issue. He asks me if I'm still carrying the photograph of Emma he gave me, and I tell him that it's in my wallet. He asks me to take it out and take a look at it, and I do. He tells me that her life is in my hands, that she's alive somewhere, that money isn't an issue, and reminds me that I'm doing this for Emma and for him, not for the police. He reminds me that when I find Cooper Riley that I'm to go to him first, that I'm to give him a few hours alone with Cooper Riley.

"Okay," I tell him.

"Promise me," he tells me. "Promise me Riley will pay for what he's done."

"I promise."

I hang up and call Schroder. "Any hits on the fingerprints from my house?" I ask him.

"Nothing. There were some good ones too. So it wasn't Melissa and it wasn't somebody with a record . . ." he says, then trails off. "Hang on a second," he says, and he takes the phone away. I can hear muffled voices but not what they're saying. He comes back a moment later. "Listen, I have to go."

"Wait a second. Maybe this guy we're looking for was young and didn't get a criminal record, but got a medical one instead."

"What are you getting at, Tate?"

"I got something for you," I tell him. "This is important. I know who took Cooper Riley."

"Yeah? Who?"

"An ex-patient from Grover Hills. His name is Adrian Loaner.

If he was just a kid when he went there, there'd be no criminal record."

"Uh huh. Good job, Tate. We'll look into it."

"Hang on," I say, his lack of enthusiasm telling me what I need to know. "You already knew?"

"Of course we knew. What, you think we can't function without you?"

"How long have you known?"

"Listen, Tate, I have to go."

"Can you meet me?"

"What?"

"With some corpse dogs."

"Oh man, are you shitting me?"

"Grover Hills."

"Look, Tate, we know what we're doing."

"Grover Hills . . ."

"We're already out there."

"You find anything?"

"We sure as hell found a lot more than you did."

"You found Cooper Riley?"

"Not yet."

"But you found somebody."

"A couple of bodies."

I break out in a cold sweat. "Emma Green?"

"No," he says, and I breathe a sigh of relief. "Listen, Tate, don't even think of coming out here."

"I'll be there soon," I tell him, and I hang up.

It's closing in on seven o'clock by the time my car is hoisted up on a hydraulic lift. It's an anxious wait, and I end up pacing the footpath outside, looking at the other cars parked around the shop wondering how hard it'd be to steal one. Each of the wheels are taken off. It takes ten minutes per tire to replace, then the car is lowered and I'm back on the road.

I still get somewhat lost on the drive back to Grover Hills even though I was there earlier today. The sun is in my eyes for most of it, creeping under the angle of the sun visor, so when I do turn corners and head in different directions I have bright lights dancing in my vision. I pull in behind one of the patrol cars at Grover Hills. One side of the building is lit up with the sun reflecting in all the windows, the other sides are dim in the shade. I have to shield my eyes as I look for Schroder. The building hasn't been cordoned off because there's nobody out here to protect it from. There are around thirty people working the scene and about half of them watch me get out of the car, but nobody comes over. They seem to know who I am, and Schroder must have told them to let me though. He's standing next to a man with a beard and a comb-over. He breaks off the conversation and comes over. His shirtsleeves are rolled up and dust and dirt has settled into the folds.

"Jesus, Tate," he says, shaking his head.

"Why don't you just give up on the indignation, Carl, and accept I'm part of this. Let me help you. That's what you wanted from me when you picked me up from jail, remember? My help? Stop bullshitting me by pretending you want me out of here when you need all the help you can get."

He seems about to argue, and he already has his hands ready to form the angry gestures that go along with it, but then they drop to his sides and he smiles. "You've got a point," he says, "and cutting out the bullshit you put me through would save me a lot of time, and is probably good for my heart too."

"What have you got?"

"So far we've got two bodies."

"So far?"

"Yeah. We're looking for more. One of the two we have is fresh."

"How fresh?"

"First body we're talking about years. Second body the medical examiner says around twenty-four hours. We think her name is Karen Ford. We're still waiting to confirm an ID, but everything matches. She was a street worker reported missing this morning. She's twenty years old," he says. "Twenty years old. Jesus."

"Got a murder weapon?" I ask.

"Not yet. And there's more. You see the cell downstairs when you were out here? We got blood down there."

"I saw it," I tell him. "The residents here called it the Scream Room."

"What?"

I tell him about Jesse Cartman. Schroder stays dispassionate for the first ten seconds before rolling his hands into fists and slowly shaking his head. When I tell him about the Twins, he's gritting his teeth so hard I'm worried one of them is going to snap away and bite me in the face.

"Jesse Cartman isn't exactly a reliable source of information," Schroder says, but I can tell he partly believes it the same way I believe it, especially now that bodies are showing up.

"You're going to have to make some calls," I tell him. "The staff knew what was going on. If it's even remotely true, you've got multiple cases of assault and murder and God knows what else stemming from this room."

"Jesus," he says. "It's going to be a nightmare."

"What about Emma Green? Any signs she was out here?"

He shakes his head. "We found some fresh prints in the downstairs room on the inside of the iron door. They match prints we took from Cooper Riley's office. We've been searching the other rooms and have found no sign of Emma Green, only signs of Karen Ford. Looks like she was tied up in one of the beds. Also we got some Taser ID disks on the floor in the basement. There were a couple on the couch and a couple under it, about twenty short of what there should have been so Adrian tried cleaning up."

"You've run the serial numbers?"

"Yeah. It's a dead end. It was part of a batch that was stolen five years ago in the US. Two hundred Tasers in total went missing and made their way around the world, along with about a thousand cartridges."

"How the hell would Adrian get something like that?" I ask.

"Maybe it belongs to Cooper."

"He was shot by his own Taser?"

272

Schroder shrugs. "Maybe."

"So Adrian was keeping Riley locked up in the basement," I say. "As a prisoner. Which means if he's not in the ground here, he's probably still alive. Maybe Cooper did something to him years ago in the Scream Room when Adrian was a patient here. What about the blood?"

"Too early to have made a match. Looks fresh though. Probably belonged to Karen Ford. We got some other stuff too. Clothes, some personal belongings, some utensils, even some plates. Found them in cardboard boxes stuffed in the taller grass near the tree line," he says. "Looks like Adrian left in a hurry and didn't have room for everything. How did you figure out Adrian Loaner?" he asks.

I tell him about the halfway house. "You?" I ask.

"It was simple. We spoke to some of the staff that used to work here. We showed them the composite sketch and we told them about your cat. They gave us a name of somebody who used to dig them up who looked like that sketch. I sent somebody to the same halfway house and learned pretty much what you learned. We heard you'd already been there. What took you so long to get here?"

"Car problems."

"We brought out a couple of the corpse dogs to take a look around before upgrading to the ground-penetrating radar. The ME thinks the other body has been in the ground at least ten years. We've started to expand the search."

Somebody shouts out from behind the building and a few of the detectives start making their way over. I follow Schroder in the same direction. I ask him what he knows about Adrian Loaner, and he doesn't know much. A group of detectives are forming a half circle. I can see piles of dirt through the gaps between them. We cross the shadow line formed by the building and step into the shade to the south, the air much cooler. There are already two open graves on this side, each with dirt piled waist high next to them, the soil on the bottom dry and thin, the stuff on the top thick with dark clods. The detectives have gathered in front of a third pile of dirt. We step into the group. Everybody is looking down at the half-excavated grave, a skull and part of an arm exposed, no flesh attached. Suddenly Jesse Cartman's story doesn't seem as crazy.

"Jesus," Schroder says. "What the hell are we digging up here?"

Nobody answers him. The person doing the digging has stopped digging for the moment while somebody else takes photos. The digger doesn't pose against the shovel and smile. He just waits until he can carry on, much slower now. There's an overwhelming feeling spreading through the group—nobody here thinks we're going to be stopping at only three bodies.

Laying on a blue tarpaulin about ten meters from one of the fully open graves is a woman wearing a shapeless dress with a large bloodstain on the front. Karen Ford. Right now her friends and family are somewhere looking for her and praying she's still alive, praying she's gone away for a few days, but for a woman in Karen's line of work, they'll know she's gone away forever.

"I fucking hate this job," Schroder says, noticing me looking over.

"It would raise some serious red flags if you didn't," another man says, the man Schroder was talking to when I arrived.

"This is Benson Barlow," Schroder says, introducing us.

Barlow's comb-over is being backlit from the sun, making it look even thinner than it is. His face is shiny from suntan lotion and looks red. He has a deep, smooth voice that could talk a suicide off a ledge. I shake his hand.

"I've heard about you," he tells me.

"And you are?" I ask.

"He's a consultant," Schroder tells me.

"A psychiatrist," Barlow adds.

"We worked together a couple of months ago," Schroder says. "It made sense that since we're dealing with patients from here, he may have some insight that could help us."

"Some of them I dealt with over the years," Barlow says.

"Adrian Loaner?" I ask.

"Unfortunately, no," he says.

"Loaner does have a primary psychiatrist who he has to check in with twice a year," Schroder says. "Doctor Nicholas Stanton."

"I actually know Stanton," Barlow says. "He's a good man."

"But unavailable," Schroder says. "He's on holiday somewhere in a different time zone where it's cooler. We're working on a warrant to get his patient files."

"And how's that going?" I ask.

"A warrant to get patient files from a psychiatrist? I'd have more luck talking my wife into giving up her credit card," Schroder says.

"Loaner only had to check in twice a year?" I confirm. "That doesn't sound like much."

"It's not much," Barlow says, "but it is what it is and, remember, it's not my fault, it's not Doctor Stanton's fault, it's the number the courts and the government doctors came up with."

"So tell me," I say, "where would Adrian have taken Cooper now?"

"Somewhere familiar to him," he says. "That's all I can tell you."

"That's not much," I say, "and not something we hadn't figured out."

"Listen . . ." he says, but I put my hand up and stop him.

"I'm sorry, I didn't mean to sound dismissive," I say. "It's just been a long day."

"It's okay," he says, nodding slowly. "It's something all psychiatrists have to get used to when we're dealing with cops." He looks at me to say something else and I have an idea what it is, but I don't give it to him. He carries on. "First some ground rules," he says. "This is all speculation. It's science, I'm nothing like one of those psychic assholes you see on TV. What I'm saying has merit. In my opinion there's a chance he'll come back here. First of all this is his home. He won't want to leave it behind for too long. He's been forced to leave his home and therefore he'll be feeling stressed and upset, and stressed people like to return to the things that comfort them. That means anybody involved with the case should keep their pets locked inside tonight. You may consider posting some unmarked cars outside each of your own houses since each of you make targets, though in your case, Mr. Tate, it's perhaps too late. That aside, I think you'll also find he's eager to return here. This has been his home for many years and he'll be watching closely. In fact, he may even be out there now," he says, and we all look out to the trees and the road looking for a madman looking in. "I would set up some patrol cars to intercept anybody who comes this way."

"Have you read Cooper Riley's book?" I ask.

"Just how did you manage to get a copy of that, Tate?" Schroder asks.

"Yes, Detective Schroder gave me a copy when he updated me on the case," Barlow says. "It's very poorly written," he adds, "and inconsistent. The man believes he knows much more than he does, and he gives that away with his conclusions. I can do a much better job. In fact it's something I've been thinking about for the last few years, and perhaps, well, I hate to sound like an opportunist, but perhaps there may even be some material here for it."

"Jesus . . ." I say.

"I know what you're thinking," he says, "but without people like me studying people like Adrian and Cooper, people like you wouldn't have a clue where to begin."

"Okay, point taken," I say, annoyed that he's made a good one. I'm just thrilled that at least somebody can make money from all this death and misery. "But there is something I still don't get."

"Just the one thing, Tate?" Schroder says.

I ignore the jibe. "Adrian wanted revenge on Pamela Deans and he killed her," I say. "If he wants revenge on Cooper Riley, why not just kill him too?"

Barlow raises his eyes and his forehead twists into a string of wrinkles. "And that's the big question, isn't it? Yes, I've been giving it some thought. I don't believe revenge is the motivation behind Cooper Riley's abduction."

"No? Then what?" I ask, genuinely curious.

"I think it's fascination."

"Fascination?" Schroder repeats.

"I think when Cooper Riley was coming out here conducting his interviews and his tests, I think Adrian became obsessed with him."

"You think he's taken Cooper to own him?" I ask.

"It makes sense."

And it does make sense. I should have seen it earlier. Should have figured it out from the moment I saw the cell downstairs.

"If he's that obsessed, why wait three years?" Schroder asks.

"He will have needed to build the courage to act," Barlow says, "and needed to acquire the tools. If it was about revenge then Cooper would already be dead. I'm certain of it. You say Adrian used a Taser? Why not use a knife, or a gun? No, it's not about killing. It's about collecting."

Ritchie Munroe said he taught Adrian to drive. That had to be part of it. Until recently, Adrian didn't have the means to bring somebody out here. It's not like he could have put Cooper into the trunk of a taxi.

"You think Adrian knew Cooper was a killer?" I ask.

"It would suggest a greater degree of intelligence than we first thought," Barlow says. "It's more likely a great degree of luck."

"You think he just happened to be following Cooper and found out he was a serial killer?" Schroder asks.

"The alternative would mean he's better at doing our job than we are," I say. "There's no way he could have figured out Cooper was a serial killer."

"Our job?" Schroder asks.

"You know what I mean."

"I agree," Barlow says. "The question now is just how much longer is Adrian's luck going to hold out?"

Only it's not Adrian's luck I'm thinking about. It's Emma Green's. She was lucky Cooper was abducted, but it could mean she's been without food and water since Monday night. I know on average a person can last around four days, give or take, without water, but these aren't normal conditions. With the heat wave . . . well, it comes down to how hot it is where she is. The pile of dirt at the latest grave gets bigger as more skeleton is exposed. I look out at the grounds and the graves still yet to be found, praying to a God who abandoned them to not abandon Emma Green and to let me find her alive.

"Loaner is an unstable person, Detectives," Barlow says, "and under the right stress conditions, he'll be capable of anything—and right now, he's stressed. Taking over his home like this, trust me, if Adrian knows what's going on out here he's going to enter full panic mode, and that means he's going to be capable of almost anything."

"And Melissa X?" I ask, and I look over at Schroder.

"He knows about her," Schroder says, giving me the okay to keep talking.

"Anything happening there?" I ask.

Schroder shakes his head. "We're talking to her friends and family and trying to build up a profile," he says.

"She's not the same person she was before Riley attacked her, assuming that's what happened," Barlow says. "Part of her has taken on the role of her dead sister, and is looking for revenge."

"And the other part?" I ask.

He shrugs. "I couldn't tell you. Some would suggest the other part is pure evil, but I don't think that's the case. The person she is now, that's a product of her past. With the right medication and the right help," he says, but doesn't finish the sentence, because both me and Schroder are staring at him as if he just doesn't get it. Not everybody is meant to be cured—some people are meant to be locked away forever. It wasn't Natalie's fault she set foot on this path, but she's killed innocent men while on it, and for that she has to pay.

chapter thirty-nine

Cooper has taken his shirt off. It's bunched beneath his head; not the most comfortable pillow, but it's not exactly the most comfortable room either. He's thinking partly of Emma Green and wonders if she's going through the exact same thing. At least she has water. Who knows, maybe after four days being tied up she's found a way to free herself, but if she has, there's still no way she can get out of the room. Mostly he's thinking about Natalie Flowers, and what he's going to do to her when he gets out of here. He'll combine what he knows about her with what the police have found out about her, and he's going to track her down and make her pay. He'll see how she likes having parts of her body crushed with a pair of pliers.

He spends some time thinking about how that's going to feel, and it is going to happen. First Adrian, and then Natalie. He understands his profession enough to know that these other women he's been hurting are replacements for Natalie, and he wonders what will happen once he's killed her, whether there will ever be any other urges. It interests him on a purely academic level.

His body is bathed with sweat. He has absolutely no way of knowing what time it is. It could be midnight. It could be noon. His body clock is completely out of whack. This must be how a roast chicken feels, he thinks, and undoes the front of his pants and separates the material a little. He needs water. He needs fresh air. He doesn't know how long Adrian has been gone. Doesn't know if the crazy son of a bitch is really going to try and abduct his mother. He hopes not. Throwing his mother into the mix will complicate things.

He can hear footsteps outside the door. Running. His first thought is that he's about to be rescued. His second thought is that rescue could end up being a problem. The slot is thrown back and light comes into the room but not as strong as before. It's evening. Maybe around eight o'clock.

"Tell me, honestly," Adrian says, and he's puffing. "How many girls have you killed?"

"Why?" Cooper asks. He makes his way to his feet and puts his shirt on. He doesn't like the idea of Adrian seeing him half naked. He walks over to the slot and rubs the base of his sore back a little.

"The police showed up at the Grove," Adrian says. "It was just like you said. They're looking around."

"Jesus, have they found anything?"

"I don't know. I don't know. I don't know. I . . ."

"Calm down, Adrian. How many of them are out there? Just the one car? Two cars?"

"Lots of cars," he answers.

"Describe it to me."

"Geez, I don't know," he snaps. "Ten or more cars. What's the difference? There're people walking around with weird-looking equipment looking at the ground, kind of like lawn mowers but not lawn mowers."

"They're looking for bodies."

"What they're doing is walking through my home! They're ruining it with their . . . their lights and equipment and touching everything. I thought it would be good going out there, I thought they wouldn't come. You said if they did they would just look around and leave! I went into the trees up on the hill and waited for them to go but they're not going. They're all walking and searching and *invading* my home. Our home!"

"Listen to me, Adrian. It's going to be okay. But you have to be careful not to get caught, Adrian."

"I wish I knew who each of them were," Adrian says, not listening, and there is blood in his hairline and while he talks, he digs a finger into it and starts scratching. His other hand goes to his neck and starts scratching at that too. Cooper can see welts beginning to appear. "I should invade their lives in the same way. I should make a list, a list like I made with those mean boys, only this time instead of killing their pets I'll kill them. I'll visit each and every one of them. Let's see how *they* like having *their* homes invaded!"

"You're bleeding," Cooper says.

"What?" Adrian pulls his fingers away and looks at them. "Sometimes I get itchy," he says and goes back to scratching. "But you were right, Cooper. You didn't lie or trick me and if there's a silver lining here then that's it."

"Listen, Adrian, you need to focus here. The woman last night, the one we killed," Cooper says, including Adrian in on the killing, "where did you bury her?"

"I hid up in the trees and nobody knew I was there," Adrian says. "When I was young I used to dream of escaping to those trees. I'd imagine what it would be like picking fruit and cooking rabbits and never having to deal with people again."

"You hid the girl up there?"

"Those dreams led me to think about getting cold and lonely and struggling to survive."

"Adrian!"

"What?"

"The girl," Cooper says, talking slowly, talking calmly. "Did you hide her up there?"

"What? No. How many?"

"How many what?" Cooper asks.

"How many girls have you really killed?"

"Why? I told you already."

"How many are buried at Sunnyview?"

"What? I don't know, a few, I guess."

"How can you not know?" Adrian asks, and Cooper is worried that if he keeps scratching himself at the current rate he'll bleed to death in the corridor and then he'll never be getting out of here.

"Calm down, Adrian."

"How many?" Adrian asks, almost screaming now. Spittle flies from his lips through the slot.

"One. There is one buried there," he says.

"The girl you took out there on Monday night?"

Emma Green? No. Emma Green is still alive, at least he thinks she is. And if this is Sunnyview, then Adrian would have found her already. Okay. There are two possibilities. Either Adrian hasn't checked all the rooms—and really, there is no reason he should—or they're not at Sunnyview. Which means they might be at Eastlake, which means Adrian has been lying to him.

"What are you going to do with her?" he asks, avoiding the question. Let Adrian think what he wants to think.

"I just need her, that's all."

"Why?"

"I just do."

"If I tell you, will you let me out?" Cooper asks.

"I'll think about it."

"Then I'll think about telling you."

"But I need to know," Adrian shouts, and he bangs his hands against the door. "Please. It's important. I have to know. *Have* to!"

"I can show you."

"No, no, you have to tell me."

"Why?"

"In case the police find her," Adrian says.

"You're lying," Cooper says.

"Please, I just really need that body. I promise when I get back things will change. You want water, right? And you said it's too hot, right? Tell me where she is and I'll give you water and fresh air. If you don't tell me then that means you don't want to be my friend so I may as well close this slot and never come back."

As much as Cooper would love to never see Adrian again, being locked in here would be an awful, awful way to die.

"I'll tell you where she is," Cooper says, "and then we start working as a team, okay?"

"Okay."

"But first, Adrian, you still haven't told me where the girl from last night is."

"In the ground, of course."

"How far away from the building?"

"I think the police have already found her," Adrian says.

"Shit," Cooper says, banging his fist against the door. The body will give them a whole lot of evidence to work with. "And the knife?"

"The knife is here," Adrian says. "I would never throw it away."

Good. That's at least something. "Listen to me, it's time you let me out. I can't afford to get caught. Neither of us can. We have to get away from Christchurch. We have to try and leave the country. If we work together we'll be okay, but you have to start by letting me out and we have to trust each other."

"You said you were going to tell me where the girl is," Adrian says, almost whining.

Yeah, he knows what he said, but his mind is all over the place, probing at every possibility. "There's a path that goes around the back," Cooper says, giving him directions to the girl who gave up on him last year and died. "Keep following it, it follows a low brick wall. You come to the end of that brick wall and you turn right. Walk fifteen meters parallel to the building and you'll find a ditch. Follow the ditch further from the building another twenty or thirty meters and you'll find a tree that's fallen over. Cross over that tree, walk another ten meters, and that's where she is."

Adrian closes the slot.

"Hey, hey, Adrian," Cooper says, banging against the wall, but Adrian is gone, and all Cooper can do is lie back down and wait.

chapter forty

Adrian feels agitated. He needs to do something to release the anger and there are only a couple of things he's good at. His face is hot and he digs at the itches and flicks the hair off his forehead as he runs back out to the car. He'd left it running. It's not like there was anybody out here to steal it. Up on that hill looking down at those men, they all looked like ants. He pinched his forefinger against his thumb and pretended to squash them, then he turned his fingers into a gun and pretended to shoot them instead. It's what he should have done to those boys back in school. Should have gotten a gun and finished them off instead of killing their stupid pets.

He snaps off a branch from the tree the car is parked under and uses it to get at the itch centered in his back. It tears at his skin but it's immediately soothing. The backs of his arms are starting to get blotchy, his skin raised up and raw-looking. This only ever happens when the stress arrives quickly. He snaps the stick in half and throws it onto the driveway. He wants to scream, to release some energy. He would get like this on occasion during his Grover Hills years. Things would upset him, and he wouldn't be able to calm down.

Things like eating nothing but mashed potatoes for a hundred days in a row or not being allowed to go outside for an entire summer. He would panic and scream and he'd be put into the Scream Room and left there for a couple of days, sometimes he'd be beaten. Other times he'd be left alone until his frustration faded and he'd forget why he was so mad. More than once he'd be left down there and he'd beat his hands bloody on the door, begging to be let out.

He gets into the car and drives fast down the driveway. It's getting dark out now, with shapes in the distance only shadows within shadows now. It feels good to be on the move again. It releases the pressure in his chest a little, but it's nowhere near enough.

His home is no longer his home! Even at the halfway house the Grove remained out here safe and untouched and waiting for him, and now . . . and now these people have ruined it! Why are they being so mean to him?

He knows the roads out here, and stays well away from the main ones in case there are cop cars about. After all, he's still driving a dead girl's car. He reaches the highway without seeing anybody, then it's a trip further west until another set of back roads. There isn't much in the way of traffic. The sun gone now, but the sky not yet black. There are no other cars around and he goes beyond the speed limit, something he's never done before, the headlights swaying across the roads as his shaking hands move the wheel. He keeps his grip tight. He's doing nearly 100 kph and his heart is racing. He has never driven this fast before.

He knows Cooper thinks their temporary home is Sunnyview, but Cooper doesn't know everything. Adrian has driven here twice. The first time was when he was learning to drive and Ritchie thought it would be fun for them to learn on back roads without risk of being caught. They drove here and parked at the top of the driveway, both of them too nervous to go any further, both of them daring each other and laughing. The second time was Monday night when he followed Cooper out here when Cooper had the girl in the trunk of his car, and that time he stayed well back in case Cooper heard him.

This time he pulls up the driveway, there is nobody to dare him, nobody to laugh with. Sunnyview is a much bigger building than Grover Hills and he doesn't like it; it doesn't have the homey feel that the Grove has. It's more modern, it's made from brick and it's more boxy and in better condition and life may have been different if he'd been sent here instead. The lawns are overgrown with patches of thistle coming through, and around the back it's knee length and tickles at his legs and he hates it. The skin on his back tingles as he carries the shovel and follows the path by the brick wall, using a flashlight now to light the way. At the end he turns left and takes a few footsteps before remembering he was supposed to go right. He should have taken notes. He knew it at the time, but he thought he would do okay. The sky is mostly dark now, purple way in the distance. There are big trees only a short distance away and thankfully Cooper didn't bury the girl in there otherwise he'd never find her. He runs in line with the building and actually trips into the ditch. It's about a meter lower than the normal level. He follows it looking carefully at the dirt. He finds the tree. It's a silver birch and the branches are all brittle. He climbs over it and it snags at his shirt and tears a small hole in it. He reaches back and drops the shovel and his foot gets tangled and he falls into the ditch, tearing his shirt even more. He picks up the shovel and bangs it flat against the ground twice, then tosses it forward a few meters, bangs his fists into the ground, and starts to cry. This isn't the way it was supposed to be.

It takes him a minute to get back up. His shirt is ruined. He finds the shovel and carries on. He has a headache. He counts out what he thinks are ten meters. The dirt looks different, it's raised up a little at the ten-meter mark, and he stabs the shovel into the ground. His itches fade as he digs, but he doesn't have to dig long before he finds her.

For a girl who has been dead only a couple of days, she is a real mess. In fact she is so much of a mess that he wonders if this is the girl at all and not another of Cooper's victims. After all, he did say he'd killed six people.

He is frightened that if he picks her up she is going to fall apart. And anyway, he doesn't want to touch her with his fingers. There are bugs and worms squirming around in her body. He looks around, sees nothing useful, then decides to use his shirt. After all, it's already damaged. He takes it off, wraps it around the dead girl's foot, and pulls.

The foot remains attached to the body, and the body slides up and out of the grave, lots of dirt stuck to it, some ugly-looking bits of flesh being left behind. He scoops her up. He keeps her held away from his body. He thinks if he tried dragging her all the way back to the car, there wouldn't be much of her left by the time he got there. He carries her around the silver birch tree instead of over it. He gets her back to the car and into the trunk. He leaves his shirt with her.

He needs to clean up. He's covered in dirt and what he thinks might be bits of the dead girl.

He takes a flashlight up to the main entrance of the building and tries the door. There is a chain going across the handles with a padlock that looks much newer than the one he smashed from the Grover Hills doors. He steps away and returns with the shovel. He rests the flashlight on the ground so it's pointing at the chain, gets a secure grip on the handle of the shovel, and swings. The first swing he misses the lock completely, and the edge of the shovel slides down the door and into the concrete step, vibrating through his hands, a few small chips of cement flicking up and getting him in the lip. When he swings again, it's out of anger. He hits the door three times before connecting with the chain, and when he does connect nothing happens, not until a few swings later when he hits down on the chain with enough force that the door handle it's attached to splinters away. He's curious—curious as to what it's like inside, curious as to what his life may have been like if he had been sent here instead. The hallways and rooms are as black as a cave, and the flashlight struggles to penetrate the dark. He leaves the shovel behind and moves through the building slowly, comparing the rooms to those of the Grove, the flashlight always keeping ninety percent of his surroundings in the dark. He finds a bathroom and rinses himself down. The water is ice cold. He carries on. He finds a strange-looking room unlike anything he has back home. It has a padded table bolted into the middle of the floor, arm and leg restraints connected to it. There are lots of power sockets around the walls and spaces on the floor and on benches where big pieces of equipment used to be, and a piece of wood with bite-marks in it with a strap connected to each end. He thinks this is one of those rooms where people used to get electrocuted when people thought that kind of thing helped. They'd put wires on you and turn up the voltage and it was supposed to fix up your brain. Geez, back then they'd even slice out part of your brain because the doctors thought it would help. He hopes they don't do that kind of thing anymore, and he's thankful that's one thing he never had to go through at the Grove. The basement was bad, and some of the things the orderlies did to him down there were worse, but he thinks he would still choose that over having bits of his brain cut off.

The naked girl in the next room comes as a complete surprise. His heart jumps in his chest when he sees her and he almost drops the flashlight. It's the girl Cooper brought out here the other night, the girl Adrian was sure that Cooper would have raped, killed, and disposed of by now, and yet here she is, so the girl he dug up is definitely a different girl. She doesn't look dead, and as if to confirm it, one of her arms moves slightly toward him, a spasm, like a cat chasing mice in a dream. There is duct tape across her eyes and two empty water bottles on the floor next to her. Her arms are tied behind her.

When he followed Cooper here on Monday night, he had hidden his car off the side of the road and approached on foot. At the driveway where he and Ritchie had stopped that day, he argued with himself what to do next, wanting to creep forward to get a better look but afraid he'd get spotted. He was brave enough to go as close as the Sunnyview entrance, but no further. He couldn't hear what was going on inside, but he didn't have to hear or see to know. He ran back down the driveway and down the road to his car. From Sunnyview he drove into town and left his car on the side of the road and took the car that had belonged to the girl Cooper took. This whole time he just assumed she was dead, and finding her alive is a blessing.

Already he is thinking what he can use her for.

Ultimately she'll be another gift to Cooper, but he doesn't want her being part of a test like the last one turned out to be. He wants something greater for her, and the universe wants something greater for her too—that's why he found her here.

But first she needs his help.

"I'm here to help you," he says.

She doesn't answer. He needs to get her some water, but he's afraid if he gives her some now she'll regain enough strength to try and run away. He carries her outside. She groans a little but doesn't speak. Her skin is hot to touch. It's hard to fit her in the trunk of the car because of the dead girl already in there, but with some perseverance he gets them snuggled up tight. He leaves the duct tape over her eyes so she doesn't have to see the view, but he knows she must be able to smell it.

Before he closes the lid, he gets the rag out of the front seat and pours the chemical that puts people to sleep, then holds it over the girl's face. She doesn't fight it, and a moment later she's asleep. He closes the lid carefully, not wanting to snap some fingers or a limb. Then it's back on the roads again, following them through the darkness and back toward their new home, the itching almost gone now, just one more thing to do before returning to the new home to see Cooper.

chapter forty-one

I wonder if Jane Tyrone and Emma Green knew each other. I wonder if they had more in common other than being young and blond and the type of girl Cooper Riley wanted to rape and murder. I try not to think about the hell Karen Ford went through here with one mentally unstable man and one madman. Whatever the relationship is between Cooper Riley and Adrian Loaner, there's no doubt that Karen Ford suffered. Her body is a mess. There is glue residue and torn skin around her lips with a drinking straw hanging from her bottom lip. I try not to think about her last few minutes but it's all I can think about—what a fucking cruel place to die.

The team of police searching the area has expanded over the last hour. So far only the one extra body has been found, this one has also been in the ground for several years according to the medical examiner, as many as twenty. Dozens of high-wattage halogen bulbs have been strung up around the scene. Moths are attracted to the lamps, they fly in at full speed, some of them impacting against the lamps and burning, others basking in the light as they dance in the air. From a distance it all looks like some archaeological dig, or a group of scientists unearthing an extraterrestrial find. So far no sign of Emma Green. Fingerprints taken from her flat, from her hairbrush and the books she was reading, have been run up against fingerprints found at Grover Hills and so far no match. Grover Hills is Adrian Loaner's hiding place, but it wasn't Cooper Riley's.

Schroder has made some calls to some of the staff who worked at Grover Hills. The first call he made seemed to be going well until he mentioned the Twins. Then he was shut down. The woman he was talking to said she wanted a lawyer. Every phone call since has followed a similar pattern.

"They're lawyering up," Schroder tells me. "Getting anything out of them is like getting blood out of a stone, and this is why. They knew shit was going on there. We're going to have to start getting warrants and bringing them in for questioning, and this is going to take a fuckload longer than it should."

Over the last thirty minutes media vans have started showing up. Men and women in expensive-looking outfits have been pouring out of vehicles and hitting the dirt roads, unable to pass the cordon that was erected only minutes before the first van arrived. Others are circling the perimeter, heading toward the trees on the hill in the near distance, all of them hoping for a better shot, wanting so desperately to be the first to share the tragedy with the rest of the country, to have their smiling faces on the ten-thirty news tonight to speak of horrors unburied, all of them aware the more bodies we find the bigger the story, the longer the story can survive, the better the ratings. At this point they have no idea what story they're covering, only that for this amount of police attention they know it's a big one. Emma Green and Cooper Riley are names that will pass across the airwaves as TV anchors bounce theories back and forth with the journalists live at the scene. As I watch them, a BMW that can only be a year old at the most pulls up and Jonas Jones steps out, the psychic here to *predict* that there are bodies in the graves. I allow myself a brief smile as I imagine what it would be like if a small earthquake opened the ground beneath the media and the city was suddenly short a couple of dozen journalists, but the smile disappears when I realize only more would come to replace them, only now with more to report on, bigger smiles and bigger news and bigger ratings.

"We're running out of time," I say, and Schroder nods. I turn toward Benson Barlow. "Who killed Karen Ford? Adrian Loaner or Cooper Riley or both of them together? And who abducted her? Did Riley abduct her and they were both taken by Adrian, or did Adrian take her by himself, and if so, why?"

"It's possible Riley and Loaner may start working together," Barlow says. "There are many cases of relationships between killers where one personality dominates over the other. I say it's possible, but I imagine highly unlikely. Riley won't have any time for Loaner. I think you'll find if an opportunity comes to kill Adrian Loaner, Cooper Riley will take it. If he's still alive, Cooper will be doing what he can to manipulate his way to freedom. I would imagine Adrian is trying to please Cooper, and the girl was a gift to him."

"Jesus," I say. "So you think Cooper Riley is still alive then."

"Until the novelty wears off, yes."

"And Emma Green?"

"If she's still alive, it won't be for long. That's one thing I can be certain of."

"We don't know anything for certain," Schroder says. "For all we know Adrian might try eating Cooper." He puts his hand on my shoulder to steer me away from the graves. "Look, I know you're not going to give me any peace, and like you said, there are things you can do that we can't."

"What are you asking, Carl?"

"I don't really know," he says, but I think he does know, he just doesn't want to voice it. He looks back to see if Barlow is following, but he isn't. He opens up his car door and leans inside. He pulls out four folders. One each for Adrian Loaner, Cooper Riley, Karen Ford, and Jane Tyrone. He holds them against his chest. "Look, Theo, you have a way of finding people and finding out about them, and if Emma Green really is still alive . . . just, I don't know, I want to say just do what it takes. I guess that's what I am saying. Do what it takes, and in your case dial it back a little."

I nod and he hands me the folders. The one with Adrian's name on it is by far the thinnest of them all. I open it up and there's a photograph of him from the institution. I don't know when it was taken, but it doesn't look much like the sketch I tore from the newspaper.

He leans back into his car. "Don't lose this one again," he says, and hands me the Melissa X file, only now it's thicker and the front of it says *Natalie Flowers / AKA Melissa X.*

I get lost on the way back home. There is no point in hanging around at Grover Hills, and there aren't any names jumping out at me as to who to speak to next. It's dark and there's no other source of lighting on these roads other than what's coming from my car and the sliver of pale moon. Nothing is recognizable, and certainly nothing looks the same as it did this afternoon. I have no idea how the media made it out here, and can only assume that in the deal they made to sell their souls, the Devil threw in GPS as a bonus. I drive up and down a wrong set of dirt roads until lucking my way back into what I'd deem civilization. The highway gets me back onto the road to town where traffic is thick but so far flowing quickly, and for the first time in my life I make it through town hitting less than half a dozen red lights.

The Friday-night crowd is spilling into town, guys in tight T-shirts with big biceps and girls in jeans so tight they look painted on. Shiny cars with bright paint race the streets, tires spinning at every intersection with smoke hanging in the dry air. Other cars are parked in groups, teenagers in black hoodies leaning against them as they laugh and smoke and drink beer and give the finger to anybody driving by, all of them in jeans way too low, showing way too much, making me want to way too much run all of them over. It's such a different world from the one I just left, and these kids have no idea just how lucky they are.

I park the rental in my driveway. Nobody from the media shows up. Plenty of them yelled questions at me as I drove through them earlier, most of them recognizing me and asking if I was back on the payroll. In my study I open up the four new files and spread the contents across the desk and set the Melissa X one to the side for later. As much as I want to find Natalie Flowers, she isn't the one who kidnapped Emma Green, she isn't the one who abducted Cooper Riley. There is a connection to her, but not a relevant one that will help us find Emma. Even if we found Natalie within the hour it wouldn't do Emma Green any good.

I pop open a Coke and start reading. Adrian's file is only one page. It has his name and age and when he was committed but it doesn't have the reason why. Medical privilege and all that. Which means we'll never know what made him crazy. It lists the halfway house as his current address.

The file on Cooper Riley is the thickest one. It traces back his history from when he was a child, his education, university, becoming a criminologist and then a professor. Karen Ford's file is thin because she was only reported missing earlier today. She was a known prostitute, but since prostitution isn't illegal in New Zealand, she doesn't have a record. Jane Tyrone's file is thick. It has all the information from the investigation into her disappearance last year. There's a photograph of her, a smiling happy-looking girl in the prime of her life. I look though Emma Green's file, but there isn't much that I already didn't know. We know who took her, and we know who took Cooper Riley.

If I pressed Ritchie Munroe, if I threatened to take Melina away from him, would he know anything more about his best friend? I wonder how easily Adrian was able to make his way to and from Grover Hills. I wonder if Cooper struggled with the drive the first few times. Jonas Jones wouldn't—he'd have used his psychic abilities. But for the rest of us, driving out there is a challenge. I figure Cooper would drive out there then drive to one of the others to conduct more interviews to save on petrol.

"Damn it," I say, slapping the desk. How could I have missed it?

I missed it the same way we all missed it, but it's no excuse. I grab my cell phone. There are two more buildings almost identical in nature to Grover Hills. Both are abandoned. And Cooper Riley knows that better than anybody. Barlow said Adrian would want to return somewhere familiar to him, and though Adrian never grew up in either of the other two places, the similarity may be enough. In fact, that similarity may be all he has. And for Cooper Riley, what better place to take Emma Green? There could be other rooms like the Scream Room, and there are certainly going to be some padded cells.

I dial Schroder's number. I walk through the living room to the French doors. Schroder answers and I open the door to step out onto the deck, wanting to escape the hot air inside.

"Oh fuck," I say.

"Tate?"

"She's here," I say, and the words are thick and catch at the back of my throat.

"What?" he asks.

"Barlow . . ." I have to hold a hand up to my mouth. "Barlow was right."

"What are you talking about?"

"Only it wasn't the pets we had to worry about."

"What are you talking about?"

"Jane . . . Jane Tyrone," I say, and her name is covered in the taste of vomit.

"What about her?"

The corpse has the same hair but beyond that it's a mess, any of the features blurred by five months of rot and decay. "She's hanging from my roof," I say, and I crouch down and throw up off the side of the deck and onto the lawn.

chapter forty-two

Adrian feels better. The itching has gone, his skin feels cool, he feels relaxed and at peace. Digging up the dead girl was a new experience, and he has to admit, an even more rewarding one than he was used to. He could have done without the mess and the smell of her, but ultimately digging up cats is child's play compared to digging up and hanging the dead girl.

Like using an ATM at a drive-through, it's character building. One brought about by a need he never thought he would have. Seeing those people at Grover Hills triggered something inside of him, something Cooper would label as *rage*, and he knew digging up the girl and hanging her from Tate's roof would make the rage disappear.

All those times he was locked in the Scream Room with blood running down his thighs and the skin on his face scuffed from the cinder blocks, he would drift away from the cold room and take himself back to the boys who hurt him, and in his thoughts he would kill them, he would kill them the way his friends at the institution had killed others. When he was a boy, digging up the animals was a waste of time. He knows that now, he's experienced it now. All those years ago he should have been killing the boys who had hurt him and stringing them up for their parents to find.

He's back in Tate's neighborhood, and he's nervous being back. During the drive here he looked at every car as a potential police car. He was beginning to regret taking her car. He should have kept the car he started with—the police wouldn't be looking for it. In this weather it wasn't that odd walking the streets without a shirt on, but it was odd carrying a dead girl, so he parked outside the house and carried the dead girl through the side gate into the backyard. The other girl, the alive one, was still asleep.

Then he went and moved his car to the end of the block and around the corner and came back. Since stringing up the girl he's been waiting behind Tate's garage, waiting for the reaction. From his vantage point he isn't able to see it, but he certainly hears it. He can hear him talking on his phone, then silence, then gagging as the ex-policeman starts throwing up on his lawn. The sound of it makes Adrian feel sick too, and for a frightening moment he thinks he's also going to throw up. He sucks in a deep breath and holds it and the feeling disappears.

He moves around the garage and down the back of the house, staying against it. Light is coming out of the dining room and kitchen windows and hitting the lawn to the side of him. He can see the grave where the cat was buried, dug up, and it looks like buried again. He reaches the end of the house. Tate is crouched off the side of the deck, the phone is still in his hand. He can hear the person on the other end of it, a tinny voice asking Tate over and over "What's wrong?"

He's positive he hasn't made a sound, yet he senses that Tate knows he's there. There's a pause, no longer than a second, but it feels like a minute in which both of them hold their breath. Tate has vomit on his chin and his face is covered in sweat, the living room light reflecting off it, the phone is hanging down in one hand and in the other . . .

"No," Adrian says, barely getting the word out before the gun comes up toward him. Adrian has never seen one in real life. He thought Cooper would have owned one, or the Twins, but the closest he's ever come to seeing one is on a TV screen. Adrian pulls the trigger on his own gun, which isn't a gun at all but only shaped like one, and the twin darts are propelled from the Taser and hit Tate in the chest and his body contracts and the gun goes off, an explosion of sound followed quickly by the impact of a bullet splintering into the wooden fence behind him.

The Taser does the same job it's been doing on everybody else and gives him the same result. He keeps his finger on the trigger, thousands of volts pouring from the Taser down the wires into the barbs embedded into Tate's body until his eyes roll up and he flops onto his back, four limbs all useless and laying in a heap. Adrian rushes forward and holds the rag over Tate's face. He isn't able to struggle. A moment later he's unconscious.

There was a small fright with the gun, but other than that none of this could have gone any better, plus now he has a gun to add to his collection!

"Welcome to my collection," he says, and can't hear the words over the ringing in his ears. He tugs at the barbs in Tate's chest and they're caught in there pretty deep but he manages to get them out by tugging harder. He winds them around the weapon and jams it into his pocket. He picks up the gun.

The cell phone is on the ground next to Tate's hand. It's still on, and whoever is on the other end is still listening. He stomps on it, a sharp stab of pain shooting up his leg on impact. It doesn't break on the first hit, rather it sinks slightly into the ground. He stomps on it a second time, this time it breaks into two pieces and the pain in his leg is more intense.

The ringing in his ears is starting to die down, and he can hear voices. He looks around at the houses next to him and lights that weren't on before are on now. There are people staring at him from one of the windows. He points the gun at them and they duck away. They've heard the gunshot and they've called the police. He crouches down and gets Tate over his shoulder, but manages only one step before his right leg gives out and he falls over, Tate landing on top of him. He rolls the deadweight off him and when he tries to stand the pain returns, the same pain as when he broke the cell phone. He reaches down and touches his leg and his hand comes away with blood. He rolls up his pants leg. There's a groove of flesh missing across the side of his outer thigh where the bullet Tate fired chewed through him. Blood is flowing from it steadily. He never even felt it happen, and now that he's seen it it's starting to hurt bad. There's no way he can carry Tate and get to the car quickly now, and the police are on their way because the damn nosy neighbors would have called them.

"This isn't fair," he says, reaching the side gate. "*Fairness is only for winners,*" his mother used to say, not his real mother, but the one he set on fire. He guesses that wasn't fair on her being set ablaze like that, and guesses that means she wasn't a winner. He moves over the front yard onto the street, gritting his teeth as he covers the distance to his car. He holds one hand firmly against the wound as he drives, and is several blocks away before he hears the first of the sirens.

chapter forty-three

For the first thirty-eight years of my life I'd never been shot by a Taser. Now it's my second time within the last year. Don't know if that means I'll go another thirty-eight years before getting shot again two more times, or whether I'm going to get shot every year now until I'm seventy-six. Last time it was my lawyer, this time it's an ex-mental patient. I don't know which is worse, but I do know who would bill me more.

I can see the stars and I can feel the ground beneath me, but I can't move anything and just keeping my eyes open is using up all my resources. There are a few voices and somebody says my name a couple of times but it seems like all the words are being dialed in from one of the stars above me. Shapes move above me but they don't stay still long enough to snap into focus, but I think they're faces. Eventually I'm moved. I know this because the stars swirl around a little and then I can see the eaves of my roof rolling by and then the ceiling of a van comes into view. I close my eyes and can feel my head spinning. I think I nap for a little while and when I open my eyes I'm not sure how much time has passed, but I can feel my arms and legs even though I can barely move them.

"It was a mistake letting you out," Schroder says, leaning over me.

"I'm starting to think the same thing," I say.

"Huh?"

"I said I'm starting to think the same thing."

"Whatever you're saying might sound comprehensible to you," Schroder says, "but all I can hear is *wubwubwubbubwub*."

"Sorry."

"Huh? Look, just relax. I'll come back in a few minutes, hopefully you'll be better."

My mouth tastes like I've bitten into a very raw piece of steak. I can taste what may be copper or may be blood but is whatever chemical Adrian used to knock me out. I close my eyes and try to focus on one limb at a time. I can move fingers and toes but nothing more. I go through each limb again. I can make fists. I can clench my feet. I keep going through them until I can bend my arms, then my legs. I sit up and my head swirls and I pass straight out.

When I come to again Schroder is back. "How you feeling?"

"Like shit."

"That matches up with how you look. Jesus, Tate, isn't there anybody left in this city you haven't pissed off?"

I'm seriously starting to doubt it. I sit up, much slower this time. I'm dizzy and hungry and thirsty and I can't remember the last time I ever felt so exhausted. I have a headache made up of sharp waves that arrive one after the other, each feels like my brain biting at the back of my eyeballs. The ambulance looks cluttered and it's a miracle the paramedics can ever know where anything is. I swing my feet out over the edge of the gurney and things swim out of focus for a few seconds but return.

"What the hell happened?" Schroder asks.

"I don't . . . don't really know."

"You were attacked while you were on the phone to me."

"You rang me?"

"No, you rang me."

"Hang on," I say, and I close my eyes and try to remember. I can remember eating a burger. I remember walking through the gardens, all the flowers, the river, lush lawns and healthy-looking trees even in this heat. I remember the bodies at Grover Hills, the guys in their gang patches with the mean dog. Then I'm walking through my house and dialing the phone, I opened the door and there she was. Is that why I was calling Schroder? To tell him about the body? No, no, I was on the phone before I saw her . . .

"She was hanging from my roof somehow."

"Jane Tyrone," he says, reminding me.

"He shot me with a Taser and drugged me."

"We know, and no doubt it's how he's taken the others. There's something he said to you."

"Huh?"

"Not long after the gunshot. Probably when you were unconscious. He said, 'Welcome to my collection.' So Barlow was right and Adrian is obsessed with Cooper, he's building up a collection that was going to include you. If he hadn't freaked out at the gunshot, you'd be in a locked room somewhere on display."

"Shit," I say, thinking how things could have gone differently, thinking that right now I could have been waking up in a Scream Room all my own.

"I'm missing something," I say.

"The gun?"

"No. I mean, yes, but there's something I had to tell you."

"Where'd the gun come from, Tate?"

I figure it's likely that Adrian *collected* the gun after attacking me. I think about telling Schroder that Adrian brought the gun with him, but there'd have been no reason for him to fire it.

"It was a gift," I tell him. "After my cat was strung up and Adrian broke into my house, I didn't feel safe here."

"A gift from who? From Donovan Green?"

"Why's it matter?"

"Because it's illegal, that's why."

"And if I hadn't had it, who knows where the hell I'd be waking up right now?"

"Okay, Tate, I'll let the gun slide for now, but I'm not forgetting about it. By the way, you shot him."

"What?"

"We found the bullet in the fence. There's cloth and blood on it, so it went through something. And we got drops of blood on the lawn surrounded by the Taser ID disks, and we've got blood leading up the street. Not enough to be something major, but you got him pretty good."

Schroder helps me out of the ambulance, taking some of my weight so I can step down. My first few steps are like those a baby foal will take and Schroder has to help me for a few seconds. The headache stays, though. I remember pulling out the gun. I was holding the phone in my good hand and reached for the gun with my bandaged one. It made me a split second slower. It made the grip more difficult. If I'd had a fraction longer I could have taken aim. This would be all over now. Problem is Adrian would be lying in my backyard with a bullet in his head, his brain pulped, along with Emma Green's location.

The ambulance is parked in front of my house. On the footpath are plastic markers sitting next to what must be blood drops. We head to the backyard where six people are looking around, all of them slightly out of focus. All the lights in my house have been switched on, and a couple of large lamps have been set up outside. My neighbors keep peering over the fences.

Jane Tyrone is hanging where I last saw her. There's rope wrapped around her chest and under her arms, and she's been strung up, the rope thrown around the chimney on the roof and pulled back down to lift her weight, then tied off against the leg of the picnic bench. I can imagine Adrian heaving her into the air, the actions like climbing a rope. Nobody would have seen a thing over the fence. Ever so slowly, her body is rotating a hundred degrees or so, the rope spinning, she comes to a stop going one way then slowly starts to spin back the other. Her body is bloated and there isn't much left in the way of skin, just a few patches, but mostly it's just raw-looking flesh and even bigger areas of no flesh at all. There's a large slice across her chest that must have been made by the shovel that unearthed her. She's naked, but covered in dirt. Parts of her are moving slowly, and I realize she has bugs squirming inside her. What face she has left is dark and sagging, the remaining skin is loose and her fingers and hands look like she's wearing gloves that're two sizes too big for her.

"Anybody see anything?" I ask.

"Lots of people heard the gunshot," Schroder says, "and most of them looked out their windows. We got a bunch of matching descriptions that line up with Adrian Loaner, along with a description of the car."

"That it?"

"That's about as good as we can get. At least this time he didn't take all your files."

"Remind me to thank him," I say. "So we don't know anything more than we already knew, is that what you're telling me?"

"Not true. We know he's obsessed with you."

"Can't somebody cut her down?" I ask, nodding toward the dead girl.

"Not yet."

"Jesus, Carl, she's been up there long enough."

"Not yet, Tate. You know how it goes."

"Goddamn it," I say, and I'm hit by another wave of nausea and have to crouch down before I lose balance.

"You okay?"

"No, I'm not okay," I say, sounding pissed off and wanting to sound that way. "I was ringing you earlier because there was something I had to tell you. Goddamn it, it was important."

"It'll come to you."

I close my eyes. I hate it when people say that, but I hate even more forgetting something I'm about to say before I can say it. This feels just like that. I squeeze my eyes shut even tighter in the hope it will help. I'm in the backyard, I'm on the phone to Schroder, I'm thinking about Emma Green, about Grover Hills, about places where Adrian can keep his collection. Grover Hills . . . for a while

Christchurch did what it could to hide the mental people away until one day they realized they were going to need a hundred institutions, so instead they closed down the three they had and let everybody go.

The three they had . . .

All within driving distance!

My eyes snap open. Every muscle in my body is humming with energy. "I know where she is," I tell him, almost but not quite grabbing hold of Schroder and shaking him.

"What?"

"Emma Green. It's what I wanted to tell you. I know where she is."

"Where?"

"I'm going with you," I say and head to Schroder's car. In the last few minutes a couple of vans have shown up, TV network slogans stenciled across the sides. I feel nauseous again. "And we're going to need to lose these vultures," I say, nodding toward the vans.

"You're staying here, Tate. Tell me, what's your theory?"

I open up the passenger door and climb in. "Let's go," I say, ignoring him, "and get some backup. We're going to need it."

chapter forty-four

His mother used to tell him only girls cried, and when he went down to the basement and came back with tears on his face that's what made him a girl. He never thought so. He always thought it was what those two orderlies did to him sometimes when they stripped him naked that made him a girl, or they thought of him as a girl, he isn't sure exactly which. But right now he is crying. He's pulled the car off the road well away from Tate's neighborhood and he's holding his hands tightly on his leg and there are tears streaming from his face. He cries not only from the pain but from the frustration. Nothing is working out. He always has to fight for everything in his stupid life and this is going to be no different. Why can't things just come easily to him like they do to everybody else?

Why can't people just like him?

His hands are covered in blood. There isn't anything in the car he can wrap around the wound, and if he takes his pants off to use he would be almost naked. His leg is itchy and too tender to scratch. He lowers his head and stares at the hole, tears dripping into his blood, and he imagines he's back in his room at the Grove and he's pacing the room, counting the footsteps, preferring the even footsteps over the odds, starting with his left and finishing with his right. Then he thinks about the cats, the boys who pissed on him and beat him, then he imagines putting them in the ground and digging them back up, ending their lives the same way they ruined his.

His tears start to slow, and the pressure in his chest from sobbing begins to ease. Strings of snot dangle from his nose and he wipes them with his hands, forgetting about the blood for a second until it streaks across his face. He begins to cry again. Life isn't fair. It never has been. It never will be.

His leg hurts but it's not bleeding as much now. His pants are completely soaked in blood. He can't stay on the side of the road all night. He wipes his hands dry on the passenger seat, starts the engine and drives slowly, but not too slow, not wanting to attract the kind of attention that will get him pulled over. Blood has pooled into his shoe and makes a sucking sound when he presses on the accelerator. The wound is bad, but he knows if it were *that bad* he'd have passed out or died from loss of blood. He has no idea how to treat the wound or take care of it. In the past, cuts that were bad were bandaged for him by one of the nurses or his mother, and since leaving the Grove he's never needed a doctor or a nurse to take a look at anything. What he needs is his mother, either one of them, but one's dead and so is the other and he has never felt their loss as much as he feels it now. He truly is alone with nobody to care for him, he's out of mothers, out of old people, his best friend left him for a girl that isn't even real, and those at the halfway house never warmed to him the same way ninety-nine percent of everybody else never warms to him.

Including Cooper.

Friendship is such a simple thing for others, but not for him. And he's being naïve if he thinks Cooper really wants to be his friend. Although Cooper was right about the police.

He begins driving, heading back home, unsure if Cooper will help him, trying desperately to think of another option. Each turn is painful as he switches from accelerator to brake. There aren't many people on the streets, not in the suburbs. People don't go out much at night. He learned not to. At night the last place he ever wanted to be was outside the walls of the halfway house.

He could go to the hospital. He couldn't go in, but he could get one of the nurses coming out to help him. She wouldn't want to at first, but he would make her do it. He could hold a gun to her head and she wouldn't say no. The problem is somebody might see him. The hospital is a public place.

What then?

"Why couldn't you have helped me?" he says, talking to his second mother. If she had helped him in the beginning, none of this would have happened.

He pulls over and stops the car, thinking, thinking, the only person who would help him is somebody who doesn't know him already, somebody who hasn't formed an opinion.

chapter forty-five

We split into two teams. Schroder lets me come along this time. We head to Eastlake House full of enthusiasm and determination, and the other team heads to Sunnyview Shelter. We know that Adrian Loaner has a gun and therefore armed-offenders units are coming along for the ride. The drive takes us out of town and back past the prison and the fields full of crops and animals but none of it is visible in the dark. There aren't any streetlights on the motorway, just faded white lines down the center of the road keeping traffic on one side from smacking head-on into traffic on the other. Red and blue swirling lights belt out from the top of the cars, a string of vehicles consistent in their urgency, the lights warning anybody ahead of us to get the hell out of the way.

Schroder is armed and so is everybody else and I'm the only one who isn't. I've never seen him drive so fast and it doesn't mix well with the headache and nausea I still have. We hit another section of unpaved roads and Schroder barely slows down, not until the roads become a maze. The dirt streets all look the same and the GPS unit on Schroder's dashboard doesn't seem to have any better idea where Eastlake is than we do. In the end all the patrol cars slow down and a bunch of us get out and stand on the side of the road, the flashing lights coloring our skin first red and then blue and then merging to purple. The urgency and frustration is evident in the way everybody starts swearing about how hard it is to find anything out here. One call to the media and we could have followed them. The air is warm and sticky but fresher out here than in town. An entire community of moths, maybe a thousand or more of them, are hanging around in the headlights, the occasional one straying into our faces. We get out maps and bounce out some ideas and finally decide on a direction. Schroder takes the lead again and we sit in silence as he drives, a few minutes later bringing us to a stop a hundred meters from a driveway lined with oak trees. He kills the lights and the other cars line up in single file behind us and do the same. The night goes dark. There is no light pollution out here from the city, and the stars are as clear as you'll ever get without flying up to greet them. Pale light is thrown out over the fields from a moon that in a few days will be full, there are shapes out in those fields, fence posts and trees and black objects the size of cars that could be just about anything.

"Wait here," Schroder says.

"You've got to be kidding me."

"I mean it. You step out of that car and I'll shoot you myself."

"Don't make me beg. Damn it, Carl, you're only here because of me."

"Maybe you're right. You should put yourself in the line of fire. It'd be worth the paperwork just to get rid of you."

I watch through the windshield as the armed-offenders unit slowly moves forward, six people dressed in armor as dark as the night, and they fade out of view about ten meters ahead of me. Schroder goes around to the trunk of the car and puts on a bulletproof vest. I get out of the car and he hands one to me. I put my arms through the holes and strap it on tight. Out of the car I can feel the tension in the air, and I'm certainly contributing to what's feeling like a trigger-happy mood. If there are any scarecrows out in the fields they're in danger of being shot. Emma Green is in this building somewhere, she has to be, and if not then she's in Sunnyview.

I follow the team with Schroder who has his hands tightly on a pistol, but I fall back with each step because of my knee. By the time they reach the driveway, I'm already twenty meters behind and frustrated. The road is hard-packed dirt and the heat of it is coming up through my shoes. The unit ahead splits up, two go left, two go right, and the other two go straight ahead. Schroder waits for me, then we follow the two straight forward at my pace, and come to a stop twenty-five meters back from the door. The building looms up out of the ground, the front of it lit up by the moon, it looks pale white and run-down, the ivy climbing the front of it so black that it looks like strings of holes in the walls. It looks like the sort of place we should have come armed with crucifixes and holy water. There are no cars out front. One of the teams makes it around the back and I can hear a voice coming through Schroder's earpiece but can't make it out. He puts his finger against it and listens carefully, cocking his head slightly to the side.

"No cars around the back," he tells me.

"Doesn't mean they're not here," I say. "Might just mean that Adrian is out and not back yet."

"Well, if he's on his way back we'll get him. We've got two units hidden a few blocks back. No way anybody is getting past without getting pulled over."

The team in the middle reaches the door. One of them stands off to the side, half crouching while pointing his gun ahead as the other person swings a metal battering ram that opens the door quicker than a key and echoes across the fields. Flashlights are switched on and the team disappears. There are loud footsteps as they make their way quickly through the building. I want to join them but Schroder puts his hand on my shoulder.

"Give them time," he says.

We give them five minutes. The moon reflects off some of the windows but the light seems to be absorbed by others. There are constant updates coming through Schroder's earpiece. None of the shapes out in the field move. Flashlights appear in all the windows. We can hear the officers moving around inside. There's the occasional stuck door being shouldered open, the odd floorboard creaking. Then the scene is clear and we move into the building.

The building seems much bigger than it ought to be up close, and even bigger inside. We step in through the main door. The framework has been splintered from where the team knocked it in. The air is dry and has the texture of dust. We start on the ground floor and make our way upstairs. We take a good look around, there are padded cells that are empty and no basements with thick iron doors and scream rooms. There is leftover furniture abandoned, a few broken windows, but no vandalism, just like Grover Hills. The living arrangements are crowded, small rooms that would take two people and I can't imagine there was much hope for anybody living out here, and I think about my wife, about her care home, about the room she has all to herself even though she's not aware of it, and I can't help but think the people sent here could have done better if they had rooms and care like that. How hard was it for the nurses and doctors to care about people who'd done really bad things? Surely many came here with good hopes but ended up being burned too many times until they just treated everybody like shit.

No scream room. No basements with thick iron doors. No Emma Green, no Cooper Riley, no Adrian Loaner, and no indication they were ever here.

"Shit," I say, voicing my anger. "We chose the wrong one. She must be at Sunnyview," I say, but nobody is listening. The armed team is going back through the rooms, and one man is covering the room I'm in with Schroder, while Schroder is on his cell phone, so I'm talking to myself.

Schroder is slowly shaking his head and I have a real good idea of what he's about to tell me and a real bad feeling about it. He slips his cell phone back into his pocket.

"Don't tell me," I tell him.

"It was a good idea, Tate, and nobody here rejected it, but that was the team at Sunnyview and it's empty."

"No way," I say, punching the padded wall of one of the cells. "It can't be. They have to be there or here. Have to be."

"There are signs somebody was there," Schroder says. "Apparently there's a new chain and lock hanging from the door that's just been smashed, there's dirt on the front steps, and there are some empty water bottles in one of the padded rooms. Forensics are going to take a look around; it's possible she was being kept there, and just as possible some homeless guy was using it for shelter."

"Emma's still somewhere."

"I know. She's just not here."

"Then where?" I ask, hitting the padded wall again, this time not as hard.

"I don't know. But it has to be somewhere big enough for four people."

"Why four?"

"I got another call while I was on the phone to the other team. Adrian's collected another person."

I almost can't believe what I'm hearing. "Jesus," I say, "are you joking? Who?"

"He's taken Cooper Riley's mother."

chapter forty-six

The bandaging is tight but it makes the wound feel much better and Adrian is thankful for her help. He did to Mrs. Riley what he did to her son, and she rode in the trunk of the car in the same style too. Cooper would want him to have treated her worse than that, but of course he'll never admit to it. He didn't need to use the Taser though. He only needed to point the gun at her and hold the rag over her face, and it was enough. Cooper's mum had to be a hundred years old and was never going to put up much of a struggle, and she didn't, not when he told her he was taking her to see her son.

He should have thought of her immediately, especially after his conversation with Cooper that morning. But instead he sat parked on the side of the road for twenty minutes before her name tumbled into his head. This time, as he had predicted, there were no cars outside her house when he got there. He parked in the driveway and he planned what he would say, but at the door those same words tangled in his mouth and he said nothing that made any sense. So instead he cried and he pointed the gun at her and told her he would kill her if she didn't help. When they were done, he found some clothes in the back of a wardrobe before putting her into the trunk of the car alongside the other girl.

By now the police will have unearthed some of the bodies at the Grove. He doesn't know how many are there. Grover Hills ran for over fifty years before he got there, and he imagines records of patients back then would have become as lost or as buried as some of the patients. Could be there were other orderlies, other "Twins" who tormented other patients and put them in the dirt. There might be a hundred graves out there. He never saw any ghosts but he's never believed in them, and he suspects the two things are related, that you can only see what you believe. He must remember to ask Cooper about that. If there are ghosts, is it possible the ghosts of the Twins are haunting the ghosts of those they killed out there, their souls tormenting other souls? Ever since that first visit down to the Scream Room, the Twins have been haunting him; in fact, it's only been since he killed them that they've finally left him in peace. They took him down to that basement eighty-seven times over the twenty years he was there. He doesn't know how many times a year that is. Sometimes it was once a month. Other times twice a year. One year they only took him down there on his birthday. Eighty-seven times. He doesn't like that it ended on an odd number. It was the irregularity of it all that frightened him the most. You just never knew. Any minute they could come and take you.

And then he took them.

First one, then the other. He knocked on the door and swung the hammer the moment it was opened. He forced his way inside, but it didn't take much forcing at that point. He finished off one of the Twins then sat quietly in the living room while waiting for the other to come home. A hammer to cave in the backs of their skulls. No need for any discussion. He didn't care what they had to say, and for years they'd told him to shut up. The Twins lived together, neither of them married, a modern three-bedroom house in a nice neighborhood with a garage door that automatically opened with the touch of a button—something he'd never seen before. There was nothing there to suggest they were so mean and cruel. Nothing to suggest they had missed the Grove so much that they had built their own Scream Room. No, those suggestions were all kept for the farmhouse they kept an hour out of the city. He knows that because even before he thought about returning to the Grove, he had been following them. He had seen the farmhouse from a distance.

The farmhouse is more open than the Grove. Lots more ground with low wooden-beam gates between paddocks fenced off with wire. Lots of different types of grass and weed are devouring the landscape, no animals anywhere, just a million bugs making sounds in the night. He wonders what used to be farmed here, if there were ever any cows and sheep and chicken. He imagines growing up in a place like this, going to one of the small schools in one of the small towns nearby, where kids who live on farms are shipped to by bus five days a week. Winters sitting around the fireplace, summers riding horses and lying under trees and eating fresh fruit. When the hunt for Cooper has died down, he should look at getting a horse and planting some apple trees. He'll plant orange trees too, and whatever else he can plant.

In hindsight, it might have been better to have brought Cooper out here in the first place. Nobody has any reason to visit, only the Twins, and they won't be visiting anymore. There must be graves out there among that tall grass, other victims of the Scream Room built inside, a room with padded walls and little acoustics and you could scream and scream in there for a thousand years and never be heard. Since he's heading down the path of hindsight, he should have locked the Twins in the Scream Room at the Grove and just left them there. Starvation would have taken care of them. Let them stay down there and let them scream their throats raw and never be heard, one of them eventually eating the other to live longer. He wishes now he had thought to do that. They were lucky to have only been hammered. With what they did to him, to the others, to what they've done in the Scream Room they built out here, they deserved much worse.

The key for the farmhouse is now hanging on the same set of keys for the stolen car. He checks on the mother and lays her down on the driveway, then pulls out the girl. He has to drag her because his leg is too sore to carry her weight. She's still asleep, and in her sleep she doesn't look happy and he guesses she didn't enjoy the earlier ride, jammed up against the girl he dug up. He gets her up onto the porch and inside and lays her down in the hall. He grabs a glass of water and comes back to her and tips it toward her mouth, but it runs over her face and soaks into the carpet. She is no good to Cooper like this, and what kind of host would he be offering her to him like this anyway? She groans a little, and he isn't sure whether she's asleep or partly awake. He drags her into one of the bathrooms where it's much cooler, his leg too sore for him to carry her. He fills one of the tubs with cool water and slides her inside. She blinks and focuses on him but still doesn't say anything.

"I'm going to make you better," he says, and he puts water onto his fingers and rolls it into her mouth. This time she swallows. He smiles. Then his smile disappears. He can't find the glue. He took it out of his ruined pants back at Cooper's mum's house and put it into his new pair—didn't he? Ever since the beating Adrian took as a kid, he's been fully aware anything he puts down he may never see again. He can take his watch off and sit it on a table only to find it two days later under the bed or outside in the garden. He can put down a key and turn his back on it and it'll disappear. Screwdrivers, coins, books, even shoes—it doesn't matter. And it's frustrating. It makes him crazy. He should have been a magician.

Now the glue, which he knows he brought with him, is missing, and how else is he supposed to be able to keep the girl's mouth closed?

The glue was something that his mother—his Grover Hills mother—used to use on him. He'd be down in that basement yelling so loudly because he was scared to be down there, and she'd come down with a couple of the orderlies, not always the Twins—though sometimes it was one or both of them and sometimes different people completely—and they'd hold him down and put the glue between his lips and pinch them shut. Most of the time when his mouth was glued he'd work at it with his fingers. He'd dampen them in the bucket of water and slowly pry them apart, a little at a time, trying not to tear the skin but usually failing. A couple of times there was too much glue, or a different kind, and for some reason no matter how hard he tried he couldn't get his mouth open, and when they finally let him out of his cell they'd rub alcohol or turpentine or something that tasted real bad across his mouth, rubbing it into the slowly widening gap and it'd hurt bad and taste even worse and roughed up the skin for days. The straw was his idea. He knew what it was like when you got thirsty and couldn't drink.

He'll do the same for this woman, once he finds the glue.

He just has to find the straws too.

He smiles at her, noticing for the first time just how attractive she is, and he blushes at the thought. He drips some more water into her mouth before pulling her out and, keeping her wet, he ties her onto one of the beds then heads outside for Cooper's mother who has rolled onto her side and is in the process of trying to get to her feet.

chapter forty-seven

Schroder goes to Cooper Riley's mother's house. He's going in the hope a map fell out of Adrian's pocket with a big circle around the location where he's holed up with Cooper and his mother and maybe Emma too.

I catch a ride with one of the officers heading to Grover Hills. I figure I can do more for Emma there than I can from a motel room. The officer doesn't make much conversation on the way. He's not somebody who was in the department when I was three years ago, so he doesn't know anything about my history, which feels nice. He also doesn't get lost—he's made the drive a couple of times today and can pick the difference between one dirt road over another. Maybe he grew up on a farm or the training these days is better than it was for me. Sunnyview and Eastlake were a bust, but forensic crews are still being sent to both to check for fingerprints and blood and to scout around the grounds for bodies.

We drive through the perimeter the media have set up around Grover Hills and questions are yelled at us and spotlights pointed at us and the officer is blinded by one of the cameras and clips one of the reporters with the side of the bumper. She is sent flying into the dirt. She gets up screaming abuse at us and threatening to sue before realizing her mistake, that being more hurt means a bigger story and more compensation, so she goes quiet and collapses into a heap. Every camera lights her up and she lays there in a caricature of pain. The officer stops the car and gets out and takes a couple of steps toward her, but is blocked by cameras and more lights all pointing at him now. He raises his hands to shield his eyes. I leave him to it and walk toward the building, passing a couple of cops coming back my way to help their colleague.

Two more bodies have been found since I've been gone, both of them in the same grave. There seems to be no pattern as to where the bodies have been laid out, probably because the people doing the digging were crazy. Nobody gives me so much as a second glance as I walk over to take a closer look. The two bodies are fresh-looking, lots of skin slippage, dark veins protrude from underneath their skin as if they are worms feeding and burrowing their way beneath the blotchy surfaces. My stomach turns for the second time tonight. One man is wearing jeans and one is wearing shorts and they're both wearing T-shirts that are stained with fluids that have seeped from their bodies.

One of the medical examiners, a woman by the name of Tracey Walter, comes over. Last time I saw her was when I was working on the Burial Killer case. Back then she had black hair tied into a ponytail, now it's been dyed blond but the style is the same. She always has an athletic look about her, as if she might break into a jog at any time.

"Who let you in?" she asks, at least grinning as she says it.

"Schroder asked for my help."

She offers me her hand. "It's clean," she says, then seems to struggle holding it there as I shake it. Last year she was pretty angry with me and I don't blame her. I almost got her fired when I stole evidence from her morgue.

"So what can you tell me about these guys?" I ask.

"Nothing," she says. "No way in hell Schroder asked you for an opinion."

"He did. Just not on this case," I admit. "Come on, Tracey, I'm trying to find Emma Green."

"And you'll stop at nothing."

"Is that such a bad thing?"

"It is for the people who get in your way, even the innocent ones."

"Any idea who they are?" I ask, nodding down toward the two men.

"Not yet," she says. "Bodies haven't been touched yet."

"Then let's touch them," I say. I crouch down on the side of the grave and tug sideways at the shorts on the closest victim, twisting them until I can get to the back pocket.

"What the hell, Tate?"

I come up with a wallet and hand it to her probably an hour or two earlier than the plan, but there's no time to mess around with protocol. There's no cash, and there are no credit cards and no license. I reach into the second grave. Same tug on the pants. Same trick. The back pocket comes around the same way and a wallet with the same amount of nothing inside it comes free.

"Great," she says. "Thanks for being so helpful."

Close to the side of the grave, I take a better look at the bodies. "You notice how similar they look?" I ask.

"In what way?"

"Same height, same hair color, same bone structure," I say. Rot and decay has taken some of the details away, but there's plenty of skin and flesh left to see the similarities. Tracey crouches down and shines a flashlight into the face of one, then the face of the other. The eyes are milky white with dark brown centers.

"It's hard to tell right now," she says, "but they certainly do look alike. They could be brothers."

"Brothers?"

"Yes. Related."

"I know what you mean," I say, getting back up. Brothers. Twins. Orderlies. "How long have they been in the ground?"

"No longer than a week," she says. "Why, does that mean something to you?"

"Possibly. I gotta go."

"You know who they are, don't you?"

"I'm working on it," I say, but I'm not sure she hears me because I'm already racing off looking for a car I can borrow.

chapter forty-eight

The cell door is open and the air coming in is slightly cooler than that already in the room. In the doorway is Adrian, he's holding a gun and a Taser, and standing next to Cooper is Cooper's mother. Cooper can see the corridor behind Adrian and this isn't Sunnyview or Eastlake, he doesn't know where in the hell this is.

"What is he talking about?" his mother asks him.

He turns toward her. There is enough artificial light coming from the corridor behind Adrian to see her clearly. Wherever they are, they have power. This could be a house. In town somewhere? No way of knowing.

"I don't know," Cooper answers, and his mother, aside from looking scared, is suddenly looking every one of her seventy-nine years, plus some. For the last few years she has had a look on her face as if she's been sucking on a lemon, now she looks like that entire lemon has been jammed into her mouth. Her gray hair is a tangled mess, and even if Adrian Tasered her he's still surprised he got her out of the house without her clawing her way back in for a comb and lipstick. She's wearing a nightgown that has all the shape

323

of a rectangle that he gave her two years ago for Christmas because he found it on sale for ten bucks. "You can't listen to anything he says. He's completely crazy."

"I'm not crazy," Adrian says. "Look, look at the blood on him. He's a killer."

"I'm not a killer," Cooper says. Two minutes ago his mother was led into his cell at gunpoint and there wasn't a damn thing he could do about it except stand at the back and watch unless he wanted to get shot. She came running toward him and almost rolled both of her ankles on the padded floor and he caught her before she fell. He hugged her hard, he didn't want her being here but he was grateful to see her in a way, which made him feel immediately guilty, and she was grateful to see him too, to see he was still alive. Somehow Adrian has upgraded from a Taser to a gun. A Taser wasn't great against two people, but a gun was. A gun could be good up against ten people if none of them had guns either. So Cooper stood back as the cell door was opened and in came his mother. He loves his mother but having her here has complicated things. A lot.

"Why continue to lie? You don't need to anymore," Adrian says. "This is your chance to unburden yourself of all that hate, that hate that made you go and kill other people. Seven now."

Two, Cooper thinks, and even then it was really only one. But it will certainly be two once he gets out of this cell. Damn it, the sick fuck is even wearing some of his dad's clothes, clothes that his mum should have thrown out nearly forty years ago when he walked out on them, but for some reason she kept. "I'm not a killer."

"Nice people don't raise serial killers," Adrian says, looking at Cooper's mother. "So why care about trying to keep her happy by lying? She isn't a nice person."

"Young man, you really need some serious help," his mother says, and it's the same tone she used to use on Cooper when he was a young boy and he wouldn't finish his dinner or mow the lawn or was mean to his sister. The same tone she used on him when he stole the car. He's half expecting her to make Adrian write a letter to his future self. "I don't know what game you're playing at here, but somebody is going to get seriously hurt."

"I can prove your son's a killer," Adrian says.

"That's bullshit," Cooper says. "Don't listen to him."

"He was driving girls out to Sunnyview. It's a closed down mental hospital and it's abandoned, and he'd keep them there for . . ."

"You're crazy," Cooper says to him, cutting him off. "Don't listen to him, Mum. He's an escaped mental patient. I used to interview him a few years ago for my book. He killed his family with an ax. He bit off their fingers and used them to draw pictures on the walls."

"Oh my God, that's awful!" his mother says.

"Wh . . . what? I did no such thing," Adrian shouts. "Tell her, tell her the truth!"

"The police found him wearing a dress."

"You're lying!"

"It was his sister's dress and it was too small for him but he wore it anyway."

"You poor boy," his mother says to Adrian, "what kind of mother did you have to have raised you so wrong?"

"It wasn't their fault," Adrian says. He moves the gun from Cooper's mother back to Cooper, and Cooper doesn't like the look of his shaking hand.

"You had more than one?" she asks.

"I only killed one of them," Adrian says, yelling now, and Cooper puts his arm in front of his mother and steps slightly in front of her. "The other one . . . the other one died naturally," he says, "and I never ate any fingers or wore a dress! I would never do that!"

"I want you to let her go," Cooper says.

"Are you sure? Is that really what you want? For your mother to be free to tell the world what kind of man you really are?"

It's a good point, and one that he's been thinking about since Adrian first threatened to bring her back here.

"I helped you," his mother says. "I bandaged up your leg and this is how you repay us? You're so rude and so ill-mannered. If I were your mother I'd be ashamed right now."

"Mum," Cooper says, and gives her a look that suggests it's time she shuts up.

"Don't you look at me like that, Cooper. I'll speak my mind."

She's going to get them both killed.

"I knew she was a nasty lady," Adrian says. "It's just like the books said. Think of what she'll tell everybody if I let her go. She may not believe me, but the police will listen to her, they'll figure things out, they'll know I'm not lying."

"Let her go," Cooper says, only he doesn't sound convincing and he's sure his mother will hear it in his voice, and she does.

"Cooper? Is any of what he's saying true?" she asks, stepping back in front of him and turning to look him in the eyes.

"Of course not," he says.

"All of it," Adrian says.

"Shut up, young man," his mother says, throwing Adrian a glare before turning back to Cooper. "Tell me you haven't hurt anybody," she says.

"He's mad," Cooper says. "I swear to you he's mad and he's making it all up."

"Promise me. Promise me you haven't hurt anybody," she says, and it sounds like she's telling him off.

"Look at all the blood on his clothes," Adrian says, and he sounds desperate to convince her. "Ask him how it got there!"

"I was trying to help somebody," Cooper says. "There was a girl. Adrian stabbed her. I tried to save her, but I couldn't," he says, and suddenly he feels like a kid lying to his mother, wanting nothing more than for her to believe him, and if she does, what then? How can he convince her not to tell the police that Adrian kept calling him a serial killer?

He doesn't think he can. His mother is nearly eighty—and eighty-year-old women say a lot of random shit all the time, and some of that is going to stick somewhere. There must be a way he can walk out of here with her, he can play the part of the victim and the hero assuming the photos haven't been found.

"She bled out all over me and it was awful," he says, "really awful. I tried so hard to save her but . . . but I couldn't," he says.

His mother takes his hand. "It's going to be okay," she tells him.

"He told me where the dead girl was," Adrian says. "How did he know? That's what the police are going to ask!"

"What dead girl is he talking about?" his mother asks. "The one you tried to save?"

"A different one," Cooper says. "He's killed many."

"What about the thumb? He cuts people's thumbs off and collects them in jars! I've seen it!"

"You're the one who cuts them off," Cooper says.

Adrian raises the gun, and Cooper steps further around in front of his mother. It could all end right now. Then Adrian smiles. "I understand why you're saying these things," Adrian says. "It's because you're scared."

"It's going to be okay," his mother whispers, her hand tight in his.

"Don't cry," she tells him, and he wasn't aware that he was. He reaches up and wipes at his eyes. "You'll get us out of here," she tells him.

"I'm sorry," he tells her.

"It's not your fault we're here," she says. "You can't be responsible for others, especially for a young man badly deranged."

"I'm not deranged," Adrian says. "Tell her, Cooper, tell her about the girl I found that you kidnapped. Tell her!"

"What girl?" Cooper asks, knowing that Adrian must have found Emma.

"The girl you left at Sunnyview. You were going to kill her."

"What the hell are you talking about?" Cooper asks.

"I'll show her to you," Adrian says, "to both of you. I have her tied up."

"You have a girl here you kidnapped?" Cooper's mother asks, and she's asking Adrian.

"I saved her."

"You saved a girl who you have tied up. Are you planning on hurting her?" she asks.

"You don't understand," Adrian says.

"Because you never make sense," Cooper says to him.

"You're scared of her," Adrian says. "You've always been scared of her because she's dominated you your entire life. It's what you wrote about in your book. It's what they all write, all the people who know stuff about serial killers. It's why she's here. And you're lying. I never killed my family. Never had a sister whose dress I never wore."

"Let us go, please, please, I'm begging you," Mrs. Riley says.

"I can't. He's too valuable." He looks back up at Cooper. "Wait here," he says, and he closes the door and disappears.

"Thank God you're okay," his mother says, and embraces him.

"I'm going to get us out of here," he tells her. "I promise," he says, and all he has to do is ask her not to go to the police until he's found out whether or not they know he's a killer.

"He's back," Cooper says, hearing the footsteps outside the door. The door opens outward and Adrian is back, the gun still in his hand, no chance of grabbing it.

"I'm doing this to help you," Adrian says.

"Doing what?" Cooper asks.

"This," he says, and he lifts the bottom of the shirt and clipped to his belt is a small Walkman. Adrian presses play, and Cooper can hear his voice coming back at him, Adrian's voice too, and in that moment his mother's fate is set. At seventy-nine years old, she has had her life. He has to cling to that, and he likes to think she would sacrifice herself to save him. That's the kind of woman she is. He loves her. He just loves his freedom more.

chapter forty-nine

I've gotten a little more used to the roads now and only make two wrong turns leaving Grover Hills. I pull over at one point and fiddle with the unmarked patrol car's laptop computer, dirt from the road slowly drifting by as I look up the address I want, and when I have it I turn up the volume on the police band and listen in to the reports coming from different parts of the city. Neighbors of Cooper Riley's mother have described Adrian Loaner and Emma Green's car as being seen in the driveway. It was one of the neighbors who called the police when he saw her being put into the trunk of the car. Bloody clothes have been left at the scene, and bandaging and medical tape and bloody rags were left on the dining room table. Adrian went there and forced Mrs. Riley to help him. More information comes in as I drive. An empty grave has been found out at Sunnyview, most likely the location where Jane Tyrone was buried. Fingerprints found inside one of the padded cells has matched those taken from the hairbrush from Emma Green's flat. The background images in the photos Cooper took match those of one of Sunnyview's padded rooms. Corpse dogs are running the grounds while they wait for ground-penetrating radar to arrive.

When I get into town I get caught up in a traffic jam. It's almost eleven o'clock and hundreds of teenage drag racers with nothing better to do are out in their cars, cruising the four avenues surrounding the central city, proving to their friends and other drivers that they have a volcano of testosterone just waiting to be released, proving a point to the council and government that even though cruising in packs in their modified cars is now illegal they just don't care, and proving to me that teenagers with this dickhead mentality are nothing more than sheep in their desperation to feel accepted. I listen to the police channel in the detective's car, learning that there's an estimated fifteen hundred drag racers circling the streets. Neon lights line the bottom of some cars, bright paint works, lots of chrome, and big mufflers, intersections are blocked and the police are just too busy with other things to care. Passengers in the car in front of me turn to give me the finger. I stare at them thinking about the man who killed my daughter, and how there's a lot of room out in that forest for more graves. The line of traffic passes a parked car that's been set on fire. I can see the lights from fire engines about four blocks away unable to get any closer. I manage to turn left onto a side street about a minute later and get clear of it all.

I drive out toward Brighton where the houses are a little more run-down and where there are fewer people to care. This part of the suburb on the edge of the beach is in need of one half-decent tidal wave to clean it up. I come to a stop outside the address I looked up, it's a small worn-down house that can't have many more than a couple of rooms, the kind of place where you're being screwed if the landlord is charging you anything more than two figures a week. The lights are on inside, which means I won't be waking anybody, but when I knock nobody answers. I knock a few more times and give it another minute before walking around the house, looking in the windows.

Jesse Cartman is sitting in the living room staring at a TV set that is switched off. He's completely naked except for a photo album lying on his lap, and two cocktail umbrellas lying on his stomach. His eyes are wide open and unblinking. I tap on the window and he looks over at me. He stands up slowly and the album slides off and hits the floor and he comes to the window close enough for parts of his body to press against it. The cocktail umbrellas have stuck to the sweat and gotten tangled in the hairs on his belly.

"Detective," he says, the word coming out so slowly it's like he's speaking underwater.

"I need to talk to you," I say.

"Detective," he repeats, just as slowly.

I make my way to the back door. It's locked but doesn't hold up to much of a kick. I figure the landlord won't notice the busted doorjamb the same way he hasn't noticed the building getting ready to fall over. The house smells of cat piss but I don't see any cats. Cartman is still standing in the living room facing the window staring out at the overgrown garden.

"Hey, Jesse," I say, and he doesn't turn around. "You forget to take your meds?"

"My meds," he says, still staring outside.

"Where are they?"

He doesn't answer. The house is small enough to find the bathroom in about four seconds. The floor is tiled with mold growing in the grouting. The bathroom mirror is cracked and the glass is pitted. I open the cabinet and find a couple of containers of pills. I read the labels and have no idea what they are.

Back in the living room he's still facing the window. He's so close to it there's no room to see his reflection around him. "You need to take some of these," I say.

"I'm hungry."

"Come on, Jesse, it'll help."

"I don't want help. I just want to forget."

"I need your help, Jesse."

He doesn't answer. I walk over to him and put my hand on his shoulder and he slams his head forward into the window. It doesn't break and he bounces back. This is not the same man I spoke to earlier today. That man wanted to take his medication to get better. That man was reminded about things and this is the man who can't remember them. I lead him back to his chair expecting him to resist but he doesn't.

"Listen, Jesse, it's very important you listen to me."

"I'm still hungry," he says. There is a bump forming on his forehead that he doesn't seem concerned with. I shake out a couple of pills and try handing them to him but he won't take them. He doesn't even look at them or seem to know they're there. I'm not even sure that he knows I'm here. There's a large bite impression on the inside of his arm that no doubt lines up perfectly with this teeth. He's hungrier than I thought.

"I need you to tell me about the Twins."

"She was so beautiful," he says. "So innocent. I just had to taste her. Had to. It wasn't up to me, but it kept saying to do it, over and over at night when I was lying in bed he'd tell me and so I did, it was the only way to shut him up. He lived inside of me, this monster with no name."

I look at the photo album. He's talking about his sister. The picture of them staring up at me is nothing like the last time I saw him and his sister together.

"So much blood," he says, "and I hate . . ." He stops talking. Just in midsentence he stops and he closes his eyes and starts slowly rocking back and forth, just little movements at first, increasing into bigger ones until he tips out of the chair and sprawls on the floor facedown. I jump onto his back and pull his head up and open his mouth and jam a couple of pills in there and hold his mouth closed and pinch his nose shut and he doesn't resist. He swallows the pills.

I sit him back in his chair and he stares ahead like nothing happened.

"The Twins," I say. "Were they actual twins?"

"She tasted sweet," he says. "Like candy."

Somehow I don't think she did. "Jesse, listen to me, think about Grover Hills."

"No."

"Please."

"No Grover Hills."

"There were two orderlies there."

"The Twins," he says.

"Were they brothers?"

"They were twins."

"Do you know their names?"

"Buttons knows."

"What?"

"Buttons," he says, and he stabs his finger into his forearm. "Buttons was there too."

"Buttons is a cat?"

"Not a cat," he says. "Buttons," he adds, then holds his fingers up to his mouth and pretends he's smoking a cigarette before stabbing it into his arm. A moment later he tilts his head back, closes his eyes, and falls asleep.

chapter fifty

Adrian can't sleep.

One reason is his leg. The bandage has gotten bloody because the wound beneath it keeps itching and he can't stop scratching at it. He keeps digging his fingernails into the itch trying to find relief only it doesn't work. Cooper's mother told him he'd need to get stitches, but he had stitches all those years ago when he was badly beaten and pissed on and he didn't like them then and can't see any reason why that will have changed.

Another reason he can't sleep is he can't switch off his mind. He never did find the glue, even though he is absolutely sure he took it from the pocket of his last pants and put it into the pocket of the ones he took from Cooper's mum's place, but the problem is the more he thinks about it, the less certain he becomes, the more his memory of the event starts to change. He can remember setting it on the bed with his old clothes when he emptied the pockets, but nothing after that.

He thinks about Theodore Tate and how he could easily have lost his life tonight if Tate didn't have a bandage around his gun hand.

That's what slowed Tate down, he's sure of it. He thinks about the Twins, he thinks about the people he met at the halfway house, he thinks about his mother and he thinks about his other mother. He can't stop thinking of people and it's keeping him awake. He thinks about the look on Cooper's mother's face as he played the tape. He only had to play a few seconds of it before closing the door, knowing what would happen next, but she deserved it. She was a bad mother. Bad mothers deserved what they got.

The bed isn't comfortable. One of the Twins—he isn't sure which one—slept on this bed, and that's another picture he can't get out of his head, a man who treated him so badly would come here at night and roll in these sheets, his skin flaking into the creases of the bed, into the folds of the pillowcase, and now it's sticking to his own body, making him itch.

In the end it all becomes too much for him. The window is open and the curtains are moving slightly on the breeze, brushing against the windowsills. He turns on the light. His pajama bottoms are soaked in sweat and there is blood on the right-hand side. He tugs them off. The bandage has gotten loose and saggy. It's across his thigh, about equal distance between his knee and hip. He holds on to it as he walks outside so it doesn't slip down his leg. He doesn't know what the temperature is, but it's still warm. He knows it's after midnight but not by much. Much warmer than usual for this time of night he suspects—not that he's normally outside at this time of night. Back at the Grove he was locked in his room, which was always hard if you needed to use the bathroom, because you had to wait. At the halfway house the only reason you'd step out the doors after dark was if you wanted to commit a crime or be a victim of one.

He lowers the bandage. He scratches at his leg. More blood and more pain and something yellow oozes out, but relief from the itch for those few seconds as his fingers scrape over it. He could try to get Cooper's mother to help him again, but he's pretty sure she isn't going to want to do that no matter how hard he tries. Anyway, he's angry at her for not believing him. Her son was the one covered in blood, he was the one who put the knife into that girl, and yet he looks like the good guy. It annoys him. He didn't think Cooper would do that to him. They were meant to be friends, weren't they?

He wishes he could work on the wound himself. It needs to be cleaned, he knows that. It may get infected. Sometimes infected limbs have to be cut off. He knows that too.

He can't help himself. He begins crying at the thought. He turns and sobs into the pillow, for the moment not caring about the last person who laid on it, only thinking of a future with one leg, pacing the room and struggling to end on an even number when you have an odd amount of limbs to begin with. When the sobbing dies down, he limps to the bathroom and goes through the medicine cabinet. There's a lot in here, but on closer look he sees dates with *exp* in front of them. They must be explanation dates; the dates explaining when the medication is no longer any good. Many of the things in here went bad a few years ago. He doesn't know if *bad* medicine just means it won't work, or won't work as well, or make him even worse. There is an antiseptic cream that was good up until two months ago, surely that's okay. The painkillers all went bad a few years ago. The bandages must stay good forever. And there's some kind of medical padding that looks like it'll help. Some sharp scissors for cutting things to fit. A safety pin for securing the bandage. He closes the cabinet and stares at the mirror. His face is flushed and there's a slight rash starting around the edge of his hairline, which he hopes is from the heat and not from some infection climbing through his body. He doesn't want to die. Not now when life is so good.

He holds the back of his hand up to his forehead like he's seen people do and his forehead feels warm. A fever? Or just the result of stress and a very, very hot day? He cups his hands under the tap and fills them with water and splashes his face. He immediately feels better, but without his fingers pinching the bandage on his leg tight it slides down to around his foot. His tears become lost in the water on his face. He wishes his mother was here. Either one.

He turns on the shower. He steps inside and lets the water run over his leg. He can feel the infection being washed away from the surface, but at the same time he can feel it inching its way through his body. He doesn't have to see it to know it's there. He scrubs at the wound with a facecloth. The gash is about the length of his finger and about as deep and as wide, a long furrow that an inch to the left would have had the bullet missing completely and an inch to the right have had it buried deep into his leg, severing one of those thick veins in there that would cause him to bleed out. It's not bleeding as much as earlier, even with all the scrubbing, but it is still bleeding. The shower feels good. He has the water temperature set so it's cool but not too cold. He spends enough time in there for the pads of his fingers to wrinkle, then he climbs out and dries himself down. The itch has faded, but he still needs to do something with the wound.

He doesn't want to lose the leg.

Doesn't want to die.

Can't go to hospital.

Doesn't want to lie down in the same bed as one of the Twins because the infection would only become more infected.

He goes outside and holds a clean medical pad over the wound, carrying Cooper's manuscript with him. He sits on the porch. There's a wooden swing chair that would fit two people, he rocks it slowly back and forth and it relaxes him. It's too dark to read yet, and he can't be bothered going back inside to turn on the porch light. The fields around him look pale blue from the moon. In four or five hours the sky will start to lighten. He's never seen that happen before, and suddenly he is desperate to watch his first sunrise, liking the idea that one day he and Cooper may sit out here on the porch enjoying it together.

chapter fifty-one

I hit the same string of drag racers. They're going just as slowly, flashing their lights and tooting their horns and I have to drive alongside them at an intersection that I can't get through because they've blocked it. I get boxed in and flick on my sirens, but it only makes things worse because then they purposely keep me trapped. It takes me fifteen minutes to get past them. The police radio spits out more news, mainly that there are now over two thousand drag racers on the roads, so far six arrests have been made and six cars impounded, and one pedestrian run over and in the hospital with minor wounds. Drag racers are outnumbering the police, outnumbering all the gangs in the country, they're an epidemic for which there is no solution.

I park outside the halfway house wishing I was armed. There aren't any gang members walking any dogs up the street so I take my chances and step out. It's still at least seventy degrees and the armpits of my shirt are soaking wet.

Buttons is sitting on the porch out front with a beer in one hand and a cigarette in the other. It's almost one-thirty. He's still wearing the same fedora and shirt and looks the same amount of out-of-place as he did when he answered the door for me earlier today.

"You're up late," I tell him.

"I don't sleep much. Never have. I knew you were going to be coming back," he says. "Ritchie is upstairs in his bedroom, most likely fast asleep. He doesn't know much, you know."

"I'm not here to talk to him," I say.

"Yeah? You after the Preacher? He's inside somewhere."

I shake my head. "I'm here to talk to you. Jesse Cartman said you'd know about the Twins."

"Jesse Cartman said that now, did he?" he asks, then takes a long drink. "What else did he say?"

"He called you *Buttons*," I say, looking at the inside of his arm where all the cigarette burns are lined up in a row, each about the size and shape of a button. "What's your name?" I ask him. "Your real name?"

"Henry," he says. "Henry Taub," he says, and doesn't offer me his hand.

"You were at Grover Hills?"

"For nearly thirty years, son," he says.

"Preacher didn't mention it," I tell him.

"He wouldn't have," Henry says. "He's good like that."

"So you know everything that went on out there."

He smiles meekly. "Almost. You want to know about the Twins, right?"

"How'd you know?"

"I always knew somebody would want to know. What did Cartman tell you, son?"

"That they were letting people die down in the Scream Room."

"You believe that?"

"No, but there are some bodies showing up."

"Hmm, is that so? So, what do you believe?"

"I believe they were doing something down there."

"You'd be right to believe that, but foolish to believe much else of what Jesse Cartman tells you. The boy's not right in the head," he says, tapping the side of his hat. "None of them are."

"And you?"

"We all believe what we're saying, son, but there's a big difference: I'm believing things the way they actually happened."

"Then fill me in."

He takes a long swallow of beer. "I s'pose I could," he says, "but the way I see it, you've been paying everybody else for their side of things. Why should I be no different?"

"Because you seem like a man with some pride," I tell him, "and not somebody who'd hold back when what he tells me could save the life of a seventeen-year-old girl."

"That's true," he tells me, "but a man still needs to know where his next drink is coming from."

"I'll fix you up when this is over," I tell him.

"Is that you believing what you're saying, or you saying the way it's going to be?" he asks.

"That's the way it's going to be. I promise."

He takes another sip and then stares at me hard for a good few seconds, *taking my measure* as I'm sure he'd say. "Sounds good enough to me," he says, finishes his beer, and opens another. "Can I get you one?" I shake my head. "It started out innocently enough, you know," he says. "Way back fifteen years, give or take a year or two. Young fella came along. Real cocky little shit. Not much more than twenty. Could have been twenty-five, but no older. We all knew he wasn't crazy, just mean, and mean and crazy are two different things, only the courts didn't see it. He used to brag about how he fooled them. Used to tell us how clever he really was, and how he was going to be free in a couple of months. Courts placed him with us because he killed a girl. Just killed her because he felt like it, he told us. A young pretty little girl not much more than ten. He was with us a week when that girl's dad came along. I can still remember seeing him outside in the parking lot. He looked nervous, like he was summoning up the courage to ask a pretty big question. You ever seen a man like that? The pain of what he wants to ask is written all over his face. I took one look at him and knew what he wanted. Then he just chose somebody. Saw somebody in a white uniform and went

340

up to him, and that person saw the same thing I did. Never knew what he said, not exactly, but I knew what he wanted. We got TV in there. Some of us knew what was going on out in the world, and I knew who he was. The orderly he spoke to was one of the Twins. Back then the Scream Room was only a punishment. Bad things happened down there, but not real bad. The dad, he offered them money. Told them he'd like some time alone with the guy that hurt his daughter. The Twins, they sold him that time. The guy returned that night after most of the staff and nurses had gone. I saw him pull into the parking lot through my window and an hour later I saw him pull away. That boy, we never saw him again."

"How often did this happen?"

He takes a long swallow of beer and wipes his mouth with the back of his hand. "Just that time. There were rumors. You think rumors are bad out here? Son, rumors are nothing compared to what goes around in a mental institution. You listen to the patients in there and you'd be believing Elvis was living out there along with Jesus. But that was the start of it. After that, the Twins, they changed. They got off on it somehow. The Scream Room became not just a room for punishment, but a room for pain. They'd take us down there and hell, most of us, we deserved every second of it. It was as though two demons were unleashed, two mean demons who just loved to beat the shit out of everybody and humiliate the hell out of them. With the boy they killed, I accepted that. An eye for an eye and all that. Was biblical. But what they became . . . they deserve to rot in Hell for that."

"They're already there," I tell him. "They got themselves killed."

His eyebrows raise up. "They did now, did they? Well, I can't say that's a real shame, now. Who got them?"

"Adrian Loaner."

"No. Adrian? Well I'll be damned. Never knew that boy had it in him."

"You sound proud of him."

"Proud? I don't know if that's the right word. I do know if anybody deserved to hurt those fellas, it was Adrian."

"Who were they? The Twins?"

"What do you mean, son?"

"I mean who are they? You know their real names?"

"Sure I do. Murray and Ellis Hunter."

"Hunter?"

"That's what I said."

The name is familiar. A few months ago when I was in jail, a man there named Jack Hunter was stabbed. Schroder came into the prison to see me and ask if I'd look into it, see if I could figure out who'd done it.

"You know where they live?"

"Now why'd I know a thing like that?"

"Because I'm thinking Adrian is hiding out there."

He shrugs. "That's a pretty big theory," he says, "but it's not impossible."

"Not impossible at all," I tell him. After all, if Murray and Ellis Hunter are dead in the ground at Grover Hills, then that means they have a home somewhere that they're not looking after. That means an empty building, and Adrian has to be somewhere and the Hunter house is looking like a good bet. "How long they work at Grover Hills for?"

He pulls a handkerchief out from his pocket. His clothes are immaculate, his shirt is still buttoned up, and his tie nice and tight, but the handkerchief is the dirtiest one I've ever seen. He wipes it around the back of his neck and it comes away wet. "They started a few years after I was there. And they left five or six years ago. Was a hell of a surprise to see them go. Never knew where they went. Adrian kill them back then, did he?"

"No. He killed them at some point in the last week or two. Along with Nurse Deans."

He whistles, like he's just inspected and appreciated a car that can travel much faster than he'd previously imagined. "She was a real piece of work, that one. Listen, son, I don't know what happened between when they left and when they died. If I were to have at a guess, I'd say they did nothing good. Those boys were evil. The patients were bad but most of them were just wired up wrong is all. Nobody liked it, but you couldn't blame them for it. Those boys, I'd bet my bottom dollar they carried on hurting people well after they left the Grove."

"And you? What's your story?"

"My story is my story," he says, and he tries to offer a kind smile that doesn't quite fit right on his face. "Don't forget we made a deal," he tells me.

"I'll be back," I promise him.

I try to use the police computer to look up the Hunters but at some point in the last hour I've been locked out, it asks for a password that I don't know. So I drive deeper into town. Cell phone technology has made phone booths pretty much redundant in most parts of the world, but not here in Christchurch where many people are still living in the stone age. I find a phone booth a block away from the police station next to the Avon River, where four teenagers in their boxer shorts are currently going for a drunken swim. Back in the nineties, to combat underage drinking, the government lowered the legal drinking age, so suddenly thousands and thousands of youths across each city were no longer breaking the law, hence making it no longer an issue. Only the government couldn't see what a bad idea that was. They opened the floodgates, and now, years later, the country has one of the biggest underage drinking problems in the world.

I flick through the phone book. Half of it is missing but thankfully it's the half starting from M. There's almost a hundred Hunters in there. Two of them belong to the brothers. I check the initials and find an M and E Hunter on the same line. Maybe they lived together. They did everything else together, so why not? I figure it's worth a shot. I figure since Buttons didn't know their address, then Adrian wouldn't have known it either. Yet Adrian found them, which means it can't be hard to do. He probably looked them up in the phone book. Probably saw the same initials and started with that one. I decide on the same thing.

I pick up the phone. It's sticky. I miss my cell phone. I drop some coins into the slot. I have to press the receiver tight against my ear to block out the loud music being pumped from every open doorway of every open bar and every passing car. I dial the number and nobody answers immediately, which I figure to be a good sign, then an even better sign comes along: an answering machine picks up.

"You've reached Ellis and Murray and we're out and you know the deal, so go ahead and leave a message if you want."

I don't bother leaving a message.

The adrenaline is starting to pump. It's closing in on two-thirty and the drag racers have either moved on or all broken down on another stretch of the four avenues because I don't get caught up in traffic again. I race through the streets doing about 20 kph over the limit, passing a couple of speed cameras, which flash at me, but I'm in a detective's car so the tickets will be waived. The Hunters live in a part of the city where there aren't any junked-up cars resting on front lawns. In fact it's a nice neighborhood where most houses look no more than ten years old and you can drive for five straight minutes without passing any crime scene tape. I find the address and there aren't any cars parked out front. I pull over a block away and grab a flashlight and make my way back. My heart is racing. Adrian has my gun and a Taser and who the hell knows what else. First thing I check is the garage window. There's one car in there that doesn't belong to Emma Green, and a space for another car. There aren't any lights on inside the house. I shine my flashlight on the back door and crouch in front of the handle. I use a lock-pick gun. It only takes a few pulls of the trigger and some good placement and thirty seconds to make my way inside. Not as quick as kicking down the door, but the door here looks far more sturdy than Jesse Cartman's house, and back there I wasn't trying to be quiet. I step into the hallway. I can hear the *beep beep* of an answering machine. It sounds frantic. It sounds like it's desperate to unload its secrets. I use the flashlight to light my way, stepping carefully. In the living room there are photos of Murray and Ellis Hunter and there's no doubt they're the two men I saw in the ground. There's a large patch of blood in the center of the living room with hair and what could be bone fragments stuck in it. There is more blood leading from the front door and drag marks in the carpet.

I go from room to room. Nothing. And nothing to suggest Cooper Riley or Emma Green were ever here.

"Damn it," I say, kicking at one of the walls and putting my shoe through the plasterboard. White dust settles onto the carpet from the hole. It looks like cocaine, and reminds me of a case I worked with Schroder five years ago, where we busted into a house and a guy dropped his drugs onto the carpet by accident, then dropped onto his knees and began snorting them, trying to hide the evidence, and he snorted so much in that few seconds that it almost killed him.

Where the hell can Emma and Cooper be? There aren't any more abandoned mental institutions. Best I can think of is Adrian is holed up in the house of another victim. I close the back door in case Adrian is planning on coming back. Hope that he's going to return is all I have. After everything I'm still back at square one with no idea in the world where Emma Green is being held.

I think about what Buttons said, about the twin boys being evil. There was no doubt in his mind the Twins carried on hurting people, probably even killing some. I start looking around the house not exactly sure what I'm looking for, but I go through everything. Maybe there'll be a scrapbook or something. I switch on the computer. I read through emails. I check the attic access in the ceiling to see if anything is hidden up there, I check beneath the carpet in the bedrooms in the corners, and an hour into the search I check the closets for loose floorboards and my search pays off. Beneath the house is a cardboard box. I open it up. I lay the contents on the floor side by side. Nine wallets in total, each of them with credit cards and driver's licenses and photos of children or wives, none of them with any cash. Three of the names I recognize from my last few years on the job—names of people who dropped off the face of the earth. Another one I think I recognize but can't be sure.

The computer is still switched on. I spend twenty minutes running the rest of the names through the news database online, along with the ones I remember. Nine names and each of them comes back with a story. Nine men all gone missing dating back to the time Buttons said the Twins left Grover Hills. Nine men who were never found. A different range of men, family men, single men, a lawyer, a plumber, a couple of unemployed men, the youngest nineteen years old, the oldest forty-five. Each of them sharing in common a very bad fate according to the cardboard box hidden beneath the floorboards in the closet.

Buttons said the Twins got their first taste of what they could do when that man approached them wanting revenge. Since then they spent years at Grover Hills using the Scream Room as an outlet. Then one day they just up and left. They built a Scream Room of their own. Had to have. But where? Certainly not here. Not in this part of the city. None of the rooms here would stop a scream from traveling outside, and in a neighborhood like this somebody would have called the police.

So where? Where in the hell is their torture chamber? And if it's in a house, why not live there? Why bring the souvenirs back here?

Because this is their home. Maybe this is closer to where they work. And they needed the souvenirs here for when they're not visiting their other place.

I go back through everything. I go through their address book. I stop on a name I recognize. Edward Hunter. It was his father who was stabbed in jail. Edward was in jail too, but not till a few days after that. Edward was sentenced for killing two men. His father Jack was sentenced twenty years ago for killing eleven prostitutes. Are they related to Ellis and Murray? Is there a family trait that makes these men want to hurt people?

I go through the rest of the address book. I head out to the car in the garage and check for a GPS unit in case there's a location plotted on it, but there's only a map and the map doesn't have any circles or crosses scrawled across it. I go through files and boxes of bills. I find tax statements but only for this address. If they own property somewhere else there's no record of it here. If they're paying for power for another house, the bills are getting sent to that address.

There's a Scream Room somewhere, it could be a cabin in the woods, it could be a house with a soundproof basement, but nothing in this house tells me where.

It has to be somewhere. It's who they are. A Scream Room is what makes them tick.

And I'm wondering if Edward Hunter might have an idea where that is.

I'm suddenly hit by a wall of exhaustion. It's almost six-thirty and it's daylight by the time I leave the Hunter house. It's a slow drive home, not because of traffic—the roads are empty—but because fatigue is trying to convince me that nothing would feel better right now than driving into a lamppost and falling asleep.

There are patrol cars and crime scene tape outside of my house and I completely forgot that I wasn't supposed to return. I switch cars, getting back into the rental, then drive to the nearest motel I can find, a place that looks okay in the dim early-morning light, and I figure since only two of the neon letters in the word *vacancy* are busted it can't be that bad a place. The clerk behind the desk is asleep when I step through the doors but he snaps to attention pretty quick. He swipes my credit card and five minutes later I'm in a room that smells of furniture polish. I phone home and check my messages, of which there are four. One from my parents, the other three from Donovan Green. He tells me he's been trying to get hold of me all night but the cell phone he gave me is switched off. I figure Schroder is asleep, so rather than waking him on his cell phone, I call the police station and leave a message for him. I give him the Hunter address and a brief rundown of what he'll find. I also tell him to send somebody to check on Jesse Cartman. I don't call Donovan Green.

I set my alarm for eight o'clock, which is a little over an hour away. I don't bother getting undressed. I just take off my shoes and lie down and stare at the ceiling and think about what Emma Green is doing right now.

chapter fifty-two

The sunrise is something he'd like to see again. Hopefully next time it won't be when he's in so much pain. He napped a little during it, and a lot before it, the previous hours disappearing into a haze of dreams in which he saw his mother and his other mother, in which he even saw his father before his father disappeared from his life when Adrian was still in primary school, walking out on the family the way some men do when they're offered simpler lives with their secretary.

He saw the good part of the sunrise. The sky lightened and for a while the sun seemed to refuse to appear, something holding it back, some entity wanting this day born into darkness. Then the tip of it broke the horizon, coming up out of the fields that trailed out as far as he could see, pouring golden light into the morning, an instant warmth, the world waking up around it. It slipped quickly into view then, the thing holding it earlier now shoving it forward, then it was angling upward, creating long shadows through the trees. He napped again a little afterward but never really fell asleep, his itching leg keeping him from drifting off completely.

The sun is up over the trees and the shadows are shorter but not by much when he goes back inside, his leg still sore to walk on but better since he rubbed the cream into it. The piece of medical padding he held over it has stuck to the wound and when he tugs at it there's a tearing sound and a lot of pain to go along with it, so he stops tugging. Somehow he's going to have to remove it and re-dress it and somehow it needs to heal. He can't lose his leg. He rummages back around in the medicine cabinet hoping he'll find something in the daylight that hid from him in the dark, but there's nothing. He doesn't understand what half of it is for, and there's a pair of false teeth on one of the shelves that looks very creepy with dots of mold and fuzz around the gums. He guesses he'll have to drive into town at some point today and pick up some supplies. There's some food in the fridge, some from his mother, some from the Twins, but not enough to get them all through the next few days, but it's fantastic having a fridge with power. There's a reality slowly kicking in, and that reality tells him he can't afford to keep too many parts of the collection at the same time. He'll have to take care of Cooper's mum and the girl today too. And it's not such a bad thing he wasn't able to get Theodore Tate.

He puts on a pair of shorts and a T-shirt and pads barefoot into the kitchen. There is orange juice in the fridge that he brought from the Twins' house, along with some fresh eggs and bread from his mother's house that isn't as fresh now. There were already a few food items out here, but mostly junk food, like bags of chips and a fizzy drink of the kind he was never allowed to drink growing up and doesn't want to drink now. He pours himself some orange juice and puts some bread in the toaster and puts on a pair of shorts while waiting for his toast to pop. He sits at the kitchen table and reads the newspaper he gave to Cooper yesterday. He learns the name of the girl he found last night. Emma Green. He reads an article about capital punishment, about the rights and wrongs of it, agreeing with both sides. The Twins deserved to die for what they did to people, but Adrian doesn't deserve to die for what he did to the Twins. And if he did, then wouldn't the people who carried out those executions on prisoners, wouldn't they be killers too, and then wouldn't they get arrested and go to jail and be next in line for the electric chair? Did New Zealand even have an electric chair? He isn't sure when they got rid of the death penalty in New Zealand, or if they even had it, and, if they did, how did they use to do it? Probably a firing squad. Not all killers are monsters. Some have their reasons.

He pours a second glass of juice and tucks the Taser into his pocket and grabs hold of the gun and opens up the bedroom door where Emma Green is tied to a bed similar to the one he slept in. He thinks this one was perhaps the master bedroom for whoever the Twins killed out here before taking it over. The furniture is old-fashioned with lots of curves and engravings, and the bedspread has lots of flower patterns over it. The window is open and the air is warm and the girl is fast asleep and he stands motionless staring at her. He wants to smell her hair and use his finger to stroke it from her face. After a few minutes she starts to stir as if sensing him. Her eyes flutter open and fix on him. She pulls back in horror.

"I'm the one who found you," he says, "and helped you. See, I have something for you to drink."

"What . . . what do you—" she says, then starts to cough. Her body tightens as she tries to cover her mouth with her hand but her hands are tied up around the headboard. "Do you, you, want?" she asks.

She's naked, but last night when he tied her to the bed he draped a sheet over her. He realizes now that she thinks he's the one who took her. Didn't she see Cooper?

"Please, I'm not the one who abducted you," he says. "I'm trying to help you." He steps toward the bed and she has no more room to pull back from him. He holds the glass out toward her. "I want you to drink this," he says. "I want you to feel better."

Before she can answer, he tips the drink toward her mouth. She gulps it down eagerly.

"Don't you remember me?" he asks, while she's still drinking. "I helped you. I put you into the bath and helped cool you down and gave you water and took the duct tape off your eyes."

He pulls the glass away. She slowly nods. Her lips are wet with juice and there are drops on her chin. He'll have to pick up some more glue when he's getting supplies today.

"I remember," she says. "You put me in the trunk of a car against something that smelled dead," she says, "but if you didn't take me, why do you have me tied up?"

"It's complicated," he says, and it always is. "I'm the man trying to help you," he says, which isn't exactly a lie. He wants to help her get better so he can give her to Cooper.

"But you kidnapped me," she says.

"No, I found you," he says.

"Then why tie me up?"

"It's complicated," he says again, and he likes this answer. He'll use it on Cooper too when Cooper starts asking him things he doesn't want to talk about.

"If you didn't kidnap me," she says, "then can you untie me? And I need food too—I haven't eaten in days."

"I'm going to untie you," he says, "and give you some food, but first you need to understand that there's no way you can understand what's going on here. If you help me I can help you, and then you can eat and I can take you home," he says, and the first part is true but the second part isn't, and he can feel himself blush. He hates lying to somebody so . . . so pretty.

"Help you?" she asks. "What exactly do you want me to do?"

"I'm hurt," he says, and he looks down at his leg. With the gun still in his hand, he tries to roll up the leg of his shorts but the Taser in his pocket stops him. He takes it out and rests it on the chest of drawers behind him where it is well out of Emma Green's reach. Then he rolls his shorts up to reveal the medical padding. "I was shot last night and there's an infection and I need you to clean it and bandage it."

"I'm not a nurse," she says.

"But you're a woman," he says, and in his experience all women seem to know what to do. "Please, help me with my wound and I'll let you go."

"How do I know you're not lying?"

"I don't lie," he says, lying and feeling bad about it.

"So what exactly do you want me to do?"

"Clean the wound and bandage it. I want you to make me feel better."

"And for that you'll let me go."

"Of course."

"You promise?"

"On my mother's life."

"Then you'll need to untie me."

"I have a gun," he says, waving it back and forth slightly even though surely she's seen it by now. "If you try to escape I'll shoot you. Please, don't make me do that, it really is the last thing I want to do," he says, and this time the entire statement is true.

"Where's the first-aid kit?"

"There are some things in the bathroom," he says, "but I don't know what everything is and most of it is old anyway."

"Then untie me and bring everything you have back in here."

"No. I'll get everything first and then untie you."

He heads back into the bathroom. He stares at the mirror. The rash is still there with the same intensity, but he's no longer flushed—if anything he looks very pale. Like a ghost. He scoops everything into a plastic bag and carries it back into the room. He returns to the bathroom and fills a bucket with warm water and finds some cotton balls and a couple of clean cloths.

"It will be easier if you take your shorts off," the girl says.

"Ah . . . I don't know. I think it'll be okay," he answers, remembering the time he vomited on the prostitute.

"They're going to keep getting in the way."

"It's just that . . . that . . ." he doesn't know how to finish. He's never taken his pants off around a woman before, except for last night when Cooper's mother helped him, but she was more like a mother and less like a woman and that's a big difference. "The shorts stay on."

"Okay. It's your decision. You need to untie me."

"I know."

"And I'd like another drink."

"When we're done."

"You promise you're going to let me go?"

"You sound like you don't believe me."

"I do believe you," she says. "After all, you saved me from whoever took me, and for that I'm thankful."

Adrian smiles. He likes her.

"What's your name?" she asks.

"Adrian," he tells her. He had never planned on telling her his name, and can't believe how quickly he's told her now.

"I really like your name, Adrian."

"You do?"

"Of course," she says, smiling at him, and wow, what a smile! He can feel his heart beating. "It reminds me of classic romance novels."

"It does?"

"Sure it does," she says. "Adrian . . ."

"Yes?"

"Oh, nothing. I was just saying your name. I like it."

He's pleased that she likes it. It makes him feel . . . warm inside.

"My name is Emma," she tells him. "Emma Green. I'm glad you're going to take me home, Adrian, because my family will be worried about me. My mum especially. I can imagine she will be crying a lot, and so will my dad, and I have a brother too. My mum has cancer," she tells him, "and is dying."

"Does she really have cancer?" he asks.

"Of course she does. I wouldn't make up something like that."

"Do you read books about serial killers?" he asks, then adds "or books about psychology?"

"What? No, no, never. Why?"

"No reason," he tells her, and he's suspicious that she's trying to relate to him. She's using his name a lot, and the story about the mum with cancer is supposed to make him feel sympathetic . . . that's what he read in the books about serial killers, but if she doesn't read those books, then she wouldn't know to say these things. She's not trying to trick him—she's a nice person. Hanging around with people who aren't nice is making him look for things that aren't nice in nice people.

"Do you have any antiseptic, Adrian?" she asks.

"Huh?"

"Antiseptic."

"Oh, yes, sure."

"Can I have some?"

He moves around the bed and unties the ropes. She sits up, carefully so the sheet doesn't drape from her body. She rubs at her wrists while he unties her feet. Her wrists are red and the skin is broken and it must be hard being tied up for nearly a week the way she was, and he's annoyed at Cooper for doing that to her. Cooper could have just locked her in a room. When her feet are free she slowly leans forward and rubs at her ankles.

"Can I have the antiseptic?" she asks.

He passes it to her. She takes off the lid and starts to rub cream into her ankles and wrists. He watches her work, going from limb to limb, and he wants to offer to help but he doesn't. He likes the idea of rubbing cream into her and helping her, but he doesn't think she'll like the idea as much.

"It really hurts," she tells him.

"I'm sorry. Next time it'll . . ." he stops talking, realizing his mistake. He looks down, unable to look her in the eye, waiting for her to pick up on it, waiting for her to say *Next time what? You said you were letting me go.* He doesn't know how to finish his sentence, and thankfully he doesn't have to because she lets him off the hook.

"Let's take a look then, shall we?" she says, missing his comment, and he is pleased. "What happened?"

"Somebody shot me."

"Oh, you poor man," she says, and her voice is soothing and already his leg doesn't seem to hurt as much. The image that comes next is immediate—he sees himself sitting with this woman on the porch watching a sunrise and not with Cooper. His chest is warm

354

and he feels a little light-headed and he isn't sure what's going on. Her wrists are shiny from the cream. He can't stop looking at them.

"It doesn't hurt that much," he says, but it really does. He doesn't want her to know how much pain he's in. "You know, I've had worse," he adds and immediately wishes he hadn't.

She tucks the sheet beneath her armpits and clamps her arms down on the outside of it. "Is that everything in the plastic bag?"

"Yes."

"We should start by washing the wound," she says. "Is that okay? Do you want me to do that for you?"

"Okay."

"You have nice legs, by the way," she says.

"Oh. Oh, really?"

"Surely, Adrian, you've heard that before?"

"Umm . . . no. Never."

"Never? I find that hard to believe," she says, and her smile makes him smile. "Now, do you have any cotton balls?"

"In the bag."

"Then let's get started."

He hands her the bag and she goes through it, placing the items on the bed next to her. Along with the antiseptic, there are other ointments, bandages, gauze pads, tape, a safety pin, pills, creams, a pair of scissors. He keeps his eyes on the scissors. He wants to take them away from her, but at the same time he doesn't want to say anything mean to her. He needs to take them away without sounding like he doesn't trust her. He's really starting to think it would be a waste if he gave her to Cooper.

"Is that pad stuck on the wound?" she asks, leaning forward to get a better look. Her hair is draped down her back, the sheet open like a curtain through which he can see her spine, it looks like a row of knuckles down her back, her skin is smooth and pale. The skin on her neck is tight and there are beads of sweat sitting on the surface. He has the urge to run his finger over them and send them dripping down her body.

"Yes," he hears himself saying.

"We're going to need to remove it."

"The leg?" he asks, the image of him pacing uneven laps in his room comes back to him, and he can feel the blood drain from his face. He wants to be sick.

"No, the pad," she says. "That would be awful if we had to remove the leg," she says, and she says it in a way to not make him feel stupid about his mistake. He doesn't know why he thought she meant the leg—it makes no sense. He feels silly. In the past others would have laughed at him for getting something so simple so wrong.

"It's going to hurt," she warns him, "but I sense you're not going to have a problem. Here, let's soak it first. It should come away easier."

"Okay. Thank you."

She soaks one of the cloths in water and he watches her fingers, her arms, the way her hair sticks to her face. His heart is racing. She squeezes the cloth and he loves the way the water sounds sprinkling back into the bucket. It makes him want to go for a swim, something he hasn't done since he was a boy. She places the cloth and holds it against the pad on his thigh and she looks up at him and smiles and his legs are starting to turn into jelly. He wishes he were sitting down. She peels the corner of the pad away. It's still stuck but not as bad.

"Just a little longer," she says. "Or I can just rip it straight off. Would you prefer that?"

"Yes," he says, and the word hasn't been out of his mouth for more than half a second when *rip*, it's torn from his thigh. "Ah," he says, "ah that . . ."

"Was really brave of you," she says, and smiles at him.

He smiles back, hiding the pain. She reminds him of Katie, Katie the girl he fell in love with, only Emma is much nicer than Katie. Far more beautiful, and friendly, and even though she's much younger than Adrian he can feel himself falling. It's as if he's thirteen again. Of course his mother would say he's becoming obsessed, but his mother would be wrong.

"Now, let's take a look," Katie says—no, not Katie, Emma. When they're sitting on the porch watching future sunsets, he's going to have to be careful not to make that mistake. "Hmm, it looks nasty. Let me wash it down," she says, and she soaks some cotton balls in antiseptic.

"It's old," he says, nodding toward the same antiseptic she put on her own wrists and ankles.

"This stuff lasts forever," she says. "Trust me, they only put expiration dates on it to make sure you keep buying more. It's perfectly safe."

"Are you sure?"

"Of course I'm sure. I used it, didn't I?"

She did, but she didn't know it was old, and he feels bad about not having told her before she used it on herself. He has a decision to make—does he believe her or not? Does he trust her? He decides that he does. She's a nice person, that is obvious, and nice people can be trusted.

He nods. "Okay," he says, "use it on me."

She smiles. He never wants to see her not smiling. She pads two cotton balls against his thigh, then slowly wipes them downward. "You're doing really well," she says. "Not much longer to go."

"Okay."

"You really should get stitches, Adrian."

"I can't."

"Then we'll do the best we can. Now, I need to cut some gauze into the right size."

"I'll do it." He leans over to the bed and picks up the gauze and the scissors. "What size?"

"Just a little bigger than the wound."

"Oh, of course." He uses the scissors then hands her the gauze. He puts the scissors into his back pocket. She holds the gauze in place and puts another medical pad on top of it.

"Now I need you to cut some tape to the right lengths."

"How long?"

"Just a little longer than the pad."

She passes him up the tape. It's difficult because he's still holding the gun, but he manages okay. He cuts a piece at a time and hands it to her and she sticks it across the edge of the pad and across his thigh. When all four are in place she lets go and leans back.

"Looks good," she says. "How does it feel?"

"Much better," he says, and he smiles and she smiles back and this is perfect, just perfect.

"Okay, now, where's the bandage?" she says, turning back to look at the contents on the bed. "Ah, there we go," she says, picking it up. "Now I'm going to put this on tight, but not too tight, okay, Adrian? Let me know if it hurts."

"It won't hurt," he says, his heart fluttering, liking how his name sounds coming from her mouth. He can see what Cooper saw in this girl, but what Cooper was going to do to her was wrong. Very wrong. He will never let Cooper hurt her. Never.

"Just let me know if it does," she says. "I don't want to hurt you, Adrian."

"And I don't want anybody to hurt you."

She puts one hand on the inside of his thigh and he can feel himself stirring and is embarrassed about it. She reaches the bandage behind his leg and takes it in her other hand then starts pulling it around. She repeats the movement over and over, crisscrossing the bandage until it's nice and secure and covering about half of his thigh.

"Now you'll need to do this again tonight, so if you like I don't mind staying for the day, and tonight after I re-dress the wound you can take me home? Is that okay, Adrian? I need to see my parents. I love them so much and miss them."

"Sure! Sure," he says, excited.

"How does it feel?"

"Good."

"Now you'll need to use both hands to hold the bandage," she says, "one here on this side and one on this side, just until I can pin it into place. Be careful with that gun and don't shoot yourself in the foot. I'd hate for you to hurt yourself, Adrian."

"Okay." He lowers his free hand and holds the bandage, and he lowers his gun hand and does the same, extending his grip along the side of the gun to the bandage, the barrel pointing to his foot.

"You got it?"

"Yes," he says, wishing things had gone this easy with Cooper.

"Now don't let go. Keep lots of pressure."

"Okay."

"Now, what else do we have here," she says, turning toward the bed, then she comes back with the safety pin. "Let me secure it with this," she says.

He's thinking about the sunrise, about how, if he's allowed, he'd like to hold her hand as they sit on the porch, a nice warm wind, both of them drinking orange juices. He's thinking about a future with her, about the sun coming over the tops of the trees and shining in her hair and he's thinking about how beautiful she'll look. He's picturing himself on the porch at the opposite end of the day, watching the sun set behind the mountains in the distance, Emma cuddled up next to him for warmth. He's thinking about holding the bandage nice and tight, and he can't think of too many things at the same time because he'll end up forgetting things.

Her hands brush against his, and he watches her fiddling with the safety pin, poking the point just so it will slide beneath the material. Her hand touches more of his hand and she tries to get a better angle, and then her hand is on his hand and then . . .

The gun goes off. Her finger is jammed against his finger, which is resting against the trigger. The barrel is still pointing down at his foot. Two toes have completely disappeared, replaced by a pulpy mess that looks like a crushed tomato. He doesn't even feel any pain, it doesn't have time to register before Emma's arm swings upward, the safety pin is in her hand and it's bent open, he gets a real good look at it because it comes racing toward his face. His hands are still on the bandage, still on the gun, and he's still not letting go just as she told him, at least until the pin hits, enters, and sinks down deep into his eyeball, right up to the small O-shaped hinge. Then he lets go with both hands and screams.

His hands race up to his face and the gun hits him in the side of the head hard enough to give him an immediate headache, but he hangs on to it. He squeezes his eyes closed and his left one closes across the pin but won't seal shut, letting in light, allowing him to see the shaft of the pin as it trails out of his blurry perspective. There's an immediate flow of tears. The pain comes from his eye and from his foot at the same time, both far worse than anything he ever felt in the Scream Room. The pain has a weight to it, it's heavy inside his head pulling his gaze to the floor, a sharp intense pain that starts at his eye and detours through his brain before spreading to his shoulders, and from his foot a dull ache races up his leg into his belly. He touches the pin with his free hand wanting to pull it out and the pain widens, and immediately he vomits, no warning of it, stomach bile spilling over his chin and down the front of his shirt. There's a sudden ache in his groin and his entire body burns with pain and he doesn't know what's happening.

The girl is screaming at him but he can't absorb the words, they're all insults, even if he can't focus on them he can recognize the tone, and the pain explodes in his groin again and he realizes she's kicking him. He puts his arm ahead and pulls the trigger and the gun goes off and he can't see if he hits the woman or the wall, and he fires again and then again, the sound deafening, hurting his ears. He staggers to the side leaving one of his toes behind, another barely hanging on, and he can't maintain his weight on his foot, he buckles and trips over the bucket and hits the floor, his bare feet soaked in the process, his body banging against the drawers and the Taser landing in his lap. He pinches his fingers on the safety pin, takes a deep breath and pulls. He can feel his entire eyeball being brought forward and the pain is too intense and he has to let go, it's as though the pin is much longer now that it's inside of him, so long it's gone directly into the center of his brain. He opens his good eye and has to hold it open with his fingers to stop it from closing. Something oozes down the pin and drips onto his cheek. He looks around the room and he's alone now. He takes another grip on the safety pin, puts down the gun, pushes his other fingers against his eye to stop it moving, grits his teeth, and pulls as hard as he can.

chapter fifty-three

The alarm clock goes off and I wake up feeling even more tired than before I went to sleep. It reminds me of how I used to feel last year when I'd wake up every morning with a hangover. I spent months on end trying to drink away the memories of the bad things I thought I'd done before crashing into Emma Green sobered me up for good. A couple of cups of coffee go a long way to bringing me around. I take a cold shower and drink another coffee before settling up with the hotel clerk, this one a different guy from two hours ago.

The roads are full of early-morning weekend traffic. Most people have the windows down with their arms hanging out the window, some of them with cigarettes between their fingers with smoke trailing into the air. There are no early indications that today is going to be any cooler than yesterday. I think of Buttons and what he said about rumors in a mental institution, and wonder how much of what he said last night was true. I hope Jesse Cartman is doing better this morning, that he'll take his medication today and not be found with his hands buried in somebody else looking for the soft meat. There's a delay up ahead, a couple of the teenage drag racers from last night have crashed, shutting down one of the lanes, so we're all bottlenecked up to and through an intersection, the heat cooking us all.

I make it through the city. I drive out past the airport taking a road with a view to the runways, an incoming plane low enough to shake the car. There are a few dozen people parked off the road, caught between reading newspapers and watching the planes come and go. Out past more paddocks and more farmers and I should just buy a house out here because it'd mean less commuting.

I don't get all warm inside at the thought of returning to the prison. I have to go past a guard station and show some ID before I pull into the parking lot where there's a small scattering of other visitor vehicles. It all looks exactly the same as it did a few days ago when I was stepping out of it. Same shimmering blacktop. Same dust floating up from the exercise yard. Same machines and same scaffolding and same work crews extending the prison walls, making more room for the new arrivals being bused in on a daily basis, not having to work too fast because the prison just keeps on busing them back out. The entrance betrays what it's really like inside. A nicely landscaped garden around the parking lot that's turning brown in the sun, a large double set of automatic glass doors, all modern styling with furniture inside only a year old at the most. There's a reception counter with about four people behind it, all of them look like they should be on the other side of the bars, especially the woman who speaks to me. She has dark black hair along with a small reserve of it lining her upper lip. She looks at me as if trying to figure how many pieces she can break me into, and I imagine it would be a lot. She has to be at least twice my weight, and she's carrying most of that in her shoulders and chest.

"I'd like to see a prisoner," I tell her.

"You have an appointment?"

"No."

"You just say no?"

"Yes."

"You can't just come down here without making an appointment."

"Then I'd like to make an appointment," I say.

"For who and for when?"

"For Edward Hunter, and for now."

"I just said you can't come here without making an appointment."

"I just made one."

"No you didn't," she says. "You just asked to make one. It's a big difference."

"Please, it's important."

"That's what everybody says."

I think about calling Donovan Green. Asking him for some more money to grease the transition between not seeing Edward Hunter and seeing Edward Hunter, then figuring it's too risky. The woman looks like she'd be happy because most of her income is being blown on steroids, but sad because she'd have to split it with the others behind her. "Please, it really is important," I say. "I think he knows something that can help me find Emma Green, the girl that's missing. Please. Her father sent me. He's desperate. And what can it hurt letting me see him?"

She takes a good ten seconds to think about it. Weighs up whatever options there are for and against, and comes to the conclusion that helping me out may end up being her good deed for the day.

"Don't make this a habit," she says.

"I won't. I promise."

"It'll take ten minutes. Sit down and wait, and if it takes longer, don't complain."

I sit down and wait and I don't complain, even though I can feel each of the minutes ticking away.

chapter fifty-four

The screams are loud, muffled somewhat by the padded walls of the cell, but high pitched enough to come through and for Cooper to know they're being made by a woman. Probably from Emma Green. There's a second gunshot, then three more, and Cooper is desperate to know what's going on. Have the police arrived? He hopes not.

His mother is in the opposite corner of the cell. He can't see her—he still can't see a damn thing in here and has no idea whether it's even morning yet, and his bladder is so full that fluids must be starting to back up into his stomach and his groin feels like it's going to pop. His mother isn't talking to him, or even looking at him now, and for that he truly hates himself. He starts banging on the cell door. He has to bang hard to produce sound loud enough to be heard, and he uses his shoe like he did back in Grover Hills.

"Hey, hey, what's going on out there? Adrian? Hey, let me out of here. Let me out, let me out, let me out!"

The screaming stops. There is no more gunfire, only silence. He keeps banging at the padded door.

Then the slot at face height opens up.

"Who are you?" Emma Green asks.

He almost jumps at seeing her face. In a weird way it's like seeing a ghost. "Who . . . who are you?" he asks, trying to sound like he doesn't know. "Please, please, you have to let me out of here," he adds, trying to hide his shock at seeing her. "He's crazy. He's going to kill us."

"You look . . . kind of familiar."

"Please, we have to hurry."

"Oh my God, you're one of my university professors! What the hell is going on here?"

"I don't know," he says, and right now he really doesn't. Somehow Emma Green has escaped. The screams must have come from Adrian. The gunshots must have been Emma Green shooting him! It's perfect. All absolutely perfect. "Listen, what's your name?" he asks.

"Emma."

"Listen, Emma, I've been captive for . . . I don't know, I've lost track of time. Please, please, you have to let me out of here. You killed him, right? The man who took me?"

"No. He's still alive. I only hurt him," she says, glancing over her right shoulder to look down the corridor.

"You shot him, right? Please tell me you shot him."

"He was shooting at me."

"Oh, fuck, so he's still out there? You have to hurry. You have to let me out, you have to let me out now!"

"Are you in there alone?" she asks.

He steps aside so she can see into the room. "My mother is in here with me," he tells her.

"What's wrong with her?"

"It's what I'm trying to tell you. He killed her. Last night he killed her right in front of me and there wasn't a thing I could do," he says. "It was the worst . . . the worst thing in the world." And it was the worst thing. He wrapped his hands around his mother's throat and he told her he was sorry over and over as her eyes bulged forward and he took her life from her. He loves her, but he loves his freedom even more. There was no other way. The police would question her. She would tell them a crazy man thought her son was a serial killer. The police would wonder if there was something to that, on account of one of his students going missing. Two students, if you counted the one from three years ago.

"Oh my God," she says.

"Please, you have to let me out."

"Hang on a second."

She takes a step back and the door opens outward into the hall. The relief washes over him. He can feel the excitement of killing Adrian. He can taste the excitement of being alone with Emma Green. For the first time he notices she's completely naked. He steps out of the cell. This isn't Sunnyview or Eastlake. "Where in the hell are we?"

"I have no idea," she says. "But I think there are two of them."

"What?"

"Somebody took me on Monday night," she says, "and left me in a building somewhere. Then somebody else took me from that building and brought me here. It wasn't the same guy."

"Where is he now? The one you hurt?"

"That way," she says, and points down the hallway.

The hallway is part of a house. Just a normal house with a padded cell and not a mental institution that's been abandoned. The hallway is carpeted and wider than what he's used to. There are old-fashioned side tables against the wall with ceramic knickknacks on them, some watercolor paintings that don't look very good and were probably done by the owners of the house. He takes two steps toward the room Emma said she came out of and the door flies open and Adrian appears, blood and fluid streaming down one side of his face, the palm of his hand hiding some kind of mess, his foot is bleeding and looks like it's been clubbed with a hammer. He levels the gun.

"Jesus," Cooper says, and he grabs Emma and shields her from what's coming, covering her with his body, an instinct he guesses coming from the Cooper Riley that predated his divorce and Natalie Flowers. The bullet hits the wall well wide of them and he figures two things right then: Adrian has probably never used a gun before today, and his accuracy is off because he's only using one eye.

"You're my friend," Adrian yells, and there's another gunshot, this one closer.

"Let's go," Cooper says, and he rolls off the girl and grabs her arm and pulls her upright. The room they just came out of would provide immediate safety, but he'll only be back at square one, locked away at Adrian's mercy.

Unfortunately it's their only option. The door is opened across the hallway, and to get past it they'd have to close it, it'd take an extra second or two and he just doesn't think they have that long.

"I thought you liked me," Adrian says, and Cooper isn't so sure he's the one being spoken to.

He pushes Emma into the room and dives after her. The impact of hitting the ground is all the convincing his bladder needs to let go, and a quarter of it is emptied before he can get it back under control. He guesses he has five seconds to make a decision before Adrian either locks the door or shoots them.

"Do you have a weapon?" he asks.

"What? No, no, of course I don't."

He looks around the room. His pants are soaking wet, and his bladder is desperately trying to let go again. In fact, it's more painful than before. There was nothing in here earlier that could help, and nothing now.

Except his mother.

His mother doesn't have to have died in vain.

chapter fifty-five

A guard comes and tells me to follow him. He has a large forehead creased with stress, and a lower lip that sticks out half an inch past his upper one, the kind of lip you wouldn't want to have when you've got a bad cold. He escorts me past a metal detector where I'm frisked for any concealed weapons or drugs. It's all caught on security camera from about four different angles, which must be switched off most of the time going by the amount of drugs and weapons that make it in here. I'm led into the visitors' room, which is on the other side of a set of bars that slide open as we approach. The visitors' room has a dozen or so square tables in it, all of them marked in some way, chips in the edges, lines and creases where things have been dragged across them, small words etched into the wood. A few of them are occupied with people in jumpsuits sitting opposite loved ones in summer outfits. The room is air-conditioned and doesn't give the visitor any indication of how hot it gets in the cells this time of the year, or how cold it gets in the winter. The last four months I always approached this room from the other side. This time I'm given a small speech by the guard on things I can't do. Edward Hunter is sitting behind a table with his hands in his lap looking at me and trying to place how he knows me. I sit down opposite him and neither of us offers to shake hands.

"Thanks for seeing me," I tell him.

"I don't remember speaking a single word to you when you were in here," he says, "what could be so important that you had to come back?"

"There's a missing girl."

"There are lots of missing girls," he says. "My daughter went missing once and she died, why should I care about anybody else?" His voice sounds neutral, like he's being chemically balanced. He speaks with no emotion when he talks about his daughter. He sounds drained, empty. His wife was gunned down in the same bank robbery Schroder was talking about, the bank where Jane Tyrone worked. Edward's daughter was kidnapped and held ransom for money, and Edward went after the men who had her. What he did to those men for killing his family is the reason he's here.

"I'm sorry about what happened to your family," I tell him.

"I know you are. Your daughter was killed too," he says. "Did you kill the person who hurt her?"

"Please, I'm here for your help."

"You did. I can tell," he says. "Do you have a monster living inside of you? Mine likes the taste of blood."

If Edward Hunter isn't on any kind of medication, I sure as hell hope he starts getting it. If he's already on some, then they need to up the dose. His words make me think of Jesse Cartman. Without a doubt there was a monster inside Jesse Cartman that was desperate to be fed.

"Her name is Emma Green," I say, moving forward. "She was kidnapped Monday night and I think she's still alive. She was taken by a man named Cooper Riley. Then they were both abducted by an ex-mental patient named Adrian Loaner."

"Sounds like you know everything there is to know."

"I don't know where they are."

"Well, nor do I. I haven't even heard of those people. I don't get

369

out much, you know. And I don't like the news. What's there to like? Same stories every day with different names. Nothing to like about that at all."

"What's your relationship to Murray and Ellis Hunter?"

"Huh? What?"

"Murray and . . ."

"I know. I heard you. They're uncles, on my dad's side," he says, and for the first time he's engaged with the conversation. "I hardly know them. I didn't see them for years after my dad was, you know, arrested. I saw them at my grandparents' funerals, and that was it. I hardly even spoke to them, and if I saw them on the street tomorrow I wouldn't even recognize them."

"They used to work at Grover Hills."

"What's that, some kind of retirement village?"

"Not quite," I say, then explain it to him.

"So what do you want to know about them?"

"Any idea where they live?"

"None. Why? You can't find them?"

"They're dead."

"What . . . you mean . . . what? How?"

"Murdered."

"Jesus," he says. "By who?"

"Adrian Loaner."

"The man who has Emma Green."

"He used to be a patient there. Everything suggests your uncles used to abuse him, along with others."

"Oh, I see," he says, reaching up and gripping the edge of the table. "Now I see why you came here. You think they have the Hunter gene, right? The one that makes us blood men. My dad had it, I have it, and now they have it too."

Two of the guards look over but don't approach us, though they look like they're getting ready to. I keep my voice low. "They hurt a lot of people, your uncles. Killed a lot of people too so it's looking."

He shrugs. "So they got what they deserve," he says, dismissively.

"I guess they did."

"So why are you here?"

"Because they had to take their victims somewhere."

"I told you, I don't know where they live."

"I've been to their house. It was full of souvenirs of people they've killed."

"Fucking gene," he says.

"They didn't take their victims there. So where? Any ideas?"

"Like I said, I just don't know them. I really don't. I wish I could help you. I could if I knew anything, but there's nothing."

"There has to be something," I say, the frustration and exhaustion starting to get the better of me. "Please, there has to be something."

"I'm telling you, if I knew I'd tell you. I get that there's a girl's life on the line, okay? I get it. I just don't know where they are. I haven't seen them in about six years."

"Since the funerals of your grandparents."

"Yeah. That's what I said earlier."

"That's the same time they left Grover Hills."

"So?" he asks.

"So it means when your grandparents died, they quit their jobs. Why would they do that?"

He shrugs. "I don't know."

He doesn't know, but it's taking shape. They quit their job because they no longer needed the Scream Room at Grover Hills. They had somewhere to build their own. "Your grandparents. Where did they live?"

"They moved ages ago. I used to live with them when I was a kid. They had a pretty nice house near town, but they always wanted something bigger with a lot of land. It wasn't long after I moved out that they bought a farm before retiring. They worked that farm for . . . let me think . . . seven or eight years, I guess, before my grandfather died. Not long after grandma died too, I think it was because she missed him so much."

A farm. It's perfect. "What happened to it? The farm?"

"I don't know. It was sold, I guess."

"But you don't know?"

"I think they left it to their kids, to Ellis and Murray, and I always just figured . . . shit, I just figured they'd sold it, but you don't think they did, do you? You think this is where they were taking their victims?"

"Where is it?"

"You're going to need a map," he says.

"I got one in the car."

"Then grab a pencil. You're going to need directions."

chapter fifty-six

His collection is escaping. All the hard work, all the planning, it's all turning to ruin. He no longer feels any pain in his leg from the gunshot last night, and even his foot doesn't hurt compared to what's going on in his head. His foot, his poor damaged foot, how will it heal? Can the toes be saved? His eye, his poor damaged eye feels like it's on fire.

The safety pin is gone. It's back on the floor in the bedroom where Katie betrayed him. He will never trust her again. She failed him when he was a kid, she failed him when he tried paying her for sex a few months ago, and now she's failed him again. Almost as much as the pain, that betrayal hurts. He doesn't know how many bullets are in the gun but he knows it wouldn't be wise to use them all up, so for the moment he's stopped shooting. He isn't even sure he wants to shoot his collection. Things can still be saved. All he has to do is close the cell door and give it some time and he'll try, he'll really, really try to forgive them, and he can use Cooper's mother or Katie to help him heal. He can still have his sunrise on the porch with Cooper one morning and Katie the next.

Like the Preacher told him, he just needs to have a little faith.

Right now he just has to close that door.

He can barely take any weight on his leg, and when he walks only the heel of his foot touches the ground, and his shoulder slides along the wall as he leans against it. He keeps the gun ahead, the end of it trained on the doorway to the Scream Room.

Cooper's mother comes out. Her eyes are half open and her face is sagging. She's upright but standing kind of funny, the same way a puppet would stand in a puppet show, limbs all loose and not in control. She comes toward him and he takes a step back. He didn't expect this. He levels the gun at her as best as he can, his hand shaking, his entire body sore. His free hand covers his eye.

"What do you want?" he asks.

She doesn't answer. He takes another step back and the weight goes onto his foot and his leg buckles and he almost falls.

"Don't make me shoot you," he says, talking loudly over his ringing ears.

Closer. Closer still.

"Get back," he says.

He pulls the trigger. Twice. One shot into the ceiling, the second into the woman's chest. Instead of flying backward like people do in movies when they're shot, she is launched forward. He takes another shot at her, this time getting her in the stomach, and she keeps coming at him and he lifts his arms to stop her from hitting him, even taking his hand from his eye as she crashes into him. He stumbles back and this time there is no way his foot can maintain his weight and he tips over, his body lying flat and his head wedged upright against the wall, which now has a dent in the plasterboard. He pushes her off. She rolls onto the floor next to him, her face staring up at his.

Cooper is standing in front of him, and Cooper looks mad. The front of his trousers are soaking wet, and there is still blood all over his shirt from the girl two nights ago. Has it been two nights already? The same view also includes Adrian's foot, and the second of the damaged toes is missing now and he isn't sure when it came off.

He raises his gun, only the gun isn't in his hand anymore, instead his hand is empty. He's defenseless, just as he was all those years ago near his school when he was on the ground being pissed on, and he gets that same feeling that he got then when he knew what was coming. Cooper bends down and picks up the gun then steps in close.

"It hurts," Adrian says. "Please, Cooper, help me. You're my best friend."

Cooper crouches down and puts the barrel of the gun against Adrian's chest. Cooper smiles. Adrian smiles too. Everything is going to be okay. The gun barrel is hot. A moment later it feels like he's having a heart attack. Every muscle in his body is cramping, and no longer does his eye seem to hurt. The world flashes brightly, like when the doctor used to come by in the hospital and shine lights into his eyes. Everything flares white again as the gun barrel gets hotter. Then the world darkens. There are twin pools of blood draining down his chest. He watches the world fade through the one eye that can still see.

He watches Katie, his beloved Katie over all these years, come out of the room, naked and beautiful and he would never give her to Cooper, never. Cooper stands up and approaches her.

And the last words Adrian hears are Cooper's as he talks to her.

"There's something I should tell you," he says, turning his back on Adrian and raising the gun to Katie, "because so far I haven't been completely honest with you."

And then Adrian sees himself on the porch, an old man now, watching the sunrise with Katie by his side, Cooper no longer part of their lives, the sunrise starting to fade, fading to night, his hand in hers, dark now, and then gone.

chapter fifty-seven

I think about my promise to Donovan Green. He wants his five minutes with Cooper Riley, and if Adrian Loaner wasn't involved, maybe I'd give it to him. Instead I call Schroder. It's the best thing for Emma, for Schroder, and for me. I need things to stay good between me and Schroder. No doubt I'll need him in the future. The prison phone is covered in scratches, names and dates etched into it, and the guard stands next to me, listening to the whole thing.

Schroder tells me they've gotten a warrant for the Grover Hills patient and staff files and will have them within the hour. He tells me interviewing of the staff will start by lunchtime, and that everybody who ever worked there now has a lawyer. I tell him that's good, and then I give him the address where I think Emma Green is being held. He asks how I came to that conclusion and I tell him there isn't time to explain it all, that he needs to meet me there, that I'm right on this one. I have probably a twenty-minute head start on him. Anything can happen in twenty minutes. He tells me to wait and I tell him that I'll check it out and call him if I see anything suspicious.

"From where? Adrian smashed your cell phone."

"I'm not just going to stand around and wait. Twenty minutes is a long time."

"Tate . . ."

"I gotta go," I say, and I hang up.

I start to walk away from the phone, and go two paces before changing my mind. I call Donovan Green.

"You got a pen?" I ask.

"Sure."

"Then write this down," I tell him, and give him the address. "I'm pretty sure this is where Emma is."

"Is she okay?"

"I don't know. If you want your five minutes with Cooper Riley, you're going to need to hurry."

I hang up, confident there's no way Green can get out there before the police do. If Emma is alive, it's going to be a fantastic reunion. If she's dead, then I've just given Donovan her location and he's going to see his daughter's body and he's going to fall apart. But it's what he wants, it's what I'd want in his situation, and it's what I owe him.

Edward Hunter has given pretty good directions, but it's been years since he was last out here, which gives him plenty of room to be a little vague. For the most part he was confident, and for the most part that made me confident too. I compare his map against the map in the car, vowing that when this is over I'm going to purchase the most expensive GPS unit on the market. More paddocks and wire fences and if a case ever brings me into this part of the country again I'm turning it down.

The farmhouse comes into view. It's a big building with a large A-frame roof, the sides of the building painted red, the roof is black, lots of white trim around the windowsills and door. It looks like the grandparents saw a nice farmhouse in a movie or jigsaw puzzle and wanted the same one. What's missing is a steaming pie on the windowsill, but what is here at the top of the dirt road leading up to the farmhouse is Emma Green's car. I keep driving. Problem is I have to drive another five hundred meters before I can find anything to park behind that will hide my car. I check the trunk and find a crowbar for wrenching off wheels that get stuck when you're changing a flat. I jump the fence. Nothing has been farmed here in a long time, there are areas of hard dirt, areas of tall grass and even taller weed, some of it up around my knees. I move diagonally across the section staying low, approaching the house from only one side to decrease the number of windows I can be seen from, waiting, waiting for a gunshot from the gun Donovan Green gave me to ring out and drop me like a rock.

By the time I get to the building my legs are itchy and blotchy from the grass. I pause against the wall. The wood is warm and the heat soaks into my skin. There is no sign of anybody. No sounds. I look through one of the windows, struggling a little to see beyond the netting. There's a large living room suite with flower-patterned upholstery, an oak coffee table with sculptured legs, a boxy TV that must weigh a ton. It all looks very neat, as if Grandpa and Grandma Hunter are still living here. I move past the window and look into the next one. It's a master bedroom with a queen-sized bed and the blankets all thrown back. The next window is completely black and I can't see anything beyond it. It's covered on the inside with something much thicker than curtains.

I head around to the back of the house. The deck leading up to the back door groans as my body weight shifts onto it. I come to a complete stop. I give it a few seconds and there's no indication anybody is coming to check out the sound. I walk as close as I can to the wall and the groaning stops. I turn the handle on the back door and it opens freely. I step into the kitchen. It's tidy. There are lots of white tiles behind the sink and a table off center for the family to sit around. There's a calendar hanging on the wall dating back nearly sixty years showing a painting of an orchard. It's faded and the edges are creased and one of the dates has a fading circle around it. Inside the circle in a script that looks old-fashioned and has also faded are the words *Our wedding*. The sun is still reasonably low and shining in under the veranda and through the windows, casually hitting every surface and filling the kitchen with light. I close the door behind me and stop and listen. It's me and a crowbar up against an ex-mental patient with a gun and a Taser.

The kitchen is open plan into a dining room, from where there are two doors, one leading into a living room, another into a hallway. I can see into the living room and there's nobody in there. I enter the hallway. It branches off in two directions, one is up a flight of stairs, the other goes straight ahead where it turns right. I stay on the ground floor and follow the hall around the corner, passing some pretty old furniture and some paintings on the wall. There's a door wide open. The hinges have been reversed so the door opens outward rather than in and it blocks the rest of the hall. The front of the door is facing me. I step up carefully to it and look around it. There are two bodies in the hall further down. I close the door slightly so I can look into the room. It's empty inside. The entire thing is padded, ceiling and floor. There are stains on the floor—this is the Scream Room the Hunter twins built. This is where at least nine men lost their lives. Despite the heat a cold shiver runs the length of my body. Could be they kept their victims in here for only a day, or it could be they kept them for months.

I swing the door completely closed and approach the bodies. One man and one woman. The woman looks to be in her late seventies. The man is who I saw setting fire to Cooper Riley's house and tried to collect me from my own. There're a pair of bullet holes in his chest. His eyes are wide open and one of them is ruined, there's a hole in it and the area has swollen and there's been some seepage. I crouch down and check the woman for a pulse. Nothing. I don't even bother with Adrian. No point. There's no immediate sign of the gun. Cooper Riley probably has it. He probably has Emma Green too. He can't know how much the police know about him, and has to be thinking the best way he can get out of here and resume any kind of life is by making up his own version of events, and to do that he can't let anybody live.

So why isn't Emma Green laying on the floor here too?

There's a sound like a small gunshot and then a muffled scream from further down the hall. I move in that direction. There's another gunshot sound that isn't loud enough to be a gunshot. I want to rush the rest of the way, but I just keep taking one step at a time, slowly, carefully, past a bathroom and an empty bedroom and toward another one that has a queen-sized bed with Emma Green on top of it. She's naked. As I watch, Cooper Riley, standing in front of her, swings his belt down against the bedside drawers, on top of which is resting the gun and a Taser. Emma jumps at the sound. It's the noise I heard earlier. Her hands are bound behind her and she tries to push herself further into the mattress. I move forward. Either he senses me or he notices Emma change as she senses me, because he turns quickly, the large bedroom window behind him, and I think about running hard at him and trying to push him right through it, only he could take me with him and I could end up landing on a rake and he could end up landing in a pile of hay. He snatches up the gun and brings it up toward me and I throw the crowbar forward. It hits his arm and he shouts out as he lets go of the gun, both items go hurtling in the same direction, the pry bar hitting and cracking the window, the gun flying out the smaller open window to the world outside. Cooper comes forward and I meet him, he throws a fast right punch that catches me in the jaw at the same time I swing one, mine catching him in the cheek. He comes at me again and I block him, grab him, and then we're tipping over into a chest of drawers. Solid objects start littering down on us, a hairbrush, a mirror, some figurines, a couple of novels, a crossword book with a pen hooked onto it, a thick glass jar with something floating inside. Emma Green is off the bed and she's gone for the door. I push up and hit Cooper in the side of the face again, and before I can follow it up he grabs the glass jar and swings it down.

It shatters against the side of my skull, but it feels like half of it has gone right through the bone. What looks like a severed thumb hits me in the nose before bouncing away, then the fluid washes into my eyes, the pain is instant and burns and everything goes fuzzy from the liquid and from the blow to my head. I can barely open my eyes. I try to blink away the fluid but it's not helping.

Cooper leans down on me. His outline is blurry. His hands tighten against my throat. I reach for them but can barely even lift my arms. I can smell urine and sweat. I can hear creaking wood. I can taste blood. I'm quickly losing a battle against something I can do nothing about, and all I have is the hope that Schroder is about to walk through the door.

He doesn't.

Cooper's hands tighten.

I blink away more of the fluid. Pressure is building up inside my head. My eyes are going to pop out. Then something comes into view. A black object that looks like a gun but is too thick to be one. Cooper tilts his head up to see it and a moment later the end of it is jammed into his mouth.

"You fucker!" Emma Green yells and pulls the trigger.

His body goes tight for a second before going completely loose. There's a low crackling sound of volts being transferred. Tiny lights are dancing in front of my vision that turn out to be small pieces of paper with serial numbers on them too fuzzy to read. Cooper's hands slip off my throat and he falls on me, his face pressing hard against my face, the full weight of his body on me. I push him off to the side and he rolls onto his back. There are two thin wires leading from his open mouth to the Taser in Emma's hand. Her finger is still on the trigger and Cooper is jerking on the floor until she lets go.

I wipe at my eyes but things still remain blurry. I crawl away and get to my knees and when I stand up I walk sideways and crash into the wall then back down to the floor. Emma puts the Taser down and picks up the crowbar. Her hands are still tied together, but now they're in front of her. She must have hooked her feet up and through.

"Who are you?" she asks. "Who the fuck are you?"

I hold my hands over my head, ready to defend myself if she starts swinging, not sure that I'm going to be able to. "Your father, he, he sent me to, to find you," I say.

"You look familiar."

"That's, that's because . . ."

"You ran into me last year. What the hell? Have you come here to hurt me?"

"No, no, of course not," I say, trying to get my breathing under control.

Cooper starts gagging. He's trying to move his arms but he can't. His mouth is open and his tongue is swelling up. There's a bulge growing in his throat. His face is turning purple and he can't breathe. He's trying to reach his mouth but he can't.

"Your father hired me," I tell her. Sweat is mixing with the blood from my scalp and whatever fluid was in that jar. I keep wiping it from my eyes. It stings like hell. "He thought that I owed it to you and to him to find you. That's why, why, I took on the case."

"Stay where you are," she says. "Stay on the floor. If you try to move I'll start swinging. I'm not kidding."

"What about him?" I ask, nodding toward Cooper. His face is dark purple now.

"Was he going to kill me?" she asks.

"Yes."

"Then let him die," she says.

"You don't want that," I say. "You do now, but soon you'll regret it. Trust me." I push myself up from the floor. I wipe at my eyes and suck in some deeper breaths. I try to move over to Cooper. My knee isn't bending again and hurts to take any weight.

"Stay where you are," she tells me.

"He'll die."

"If you move one muscle I'll put this through your skull. You got a phone?"

"No."

"Bullshit," she says. "Everybody these days has a phone."

"Yeah? Where's yours?" I ask.

"I don't know. He took it from me."

I wipe the bottom of my shirt over my face. My vision is starting to clear. Cooper is making gagging noises.

"Why do you want to help him so much?" she asks.

"The police are on their way, but they're still five or ten minutes away, and honestly I'm just as happy as you are to stand here and watch him die. But he has information I need. There's another woman I'm looking for. Another girl that he hurt."

"I don't believe you."

"You have to trust me."

"I'm never trusting anybody again."

I reach into my pocket. I find the photograph Donovan Green gave me the day I got out of jail.

"Your dad gave me this," I tell her, and I show it to her. "He said the day this was taken you turned ten. He said all you wanted for your birthday was a puppy and when they didn't get one for you, you ran away. He told me they found you two blocks away at the park on the merry-go-round trying to talk to the birds in the trees and make friends with them. They were so relieved you were okay and when they were about to tell you off, you talked your way out of it. Your dad said you told them you ran away because you felt bad about having wanted so much from them, and not because you hadn't gotten it, and that you ran away because you were a bad girl. He knew you were making it up, but the way you said it was believable and made them feel bad and they couldn't bring themselves to tell you off. He said you've always been able to talk your way into getting what you want from him. Put down the crowbar, Emma, and let me help him."

"He told you all that?"

I nod.

She doesn't put down the crowbar, but she nods toward Cooper. "Help him," she says. "Ask him what you need to."

I move over to Cooper and crouch down next to him.

"Calm down," I tell him.

He doesn't. He isn't moving much, mostly just shudders, but I need him to stay perfectly still.

"Stop struggling or you're going to die. Now, this is going to hurt but at least you'll live. You got that?"

He stops moving.

I take the pen off the crossword book and snap it in half, giving me a plastic tube.

"What are you doing to him?" Emma asks.

"I'm going to save his life. You know what I'm about to do?" I ask Cooper.

His eyes tell me that he gets it. I pick up a piece of glass from the broken jar, put my hand on his forehead and push his head against the floor to keep him still, then drag the glass down his throat, between two little ridges. He starts struggling again. His face is covered in sweat. When the cut is big enough, I jam the tube into the wound.

He starts breathing, air going through the pen.

Sirens finally start sounding in the distance.

"The police are here," I tell her. "Go and find some clothes. I'll wait with him."

Emma leaves the room. Cooper stays where he is. His skin is returning from the purple color back to normal.

"You remember Natalie Flowers?" I ask him.

He finds the strength to nod.

"Do you know where she is?"

He shakes his head.

"Any idea at all?"

He shakes his head again.

"If you knew, would you tell me?"

Another shake of the head.

"You sent her down a path, you know that, right?"

He nods.

"People are dying because of her, because of what you did to her. You're a piece of garbage, you know that, right? The rest of the world is going to know it too because you were kind enough to take the photos to prove it. They're going to know that you're the worst kind of rapist. You know, I've been in jail, I know what it's like, but for you, well, there's a special place in jail for you. My experience in jail is going to look like a vacation compared to yours. Help me with Natalie, and maybe I'll see what I can do. Maybe you don't have to spend every day sitting on a bag of ice to keep down the swelling."

He lifts his hand slightly and signals that he wants to write something. Every breath he makes is drawn in and out of the pen, accompanied by a hollow whistling sound. I find the nib and plastic spine that came out of the broken pen and hand it to him, along with the crossword book. He tilts it toward him and writes, then puts down the pen. I take the book back off him.

He's written *Fuck You* in the margin. I look down at him, and he grins. Then he reaches to the plastic tube and pulls it out.

The smile stays on his face for ten seconds. He's controlling the situation, controlling his fate, controlling the outcome. He's avoiding jail, avoiding the responsibility, avoiding the media circus. He prefers death to the humiliation he'll have to face with his peers. His thoughts are very clear in his eyes. He's happy with the decision he's made. Then that smile flickers around the edges. He begins to turn purple again, sweat is running down his forehead. He's beating the system, but he's not looking as happy with his decision anymore. Twenty seconds into it and there is no longer any hint of a smile. He begins fumbling with the plastic tube. He lifts it up to his throat. He gets the tip of it against the cut but can't get it in there, there's too much blood and he can't get the angle right. It keeps slipping around the edges of the wound and also in his fingertips. He tries to widen the hole with his finger, but in the process he drops the tube. It rolls over the floor toward me.

Thirty seconds into it and his eyes are pleading for help. He tries to form the word but can't make it, but he mouths it over and over. *Help.*

I underline the message he wrote me and throw the crossword book onto his lap. He looks down at it, then back up at me. Forty seconds now and I've never seen such panic in anybody's eyes before.

It's hard to watch.

I don't want to watch it.

And I don't have to.

I reach down and pick up the plastic tube. I drop it into my pocket and step out of the bedroom. I walk down the hall, past Adrian, past the dead women, back past all the old furniture and antique calendar and step out the back door, away from the gagging sounds coming from the bedroom. I circle my way around the house. The gun is outside the bedroom window in the garden. I pick it up and drop it into my pocket. I look through the window. Cooper isn't moving. I didn't kill him, I could have saved him, and I'm comfortable with not doing so. I throw the tube back into the window. I don't want to have to explain to Schroder why it was in my pocket. It rolls under Cooper's body but he doesn't make a reach for it.

Emma Green is standing in the driveway. She's wearing a flannel shirt and a pair of jeans. She's still holding the crowbar. I stop ten meters away from her because she looks like she's going to swing that thing at the next person who enters her hitting zone. She keeps holding it even when the police cars pull into the driveway and Schroder, along with the other officers, jump out of the car and come over.

Donovan Green is following them, a woman in the passenger seat who must be Hillary, his wife. Emma recognizes the car and drops the crowbar and runs toward them. Before he can come to a stop his wife has the door open and her feet out, and she almost falls jumping from the car. Donovan leaves the engine running, none of them looking at me, mother and father having eyes only for their daughter. I smile as I watch them give each other the tightest embraces of their lives, and Schroder comes over. He's armed, and so are the men who show up with him. They're approaching the house carefully.

"Adrian?" he asks.

"Dead," I tell him.

"Cooper?"

"The same."

"Jesus," he says. "Tell me what happened."

So I tell him as we watch Emma and her family continue to hug each other, and as the Christchurch sun continues to try and set fire to fields around us.

epilogue

The café owner kept Emma's job for her. She didn't want to go back, but she needed the money, and anyway, she has time to kill before she heads away to the police academy. She had never thought before that she would want to be a cop, but it's all she can think about. She has quit university, has filed her application with the police force, and now she just has to wait. It could take six months. It could take three years. Hopefully she's accepted. Hopefully she has the strength to get through the months of training, and then hopefully she is posted in Christchurch so she can be near her family where she can make a difference. Despite everything that has happened to her, she loves this city. She wants to protect this city. She wants to make sure other girls like her don't have to go through what men like Cooper Riley put her through. She doesn't know whether in a few months' time she might have changed her mind, that the reality of what happened to her two weeks ago will seem different and instead of wanting to become a cop she'll be wanting to curl up in her bedroom for the rest of her life. Her parents don't support her decision. They want her to carry on with her studies.

They tell her it's too dangerous being a policewoman. She pointed out that it's equally as dangerous being a student or working at a café.

The old man who she thought was dead the night she was abducted is sitting at the table closest to the counter. He's working his way through a muffin and a coffee and also the crossword puzzle. He doesn't recognize her from that night. God, how she wanted to scream at him when he walked in! She wanted to spit in his coffee too, but she just smiled and took his money and brought out his order when it was ready.

Part of her, and she can't deny it, wants to follow him out to the parking lot when he's done and, in the morning, people will find him sitting dead behind the driver's wheel of his car. It's what Melissa X would do.

He senses she is looking at him, and he looks up, a big smile on his face.

"Best coffee in the city," he tells her.

She smiles back. "I appreciate hearing that," she says.

He goes back to his crossword. She thinks about Adrian Loaner, and how it felt putting that safety pin into his eye. A month ago if asked, she'd have said that sort of thing would never have been possible for her, not under any circumstances. She also never would have thought about following a customer into the parking lot and strangling him either.

People change. Some for the better, some for the worse. After helping kill two men, she doesn't know which of those sums her up.

She thinks about Cooper Riley, flat on the floor with his throat blocked from the Taser. She wanted him to die. She was desperate for him to die, and even though that's what happened, she's glad he didn't die from her hand. There is some relief there. He killed himself, and that took any guilt away from her—even though she isn't sure she ever would have felt any. If he had lived, he could have hurt other people. Not today, not next week, but definitely in fifteen years when he was freed from jail.

Theodore Tate made sure that wouldn't happen.

At least she thinks that's what happened.

Theodore Tate. She still hates him for what he did to her last year. But that's changing. She's heard he's wanting to be a cop again. She hopes she gets to work with him one day. She knows there are things about the world he can teach her that the police force can't, things that can make her a better cop. Things she can do to help more people.

Like pulling plastic tubes out of evil men's throats.

Okay—she isn't sure if she could do that, just as she isn't sure what really happened in that bedroom after she walked out.

The following day nine bodies were found at the farmhouse. All of them men who had gone missing over the previous few years, all of them killed by a pair of brothers who were themselves killed by the man she stabbed with the safety pin.

Yes, she absolutely wants to become a cop. She wants to rid this world of men like that.

The old man finishes off his crossword and waves at her on his way out the door. She goes over to his table and picks up the newspaper he left behind. She folds it over to the front page. There's a sketch of Melissa X, the same one they've been running since last year, only now she has a name and a photograph of when she was a student. Natalie Flowers.

Natalie Flowers was Cooper Riley's first victim.

It's an awful thought, but she wishes Cooper had killed Natalie Flowers.

Last night another body was found. An ambulance driver. He was found naked in a park with his hands tied around a tree. His uniform wasn't at the scene. She wonders if she'll make it onto the force before Natalie Flowers is caught, then wonders if Flowers will ever be caught. She carries the coffee cup and plate out to the kitchen, folds the newspaper in half, and tosses it into the bin.

acknowledgments

I would like to say a big thank-you to the team at Atria, and especially the fantastic Sarah Branham, who did an amazing job with the manuscript and I'm very lucky to have her as my editor.

I'm also lucky to have the best agent in the business—Jane Gregory, who has shown a lot of faith in me and given a lot of support—I'd be lost without her. Stephanie Glencross, Jane's in-house editor at Gregory and Company, has a great eye for detail and a great bedside manner in pointing out my mistakes.

I also want to say thanks to all the people who have bought the books and to those who have emailed me—without those kind words I'd have stopped writing by now. 2010 was a pretty bumpy year, and I'd like to thank all my friends for making sure I got through it in one piece!

And of course my parents—the two coolest people in the world—everything I am is because of them.